Also by E.E. Ho

THE WORLD OF THE GATEWAY
The Gateway Trilogy (Series 1)
Spirit Legacy
Spirit Prophecy
Spirit Ascendancy
The Gateway Trackers (Series 2)
Whispers of the Walker
Plague of the Shattered
Awakening of the Seer
Portraits of the Forsaken
Heart of the Rebellion
Soul of the Sentinel
Gift of the Darkness
Rise of the Coven
City of the Forgotten
Shadow of the Brotherhood
Betrayal of the Sisterhood
Tales from the Gateway
The Vesper Coven (Series 3)
Daughters of Sea and Storm
Keepers of Forest and Flame
Pages of Shadow and Smoke

THE RIFTMAGIC SAGA
What the Lady's Maid Knew
The Rebel Beneath the Stairs
The Girl at the Heart of the Storm

Pages of Shadow and Smoke

Pages of Shadow and Smoke

The Vesper Coven
Book 3

E.E. Holmes

Fairhaven Press

Fairhaven Press

Townsend, MA

www.eeholmes.com

ISBN 978-1-956656-25-1 (Paperback edition)

ISBN 978-1-956656-24-4 (Digital edition)

Publisher's note: This is a work of fiction. Names, characters, places and incidents are either the product of the author's imagination or are used fictitiously.

Cover design by James T. Egan of Bookfly Design LLC

Author photography by Cydney Scott Photography

To all those battling through this world armed with love, compassion, and kindness as your only weapons, this one's for you.

The lust for power, for dominating others, inflames the heart more than any other passion.
-Tacitus

Prologue

It takes three attempts to draw the circle. My hands are shaking so badly that the chalk snaps twice beneath my fingers.

I am running out of time. My sisters have surely realized I am missing, or will very soon. When they do, they will know exactly where to find me, and even our bond of blood will not be enough to save me from their wrath.

That bond is nothing now. I am the one who broke it first.

I burn my palms as I transfer the lit candles into the glass jars, but there is no other way to ensure the flames won't be extinguished by the winds on the clifftop before the ritual is over. I can instinctively feel the pull of the elements as I place each candle at its proper direction. Even without the stars or the moon to guide me, I know they sit perfectly at the points of the compass.

My circle cast, I reach for the cloth bag I have slung over my shoulder, and extract the book. I had seen it so many times in the hands of the Vespers, or else tucked away on the shelf above their hearth, its bejeweled cover winking in the firelight. The rumors about that book have flown about the town like the gulls now circling my head. Many have coveted the magic it is believed to contain within its covers. Some believe the book doesn't belong to the Vespers at all, but that they had stolen it before they embarked for the New World. All I know is that only Vesper hands have held it, only Vesper voices have whispered the incantations etched into its pages.

Only Vespers, until tonight.

I shudder when I think of what I have done to obtain it, but I shake away the doubts. They will cloud my concentration, and I can't risk any distractions. I have one chance to perform this spell, and everything must go according to plan, or everything I have worked and schemed so hard for these many months will crumble to dust.

I cannot lose him. I will not lose him.

The Darkness is near. I can feel it gathering in the sand beneath my bruised and battered knees, in the waving grasses beneath my palms. Like an oncoming storm charging the air, the pressure is building. Anticipation licks up my innards like flames up desiccated wood, and my own power roils through my veins, ready to serve me.

To serve *him*.

My trembling fingers riffle through the pages until I find the one I seek. It is blank to the naked eye, but I know better now. I have discovered the secret of the book. Reaching into the pocket of my apron, I extract a small glass bottle full of something that gleams scarlet. I pull out the stopper and tip the bottle over the page, and watch with a ravenous expression as a single drop of the viscous red substance beads up at the opening, and then drops with a plop onto the page. The slow bloom of my elated smile echoes the slow bloom of words upon the page, shining in red ink that is not ink at all. I stopper the bottle once more, and stow it safely back in my pocket.

My eyes rake over the newly revealed incantation, as I ready myself. I look up at the sky. As soon as the full moon shows itself... as soon as the clouds shift...

There is the snap of a twig and I suck in a startled breath. I wheel on the spot, clutching the book to my chest, and peer into the tree line behind me. Shadows gather there, huddled under the canopy of lush summer foliage. Are they shifting, or are my eyes playing tricks on me, spinning enemies from air? I hold my breath, listening hard, but no further sounds break the stillness. I almost turn away, and then my gaze snags on a sudden movement.

Two bright green eyes appear low to the ground, staring unblinkingly at me.

All I can do, for a moment, is stare back. My head swims and I realize I'm not breathing. The air whooshes from my lungs only for me to suck in another, panicked gasp of air. I am being watched, but by what? A mere forest creature, or something worse?

As though in answer to my silent questions, the eyes blink and begin to move toward me. The tendrils of shadow unwind from the creature as it moves out of the embrace of the trees and onto the salt-swept clifftop. Pointed ears. Arched back. White bushy tail flicking back and forth behind it like a flag of surrender.

A cat. It is only a cat.

I almost laugh, but then the recognition sets in, and I choke the laughter back down. It isn't a cat, not really. I know this creature. It is a familiar, and it belongs to the Vespers. I have seen it many times, winding its way around their legs as they work, patrolling the edges of their land like a sentry. I meet its eye as it moves closer. Its gaze is sharp and knowing, and its tail flicks in my direction like an admonitory finger.

I know what you're doing, Sarah Claire. I know what you're about.

I stand up, careful not to disturb my circle and hiss at the creature. "You can tell them, if you like. Go on, foul little beastie. Return to your mistresses and tell them what you've seen. It matters not. They are already too late to stop me."

At that moment, there is a shift in the clouds, and a beam of moonlight breaks its way through the storm-tossed dark. The moment the moonlight falls upon the circle, the candles spark, their flames leaping higher, and the circle itself turns a bright, blinding gold. I look from the moon to the circle, and then, finally, back at the cat.

"You see? Too late," I whisper.

Then I open the grimoire again, and begin to read the incantation as the cat vanishes once again into the embrace of the night-cloaked wood.

1

"And that's the story of how a familiar saved Sedgwick Cove from certain destruction."

I blinked at my aunt, Rhiannon Vesper, as she concluded her tale with a flourish of her kitchen towel. She dropped her hands to her hips, looking slightly put out.

"Usually this is the point where people applaud," she said sourly.

I brought my hands together in a hurried flurry of clapping, and Rhi gave an exaggerated bow.

"That's more like it," she said. "After all, Wren, you're theatrical. You ought to appreciate a good performance."

"And here I thought this was a family history lesson," I said, closing my notebook and reaching for a cookie. Rhi slapped my hand away with a flick of her towel.

"Give them a minute to cool, for Hecate's sake, or you'll burn your fingers off."

I groaned. The cookies smelled divine. In fact, everything Rhi cooked smelled divine, and tasted even better. It was, by far, the best perk of living with a kitchen witch.

The scent of the cookies wafted through Lightkeep Cottage—from

Rhi's little kitchen kingdom through the snug library crammed full of spellbooks and magical histories, through the French doors to the vast gardens, where the scent of vanilla and raspberry mingled with the heavy perfumes of a thousand different blooms my mother tended. It drifted up the stairs into the fabric-draped depths of my Aunt Persephone's room, as she leaned back from her sewing machine, swearing and sucking on her finger where an errant pin had pierced it. At last it found the curious nose of my own cat, Freya, who leapt down from my bed to investigate whether she might be able to partake in Rhi's most recent creation. A moment later, she appeared mewling plaintively at my ankles.

"See? Freya appreciates a good tale of feline heroism," Rhi said, gesturing to Freya, who was preparing to leap up onto the counter.

I caught her mid-leap and set her on the floor again. "I think what she appreciates is the smell of those cookies," I corrected her. I lifted Freya back down, and she glared at me. Then, as though she had silently called for backup, the other resident cat, Diana, appeared in the kitchen and sat imperiously beside Freya. They looked like a pair of queens awaiting their crowning.

"Ah yes, and the hero herself wants her reward, too, I see," Rhi crooned, and began to break one of the cookies into little pieces so it would cool faster.

"So Diana is descended from the familiar in the story?" I asked. "That's pretty cool."

"Oh, it's even cooler than you think," Rhi said, smirking. "Diana *is* the familiar from the story."

My mouth fell open. "Are you... you're not actually... be serious."

"I am utterly serious," Rhi said absently. She made a kissing sound and Diana rose sinuously to her feet and leapt lightly onto the counter.

"You mean to tell me that cat is four hundred years old?!" I gasped.

"Oh, I think she's much older than that," Rhi said, holding the cookie crumbs out to Diana, who deigned to eat them. She then glared at me as she chewed, as though in silent disdain at my incredulity. "But don't call her old, Wren. That's rude."

Rhi winked at me, and I laughed again. Every day, it seemed I discovered that some new impossibility was truth. At some point I was going to have to accept that it was just a part of my new normal.

Sedgwick Cove didn't have a typical definition of "normal." The tiny coastal town had been, from its very founding, a haven for the abnormal. The outcasts. The fairy tale villains turned friends and neighbors. Sedgwick Cove was the home of witches from all over the world, and my family, the Vespers, had been the very first. Drawn by the deep magic of this coastal place, our coven settled here only to discover that something else had settled here too—something ancient and evil that wanted the deep magic for its own. We called it simply The Darkness, and we kept it at bay by sealing a covenant with Vesper blood. As long as there were three Vesper witches in Sedgwick Cove, the Darkness could not take hold again.

And that worked... until recently.

Last spring when I turned sixteen, my grandmother Asteria had died, and my mom took me to Sedgwick Cove for the first time since I was a toddler. It was only then that I learned what my mother had run from—what she had kept from me my entire life: not only was I a witch, but I was powerful enough that the Darkness itself had been after me for years.

As far as I knew, I was just an awkward theater nerd with glasses and crippling stage fright, so this tidbit of information was a shock, to say the least.

But as it turned out, I was already acquainted with the Darkness. I knew him as the Gray Man, a mysterious figure from my childhood nightmares. When I returned to Sedgwick Cove, the Gray Man used my mother as bait to try to steal my power—power I still wasn't convinced at the time that I even had. Then I sort of accidentally-on-purpose called the elements to save myself, my mother, and my friends; and to drive the Gray Man back into the shadows. It seemed my power was there all along.

Since then, I'd been trying to learn all I could—about myself, my coven, my town, and most importantly, my own abilities. As Rhi constantly reminded me, all of us Vespers were in uncharted territory here, magically speaking. Both my mother and my grandmother had tried to protect me in different ways. But it had become increasingly clear that I would have to learn how to protect myself.

Over the summer, I had learned that there were others who sought the deep magic of Sedgwick Cove, and would do anything to harness it. The Kildare coven had been banished centuries ago for wicked magic but, unbeknownst to the rest of the town, they had returned more than sixty years ago claiming to be another coven entirely. I'd come face to face with their descendant, Veronica Meyers, on the summer solstice. She had tricked me, lured me to the source of the deep magic, convinced that I would understand it and be able to control it.

But I didn't understand it. I couldn't control it. And if it wasn't for my mother, my aunts, and my friend Eva's kid sister Bea, I probably wouldn't have lived to try. Veronica vanished, but none of us were foolish enough to think she was gone for good. And now we had another mystery on our hands—the source of the deep magic itself, and what to do now that we had unearthed it.

In the meantime, I was also learning what it meant to be a pentamaleficus—a witch of the five, who could command not just one element, but all five: earth, water, wind, fire, and spirit.

"It would probably be easier to guide you if there was a single living pentamaleficus here in Sedgwick Cove," Rhi had said over an open spellbook one day, "but as far as we know, you're the first since Sarah Claire herself."

Sarah Claire. Those were footsteps I definitely did not want to follow in. And so, I'd done everything I could all summer and fall to make sure I did the exact opposite. I didn't know where Veronica Meyers was, or what she and the Kildare coven were planning next—because, as Persi said, "They were sure as shit planning something,"—but I was determined to be as ready as I could be.

"I knew I smelled cookies!"

My mom had appeared in the doorway from the garden. Her face was streaked with smudges of earth, and she was sweating through her t-shirt, but her eyes were shining. She looked happy—really, soul-deep happy—for the first time that I could remember. It took me by surprise, until I remembered that she was using her own magic for the first time after a decade of shoving it down into the dark places of herself.

"What are you smirking at?" she asked me, as she took the stool beside me and helped herself to a cookie.

"Oh, nothing," I said, and crammed a cookie in my own mouth before she could interrogate me further. She didn't need me to tell her why she was happy. It was plain to see in every lush, vibrant petal and vine out in the garden.

"How is it going in here?" my mom asked, looking between me and Rhi.

"Rhi's trying to convince me that Diana is four hundred years old," I snorted.

My mom shrugged. "Oh I think she's quite a bit older than that."

I half-choked on my cookie. "Wait, seriously?"

At that moment Persi slunk into the kitchen, looking sulky. "You're having a cookie party and didn't invite me? Even the cats are here."

Rhi threw up her hands. "Fine, let the vultures descend. It's not like we need to restock the shop or anything."

"I mean, we won't eat *all* of them," my mom said.

"Speak for yourself. I'm making no promises," Persi said, grabbing two cookies at once, but stopping short of putting them in her mouth. "Wait, did you enchant these?"

Rhi raised an eyebrow. "I guess you'll all find out, won't you?"

We all looked at each other, shrugged in almost-perfect unison, and kept right on eating.

"Don't you have class today?" my mom asked me, looking at her watch.

"No, but I do have to drop off a paper, so I'd better get going," I said, hopping down off my stool and closing my notebook. "Do you want me to take these down to Shadowkeep?" I asked Rhi, pointing to the remaining cookies.

Shadowkeep was the Vesper-owned shop downtown. It was a typical witchy tourist trap downstairs, but upstairs it was the most expansive and specialized apothecary and supply shop any witch could hope to find. We also sold Rhi's kitchen witchery there, when they managed to escape our collective greedy clutches.

"Wait, I've only had two!" Persi whined. "Wait, no... three..."

"Oh forget it, I know a losing battle when I see one," Rhi said. "Luckily, I'm always prepared." And she pulled a basket of pre-wrapped cookies tied into little bags with twine and a sprig of rosemary.

"When did you make those?" Persi asked, sounding offended that anyone would have the audacity to hide baked goods from her.

"While the rest of you were sleeping. It's the only safe time if I want them to make it to the shop," Rhi explained.

"I can take them when I head out to open up," Persi said, her eyes wide and innocent.

"Not a chance," Rhi said flatly.

I left my aunts and my mother to battle it out over the rest of the cookies, and strapped the basket carefully to the back of my bicycle. I'd been saving up for over a year for a car, but there seemed no point in owning a car in a place like Sedgwick Cove. Maybe I'd feel differently in the winter, when the long and unrelenting cold set in, and the snow and ice turned the streets to slick, treacherous ribbons of white; but for now, I was more than content to sail down the coastal paths with the briny breeze whipping through my hair. It was hard to imagine Sedgwick Cove in winter—to me it felt like it must always be warm and bright here.

Thanks to foliage chasers, New England in general was still teeming with tourists this time of year, but no place on the Northeast coast was busier in the lead up to Halloween than Sedgwick Cove, with the possible exception of Salem, Massachusetts. The towns had very similar witchy reputations, though Salem's stemmed from the violence inflicted against supposed witches, while Sedgwick Cove's was much more rooted in the community of confirmed witches that lived there. Both towns leaned heavily into their reputations—I'd even heard that the Salem High School mascot was a witch on a broomstick—but in the case of Sedgwick Cove, the embrace was more out of safety than for tourist dollars. I hadn't understood this at first.

"But if we just advertise that this is a town full of witches, then how is that protecting people?" I had asked one afternoon, a few weeks into our move.

"It's like hiding in plain sight," my mother said, laughing as she picked through her rose bushes—not only hers because we lived at Lightkeep now, but hers because, as a green witch, they always had been. The petals brightened at her touch.

"That doesn't make sense," I said. "How can you hide while fully admitting what you are?"

"Ah, but we don't fully admit it. You remember how we set up Shadowkeep?"

Of course I knew. I was getting as familiar with the family shop downtown as I was with the rest of the Cove. The downstairs level was crammed full of touristy junk: sparkly witch hats and broomsticks, mood jewelry, candles, and housewares decorated with black cats and silly sayings like, "I'm a real WITCH before I've had my coffee." It was all campy, and even the items that claimed to be magic were not really magic at all. But upstairs, through a hidden door, the local witch population could find everything they needed to conduct their spellwork, charms, and sorcery: from rare herbs, to incense, to crystals and spotlessly cleaned animal bones.

My mother shrugged. "Shadowkeep itself is a good metaphor for the whole town. By presenting a silly, harmless version of witchcraft to the world, we can distract them from the real witchcraft flourishing beneath the surface—and the other, more nefarious things as well," she added, her amused smirk melting away.

Because we knew better than anyone about just how nefarious those "more nefarious things" were.

And so, Sedgwick Cove became a wildly popular tourist destination in the weeks leading up to Halloween. All Hallows Eve, or Samhain, as witches called it, was just one of many important days in the wheel of the year; but for the outside world, it was the one day of the year where witches had a share in the cultural spotlight. Therefore, it was totally unsurprising to find the town full to bursting with tourists, even on a weekday morning. There were people already lined up outside of the tarot shop, even though the sign on the door said it didn't open for another fifteen minutes. The Historical Center door had been flung wide, and Penelope was putting out a sandwich board advertising the walking tours that left from that corner of Main Street every hour, a queue already forming beside it. I waved at her, but her answering wave and smile seemed somewhat strained. At first, I thought it must be the stress of peak tourist season, and then I remembered that half the town was scared of me —it was one definite downside of discovering your power is coveted by the ancient evil that inhabited your town. I tried to shake it off, the fear behind the smile.

"It's only temporary, Wren," my mom kept assuring me. "They'll come to their senses."

But it had been months. If people were going to come to their senses, wouldn't they have done it by now? The thought popped like a soap bubble, though, when I spotted the next face that smiled at me. There was no fear there.

"Hi Bea!"

"Hi Wren!"

Beatriz Marin was standing outside of Xiomara's Cafe taking orders from the line out the door. Her grandmother was the cafe's namesake, also one of my Aunt Rhi's best friends, as well as one of the coven matriarchs that made up the Conclave. She was also the most powerful spirit witch in the whole of Sedgwick Cove. Since the summer, when I'd discovered I was a pentamaleficus, she had been helping me to develop my spirit abilities.

"Are you coming over tonight?" Bea shouted to me.

"Of course. You think your *abuela* would let me skip a session?"

Bea just grinned. "No way. See you, then!"

"Is Eva around?"

"No, she's got that test today! You just missed her!"

Shit, I'd almost forgotten. Eva had been obsessing for weeks over this test, which was meant to assess her abilities as a water witch. If she passed, she would be allowed to begin more advanced studies as a waterworker—a skill she'd been working toward for half her life already. I checked my watch. If I pedaled fast, I might be able to catch her before she went in.

One of the many ways Sedgwick Cove was unlike other towns was that we didn't have a typical school system. As a town populated entirely by witches, the skill sets we had to learn were not exactly to be found in your average curriculum. Most of the kids were homeschooled, which made perfect sense because each coven had their own unique magical traditions and abilities. But we all had to attend a smattering of classes at Cove Academy as well, to keep the State Board of Education out of our hair. I wasn't sure the State Board of Education would have approved of these classes, as everything from American History to Mathematics was taught through a lens of the witchcraft tradition; but, as Xiomara said, "What the government doesn't know won't hurt them... unless we decide it should."

Cove Academy was a collection of antique Victorian houses that looked down over Main Street like colorful sentinels from a grassy slope. Each was painted in its own bright palette of colors and adorned with ornate gingerbread trim that made them look like overgrown dollhouses. I pedaled hard up the hill, panting in the humidity, and came to a stop at last in front of the mint green house with a frilly front porch, and a doorknocker shaped like a phoenix in flight in the center of its cheerful, lavender door. I was relieved to see Eva sitting on the porch steps, head bent over her stack of flashcards.

I shoved my bike against the bike rack—no one bothered to lock their bikes up in Sedgwick Cove—and hurried over to Eva. She was muttering under her breath with her eyes closed, and I had to say her name three times before she looked up, startled.

"Huh? Oh, hey, Wren," she said, in a slightly manic tone.

"You okay?" I asked her, smiling sympathetically.

"Oh yeah," Eva replied, puffing herself up with manufactured bravado. "Never better. Totally gonna crush this. Supremely confident."

"So, freaking out, then?"

"Big time."

I laughed and sat down next to her. "Hey, you've got this. I've never seen anyone study harder for anything in my life."

Eva sighed. "I can't be the first water witch in my family not to become a waterworker. I just can't. I'll never live it down."

"Are there a lot of water witches in your family?" I asked.

"One in every generation, typically."

"Okay, yeah, I guess that's a lot of pressure. But if you don't pass the test, can't you just take it again next year?" I asked.

This was apparently the wrong thing to say. Eva turned on me, glaring.

"Not that you're going to fail, obviously," I said quickly. "Supremely confident, remember?"

Eva's glare melted and her shoulders sagged. She dropped her head forward into her hands, so that her braids swung down over her face like a curtain being closed. "It's not that simple. The test isn't even really about all this." She held up the flashcards. "I mean, I have to know it, obviously, but I've known it for a long time. It's about my magic. It has to be powerful enough to work the spells."

I put an arm around Eva's shoulders. "Hey, six months ago I didn't know I was a witch, and now half the town is afraid of me. If I can do that, then you can most definitely do this."

Eva laughed—it was shaky and uncertain, but at least it was genuine. She took a deep breath, and blew it out slowly before getting to her feet. She threw her shoulders back and whipped her braids behind her. "You're right. I've got to get out of my own head. I'm psyching myself out. Wish me luck. Not that I need it, of course."

"Good luck," I said and, pulling a polished piece of jade from my pocket, I handed it to her. "From all the Vespers. We all imbued it with intention."

Eva smiled, rubbing her thumb over the smooth surface of the jade before pocketing it. She started bouncing back and forth from foot to foot, and shaking out her hands. As she did so, the water splashed up and out of a nearby birdbath. She looked over at it and grinned. Then she bounded up the steps and into the house.

It was good to see Eva smile, but I still had a little knot of anxiety for her in my stomach as I walked up the steps of the next building over, this one painted in Easter egg shades of pinks and purples. Inside the doorway was a curtain of bells, feathers, and gemstones hung on braided silk ribbons that I had to part with my hands and walk through to reach the secretary. It tinkled and swished behind me as I walked into the Sedgwick Cove version of a front office.

"Well, hello, Wren," Miss Bishop trilled from behind her desk. She was a squat little woman, with silvery hair braided into ropes that hung about her ears and nested on her head, like a shiny serpent.

"Hi, Miss Bishop," Wren greeted her with a smile. "I have a paper to drop off for Ms. Boswell. Could you put it in her mailbox for me, please?"

"Of course, pet," Miss Bishop said, reaching out a hand that jangled merrily with bracelets and bangles. "Just sign the log there, if you please."

I jotted my name down along with the time, gave a last wave to Miss Bishop, and jingled my way right back through the curtain and out the door. Ms. Boswell was one of the history teachers—a tall, willowy woman who gestured violently with her hands while she taught. Her lectures were half performance art, half factual information. I was excited for her to read my paper, which I had researched using family records in the Sedgwick Cove Historical Center. I couldn't remember ever being excited about homework before; but then, why would it be surprising that magic made everything—even homework—more interesting?

As I headed back to my bike, I noticed a woman with long black hair streaked with purple. She was standing on the steps of one of the school buildings, looking thoroughly aggravated as she examined a map. Was she lost? Her expression was so fierce, I decided to just slip away before she could ask me for directions. I would have enough of tourist demands over at Shadowkeep, where I was headed next.

Little did I realize there was no point in avoiding the woman. Before the day was over, our lives would collide.

2

By the time I pedaled over to Shadowkeep, there was already a small crowd of people outside with their faces pressed to the window displays. Of all the shops on the main drag of Sedgwick Cove, Shadowkeep was perhaps the most obvious tourist trap. Everything about it, from its sagging front porch, to its impossibly lush plants, to its ancient-looking sign screamed the Hollywood version of witchcraft. Eager to avoid a scrum of people trying to get through the door after me, I cycled around the side of the house, and opened the gate in the fence that led into the garden. I leaned my bike against the inside of the fence, unbuckled the basket from behind the seat, and turned to face the shop.

There was a trick to finding the secret entrance. Only a witch could see around the glamour that hid the staircase in plain sight. It wasn't exactly invisibility—it was simply a trick of the mind that caused the passersby not to notice the stairs built up the side of the house that led to a door on the second floor. I amused myself as I walked up by waving at passersby and watching them completely ignore me. I wondered if that was how ghosts must feel, drifting invisibly along beside people, but the thought pricked at me like an unexpected thorn. I didn't want to think about ghosts right now, not when my own studies of my spirit abilities were going so poorly.

Well, *I* thought they were going poorly. Xiomara seemed to expect no better, a fact which I knew should have made me feel better, but instead festered inside me like an ulcer. Like with Eva and other friends who were coming into more advanced studies of their powers, we were all starting to feel the pressure of expanding and honing our magic. Was this what normal teenagers felt like with stuff like SATs and college applications? I'd have to ask Poe or Charlie the next time I talked to them.

At the top of the stairs, I inserted my key in the lock and twisted the rattly old crystal doorknob to let myself in. The door was so old, I could probably have opened it with one good shove of my shoulder. I'd have to talk to Rhi and Persi about replacing it—it might be invisible to most people but, as we now knew, enemies had infiltrated the Cove without detection over the summer.

"Hi Persi," I said as I entered the upstairs shop space, and found she had beaten me there. Persi merely grunted in reply—she had a screwdriver clamped between her teeth as she stood perched on a stepladder, and adjusted the height of a new shelf above one of the windows. "Do you want me to get things ready to open downstairs?"

She grunted again, this time with a nod which I took to mean "yes." I moved past her to the opposite door, and descended the stairs into the tourist area of the shop. I unlocked the old-fashioned cash register and double-checked the starting cash. Then I walked around and clicked on the many stained-glass lamps, fairy lights, fake candles and lanterns we used to light the place instead of overhead strip lighting—nothing spoiled a spooky atmosphere like fluorescent lightbulbs. I could hear the voices outside rise into an excited babble as they realized the store was waking up and getting ready to open. I tried to ignore the faces pressed to the glass as I fixed some displays, restocked a few items that were running low and, at last, turned the sign from "BOO, we're closed" to "Enter If You Dare." With a sigh, I plastered on a smile, pulled back the deadbolt, and opened the door.

"Welcome to Shadowkeep," I said, in what I hoped was a good

imitation of Persi's musical tones. "Please let me know if I can be of any assistance, magic-makers."

The rest of the morning was a blur of cheap wigs, plastic vampire teeth, and melting face paint. Nearly every visitor to the shop was decked out in their Halloween finest, despite the fact that the lingering summer heat was refusing to cede its ground to the crisp breezes of autumn. I could never remember it being this warm in the run up to Halloween. By the time Persi descended into the lower shop an hour later, Rhi's cookies had already sold out. This soured her mood, and she snapped at several customers before she got over it.

Around lunchtime, Zale and Eva braved the crowds, pushing past two girls taking selfies dressed as Elphaba and Galinda by the candle display, to arrive, breathless and grinning, at the checkout counter.

"Well? How did it—?"

"Say hello to Sedgwick Cove's newest waterworker!" Eva crowed.

"I knew it!" I cried, leaning across the counter to pull her into a one-armed hug. "Persi, I'm gonna step out for a second, okay?"

"Sure, I'm not drowning in customers over here," came the dry reply, over the heads of the customers.

"Thanks!" I called blithely, ignoring the sarcasm, and slipped out onto the porch with Eva and Zale.

"So? Tell me all about it!" I said, as we settled ourselves on a cluster of Asteria's creaking old rocking chairs.

"She flooded the Humanities building," Zale said, deadpan.

"Very funny. Wait, did you?" I gasped, rounding on Eva.

"Of course I didn't," Eva snapped, shoving Zale so hard that he fell out of his chair and into a planter full of climbing roses. Ignoring his curses, she went on. "I really thought my nerves were going to get the best of me, at first. I sat down at the practice altar, and my mind went absolutely blank. I honestly don't think I even remembered my own name. I thought I was going to pass out."

"So what snapped you out of it?" I asked. I was having a vivid flashback to the time freshman year when Poe had dragged me into an audition for the musical. My brain had similarly short-circuited, though rather than recovering and nailing my audition, I'd given up and became a stage manager instead.

"Well, I opened up my notebook and found this," Eva said. She pulled a folded-up piece of paper from her shorts pocket, and unfolded it. It was a sketch of Eva herself, but she was dressed as a superhero with a water droplet on her chest, and more little drops dancing at the ends of her long braids. Streams of water shot from her eyeballs onto a burning building, while a crowd of firefighters cheered her on.

I grinned. "Bea?"

Eva nodded. "She must have swiped my notebook last night after my mom demanded I go to bed early. That kid drives me up the wall, but sometimes, she's all right. Anyway, it made me laugh, and it was like my brain just clicked back on again. It was smooth sailing after that!"

"And she just told you that you passed right on the spot?" I asked, as Zale slumped back into his seat, grumbling.

"Yup! I'll get my actual score next week, but she said she didn't want to leave me in suspense."

"Wow, this is so awesome," I said. "We'll have to celebrate!"

"My thoughts exactly!" Zale said. "Are you free tonight?"

My face fell. "No. I have lessons with Xiomara."

"Can't you just sk—" Zale began.

"No," Eva and I said at the same time.

"It's okay," Eva said. "Let's wait for Friday night."

"Are you sure?" I asked. "I don't want to delay the celebration."

"It won't be a celebration if you're not there," Eva insisted. "It's only one more night. And anyway, my family will probably want to celebrate tonight, which means it will be hard to get away."

"Okay," I said, brightening. Weathering my lessons with Xiomara would be easier if I had a night out with my friends to look forward to. "What do you want to do?"

Zale and Eva traded a knowing look. "It'll be a new moon on Friday," Zale said.

"It sure will," Eva said, a smile spreading slowly and mischievously over her face. "The moon that ushers in Samhain. Let's introduce Wren to a Sedgwick Cove tradition, shall we?"

I looked back and forth between the two of them, starting to feel nervous. "What tradition?"

But Eva shook her head. "You'll see. Don't want to spoil the surprise. See you tonight at my house?"

They both stood up and headed for the stairs.

"What tradition?" I repeated.

But neither of them answered, still just grinning like a pair of cheshire cats.

"WHAT TRADITION?!"

"See you later, Wren!" Zale called over his shoulder as they took off down the street, cackling now.

I shook my head. I squeezed back into the shop, determined to ask Persi what Zale and Eva had been talking about, but instead was overpowered by an incredibly strong smell. Coughing, I slapped my hand over my nose and mouth, and looked around for the source of the sudden olfactory assault. Finally, I spotted Persi. She was bent low, cleaning up a pile of shattered glass with a prop broom with one hand, while pressing her scarf over her nose and mouth with the other. A pair of teenagers dressed as anime characters stood beside her, apologizing profusely and looking miserable.

"We were just trying to get it in a video," one of the girls was babbling.

"Well, maybe if you learned to experience the world with your own eyes instead of through your phone screen, these things wouldn't happen," Persi snapped. "Everyone out! We need to air the place out! No, not you two, you come to the register, please. You'll have to pay for that."

The two girls shuffled miserably against the milling crowd, which was now moving steadily toward the door amidst coughing and retching sounds.

"What is it? Incense? Perfume?" one man gasped.

"If it's perfume, it's the worst one I've ever smelled," a woman replied.

"It's a potion, and if you don't all clear out, you'll all start breaking out in pimples!" Persi shouted over the crowd. That made everyone push harder for the door. "Don't panic, just get some fresh air!"

Persi spotted me, snapped her fingers and pointed to the cash register. I elbowed my way to it with many mumbled apologies and pardons to the exiting patrons. Persi placed one of the shards of glass on the counter—the label for the contents was still attached to it, so I was able to key in the right item.

"This isn't a spell to cause breakouts," I whispered to her. "It's just patchouli oil."

"I know, but I had to say something to get them all out of here," Persi replied under her breath. "It reeks in here. We're going to have to open the windows and mop it up, and then wash it all down with bleach."

"And by 'we' I assume you mean me," I grumbled.

"You assume correctly," Persi said, smiling sweetly and pointing to the corner, where an old coat closet contained all the cleaning supplies. "But put up the sign first."

I followed the two shame-faced girls to the door, handed them their other purchases, and shut the door behind them. As I turned the lock and hung the sign that said, "Back In A SPELL!" I noticed the same woman I'd seen over at the school. She had a map in her hands and seemed to be coughing, her nose scrunched up as the two girls walked past her. They exchanged a few words, the woman threw a wary look at the shop, and then turned and continued back along Main Street. She still had a disgruntled look on her face, like when I'd seen her over at the school, and I found myself thankful she didn't seem interested in entering the shop. She had the determined air of someone who would have ignored a 'closed' sign and just walked right in.

Cleaning up the patchouli oil took so long, that my shift was nearly over when I had finished. I flipped the sign back over, ushered in an impatient stream of customers, and then called up the stairs to Persi, who had vanished up them at the first opportunity to work on some custom spellwork orders for one of the local covens. She descended the stairs and handed me a small, blue velvet bag that clinked a little as she dropped it into my hands.

"Be a lamb and drop this for Leila at the Historical Society?"

"Leila?" I asked, frowning.

"Leila Nightjar. She works there, helping Penelope lead the tours. Just ask for her, if you're not sure."

"Okay," I said. "See you for dinner?"

"No, I've got more work to do here after we close, and then I have somewhere I have to be. I'll be late," Persi insisted. "Tell Rhi for me, will you?"

I almost asked her where she was going, but decided against it. There were too many people in the store now, and Persi's nighttime wanderings were hardly the type of thing we wanted the tourists to know about.

Especially if, as I suspected, she was visiting a certain someone...

I walked my bike slowly between the knots of people who swarmed the streets—it was entirely too crowded now to attempt pedaling. What had started a couple of weeks earlier as a fun and colorful influx of costumes and tourist money had soon devolved into chaos, constant noise, and pushy crowds. I'd also realized it was the perfect cover for someone like Veronica if she wanted to sneak her way back into town undetected. How could I be sure that the faces hidden behind the masks and the face paint weren't those of Veronica Meyers, or other members of the Kildare coven? But I soon found that it was too mentally taxing to keep up that level of paranoia, and now that we were halfway through the month, I was no longer looking over my shoulder constantly.

There were still two weeks until Halloween, and I found myself longing for the peace and quiet the first of November would bring. Tourist season would officially be over, and Sedgwick Cove would settle down to hibernate through a chilly New England winter. Then I'd finally be able to help with the secret work upstairs, and learn the craft that Shadowkeep was really known for—the kind of work that currently nestled in the bag Persi had given me.

As I approached the Historical Society, a walking tour was just gathering on the corner. A motley collection of superheroes, 80's slasher villains, and a trio of glitter-winged fairies were standing grouped around a tour guide decked out in a Victorian-era black corseted dress and a witch hat. As luck would have it, she was also wearing a gold nametag pinned to the front of her dress: Leila Nightjar.

I leaned my bike against the light post on the corner, and eased my way through the little crowd.

"Right, okay, everyone have your QR codes pulled up on your phones so I can scan your tickets please!" Leila called into her crowd, and waited while everyone from Michael Meyers to Captain America fumbled for their phones.

"Excuse me? Leila?"

"Sorry, but this tour's full, you'll have to—oh! It's Wren, isn't it?" Leila asked, her somewhat bored expression brightening as she recognized me. She was an elven slip of a woman who was probably in her early thirties, but looked younger. She had a pixie cut dyed a soft shade of rosy pink, and a sprinkling of freckles across her slightly turned-up nose. Her smile, as it spread across her face, was wide and brightly white.

"Yeah, that's right. Um, my aunt asked me to deliver this to you," I said, holding out the blue velvet pouch.

"Oh!" Leila's bright smile crumpled into something like disappointment as she took the pouch carefully into her hands. "I told her I would be by to pick it up. You didn't have to go out of your way."

"It was no trouble. I had to ride right by," I assured her.

"But I..." she bit her lip, and for one alarming moment she looked like she might cry. "Did she, um... say anything else? A message to pass on?"

I frowned. "No. She just asked me to drop this off."

"Right," Leila said, attempting a smile, but spoiling the effect with her trembling lower lip. She slipped the pouch carefully into a little leather satchel she had attached to her waist. "Well, please tell her I'll... I'll be by soon. For a chat."

"Okay, sure," I said.

"It was nice to meet you, Wren. Hopefully I'll see you around," Leila said, smiling in an attempt to rally her spirits before returning to her patrons.

"You too," I said, and I meant it. I was so used to the other locals looking wary or anxious when they met me, that it was refreshing to experience a friendly greeting for once. Maybe Eva was right, and people were starting to get over it. Or maybe Leila was just the kind of person who didn't let rumors cloud her perceptions of people. Still, I felt a little uneasy as I steered my bike away from her tour group. She seemed upset about something, and I thought I knew what. Persi had a bit of a reputation as a heartbreaker. I hoped Leila's heart wasn't her latest victim, but I really couldn't invest too much of my own energy in the situation. Goddess knew I had my own problems.

I hopped on my bike and began to pedal as soon as I was free of the crowds, delighting in the sea breeze that whipped through my hair, filling my nostrils with the tang of the ocean, and leaving a salty residue clinging to my bare arms and legs.

Lightkeep Cottage appeared over the crest of the hill and, with it, the same dark-haired woman I'd spotted several times that day. She stood at the garden gate, and looked around at me the moment she heard the crunch of my tires over the gravel of the drive.

"Hi. Can I help you?" I asked, as I dismounted.

"I'm looking for Lightkeep Cottage. And since the road ends just up there at the cliff, I'm assuming I found it?" Her voice was heavy with exhaustion.

"Yeah, you found it."

"And do the Vespers live here, do you know?"

"Yeah, they do."

"Thank God," she said, sagging a little. "I don't think I could have walked much further. Did you know this place isn't on Google maps? And no one in this town gives information very freely."

"What do you want with the Vespers?" I asked. If she was a member of the Kildare coven, she wouldn't draw attention to herself by asking where the Vespers lived. And yet, I still felt unaccountably nervous.

"I'm actually just looking for one. Her name is Wren? Wren Vesper?" My surprise at hearing my own name must have shown on my face. The woman eyed me suspiciously. "Is that who I've found? Are you Wren Vesper?"

There seemed no point in lying. I'd already given myself away. "I... I am."

"Wren Vesper," the young woman repeated, her face breaking into a relieved smile. "I'm not sure I've ever been so happy to see anyone in my life. I have something for you." And she pulled a black backpack around onto her hip so that she could unzip it and dig around inside.

"Sorry, but... who are you?" I asked, taking half a step back from her as she pulled something from the bag, something large and rectangular and wrapped carefully in a swath of velvet fabric.

"Oh, I'm sorry. I should have introduced myself first," the young woman said. She unwound that fabric from the item in her hands to reveal a very old and tattered book which she held carefully out to me. "My name is Jess Ballard, and I've traveled a very long way under strict instructions to give this to no one but you."

3

I didn't reach for the book. I couldn't seem to move. I stared down at it, a dozen emotions chasing each other around inside my head, making me feel almost dizzy.

Who was this stranger?

Where did that book come from?

Was it dangerous?

Was all of this some kind of trap, like I'd touch the book and turn into a toad or something? That sounded about right for Sedgwick Cove.

As I stood there, paralyzed, I heard the woman heave a quiet sigh. I tore my gaze from the book, and looked up to find her looking at me with eyes full of warm sympathy.

"Are you going to take it?" she asked. "It's kind of heavy."

I shook my head. "I... no, I don't think I... not quite yet," I whispered.

"Fair enough," she said. "I'll just put it back in my bag, for the time being. It's not exactly the kind of thing we should leave lying around, you know?"

I nodded, because somehow, I *did* know. I watched the book disappear back into her backpack. I felt an odd sense of relief as she yanked on the zipper—like the book had been staring at me, and now I was free from the intensity of its gaze.

It's a book, I reminded myself. *Books can't stare at you.*

That's no ordinary book, a voice in my head replied.

"Is it okay if we sit down for a minute?" the woman asked, after an awkward silence. "I've walked a lot today."

"Huh? Oh. Yeah, okay. I'm not sure..." My gaze darted to the house, and she didn't miss it.

"I don't think anyone's home. I rang the doorbell before you rode up, but no one answered."

I bit my lip. Rhi was down at the Sedgwick Cove Library for her monthly cookbook club meeting, I knew that. My mother was probably home, but out in the gardens somewhere, and I felt like a helpless child calling for her. As I struggled over what to do, Jess piped up again.

"I think there's a stone bench over there, a little ways along the garden fence. Maybe we could just sit there for a few minutes? I'm sure you have questions," she suggested gently.

I couldn't think of any nefarious reason she'd want to sit with me on a bench where anyone could see us. So, I nodded, gestured wordlessly to the bench, and she followed me over to it. As I sat down, the flowers around me nodded in the breeze, brushing against my legs and arms. A bright cluster of purple asters bent over the fence and nudged my shoulder.

Asters. Asteria.

Like a bolt of lightning, the memory that had been nudging gently against me like those flowers exploded into my mind, a memory trying to break through my initial fears and suspicions about this stranger now sitting beside me. Asteria had come to me while I met with Xiomara and given me a message. She had told me this would happen. What was it she said?

The girl will bring the book. Trust her, little bird.

I stared at the young woman beside me. She gave a kind of groan as she sat down and pulled a hair tie from her wrist, which she used to hoist her hair into a messy bun on top of her head, squinting into the sunlight.

Was this her? Was this the woman Asteria had told me about? I swallowed hard, my thoughts absolutely swirling now. Asteria might want me to trust her, but I still had questions.

"Sorry, what did you say your name was?" I asked, hoping against hope that she wouldn't hear the tremor in my voice.

"Jess Ballard," she repeated patiently.

"And... that book," I said, pointing down at her bag, which she had taken off her back and was now leaning against her leg. "Where did you get it?"

"It was... well, kind of an accident that I found it," Jess said. She seemed to be choosing her words carefully. "I work at a school over in England called Fairhaven. We have an extensive antique book collection, and one day some students sort of... stumbled upon that one." She hiked her thumb at her backpack, in which the book was now zipped.

"You mean it's a library book?" I asked.

"Well, yes and no. It was technically in our library, but it shouldn't have been. I couldn't find a record of it in our catalogue, and it was so different from the other books we had that I decided to get it examined properly by an expert, a Dr. Vesper. And that led me to you."

"Wait, the person who examined it was also named Vesper?"

"That's right."

My mind was whirling. I'd never asked about Vesper relatives outside of Sedgwick Cove, so I had no idea whether what she was telling me was true. Still, it sounded plausible.

"So this Dr. Vesper said you needed to give the book to me?"

Jess paused just a moment too long before she said, "With a little investigating, we were able to determine that you were the rightful owner. I left some of Dr. Vesper's notes on your family tree tucked in there, that I think will help explain."

"You said the book is... is different from the other books?" I asked. "What does that mean exactly?"

Here, Jess bit her lip. "It just... didn't quite fit in our collection. I'm not sure if someone had put it there by accident, or maybe they were trying to conceal it there. But however it got to be there, it shouldn't have been."

"And you came all the way from England to give it to me?" I asked.

"Yup."

"No offense, but that sounds like an awful lot of trouble to go to. I mean, you don't know me."

Jess lifted a hand to her lips, rather like she was trying to smother a laugh. "I suppose you're right, but... I just wanted to make sure it found its way home."

"And its home is... me?"

"So it would seem."

I took a deep breath. "Can I... see it?"

"Of course. It is yours, after all."

Jess reached down into her backpack and pulled out the book once again. This time, when she held it out to me, I took it.

The very moment the book touched my skin, a frisson, like electricity, shot up my fingers, filling my body with strange, hot energy. At once, I yelped and the book nearly fell to the gravel, but Jess shot out a hand and managed to grab it before it did.

"What was that?" I gasped.

"What was what?" Jess asked, though she sounded more intrigued than confused.

"I... nothing," I lied quickly. "Uh... static electricity, probably.

Jess only nodded, and placed the book in my lap.

Prepared for it this time, the energy that pulsed gently against my knees didn't scare me. Fascinated, I studied the book itself. It was clearly very old, bound in black leather worn smooth and gray in places, but the binding seemed tight. The edges of the pages were rough cut and the paper was thick and pulpy, like it had been made by hand. There was no writing on the cover—if there ever had been, it had long since worn away. Instead, there was a symbol that seemed to have been branded or stamped into the leather—an intricate Celtic knot at the center of a compass rose. At the four points of the compass, a jewel had been set into the leather, each a different color, each glittering in the sunlight like there was a tiny fire lit inside them. I didn't need to be an expert in precious stones to know they were real and probably extremely valuable.

"Wow," I muttered, in spite of myself.

"Yeah. That's what Dr. Vesper said too, when she first saw it."

Heart pounding, I lifted the cover and peeked inside, carefully thumbing through a few pages. The text was handwritten in different hands, some of it clear, other parts illegible, accompanied by sketches of plants, runes, and constellations. I closed it again quickly.

It was a spellbook. I was holding a spellbook.

I looked up to see Jess looking intently at me, like she was trying to read my expression.

"Did you, uh... did you look through this book?" I asked, hoping I merely sounded curious instead of nervous.

Jess nodded. "Of course. It's really cool, isn't it?"

"Yeah, yeah, it's..."

"A grimoire, I think."

I stared at her.

"That's what Dr. Vesper called it," she went on. "She said your family had a history of witchcraft. In fact, that's what Dr. Vesper studies. She teaches courses on witchcraft and other folk magic and traditions at Cambridge."

"Oh."

"Anyway, once I tracked you down to Sedgwick Cove, I realized I must be on the right track. I used to live in Salem, Massachusetts, you know. These New England towns can be steeped in occult heritage. Once I saw your family's shop downtown, I knew you'd appreciate having this. There's probably some cool family history in there."

I could feel my pulse calming down. The more she talked, the more it was apparent that this woman wasn't here to drop a bombshell or expose my family's magical secrets. It really seemed like she was just a nice young woman who found something cool that belonged to us, and wanted to return it. I finally felt I was able to return her smile.

"Thanks for coming so far to deliver it," I said. "You could have just... just mailed it, or something. You didn't have to come all this way."

Jess shook her head, laughing. "An antique like that? Not a chance. I couldn't have lived with myself if it got damaged or lost. Besides, it was a good excuse to visit the old stomping grounds. I caught up with some friends down in Massachusetts, and got to relive my college days. Seriously, it was a good trip."

"Well, thank you. It's... this is really cool," I said.

Jess' smile widened. "Good. Well. Mission accomplished, I guess." She slapped her knees with her hands and stood up, hoisting her backpack onto her shoulder again. "Any suggestions for a place to grab food on my way out of town?"

"Xiomara's Cafe," I said, without hesitation. "Best food in town, hands down."

Jess grinned. "Brilliant. I think I saw that place right on Main Street. Well, nice to have met you, Wren Vesper." She thrust out her hand.

"You, too," I replied, taking it. She gave my hand a hearty shake, waved, and headed off down the road toward town, tilting her chin back like she was trying to soak in the sun and sea air as she went. I was so rattled, so frightened of her sudden appearance, and then so mesmerized by the book itself, that I forgot that Asteria had also said something else about Jess Ballard:

She understands the Source. She's connected to the Source.

I STOOD for a long time after she left, paralyzed with indecision. Do I go after her? Even if I did, what could I say?

Hey, so the ghost of my dead grandmother came to me in a trance and told you you're connected to the Source. Would you care to elaborate? Even in my head it sounded insane.

I'd never told anyone about what Asteria had said to me that night in Xiomara's presence. Xiomara had advised against it. She thought the message was too vague, and that I should continue to reach out to Asteria for more information. And I'd been trying to do just that, unsuccessfully, all summer. Either Asteria had no more information for me, or I was getting worse at connecting with her. Whatever it was, Xiomara had advised me to keep trying until the message became clear.

Well, despite Asteria's continued silence, the message was now clear. The girl in question had arrived. She had indeed brought a book, and I had trusted her enough to take it. I looked down at it, and suddenly felt very exposed, standing out in the gravel drive. I turned on my heel and fled into the house.

Once inside, I sat down at the kitchen table and laid the book in front of me. Maybe I didn't have to chase after Jess. Maybe the answers were right in front of me. The papers Jess had mentioned were tucked into the back of the book. I pulled them out, unfolded them, and spread them out on the tabletop. There were five pages in total, all written in the same loopy, slightly messy scrawl. The first was a letter on pale blue stationery.

Dear Ms. Ballard,

Thank you for the opportunity to examine this book. My colleague was correct—this is absolutely in my wheelhouse, and I was delighted to have the chance to dig around and discover what I could about it. None of us could have been prepared for just how much this book and I have in common. I'm still reeling from it.

It turns out that this book, a grimoire, as I explained when you came to see me, is not only tied to my very niche field of study, but also to my very own family. I am actually descended, distantly but nonetheless, from the coven that created this grimoire. I have enclosed a rough family tree that explains the connection. I have long been aware of my family's connection to witchcraft. It was, as you have probably guessed, the spark that lit the flame of my academic pursuits. It has been the thrill of my career holding this book in my hands, and I shall be sorry to no longer have it in my possession. I am, however, delighted that I can return it to the relatives to whom it rightfully belongs. When you do return it, please pass along my contact information. If they would be amenable, I would love to connect with this branch of my family tree and glean what I can of our shared history.

With Gratitude,

Dr. Camilla Vesper

I set the letter aside, along with the business card that had been enclosed, which had Dr. Vesper's phone number and email address printed on it. Much like Jess, it seemed Dr. Vesper thought of this book more in the sense of a family heirloom than as any sort of legitimate magical object. For some reason, this calmed me. After all, if she had believed the book to contain any sort of real power, she wouldn't have relinquished it so willingly. Next, I picked up the family tree, smoothing out the creases in the paper so that I could examine it more closely.

It was handwritten in blue ink, a series of lines and dashes and scribbled names and dates. The name Vesper appeared over and over again; even when a female family member was joined to a man—presumably her husband, if I was reading it correctly—there was no change to her name. And what was more, the name Vesper was passed down to the children. Curious, I searched for a familiar name and finally found Asteria. I'd never stopped to consider that Vesper hadn't been her married name. I traced the line that joined her name to my grandfather's: John Templeton, and then the lines that led to her three girls: Rhiannon, Persephone, and Kerridwen Vesper.

My mother had told me her father had died of a heart attack when she was only five years old. Had Asteria changed all of their names after his death, or had they always been Vespers? Somehow, I thought it must be the latter.

"There is great power in a name. A name, known and spoken, can hold as much power as an incantation," Rhi had told me a few weeks ago, as she led me through my studies. To be a Vesper was a powerful thing, I had come to learn. Perhaps carrying on the name was part of that power. I would have to ask my mother or one of my aunts about it.

I followed the dashed ink line from my mother down to where my own name stared up at me like an unanswered question. Jess's words floated back to me on the surface of my memory.

I've traveled a very long way under strict instructions to give this to no one but you.

The words suddenly felt strange. Whose instructions? Dr. Vesper's, surely. But why? Dr. Vesper's chart was very thorough. She had included birth and death dates for all the Vespers going back centuries. She knew that Asteria had passed—there was her death date—my birthday—staring up at me like a thorn ready to prick me. And under my mother, Rhi, and Persi's names, just their birthdays followed by a dash. Dr. Vesper knew that my mother and her sisters were still alive. So why in the world would she insist that the book be passed along to me, specifically? She could do the math—she knew I was just a kid. Even if I had been studying witchcraft all my life, it still made no sense to pass the book along to me. Surely Rhi, as the oldest living Vesper, was the rightful recipient? I frowned, thinking hard, but no matter how I considered it, it made no sense that Jess Ballard had been told to give the book to me.

I set the family tree aside and with it, my questions for the time being. I looked instead at the book itself—the grimoire. Prepared for it this time, the surge of energy through my fingertips didn't startle me, though it did intrigue me. I wondered if Jess had felt the same thing when she'd handed me the book. She hadn't let on, if she had. I turned the pages carefully, through sketches and notes.

In sanguine tuo, clavis ad vim occultam

I muttered the words over and over again under my breath. I wasn't sure what language it was—Latin, maybe? They were the only words on the page. They reminded me of a dedication in the front of a novel, or a title page. The words were clearly important, set apart as they were at the beginning of the book, but what did they mean?

I flipped forward through more pages, and realized that there were many blank pages scattered randomly throughout the book. In fact, the further through the pages I searched, the more blank pages I found. What was more, when I touched these blank pages, the zing of energy that pulsed through my fingertips grew stronger.

"Wren?"

"GAH!"

I leaped out of my seat, hand pressed to my now pounding heart, to find my mother standing in the doorway to the kitchen, earth smudged across her cheeks and down the front of her overalls.

"Sorry! Did I scare you?" she asked, wide-eyed.

"No, it's... I mean yes, but don't worry, it's not your fault. I was kind of wrapped up in something," I said, as I attempted to catch my breath.

"What's Rhi got you working on now?" my mom asked, smiling as she pulled her gloves off and headed for the fridge. "Or is it homework from Xiomara?"

"Neither, actually," I said. "It's this book."

"Hmm? A book?" My mother was barely listening as she poured herself a glass of Rhi's lavender lemonade and started gulping it down.

"Yeah, this woman came by today to deliver it to me. It's... I guess it's some kind of family heirloom?"

This made my mother turn. "What woman?"

I shrugged. "I've never seen her before. She said her name was Jess B—"

"Is that the book?" She had set her glass down and was pointing with a dirt-smudged finger at the book, where it still lay open on the kitchen table.

"Yeah," I said, closing it carefully and holding it out to her. "She said she had strict instructions to deliver it to me."

My mother seemed to drift toward me, like she was in some kind of trance. I watched as with every step, her eyes widened, her complexion paled, until she arrived at my side, trembling and paper-white.

"Mom?"

"Where did you get that book?" The words were barely a whisper through her unmoving lips.

"I just told you, this woman... Mom, are you okay?"

At that moment, my mother sank into one of the kitchen chairs. For one awful moment, I thought she was going to pass out. Then she pushed her hair back from her face with shaking fingers.

"Wren, put that book down, and don't touch it again," she whispered. "We need to find my sisters and get them home. Now."

4

The air in the room was so thick with tension, I felt like I couldn't breathe it. My head was absolutely spinning with the events of the last sixty minutes. My mother and my aunts, whispering and gasping and running around digging through family records. The interrogation, all three of them asking the same questions over and over again, and me repeating the same bewildered answers.

Where had the book come from?
Who was the woman?
What did she look like?
Where did she go?
What did she say?

No matter how many times I replied, my answers never seemed to be good enough, and they would repeat the questions again, as though I would somehow answer differently. Then they all left the room and huddled together out on the porch, whispering frantically to each other, their voices only occasionally rising to a volume where I could catch a phrase or two:

"...can't possibly be the same book, there's no way..."

"...it must be a trick..."

"...but didn't you *feel* it?!"

After that, Rhi took her phone out into the garden and paced back and forth between the riotous hydrangea bushes, arms gesticulating wildly. Finally, after about fifteen minutes she joined Persi and my mom, and after a quick whispered conference, all three of them came back into the kitchen.

"Is anyone going to tell me what's going on?" I snapped, the stress and uncertainty finally fraying my patience.

Rhi leaned forward, taking the corners of the velvet wrappings and covering the book with them, being careful not to touch it. Once it was completely enclosed, she lifted it gingerly from the table and said, "Back up from the table, Wren. Go ahead, Persi."

I slid back from the kitchen table, my chair legs squeaking across the wood floor, as Persi reached down and took a hold of the tabletop. It was a round table, with a blonder wooden circle inset within a darker wood border that was carved and painted with flowers and vines and birds. I'd always assumed the design was merely decorative, but now I watched with astonishment as Persi reached beneath it and, with a couple of faint clicks, caused the entire center circle of the table to drop and flip over. Then she engaged some sort of crank and the center circle rose into place again, revealing some kind of intricate circle carved into the wood.

"Permanent protective circle," Persi explained as I gaped. "A Vesper is always prepared in her own home."

"It was our grandmother's invention," Rhi added with a hint of pride in her voice. "She had it specially made."

Once the inner section had clunked into place, Rhi set the book down once more, this time at the heart of this hidden circle, and carefully pulled the wrappings away. Wordlessly, my mother and aunts spread out around the table naturally, taking up places at the south, east, and west directions. Persi looked pointedly at me, and I jumped up from my seat to stand at the section of the table that pointed north. As I watched, Rhi pulled two stones from the drawer behind her—citrine and tiger's eye, I thought—and placed them in a little mesh pouch on the end of a string, all the while muttering under her breath. Persi and my mom began to mutter, too, as Rhi lifted the little bag so that it swung like a pendulum over the book. She swung it first in a counterclockwise, and then a clockwise motion. Then she went still, all muttering stopped, and her sisters did the same. I felt frozen with anticipation, waiting for something to happen.

Nothing did.

After about half a minute, Rhi let out a long breath. Her shoulders sagged with relief, and she lowered the mesh bag to the table.

"It hasn't been cursed. So it's safe to handle, at least," she announced.

I felt afraid instead of relieved. Could it really have been so dangerous simply to touch the book? Even though I now knew it was safe, I had a sudden desire to wipe my hands on my shorts, feeling contaminated despite Rhi's reassurances.

"What do we do with it?" Persi asked. "It can't possibly be *that* book. Can it?"

My mom sat down, pulling the book toward her while the rest of us took our seats around the table. Despite the fact that Rhi had pronounced it safe, my mother was extremely careful as she opened the cover of the book. There she spotted the same strange words I'd read earlier: *In sanguine tuo, clavis ad vim occultam.* Unlike me, however, she understood exactly what they meant.

"Well, there's one way to find out," my mom said. She reached into her gardening belt, dug out a pair of garden shears and, without any kind of warning, dug the tip of one sharp blade into the callused pad of her thumb.

I cried out, but she silenced me with a look. Then, using the hand that wasn't currently dripping blood, she flipped through the book until she found one of the many blank pages scattered throughout. With one swift, serious look at her sisters, she pressed her oozing thumb to the paper.

The effect was instantaneous. The paper sucked up the blood like a desiccated sponge, and from the place where it disappeared, lines began to appear, swirling and spreading across the surface like veins. The lines curved and looped into words and soon, the formerly blank page was covered in writing. The heading at the top read "A Spell for Concealment."

"Oh my goddess, it is," Rhi whispered. "It is. It really, truly is."

"Really is what?" I finally burst out. "Is anyone going to tell me what's actually going on here?"

My mom tore her eyes from the book with difficulty. She opened her mouth, as though struggling for the right words.

"Mom, can you, like... take care of that?" I asked weakly. "It's dripping down your whole arm."

"Huh? Oh!" My mom pulled the blue bandana out of her hair, and wiped the snaking trail of blood from her forearm and wrist before wrapping the cloth hastily around her thumb. I didn't bother mentioning that it was filthy—I was too eager to hear her answer.

"Well?"

"We'll... we'll have to perform some more tests, just to be sure—"

"Oh, come on, Kerridwen! What other tests do we need?" Persi cried. Her eyes were bright with a wild, enthusiastic light.

"I don't think we should jump to any conclusions," my mom began defensively, but Persi cut her off again.

"Jumping? Who's jumping? The conclusion is right in front of us. What else can it be but the truth?"

"The Conclave will want to—"

"Oh, screw the Conclave!" Persi snapped. "We don't need them to quaver and argue over what we can already see with our own eyes!"

"Which is WHAT?!" I shouted.

Persi turned her sparkling eyes on me. "That after being lost for centuries, the Vesper grimoire has finally come home!"

Her words crackled in the air like an incantation of their own.

"I don't understand. We already have a grimoire," I said, gesturing over to the kitchen counter where a huge leatherbound book sat propped on Rhi's cookbook stand. It was the same spellbook we'd been using for all of my lessons, the book Rhi cracked open every time she was baking or looking something up.

"That is *a* grimoire, Wren. Not *the* grimoire," Persi said, as though that clarified things.

"Huh?"

"Oh, come on!" she snapped impatiently. You know the story, don't you? Rhi, have you been neglecting to include the family history in this so-called education?"

"Of course not!" Rhi retorted, looking offended. "Don't you start criticizing me when you keep flaking out on her lessons to go off galivant—"

"Then you know the story of Sarah Claire and the night of the Covenant," Persi interrupted, ignoring Rhi's criticism.

Yes, I knew it. We'd been discussing part of it just that morning, when Rhi, in her explanation of familiars, explained about Diana's role in our coven's history. I tried to remember the story—Sarah on the cliff top, frantically trying to complete her spell before she was discovered, and Diana's arrival just as she began the incantation.

An incantation in a stolen book...

An incantation summoned with blood...

"Holy shit!" I gasped, as the pieces finally clicked together in my brain. "Is that... that can't be the same book!"

"I wouldn't have believed it myself, if I hadn't just watched your mother prove it," Persi replied. She reached forward and pulled the book toward her.

"Be careful!" Rhi complained, as Persi flipped none too gently back through the pages until she found those mysterious words again.

"*In sanguine tuo, clavis ad vim occultam,*" she read out loud, her voice vibrating with barely suppressed triumph. "In thy blood, the key to hidden power."

"That's what it means?" I whispered.

"It's Latin. The Vesper grimoire was coveted by every witch who ever encountered its magic, but the book was protected. There were lesser spells that any reader could find and perform, but only a Vesper's blood could reveal the most powerful spells contained within."

"I don't understand," I said, shaking my head. "If this book is so powerful and important to our family, why have we never seen it before? How did we ever let it out of our sight?"

It was Rhi who answered, dropping into the chair in front of her with a weary sigh. "That's just it, Wren. We're not sure."

"You're not sure? How can you not know?" I asked, incredulous.

"The fate of the book is one of the most mysterious chapters in our coven's history, and one we've been trying to find an answer to for ages. You see, it disappeared on the very night of the Covenant."

My mother also took her seat at the table, and we all looked at Rhi, expectant.

"Sarah Claire stole the book, as you know," Rhi said, her voice settling into the lulling rhythms of a story told and retold many times; and for a moment, I could imagine my mother and her sisters asking the same questions, and Asteria in Rhi's place, giving the same answer I was now about to hear. "Mary Vesper was feeling poorly, and Sarah disguised the potion in a broth she brought to the cottage. Once Mary had fallen into a deep sleep, Sarah took the book, but she knew she also needed Vesper blood in order to find the spell she needed."

My heart gave a thump. "She didn't... I mean, did she *kill*—"

Rhi shook her head. "No. She used a knife to puncture one of Mary's fingers, and collected the blood in a vial. A drop or two will suffice, as you've seen. She went to the cliffs to carry out her plan. But Diana didn't only protect the coven. She protected the book as well. She knew it had been taken almost as soon as Sarah left the house, and she followed. She roused the coven to action and they, along with the rest of Sarah's own coven, were able to stop her before it was too late."

"So they got the book back," I said.

"They did. And they used it to seal the Covenant. But after that, the book vanished."

"I don't—"

"It was Mary," Persi chimed in. "She knew the grimoire put them all in danger. It held the key, not only to binding the Darkness, but also, now, unleashing it. As long as the Vespers held those secrets close, they would always have a target on their backs. It was too risky to keep the grimoire."

"So what did she do with it?" I asked eagerly.

"No one knows," my mom answered. "Well, Mary did, of course. But soon it was put about that the book was gone, and when people asked about it, Mary would only say—"

All three sisters spoke the words at once. "'It is lost, and long may it stay so.'"

"And she never told anyone what she had done with it? No one, not even other members of the coven?" I asked.

"It seems not. If she did, they kept the secret as thoroughly as she did. Our family started over, passing spells down by oral tradition, and recording them in new grimoires; but the deepest, most dangerous magic contained in that original grimoire was lost... until now."

Until now.

We all fell quiet, staring at the book. Its very presence seemed to have sucked all the air from the room. After what felt like a long time, Persi's voice suddenly broke the silence, making us all jump.

"And now, out of nowhere this woman just... just shows up and hands you a centuries-lost book, the most powerful book of magic known to have existed? It doesn't make sense!" she ground out, pounding her fist on the table.

"It does if she didn't realize what it was she was handing over," my mom said, chewing thoughtfully on her bottom lip. "I mean, think about it. She's an academic, right? Or a librarian?"

She looked at me for clarification, but I shrugged. "She just said she worked at a school. Fairhaven, I think she said it was called. It's in England, although she didn't have an English accent."

"Okay, so let's assume academic of some kind. She finds this book, has it examined, discovers where it belongs, and returns it. That seems reasonable," Rhi says.

"But how?" Persi persisted. "How does a book lost for centuries—no, not lost, but intentionally hidden away—wind up at this Fairhaven in the first place, just sitting on a shelf for anyone to find? Did she explain that?"

"She didn't know," I said. "She told me some students discovered it in their library, but that they didn't have a record of it. She thought it had either been returned there by accident, or hidden there."

"Those students are lucky to be alive, if they even are," Persi said darkly. "Imagine someone with no magical training handling this book, let alone trying to use it?"

She shuddered, and I joined her. After all, my magical training was rudimentary at best, and I'd already had a taste of the damage uncontrolled magic could do.

"How did this woman find us?" Rhi asked, wringing her hands together. "I don't like that she found us so easily."

"I don't think it was very easy, actually," I said, holding out the letter from Dr. Vesper, along with the family tree. "This Dr. Vesper is a relative. She had already done a lot of research on our family history. She's the one who figured out who to return the book to. Jess Ballard was just the messenger."

"Hmm," my mother said, taking the papers from me and looking them over. "Well, I suppose that's easy enough to verify. But why you specifically, Wren? Why not one of us?"

"I don't know," I admitted. "I didn't think to ask that question while she was here."

"Well, we need to find her and find out. Maybe it really is all an innocent discovery, but I'd like to know for sure. Did Jess leave anything that would help us contact her?"

"No."

"Hmm. Well, we might be able to find her through this Dr. Vesper, or that school she mentioned. Unless..." My mom sat up a little straighter. "How long ago did this woman leave?"

"I don't know... an hour ago, maybe a little more?" I said.

"And did she say where she was going?"

"She... she asked where she could get food on the way out of town, and I told her to go to Xiomara's, obviously."

My mom jumped up out of her seat. "We might still be able to catch her. Come on, we'll take the car."

Before I could even process what was happening, my mom and I piled into my mom's beat up little Subaru and began speeding down the road toward town. As we got closer, the size of the crowds meant we had to slow down to a crawl. My mom, swearing under her breath about tourists, swung the car into a parking space just as another car vacated it; and we jumped out and began to weave and duck our way through the hordes on the sidewalks until we reached Xiomara's Cafe.

"Do you see her, Wren?" my mom asked, as we surveyed the line of customers snaking right out the door.

"No," I replied after scanning each face carefully.

We skirted the line and ran around the side of the building, where there was a door that led to the kitchen. My mom hammered on it and waited, bouncing on the balls of her feet. After a few seconds the door opened, and Eva stuck her head out. She looked startled to see us standing there.

"Wren! Ms. Vesper! What are you—" she began, but my mother cut her off.

"We're looking for someone who might have just stopped by." She turned to me. "Wren can you—?"

"Uh, yeah, she was like mid-twenties, black dyed hair with purple highlights, all black clothes, kinda heavy on the eyeliner?" I said quickly.

Eva frowned. "I don't *think* so, but I feel like I've seen at least a dozen girls who could fit that description today. Black clothes and colorful hair could describe like half the tourists who come in here during the lead up to Samhain. Sorry."

"That's okay. Will you text Wren if you spot someone who fits that description?" my mom asked.

Eva's eyebrows pulled together. "Sure, sure. Can I ask why you—?"

"We'll explain later, honey, we've got to keep looking," my mom said. "Thanks for your help."

Eva threw me a curious glance as she pulled the door closed. I turned to ask my mom what was next, but she was already halfway back up the narrow alleyway toward the bustling street again.

"Mom, would you wait up? You don't even know who you're looking for!" I cried, hurrying after her. She didn't slow, though, reaching the end of the alley and turning her head back and forth, scanning the crowd for any sign of Jess Ballard. I arrived beside her, panting.

"Mom, isn't this a little... overkill?" I asked.

"Huh?" she asked, not even looking at me.

"This is ridiculous, Mom. We're never gonna find her in this crowd. And anyway, she said she was heading out of town."

"We need to talk to her, Wren. We need to find out more about how she came across that book."

"I know, but this isn't the way to do it. She left us Dr. Vesper's card. Let's get in touch with her. She'll know how to reach Jess."

My mom sighed, lowering her heels to the ground. "You're right. This is a needle in a haystack situation. Let's just walk the main thoroughfare once, okay? Humor me. If we don't see her, we'll go home."

I agreed, and together we walked from one end of Main Street to the other, my mother pointing at every black-haired woman she saw and hissing, "Is that her?" over and over again until I was ready to scream. Finally, the shops trickled away, and the bustling downtown faded to a few cottages dotting the grassy dunes. Up ahead, we could see the Manor, home of the Claires, looming on the hill and marking the furthest reaches of Sedgwick Cove. My mother reluctantly admitted defeat, and we turned around and retraced our steps back to the car. When at last we pulled back up in front of Lightkeep Cottage, both Persi and Rhi were waiting on the porch for us.

"Any luck?" Rhi asked, though without much hope in her voice.

"No," my mom said, slamming the car door a bit harder than necessary in her frustration. "No sign of her."

"Damn it all," Persi cursed.

"I still think we'll be able to get in touch with her," I said. "We've got—"

"What do we do about the Conclave?" Persi asked, steamrolling right over me.

"We have to tell them," Rhi said at once.

"We have to tell them eventually, yes," my mom said, twisting a strand of her hair around her fingers like she always did when she was preoccupied. She looked at Persi, who nodded.

Rhi looked back and forth between her sisters, her expression scandalized. "Kerri, you aren't seriously suggesting we keep this from them!"

"No, not exactly. It's just... you know how they are." She raised her eyebrows as though that was all that needed to be said on the subject.

"*I* don't know how they are," I said, starting to feel annoyed now. "Can someone please explain?"

Rhi gestured toward my mother, as though to say, "Be my guest," and my mother heaved a resigned sigh.

"The Conclave is old school," my mother began, and then, seeing the incredulous look on my face, she amended, "Yes, I know, all of Sedgwick Cove is old school, to a degree. But the Conclave is particularly stuck in their ways, and they are especially fierce when it comes to security."

"Meaning?" I asked.

"Meaning that if they caught wind of this book reappearing, we'd likely never see it again," Persi answered.

"That's not true," Rhi scoffed. "The book belongs to the Vesper coven, they know that."

"And they also know what spells must be contained in this book, which means they'd be tripping over themselves to make sure it was buried again," my mom said.

"Ostara especially," Persi said, and her expression hardened into a mask. "In her mind, that book is the reason her coven was disgraced. It's why she's always been so fierce about dark magic, keeping the books locked away from her family. She will fear the temptation this book represents."

"Which means she'll fight to have it locked away," my mom said.

"Or destroyed altogether," Persi added.

"Oh, be reasonable," Rhi cried, though she sounded more plaintive now.

"Why? Ostara certainly won't be. We need to think strategically here,

Rhi," my mom said. "I'm not saying we shouldn't tell them. We should, and soon. But let's get what answers we can first."

"Such as?" Rhi asked, crossing her arms over her chest.

"Such as who this Jess... what's her name again?"

"Ballard," I supplied.

"Right. Let's track down this Jess Ballard and get the full story of how this book resurfaced. I don't think she—or this Dr. Vesper, for that matter—understand what this book really is; but we need to be sure. We also need to know who else has handled it, and whether they were able to unlock any of its secrets."

"Surely not, or they would have kept it!" Rhi said. But her voice was weak now, and Persi, sensing victory, jumped in.

"We have to be sure. And we need time to examine it for ourselves. Rhi, this book is the most important legacy our family has. Do we really want to hand it over before we've had the slightest chance to look at it?"

Rhi stood there tapping her foot. "Fine. But you have to promise me we will tell the Conclave."

"Of course we will," my mom was quick to reassure her.

Rhi's mouth twisted into a disapproving little knot, but I could see her eyes softening, and even I could tell she was about to cave. "Samhain," she finally said. "I'll give you until Samhain, and then I'm telling them myself."

Persi looked like she wanted to argue again, but my mother gave her a warning look. *It's the best we're gonna get and you know it,* that look seemed to say. Persi nodded curtly.

"Okay, Samhain it is," my mom said. "That means we've got two weeks."

I looked through the window to where the book sat on the kitchen table. Two weeks didn't seem like enough time to plumb the depths of a tome like that, but it seemed it was all we were going to get.

"How do we start?" I asked.

My mom looked over at me, startled. "Oh. Wren, honey I really think we should... I mean this book could be dangerous."

I frowned at her. "Didn't you already test to see if it was safe to handle it?"

"Well, yes, but that doesn't mean that there isn't more danger to unmask on the inside, honey."

I narrowed my eyes at her. "Are you saying you aren't going to let me help?"

All three of the sisters looked at each other now, and I realized that not one of them had planned to include me in the investigation of the grimoire.

"Jess delivered that book to me. Me, specifically," I reminded them.

"Wren, honey, you're still so new to witchcraft, it wouldn't—"

"And whose fault is that?" I asked, firing up. "That wasn't my choice."

My mom's face flushed with guilt, but I didn't care. I wasn't going to be the only Vesper left out of the most important thing to happen to our coven since the Covenant itself.

"Just... just let us get started. We won't keep you from it when we know it's safe, honey."

"But I know it's safe! Asteria said—"

But I stopped myself suddenly. I had never told them about Asteria coming to me at Xiomara's. I never told them what she had said, about the girl and the book, and how I needed to trust her. This silence was partly Xiomara's idea—she thought the message was incomplete, and I should continue reaching out until I had more information. But for me, it was more than that. My mom and her sisters thought their mother was gone—not just dead, but that her spirit had crossed over peacefully. I didn't want them to know that Asteria was restless and confused. What good would that do? Besides, her message wasn't for them—she had never mentioned them at all. Her message was for me. The book was delivered to me. Didn't that mean something?

"What did you say, Wren? What about Asteria?" my mom asked, interrupting my inner turmoil.

"Asteria... wouldn't want me to be excluded," I lied. "She wanted me to be a Vesper—a real Vesper. But I can't be if I'm always on the outside."

My mom's expression twisted, and I experienced a stab of guilt. But before either of us could say anything else, Rhi forestalled us by blurting out, "You've got to get going, Wren! You're going to be late for your lesson with Xiomara."

I wanted to argue but she was right, and Xiomara was not the kind of person you left waiting.

"Fine," I snapped. "But I'm not letting this go."

"I wouldn't expect you to," my mother sighed.

Normally, I'd have been angry that I couldn't stay and continue to plead my case, but not in this moment. In this moment, a session with Xiomara was exactly what I needed. Asteria had left too many questions unanswered. If anyone could help me find those answers, Xiomara could.

5

I had to pedal like I was being chased down by a horde of zombies, but I made it to the Marin house on time. Eva laughed at me as she opened the door.

"What the hell happened to you?" she asked.

"Running late," I panted. My face felt flushed and sweaty.

Eva just shook her head, still chuckling, and stepped aside to let me in.

I took off my shoes and greeted Eva's mom, Maricela, who was pulling a tray of something cinnamon-smelling out of the oven in the kitchen.

"Hello, Wren! Did Eva tell you? We've got a waterworker in the house!" she said, smiling broadly.

"I know!" I said, smiling back. "It's so exciting, congratulations!"

Most teenagers probably would have rolled their eyes, but Eva just beamed. This was one instance where family pride—or more specifically, coven pride—was gratifying rather than humiliating. Eva would be glowing for days over this achievement—as well she should. I wish my studies were going half as well.

Speaking of...

Xiomara appeared in the doorway to her back room, hands on her hips, looking put out about something. Her expression summoned an apology to the tip of my tongue, but I could see from the clock over the stove that I wasn't late, so I swallowed it down. Whatever Xiomara was frustrated about, I didn't think it had anything to do with me—at least, not yet.

"Hi, Xiomara," I ventured.

She merely grunted, then pointed to the table, which looked like it might collapse under the amount of food laid out on it. "Have you eaten?"

I understood by now that this was a trick question. Even if I had eaten, she would still tell me to make a plate, but in this particular instance, I was ravenous. In all the excitement of the grimoire's arrival, I hadn't eaten dinner. I descended on the table, and started loading my plate with beans, fried plantains, empanadas, and arroz con pollo. Xiomara grunted her approval.

"I'll call you in," she said, jerking her head back toward her room. "I need more time at my boveda." Then she shuffled back through the wooden beaded curtain.

Maricela watched her go, frowning, as she joined me at the table. She traded a look with Eva that I didn't miss.

"What's up?" I asked, glancing between them.

"My mother is... troubled," Maricela said, looking not at me, but at the still gently swinging strings of beads in the doorway. "She hasn't shared what it is, but something is troubling her."

"She's spending more and more time back there, and I don't mean with clients. By herself, at the boveda," Eva added, picking up an empanada and biting into it.

"She's searching for something," Maricela said softly. "Something that is eluding her."

Well, that sounded ominous. I swallowed a huge mouthful of food and cleared my throat. "I... do you think I should stay?" I asked. "If she's really upset about something—"

"If she didn't want you here, she would have told you so, honey," Maricela said. "You just go ahead and eat, and she'll be ready for you soon."

I shrugged and started shoveling food into my mouth, examining the spread on the table as I did so. It was excessive, even for Xiomara. "Did you have company?" I asked.

Eva nodded. "Extended family was over all afternoon."

"Celebrating," Maricela added, smiling at Eva again.

At that moment, Bea trotted into the room. "Mama, are there any of those empanadas left that Tia Laura—oh! Hi, Wren!"

I couldn't answer because I'd just crammed half of said empanada into my mouth, so I just waved as I chewed.

"Hurry up before Wren inhales them all," Eva said.

Eva told me more about her waterworker tests while Bea and I ate. I couldn't help but notice how often Bea's gaze drifted over to the door of Xiomara's back room. Her expression, like her mother's, seemed troubled. Finally, as I pushed a second helping of flan away, conceding defeat, Xiomara appeared again.

"We begin," she snapped, and vanished once more.

"Come up to my room when you're done," Eva whispered, as I got up from the table. My stomach gave an anxious lurch, and I suddenly regretted eating so much. I waved goodbye to Bea and Maricela, and followed Xiomara.

Lessons with Xiomara had already turned into a source of anxiety, but now I was buzzing with nervous energy as I traced her steps through the curtain and into her backroom studio. Xiomara had already seated herself at the table in her usual chair, the back of which was upholstered in faded green fabric that rose up behind her like a throne. I took my usual seat in the chair opposite her, a slightly rickety wooden rocker with a little braided rug tied onto it in place of a cushion.

"Hi," I said lamely as I settled into my seat.

Xiomara gave a strange sound in reply, something between a snort and a disgruntled grumble, as she tidied the tabletop between us. She paused in the stacking of her tarot cards, glaring at a few individual cards as she placed them back in the deck.

"How are you, Xiomara?" I asked. I felt like I was placing the words carefully, stacking them precariously one on top of the other into a teetering tower destined to topple over.

"I've been better, *mija*. I've been better," she replied, so quietly that I couldn't tell if I was meant to hear her reply or not.

"Are you... not feeling well? Because I don't need to stay—" I was already tensing the muscles in my legs to rise from my seat again, but Xiomara held out a hand.

"Stay where you are, child. I am well in body. It's my spirit that has me troubled," Xiomara replied. She looked up from her cards, caught my eye for just a moment—the usual laser focus of her gaze was clouded with confusion and frustration. As much as Xiomara intimidated me sometimes, this was the first moment I remembered feeling actually afraid in her presence.

"What is it?" I whispered. "Can I help?"

Xiomara slipped her tarot cards back into their pouch and pulled the string tight before she answered. "I'm not sure. I'm not sure of anything." She looked over at her boveda in the corner of the room, and sighed.

I'd been introduced to the boveda at my very first lesson. It was an altar, draped in a white cloth, crowded with framed photographs of Xiomara's relatives who had passed on—parents, cousins, a sister, as well as some much older photographs, daguerreotypes, and paintings of relatives from even earlier generations. These images, propped up against each other as though the inhabitants were posing for a group photograph, were surrounded by offerings—fruit and treats baked in Xiomara's Cafe, brought home and laid before these long-lost relatives as a sign of respect and also, I soon learned, as an invitation. It was at this boveda that Xiomara would convene with her relatives, who acted as her spirit guides. She described it as her own personal door to the spirit world.

"Not a door that I can open," she hurried to clarify. "No, *mija*, that door is locked. None of us have that key. There is no key. But with the help of my spirit guides, I can place my ear against the gap. I can press my eye to the keyhole. It is up to me to interpret the glimpses and whispers that they provide."

This explanation had been a comfort at the time. It made me feel better about how difficult I was finding even the simplest spirit communication. If Xiomara, the most powerful spirit witch in Sedgwick Cove, could only achieve "glimpses" and "whispers," then I could hardly expect my own powers to produce much at first. Months later, it was hard not to let the doubts creep in, even as Xiomara guided me with maddening calm, and a relaxed sense that she expected nothing better. Now, however, it was her face that was crumpled with frustration, while I sat and tried to find the right soothing words to get her to talk to me.

"Are your spirit guides... whispering more quietly than usual?" I asked her.

Xiomara was silent for a moment, leveling me with a look that said she was carefully weighing her words, trying to decide how much to tell me, and how much to keep back. I was used to this look—it had been leveled at me by Conclave members, my own mother and aunts, and many others in Sedgwick Cove since I'd arrived. How much could I handle? What could they tell me without telling me everything? I was beginning to hate that look—it made me feel infantile and untrustworthy. But as I met it now from Xiomara, all I could do was hold my breath and hope that, after so many months, she might trust me enough to tell me the truth.

And then she did.

"Do not speak of this to anyone. Not Eva, not your mother or your aunts. No one."

My pulse began to jump. "Of course."

Xiomara rose to her feet suddenly, making me jump. She moved swiftly to the doorway and peered through to the kitchen. Maricela was no longer there. Assured no one would overhear us, Xiomara walked around the table until she stood right in front of her boveda. "I have sat for many hours this last week, communing with my spirit guides," she said. Her voice was low, with none of its usual snappishness. "I have used every method at my disposal."

"And?"

"Silence."

All I could hear was the blood thudding in my ears. I turned and looked at the boveda again, at the piles of fruit, the heaps of breads and cookies, the wilting flowers dropping petals into the wax of candles burnt so low they were in danger of extinguishing themselves. I looked at the photographs, faces frozen in time, some faded and creased, winking in and out of view in the intermittent gleam of the candlelight on the glass of their carefully polished frames. They'd always seemed alive to me as they'd watched over my sessions with Xiomara. Sometimes, I'd even had to repress an urge to turn them around, so that I didn't have to continue floundering in front of what felt like a very judgmental audience. But now, it was as though someone had closed Xiomara's personal door that connected her to them. I couldn't feel them watching me anymore. A few months ago, Bea had revealed her own gifts as a spirit witch by showing me her drawings. One in particular still lived rent-free in my head, a sketch she had made of Xiomara in her kitchen at the cafe, bent intently over her work, and surrounded by the ever-present forms of her spirit guides hovering over and around her, like they were constantly whispering to her as she went about her daily tasks. I wondered, if Bea drew Xiomara now, would she be alone?

Bea...

"Have you talked to Bea about this?" I asked.

Xiomara's expression tightened. "No, I have not."

"Why not?"

"I don't want to alarm the child. She has enough to be getting along with."

"But don't you wonder if she's noticed the same thing? With her own gift?"

Xiomara chewed on the inside of her cheek, and though she didn't reply, the answer was clear on her face. She *had* wondered about it, of course, but...

"You're afraid of the answer," I murmured, and though Xiomara looked frankly annoyed at my choice of the word "afraid," she nodded.

"She has just barely begun to explore," Xiomara said. "I am not sure she understands her gift well enough to know if it has been compromised."

"But you haven't asked her. And she hasn't mentioned it?"

"No."

I wanted to argue further, but there seemed little point. Xiomara's expression was defiant. Why did adults insist on keeping kids in the dark in moments when those same kids desperately needed the light? I mean, my mother had sheltered me so hard I didn't even know who or what I was, and in the end it hadn't protected me at all—it had only delayed the inevitable, and left me woefully unprepared to deal with it. Well, I couldn't force Xiomara to talk to Bea, but there was nothing stopping me from talking to Bea myself. I was sick of these pointless curtains drawn between generations who should be working together. I would find Bea when I went upstairs and start asking the questions Xiomara wouldn't.

"What of your work over the last week?" Xiomara asked, now eyeing me beadily. "You were meant to clear your own mental connections to your spirit guides."

It was my turn to feel self-conscious now. I felt the color flooding my cheeks, and I dropped my gaze to my lap, trying to decide how best to explain.

Xiomara snorted a laugh. "That well, huh?"

My frustrations over my spirit abilities were not simply because it was taking a long time for me to access them; it was that the access was so spotty and unpredictable that I had absolutely no idea what I was doing right, or what I was doing wrong. It was like trying to grab a hold of something ephemeral, like smoke.

In my room at Lightkeep Cottage, I had my own altar that I had curated over the months with Xiomara's guidance. It was crowded with objects that grounded me in my power for all the different elements that my magic was tied to. When it came to spirit, though, I didn't know where to begin.

"Our spirit gifts come from our deep connections with those who have gone before us," Xiomara had explained. "We are tethered to them in life by blood, and in death by the magic that lives in that blood. If we can learn to tune in to that connection, to harness that magic like... well, like one of those phones you young people are always glued to, then you can communicate with those spirits to whom you are connected."

"So, spirit witches can only communicate with their own relatives?" I asked. I wasn't sure if I was disappointed or relieved. On the one hand, I had absolutely no desire to be a ghost magnet, with random departed spirits harassing me everywhere I went. On the other hand, only being able to connect with spirits I was blood-related to felt... limiting. I thought about the spirits I'd already come into contact with, like Sarah Claire. Wouldn't it be helpful for me to be able to communicate with spirits like her, even if only to stop them from whatever nefarious plot they were ensnared with?

But Xiomara shook her head. "It is a door, remember. Your ancestors act as your spirit guides. They wait for you on the other side of that door. But they can help you connect to others who dwell with them on the other side of the door, if you become proficient enough in your gifts."

If. How could such a tiny word feel so insurmountable?

Xiomara recommended placing a photograph and perhaps some belongings of my closest ancestors on the altar to help ground me in my spirit gifts. That made sense, but I didn't have nearly the close connections to my Vesper family that Xiomara had to the many Marins who went before her. I asked my mom and my aunts for help, and they produced some old family photographs of aunts and great-grandmothers and cousins I'd never met, or even heard of. Once they had been arranged on my altar, like I had seen Xiomara do, I looked at each of the faces, willing some kind of connection between us.

I spent hours willing myself to feel something—*anything*—as I studied those relatives one by one. I noticed many throughlines, like threads run through a tapestry. I spotted my mother's piercing, heavily lashed eyes, Rhi's wildly curly blonde hair, Persi's sharp cheekbones and full lips, all appearing in the various faces of these people I'd never met. I even saw, to my surprise, my own narrow, freckled nose and wide eyes sprinkled into a distant cousin's features. I tried to focus on just these things as I relaxed my mind and imagined a tunnel opening, expanding, with me waiting at one end and all those familiar yet unfamiliar faces waiting at the other.

We're the same, I spoke into the empty air. *We're connected. Please. Please reach out.*

It was hard not to take their silence as a personal affront, a commentary on not only my power, but of myself. Was I too much of an outsider to connect to my own family?

Only when I focused on Asteria's photo did I achieve any sense of connection, and it was so fleeting, so inconsistent, that I could barely trust my own senses. Had I really gotten a whiff of her perfume, or had I imagined it? Was that really her voice I heard whisper on the breeze, or was I fooling myself because I wanted to hear her so badly?

The most frustrating thing about it all was that I *had* communicated with Asteria. She had been able to reach me. I'd even seen her last spring several times. So why the silence now that I was actively trying to reach out? I began to wonder if I had created a mental block for myself—was I trying so hard that I was sabotaging myself? It was like when I had first started in theater, and I was trying to learn lines. I knew I could memorize things—I'd done it a thousand times with songs and memorable dialogue from tv shows and movies. But those lines wouldn't stick in my head no matter how often I repeated them. It was my fear, throwing up roadblocks.

But I wasn't afraid to connect to my spirit abilities. Was I?

Now, as I sat across from Xiomara, I was ashamed that I felt something akin to relief. She was struggling, too. Of course, I didn't want that for her—I didn't want it for anyone. But it was somehow comforting to know I wasn't the only one facing this problem. For the first time, I considered the fact that it wasn't just me.

"When did you first notice you were having trouble?" I asked tentatively.

"Consistently? For the past two weeks. But the very first trouble I had was right after we discovered the source of the deep magic."

I felt my breath catch in my throat. I hadn't heard anyone from the Conclave talk about what we'd discovered under the Sedgwick Cove Playhouse since the initial days after we'd found it. I'd asked, of course— but no one seemed to think I needed to know any more than what I'd gleaned from our time under the Playhouse—and I hadn't understood much of what happened that night. I held that breath, waiting to see if Xiomara would elaborate.

"As I told you when we first discovered it, I think the Source—if that is indeed what it is—is connected to spirit somehow. There is a strange energy around it, a constant psychic game of tug of war. It repels you even as it draws you in. I found it disorientating. And I heard..."

"You heard what?" I asked eagerly. I knew what I had heard—Asteria's voice, warning me against danger.

"I heard voices... spirit voices," Xiomara admitted.

"Did you... recognize them?"

Xiomara shook her head, and I noticed with alarm that her eyes were brighter than usual—like she was holding back tears.

"I cannot say for sure. But they were... calling for help."

"Calling for you?"

"No, simply calling out. I tried to respond, but it was as though they could not hear me. And that troubled me, Wren. That troubled me greatly," Xiomara said. She leaned back in her chair, closing her eyes as though she was suddenly exhausted. "I have been back many times. I have tried all the methods I know, and still, I cannot answer those cries. My words cannot reach them. And so I have done what I always do in times of confusion—I have sought out the guidance of my ancestors, of the spirit witches who have come before me, from whom I have inherited my gifts. And now they, too, are silent."

"What does it mean?"

"I wish I knew, *mija*. I wish I knew."

I sat there, looking into Xiomara's lined face, roiling with indecision. Xiomara's difficulties had nearly pushed my own desperate desire to communicate with Asteria out of my mind, but now it came flooding back. My mother and her sisters were determined to keep the discovery of the Vesper grimoire from the Conclave, and that included Xiomara. In this, at least, I agreed with them. I didn't want anyone else to get their hands on that book before I had a chance to understand why it had been delivered to me. So if that meant lying to the Conclave, I was on board. On the other hand, this wasn't just about the book anymore. Asteria had said that Jess Ballard was connected to the Source. The Source was connected, somehow, to the element of spirit. And now, the most powerful spirit witch in Sedgwick Cove couldn't seem to communicate with spirits at all, just as Jess shows up on my doorstep. It couldn't possibly be a coincidence. Was there a way to find out more, without completely giving everything away, and possibly losing the book to the Conclave? I chose my next words carefully.

"Xiomara, you remember the night we found the Source, that I came to you in the middle of the night?"

"Of course."

"You remember Asteria came to me?"

She grunted an affirmative and opened her eyes again, now surveying me as I spoke.

"She said something about the Source, remember? About someone tied to it?" I worded it so carefully, leaving out the mention of the book in hopes that Xiomara would not recall it.

Xiomara sat up a little straighter. "Yes."

"Maybe, if we're able to make contact with Asteria tonight, we could ask her about it."

"But you've had no luck in connecting with her. Not since that night."

I shrugged. "That could just be my lack of experience. Have you tried contacting her since that night?"

"No. My own spirit guides are usually much easier to communicate with than other spirits. Besides, if your grandmother wanted to send me a message, she would well and truly send it. It would be unmistakable."

"Unless the same thing that's keeping your spirit guides silent is also keeping her silent."

Xiomara pressed her lips together. She clearly didn't like this observation, but she wasn't dismissing it either. Finally, she asked, "You're saying you want the two of us to attempt contact? Joint contact?"

"I think it's worth a try," I said. If Asteria mentioned the book, I could just play dumb or deflect. This might be my only chance to connect with her.

"Very well, *mija*," Xiomara finally said with a sigh. "We will do as you have suggested. Let's see if Asteria has anything to tell us."

6

According to Xiomara, we would have better luck contacting Asteria if we were in a place she was connected to.

"You mean Lightkeep?" I asked, my heart speeding up. "I really don't want to do this in front of my mom or my aunts." This would have been true even if I wasn't trying to hide the fact that Asteria had been communicating with me. Given how spotty our connection was, it would be humiliating to try to communicate with her in front of an audience—attempting it in front of Xiomara would be embarrassing enough.

"No, we don't need to go that far. Any garden will do, as she channeled her magic through plants. We'll walk up the block to Shadowkeep and use the garden there. Her presence will be closer there and therefore easier to manifest."

Maricela watched us come out through the kitchen, her expression puzzled. Xiomara waved an impatient hand at her with a muttered, *"Regresaremos enseguida,"* as though there was no time for such mundane things as explanations. I managed a weak smile over my shoulder, hoping it reassured her, but Maricela looked troubled as I closed the door behind us.

We set off down the sidewalk in the gathering darkness. There had barely been a cloud all day, and the cloudlessness continued now, so that the stars winked down at us in an uninterrupted display. The moon was barely a sliver—the new moon would arrive the next night, and with it we would usher in Samhain. I wondered what Sedgwick Cove tradition Eva and Zale had in store for me the following night. I considered asking Xiomara as we walked, but then I realized I didn't know if this tradition was sanctioned by the adults. If this was going to be some rebellious teenage shenanigan, I didn't want to blow our cover.

We arrived at Shadowkeep, and I let us in through the gate. Instead of going up the porch steps, we cut around to the side garden, where a glamour hid the staircase up to the second level. Even though I knew it was there, I couldn't see it unless I looked at it just the right way, out of the corner of my eye. Xiomara stopped in the middle of the garden and turned on the spot, considering. Then she pointed over into the north corner of the garden.

"Asteria planted those hydrangeas herself. We should conduct our seance there," she said firmly. "And if I remember correctly... yes, the birdbath is still here."

I followed her into the clump of enormous hydrangea bushes. They formed a rough circle around a wide stone birdbath so old and overtaken by moss and vines that it looked like it had sprung naturally up from its surroundings, instead of being placed there by human hands. The water inside it was perfectly still, the sky above reflected in it like a mirror.

Xiomara pointed a finger over her shoulder and said, "Bring down one of those chairs from the porch, Wren. I'm on my feet too much as it is, and this could take some time."

I hurried over to the porch, and dragged one of the rockers back to the hydrangea bushes. Xiomara settled herself in it with a groan, and then gestured for me to stand on the opposite side of the birdbath. I went and stood where she indicated, bouncing on the balls of my feet, and shivering slightly in the rapidly cooling breeze that was rolling in off the water. Maybe the weather was starting to turn at last.

"What exactly are we doing?" I asked, after a few moments of quiet.

"We are scrying," Xiomara said.

"We are?" I asked, swallowing hard against the anxiety now sitting in my throat, like an obstruction.

I had never attempted scrying, as Xiomara knew. It was not one of the methods of spirit magic we had yet tried in our lessons together, but that didn't mean I was completely unfamiliar with it. In fact, scrying was one of the reasons I'd almost died in June.

When Bernadette Claire made contact with her ancestor Sarah Claire—the same Sarah Claire, incidentally, who had stolen the grimoire now sitting back at Lightkeep Cottage for the first time in centuries—she had strengthened that connection using a mirror that had once belonged to Sarah. She had, in essence, bound Sarah to that mirror, and used it to communicate back and forth. At the time, I had not realized there was a name for spirit communication through a reflective surface. Now, I knew that it was a very old magical practice called scrying. All the times as a kid I watched a fortune teller gaze into a crystal ball, or an evil queen demand answers from the "mirror, mirror on the wall," I had actually been watching pop culture versions of scrying. The real thing—watching Bernadette whisper brokenly into that haunted mirror—had been far more terrifying than any evil queen on a movie screen could ever be.

"M-maybe we should try a method we've tried before," I suggested, trying to sound robustly practical and logical. "We're not likely to have much success with something I've never even—"

"Wren." Xiomara's voice, as she spoke my name, was unusually gentle. "You cannot judge scrying on what you saw in the lighthouse."

Damn it. I really was a terrible actress.

"Bernadette abused the practice, and the hold Sarah had over her was already toxic," Xiomara went on. "It festered into something twisted. That is not scrying as it is meant to be practiced."

The knot of tension in my stomach loosened up. I felt my shoulders drop and let out a sigh.

"Promise?"

"I do."

"Okay, fine."

I stood on the other side of the birdbath. An owl hooted in a tree nearby. The wind whipped my hair around my face, and I brushed it impatiently away.

"The key to scrying," Xiomara said, "is to have no expectation. You must allow yourself to be open to whatever images present themselves to you."

"But we do have expectations," I said, frowning. "We're trying to get a message from Asteria."

"Yes, but a message will only come through if we put that aside," Xiomara explained. "Think of a person trying to cross a crowded room. If the path is junked up with obstacles, there is less of a chance that the person will come close enough for a message to come through. We must clear it all away, Wren, like we did in your first lesson."

I thought back to that day. I had imagined my mind as an empty stage with a single spotlight shining down on it, waiting for someone to step into the light. I looked down at the smooth, unruffled surface of the birdbath, and tried to think of it the same way—a blank slate, an empty stage.

"Now we light a candle," Xiomara said, and started digging around in the pockets of her house dress. After a bit of grumbling, she produced a lighter and the stub of a white candle. "White is preferable. Purple will also work in a pinch." She lit it and balanced it carefully on the lip of the birdbath, casting her own face in an eerie glow that made her look much older than she was.

"This must always be done in the dark," Xiomara said. "The candle should be the only source of light. We are far enough from the streetlight on this side of the house, and there's no moon to speak of. Conditions are favorable for a connection. Let's see if we can make one."

She placed her hands on either side of the birdbath's wide stone bowl. I did the same from the other side, pressing my palms firmly against the smooth, aged stone to hide the fact that my hands were shaking. It wasn't that I didn't trust Xiomara. I didn't trust myself.

"What do we do now?" I whispered.

"Close your eyes and clear your mind, just as we have done before. When you feel that you have cleansed and freed your mental space, open your eyes again and simply look. You don't need to search—keep your gaze relaxed, try not to force anything."

"And then?"

"And then we'll see what the spirit world has to say to us, if anything at all," Xiomara said.

"But if... if we're just looking for any message at all, inviting any contact... doesn't that mean that any spirit could try to speak to us?" I asked. My voice cracked, betraying my fear.

"Perhaps. But that is the risk we take when we open ourselves in this manner. Do you wish to stop?"

I stared at her, indecisive. Yes, part of me did want to stop. I was scared. But greater than my fear was my curiosity. I wasn't content to grope around in the dark, allowing my mother and my aunts to look for answers that I felt belonged to me. I couldn't be a coward.

"No."

"Very well then. Let us clear our minds. We are empty vessels waiting to be filled. Let us see what we can see."

For the first few moments of concentrating, all I could think about was the way my heart was absolutely thundering in my chest. But as the seconds passed and I deepened my breathing, my heart settled into a more relaxed rhythm. I began to hear the sounds around me, rather than my own blood pumping in my ears. I tried to reduce myself to my breathing, to the in and out, the ebb and flow, like the waves undulating in the ocean nearby. I started matching my breaths to the ocean, feeling like I was lulling myself into a kind of trance. Deciding I was relaxed enough, I leaned forward over the birdbath and opened my eyes.

I was looking into the sky, as though the birdbath was a mirror or a window right into the stars. The reflection was so clear that I gasped, and then closed my mouth so that I wouldn't startle Xiomara into thinking I'd seen something spirit induced. I focused on the patch of sky, counting the stars, examining the color, trying to decide if it was truly black or if there was a hint of navy blue.

Suddenly, something large and dark flashed across the reflection. I gasped again, louder this time, so startled that I reeled back from the birdbath, lost my grip on it, and fell backwards, landing hard on my backside. The breath huffed out of me, and my eyes squeezed shut. I waited for Xiomara's sarcastic remark about my clumsiness.

It didn't come. In fact, there was only silence—actual, complete silence. A silence that pressed on me like a physical presence. The sound of the ocean, the feel of the breeze, the quiet shushing of plants as they moved in the wind, all of it was gone.

I opened my eyes. I was alone. Xiomara was gone. Shadowkeep was gone. The garden was gone. The sky was gone. There was only me, sitting on nothingness, and the birdbath. It was as though the rest of the world had been stripped away.

"Xiomara?" My voice shook violently, echoing in the emptiness. There was no answer, no sign that Xiomara, wherever she had gone, could hear me calling to her. Shakily, I got to my feet, a process made all the more unnerving by the fact that I couldn't actually perceive what I was pushing against with my hands, or standing on with my feet. It didn't feel like anything, and yet it seemed solid beneath me—I was anchored to it, not floating away.

I stepped forward toward the only thing that seemed to have traveled with me into this void, which was the birdbath. I looked down into it. I saw the stars in an inky sky, the same stars I'd been staring at before—the stars which, I confirmed with a wary glance, were no longer winking down at me.

I tilted my head, and realized I could see more than just the stars. There were branches of trees swaying gently in the breeze and, if I lowered myself close enough to the basin, I could just make out the edge of Shadowkeep's porch roof. Inside the birdbath was the place I'd just been.

So where was I now, and how the hell had I gotten here?

I tried not to panic, but beads of sweat were already breaking out on my forehead and dampening the palms of my hands. *Okay, think, Wren, think,* I commanded myself, but my mind was nothing but blank buzzing. Nothing I'd learned so far gave me any hint as to what had just happened to me. Xiomara had made no warnings about sudden shifts in time and space, or falling through hidden magic portals. I tried to take a deep, calming breath, and felt like my lungs had turned to stone, unable to expand.

A slight rustling sound broke the muffling silence as completely as a gunshot, and I spun on the spot, staring around wildly for the source of the sound, and then promptly screaming.

I was no longer alone. A figure stood maybe twenty yards away in the emptiness. It was facing away from me, but I still knew exactly who it was. Tousled gray-blonde curls, slender, long-fingered hands, the trailing hem of her patchwork dress dragging along the nothingness she stood upon. It was Asteria.

The rush of relief I expected to feel didn't come. I stayed rigid, my hand pressed over my mouth, for some reason terrified that she had heard me. She hadn't turned at the sound of my shriek, nor did she show any sign that she was aware of my presence. Her stillness filled me with a dread I couldn't explain or control. I didn't want to be here with her. I didn't want her to turn around.

I turned back to the birdbath, reaching out into the space on the other side of it, desperate for some sign of Xiomara's presence. Would I be able to sense her there, even if I couldn't see her? But my hands groped through an emptiness as complete as the rest of the space around me. Wherever Xiomara was, she wasn't here with me. I would have to face this alone.

I turned back to the still-motionless form of Asteria, my mind in a whirl. I was the one who had been desperate to communicate with Asteria. I was the one who suggested that Xiomara and I try to reach her together. But for reasons I didn't understand, it was only me here. Maybe that was as it should be. After all, I was the one she had been reaching out to at the start of the summer. I was the one she sent the messages and warnings to. Now it was just the two of us. This realization calmed a little of my fear. Was I really going to waste this chance to talk to my grandmother on my own, just because I was afraid?

As I worked through this tangle of thoughts, my breathing finally calmed. My heart settled from a gallop to a trot, and I felt steadier. There was no reason to fear my own grandmother. I might not understand what was happening, but that was no reason not to try for the answers I sought.

"Asteria?"

I spoke it quietly. I wasn't sure if you could startle a ghost, but it seemed prudent to try not to. But Asteria made no movement, no sign that she had heard me. I tried again.

"Asteria? Asteria Vesper?"

Again, nothing. I cleared my throat, and then remembered that the volume of my voice was unlikely to be the issue. I was communicating with a spirit. The loudness of my voice surely meant far less than the clarity of my mind. I took a moment to push away every thought that had crowded in there since the moment I'd landed in this odd in-between space. I focused instead on inviting Asteria in, opening a mental door and making room for her.

"Asteria," I whispered, and felt how much further it traveled. "Asteria Vesper."

The reaction was so small I almost missed it. One of Asteria's hands, hanging limply at her side, twitched—the fingers curling in and then falling loose again. It was the first movement she'd made since I spotted her—I took heart and tried again.

"Asteria, it's me. It's Wren."

Wren Vesper.

The words fell into my head like coins into a well, echoing in the emptiness I'd created to receive them. They were quiet and dim, a faint whisper carried on a breeze I couldn't feel. The figure of Asteria was close. But her voice was very, very far away.

I chanced a step closer to her, and then another. My mouth had gone dry. Maybe if I could see her face, I would understand better. But why wouldn't she move, or even turn to look at me? It was unnatural—even for this very unnatural situation in which I now found myself. Everything felt wrong, but that felt the most wrong of all.

I began to move in a large arc, circling around Asteria with slow, deliberate steps. I was afraid of spooking her, even as I called out to her again.

"Asteria, it's me. You gave me a message, remember? About a girl and a book?"

Wren. The girl. The book. The girl will... bring the book.

My pulse quickened as hope shot through me. She was understanding. We were connecting. I was coming around the side of her now, though her face was still obscured by the curtain of her untamed hair. My memory ached for the smell of her—damp earth and lilac and rose petal. I longed for the touch of her strong, callused hands, the twinkle in her eye that always spoke of the untold mischief we might make together. I beat the longing back so that it wouldn't cloud my focus. I needed answers, not nostalgia.

"She came, Asteria. She brought me the book."

The book... has come home?

A wave of something heavy swept over me, a disorientating mixture of relief and fear. It confused me, and I stopped walking. Any moment now I would see her face. Just another step or two. But why was it so hard to convince myself to take them? I spoke instead, stalling.

"Yes, the book is home. Asteria, you told me to trust the girl."

Trust... her... you must...

"You said she was connected to the Source..."

Asteria moved for a second time. A sort of spasm rolled through her body, and she let out a strangled sort of gasp. My heart lurched, and I stumbled a few steps closer to her.

"Asteria? Are you okay?"

The Source...

"Yes, the Source. What did you mean? How is she connected to it?"

The Source... the Source is in danger...

"Asteria, I don't understand. What does that mean? Is the girl the danger?"

The Source... you must protect the Source... find the girl... we can't... we're so lost...

"Asteria, why is it in danger? From what?"

So lost... so dark... all of us trapped...

Her voice, still so far away, was broken and trembling. My heart leapt up into my throat at the sound of it, tears welling in my eyes. It was unbearable, that fear in her voice. I bridged the last of the distance between us at a run, all fear swallowed up by a deep need to comfort her. At last I reached out and, grasping her hands in mine, pulled her around to face me.

Where Asteria's face had been, there was just... emptiness. A smooth featureless stretch of void, from her hairline to her chin. It was as though someone had come and erased her.

I screamed, and the place in which we stood together shattered.

7

I woke to someone slapping my face. Hard.

"Ow!"

"Wren! *Gracias a la diosa!*"

I opened my eyes to find Xiomara staring down at me with a panicked expression. There was a sheen of sweat on her face, and her eyes were bright with fear.

"Xiomara?"

"Yes, *mija*. Sit up. Sit up and drink some of this."

I found I hadn't the strength to sit up on my own, but Xiomara was already tugging at me. She hoisted me into a sitting position against something hard and wooden, which I realized after a moment was the rocking chair she had been sitting in when we'd begun our scrying session. Before I could get my bearings, she was shoving the rim of a ceramic mug against my lips, and I sputtered as the hot liquid sloshed into my mouth.

"What is... how did you... is that tea?" I gasped.

"Enough questions. Just drink."

I blinked around. We were back in the garden of Shadowkeep. All that had vanished—the breeze, the sound of the ocean, the hydrangea bushes and, of course, Xiomara herself—had all returned, so that my senses were momentarily overwhelmed at the rush of input. I knew I wouldn't get so much as a whiff of an answer to any question until I'd done as Xiomara asked, and so I let her pour more of the bitter tea into my mouth. After a few swallows, I was grateful for it; the tea, whatever was in it, cleared away the confusion and made me feel steady and lucid again.

"Better?" Xiomara asked, with the air of someone who already knew the answer.

"Yes. Thank you."

"Can you stand?"

"Yeah, I... ugh, no. Not yet," I replied, as I tried to raise myself, and felt my head spin. "I think I still need a minute."

Xiomara only grunted in reply, and held the cup out to me again. Obediently, I forced down several more swallows, and after a minute or so I felt steady enough to maneuver myself off the grass and into the rocking chair Xiomara had previously been occupying.

"What happened?" I asked. Had it been this cold when we'd begun? I was shuddering with chills.

"You stole my question, child," Xiomara said. She was looking at me as though my face was a clump of tea leaves she was trying to read. "Tell me what you experienced, and I might be able to tell you what happened."

I hesitated, playing for time. On the one hand, I wanted to understand. On the other, I didn't want Xiomara to know about Jess and the book. Not yet, anyway. I settled on the truth—or, part of it, anyway.

"I looked into the birdbath and something moved, like a shadow. Then, suddenly I was in this sort of... emptiness."

"Emptiness?"

It was just... nothing. Silent. No sky, no ground, nothing except me and the birdbath and..."

"And?"

"And Asteria. At least... I think it was her."

"You're not sure?" Xiomara pressed, scowling ferociously.

"She wasn't facing me. It looked like her from the back. But when I saw her face she..." I swallowed hard, and suddenly I was fighting the urge to cry.

"Go on," Xiomara urged, her voice much gentler than usual.

"Her face... it was just ... gone. Like everything else that had disappeared. She had no features, just a smooth blankness."

Xiomara tried to control her face, but I didn't miss the spasm of horror that rippled over her features. She composed it almost at once. "I see. Go on."

"Her voice sounded very far away, and she still seemed confused, like the last time we spoke to her. She told me the Source is in danger, and that we have to protect it, and..."

I swallowed hard against a lump in my throat. A tiny sound escaped me, something between a whimper and a sob, and Xiomara tightened her grip on my hand.

"You can tell me, *mija*. It's all right."

"That's it though, I... don't think it is all right. Asteria said that it was dark and 'they' were lost and that 'all of us were trapped.' But she was alone, Xiomara. So who's 'they' and 'us'?"

Xiomara did not answer right away. Her brow was furrowed in concentration as she mulled over what I had just said to her. Within her grip, my fingers were starting to go numb.

"Your grandmother is troubled, that much is clear. She is also disoriented—something has happened that has confused and frightened her. She ought to know you, *mija*, but it seems she doesn't even know herself."

"But why?"

"I cannot say. I wish I could."

"Who is it she's trapped with?" I asked. "Is she talking about us? Is this a warning, like we've all been trapped somehow?"

"I do not think so. Remember child, your grandmother is not of this living world anymore. She is no longer a part of 'we' here on this plane."

A realization clicked into place. "Your spirit guides... you haven't been able to reach them."

"No."

"Do you think... when she says 'we'... could she be talking about other spirits?"

"I cannot say for sure. But I think it is a very real possibility."

"What about the Source? Why did she say it was in danger?"

Xiomara pressed her lips together contemplatively. "It seems to me that she could be speaking of the dangers we already know."

"You mean the Kildare coven?"

"I do. You said Asteria was with you that day, under the Playhouse. She spoke to you, even warned you in a crucial moment. Is that right?"

"Yes," I confirmed. It had been Asteria's voice that had kept me calm in those moments, that had encouraged me not to give in to Veronica's demands.

"And she displayed none of the confusion she seems wrapped in now, is that so?"

"Yes."

"Then it is possible she is still reliving that moment. Spirits can become confused and disoriented, reliving memories and moments from their past. Asteria might be stuck in a sort of loop of that moment when Veronica was a direct threat to the Source. Or perhaps she worries about the lingering threat, since Veronica disappeared and we have yet to track her down."

She sounded like she was trying to convince herself as much as she was trying to convince me that the threat was nothing new. The problem was, I could already tell she didn't believe it. I looked into Xiomara's eyes, and I saw my own confusion and fear and unanswered questions staring right back at me. That reflection frightened me nearly as much as my encounter with Asteria, because I'd grown used to the idea that the older witches in my life would have the answers I couldn't find. I didn't think there was anything about the world of spirits that Xiomara couldn't explain. The fact that she looked almost as lost as I felt hit me like a physical blow.

"What should we do?" I finally asked.

The question seemed to snap Xiomara out of deep contemplation. She blinked, and then cleared her throat, attempting to resume her usual no-nonsense tone, but ruining the effect with the tremor in her voice.

"There is nothing more we can do in this garden. It is late, and your mother will surely wonder where you are."

"That's it? We're just... letting it go?" I asked.

"Did I say that? Don't you put words in my mouth, child," Xiomara snapped. "I said there was nothing more we can do in this garden. There is, however, plenty that we can do, and we shall begin at once."

Chastened, I nodded.

"I am going to consult with a relative of mine," Xiomara said. "I need to know if there has ever been such silence at our boveda before, and if so, what came to pass in those moments."

"And what about me?"

"You are going to go home and behave as though everything is normal. Do not mention what happened tonight."

"I wasn't planning on it," I murmured. That was the last thing I needed, giving my mother another reason to worry. On the other hand, I was afraid I was going to lose track of the things I was hiding from people. "Are you going to tell anyone?"

"I must inform the Conclave, but I shall tell them the message came to me, not to you," Xiomara said slowly, as though she was making the decision even as she spoke it.

"Why?" I asked. "Not that I'm complaining. I'd rather not face an interrogation from the rest of the Conclave. But why lie to them?"

Again, Xiomara hesitated, and I didn't miss the fact that she didn't quite meet my gaze as she replied, "I think it best if we leave you out of it, for the moment. They are... concerned about the presence of a new pentamaleficus in our midst. They worry that it bodes ill."

"You mean they're afraid of me, too?" I asked bitterly, unable to stop myself.

"No, child. They fear the past. We are not without our prejudices and biases, as you know. Our darkest hour here in the Cove was brought about at the hands of a pentamaleficus, and the Conclave sees it as their duty to ensure such trouble does not tear apart our community again. I don't intend to give them any more reason to cloud their judgment by indulging their fear. Now come along, before your mother and aunts start beating down my door looking for you."

I knew her words were meant to reassure me, but I felt far from reassured as Xiomara helped me to my feet, and led me out of the garden and back up the street to her house. I burrowed deep into my own thoughts as we walked, repeating Asteria's words over and over again, hoping some clue would reveal itself. But no matter how many times I replayed the encounter, no sudden burst of understanding broke like the sun through clouds. Asteria's meaning remained opaque, a riddle with no discernible answer.

I stepped into the house just long enough to grab my bag and say a hurried goodbye to Eva.

"Are you okay?" she asked me, staring with the same razor-sharp gaze as her grandmother.

"Yeah, of course," I said aloud, knowing Xiomara was standing behind me, watching the whole exchange. Sure she could not see my face, I mouthed, "Tomorrow." Eva knew better than to react visibly.

"Okay, see you," she replied in a pointed tone, the subtext of which was, "You'd better explain then."

I nodded. It would have to be enough for tonight. I knew Eva wouldn't let it go, so at least I had until tomorrow to decide exactly how much I wanted to tell her.

I was barely aware of what I was doing as I pedaled my way home in the dark, which meant I almost went over my handlebars twice, but I didn't care. When I walked in the door, I could hear hushed voices from the kitchen. I followed the sound, and found all three of the Vesper sisters sitting around the kitchen table, deep in conversation. They stopped talking at once when they saw me, which normally would have aggravated the hell out of me; but in the moment, all I wanted to do was escape up to my room and think. My mom looked up, took one look at my face, and stood up, looking panicked.

"What's wrong?" she asked.

"Huh?" I stalled. Damn it, I'd forgotten to fix my face. Did I look as freaked out as I felt? "I'm fine, Mom. I'm just tired."

My mom narrowed her eyes suspiciously. "You look more than tired. You look upset."

I attempted my best teenage sigh. "Okay, well, if you're gonna make me say it, I'm frustrated, okay? For a supposedly powerful pentamaleficus, I suck at this whole spirit witch thing, okay?"

It worked. My mother's face relaxed into an expression of sympathy. "Oh, Wren, don't get discouraged, honey. You're making so much progress. It's not all going to come to you at once."

"Spirit is the toughest element to attune to," Rhi chimed in. "It's why spirit witches are so rare."

"And Xiomara is no picnic as an instructor either, I'd imagine," Persi added dryly.

I just shrugged. I didn't trust myself to say much else. I was afraid I might blurt everything out, or else just burst into tears.

"Here," Rhi said, getting up from the table. "Take this up with you, have a little treat and crawl into bed. You'll feel better in the morning."

She poured me a cup of the tea they were all drinking, and placed two cookies on the edge of the saucer. I took it from her with murmured thanks. I spotted the grimoire, still on the table between them, and swallowed the hundred questions I wanted to ask them. The book—and the questions—would still be here in the morning.

"Good night," I said.

Their chorus of good nights followed me up the stairs. I could hear they were already deep in conversation again by the time I closed my door. Freya sat on the bed waiting for me and, to my surprise, Diana was beside her, staring at me with all the inscrutable serenity of a sphinx.

Diana was one of those cats that never seemed to bother much with the humans in her orbit, and so I had never really interacted with her very much. She seemed to prefer the garden to the house, and I'd never once seen a bowl of cat food set out for her or seen any sign of cat toys or a litter box for her. Diana, like many cats, came and went as she pleased, with little regard for anyone or anything else. Therefore, the sight of her sitting nonchalantly on my bed like she belonged there was a bit surprising and— given what I now knew about her age—slightly intimidating.

"Hello, Diana," I murmured. "Didn't expect to see you up here."

She blinked at me with her one bright eye. The socket where the other had been was scarred and empty. Her white fur looked almost silver in the dimly lit room. Her tail flicked back and forth like a metronome keeping time. I crossed the room and sat on the edge of my bed, wondering if my proximity would spook her, and then deciding that a four-hundred-year-old cat was probably not easily spooked. Sure enough, she didn't so much as tense up as I sat down.

"What about you?" I asked her, my voice barely more than a whisper. "You've seen some shit. Do you have any idea what's going on?"

Diana merely looked at me, her tail like a hypnotist's pendulum ticking back and forth.

"All those Vespers you've known, all the ones that have gone before us... can you still speak to them?" I asked. "Can you feel them there, just on the other side of the veil? What do they whisper to you, huh? What do you know that the rest of us don't?"

I stared at Diana. Diana stared back.

"Of course you won't tell me," I sighed. "You might be four hundred years old, but you're still a cat, aren't you?"

Diana inclined her head slightly, as though acknowledging the truth of my words. Beside her, Freya yawned lazily. Feeling suddenly almost weak with tiredness, I changed into my pajamas and, too tired even to brush my teeth, stumbled into my bed. As I pulled the covers up to my chin, shivering, three bright eyes blinked at me out of the darkness.

I might be confused, overwhelmed, and frustrated; but in that moment, as sleep washed over me, at least I felt safe.

* * *

THE NEXT DAY dawned bright and colder than any morning we'd experienced so far in Sedgwick Cove. I'd expected to be plagued by nightmares after the events at the birdbath, but I slept so soundly that I felt disoriented when I finally peeled my eyes open. The light looked wrong coming in the window. What time was it? What *day* was it?

I sat up and put my glasses on. Diana and Freya had left their posts, slipping away to wherever it was cats went when they disappeared. I padded over to the window, stifling a yawn, and peered out over the garden. Well, that explained the weird quality of the light—the first frost of the season lay glittering over the lawn, reflecting and scattering the sunlight like a million tiny mirrors. A quick peek at the flowerbeds, however, revealed that my mother had been prepared. I had no idea what spell she had cast, but her blooms were free and clear from the frost, the moisture instead dripping from the branches and petals like rain. I wondered if the spell was one she had cast herself, or if the garden had been permanently protected from frost by Asteria.

Asteria.

I sighed as the full weight of the previous night pressed down on me. I had gone to Xiomara's house hoping for answers, and instead all I had was a new pile of more troubling questions. I had managed not to mention Jess to Xiomara, and while I still wasn't sure that was the right choice, I couldn't unmake it now. If I wanted to understand how everything fit together—the Source, the grimoire, Asteria's confusion—I needed to find Jess Ballard again.

I was frustrated that I'd let her walk away without getting more answers from her, but I'd been too surprised and wary to think straight. I knew my mother and my aunts would want to track her down as well, so at least we could work together. I was going to take Xiomara's advice and not mention the messages from Asteria until I understood more. I pushed aside the uneasy feeling that there was quite the collection of lies and half-truths and secrets piling up around me—for now, at least, I could hide them away, like cleaning my room by shoving everything into the closet and forcing the door closed. Eventually it would all bury me like an avalanche when the door burst open, but that was a problem for future Wren. Present Wren had work to do.

When I arrived in the kitchen, it was to find Rhi sitting at her laptop at the table, her reading glasses perched at the end of her nose as she squinted down at the screen. She started when she saw me, but then her face broke into a smile.

"Good morning!"

"It's weird seeing you in here with a computer instead of a mixing bowl," I said, sliding into a seat at the table, and helping myself to tea.

Rhi chuckled her high pitched laugh. "Yes, I am rather outside my element."

"What are you up to?"

"What else? Searching for our mysterious Jess Ballard, of course."

All at once, I was feeling much more awake. "Any luck yet?"

"Not as such, no," Rhi admitted, chewing on her thumb nail. "I started with what she told you—it seemed the most logical place. First, I searched Fairhaven University. It is a real place, located near Cambridge, England. Very small and very prestigious private university. But when I search her name along with the name of the university, nothing comes up."

"Really?"

"Well, they don't have a full listing of all the staff," Rhi said. "In fact, they don't have a lot of the information I'd expect a college to have on their website. It's kind of weird, actually."

My heart began to race. Asteria told me to trust Jess. But was one of the few things she told me about herself a lie?

"I did find one thing with the name 'Ballard' and Fairhaven, but it's just a wedding announcement for a woman named Hannah Ballard who had her wedding on the campus in June," Rhi went on. "Maybe this Jess is a relative."

"Maybe," I allowed.

"Did she happen to mention if 'Jess' was short for anything? It's not a name you usually see unless it's short for something else, like Jessie or Jessica."

"No, she didn't," I said. "I'm sorry, Rhi, I didn't realize when I was talking to her that we'd have to track her back down. I should have asked her more questions."

"Don't be silly, Wren, how could you have known? I'll keep searching," Rhi said. "And in the meantime, I've emailed this Dr. Vesper. I got an out of office reply, but it did specify that she'll be back in a few days, so hopefully she can point us in the right direction."

"Is there anything I can do to help?" I asked.

Rhi looked up at me over the top of her reading glasses, looking thoughtful. "You can get started on today's lessons," she finally said, in what I recognized as her teacher-y voice. I say "teacher-y" because she didn't have enough of a commanding or authoritative tone to sound like a real teacher—well, maybe a kindergarten teacher. She was just too sweet. In spite of the sweetness though, I glared at her.

"Seriously? We have this grimoire crisis happening, and you think I should do homework?" I asked.

"Yes," Rhi said calmly. "And so does your mother. We both agree that shoring up your magic is the best use of your time." She looked up at me, saw my mutinous expression, and smiled sadly. "Wren, we have to assume that all of this will lead back to the Darkness and, eventually, to you. We can't leave you so undefended as you were the last time you had to face that kind of situation."

I deflated. She was right, though I hated to admit it. Still, that didn't mean I had to be happy about it.

I therefore spent the day rather grumpily working through a steady stack of lessons as my mom, Rhi, and Persi spent time examining the grimoire, trying to research Jess and, in Persi's case, disappearing for hours at a time and answering questions related to her whereabouts like vicious attacks. I didn't ask. I knew where she was going.

She was visiting Bernadette Claire. I imagined she was the only person visiting her, aside from a dutiful few from her family coven. Bernadette had been recovering in Sedgwick Cove's Community Health Center which, aside from helping with stitches, broken bones, and fevers, also helped people recover from magic gone wrong. Getting information about Bernadette had been about as successful as squeezing blood from a stone, so I'd given up. From Nova Claire, I'd gathered that Bernadette was basically catatonic since her possession by Sarah Claire. No one knew if she'd ever recover. But if one person was unwilling to give up on that possibility, however remote it might be, it was Persi.

As the day wore on, I threw myself so deeply into my studies that when I opened the door to see Zale and Eva standing on the porch, their faces glowing with excitement, I was momentarily confused.

"Hey," I said. "What are you guys doing here?"

Zale's face fell immediately. "What are we doing here? Did you seriously forget we had plans tonight?"

I looked down at my pajama pants and sweatshirt ensemble, then at the time. "Apparently, yes. I'm sorry, you should just—"

"We are not going without you," Eva interrupted, raising a hand so close to my face that I had to stop talking. "Just march that forgetful behind up the stairs and change. We'll wait for you."

"Speak for yourself," Nova called from her car, and revved her engine.

"Ignore her," Eva said. "Go."

I looked them both up and down, noting the all-black outfits they were wearing. "Am I also supposed to dress like one of the tourists we've been tripping over for the last two weeks?"

"Black is traditional, yes," Zale said. "Sorry, we should have mentioned that. Didn't your mom or your aunts tell you?"

"No, because I forgot we were even—"

"Don't worry about it, just go change. It's gonna be cold tonight, so bundle up."

"And what exactly are we doing again?"

"No more time for questions!" Eva cried, pointing behind me up the stairs. To emphasize the point, Nova honked her horn impatiently.

"Okay, okay!" I said. "Be right back!" And then disappeared up the stairs.

As I passed my mom's room, she poked her head out. "Did I hear someone at the door?" she asked.

"Yeah, it's Zale and Eva and Nova. They invited me out with them tonight, but I forgot. Is it okay if I go?"

My mom glanced at her watch. "Sure, it's only eight o'clock. Where are you—oh!"

I watched as a realization lit up in her eyes, and then a slow smile crept over her face.

"What?"

"I just remembered what day it is."

"Does that mean you know where I'm going?" I asked, slightly annoyed. "Because I still don't."

The smile broadened into a grin. "I think I'll let your friends surprise you."

"Mom, don't you think I've had enough surprises lately?" I asked.

She laughed and ruffled my hair. "Not the good kind. And this is the good kind, honey. Trust me."

"Fine," I huffed, and bolted into my room. I dug through my closet until I found a black pair of leggings, a black t-shirt, and a black sweatshirt, which took almost no time at all, because as a theater techie, fully half my wardrobe was black. I threw them on and, because I was on edge, I also grabbed my old protective charm from Asteria and slung it around my neck. The charm was no longer active, but it made me feel better to wear it. I tucked it down the front of my sweatshirt, and bounded out to Nova's car.

"Finally," she muttered.

I opened my mouth in a fresh attempt to get information, but Eva forestalled me. "Hey, are you good? After last night?"

I froze. Had Xiomara let something slip in front of Eva?

"You looked kind of upset when you came back. Where did you go anyway?" she continued, and I relaxed just a little. I decided yet again on only part of the truth.

"We went to Shadowkeep. I've been trying to commune with Asteria, since she's my most recently departed relative, but I've been having trouble. Your grandmother thought it might be easier if we went somewhere Asteria was connected to, and Shadowkeep was closest."

"I'm guessing it didn't go well?" Eva asked with a tiny, sympathetic smile.

"No, it didn't," I said shortly.

"Try not to stress out," Zale said, reaching over to pat me on the shoulder. "Spirit work is intense."

"Maybe you're just not a spirit witch," Nova said from the driver's seat.

"Of course she's a spirit witch," Eva said. "She's a pentamaleficus."

"Maybe she's not," Nova said, shrugging. "Maybe they're wrong."

"So you think the Darkness made a mistake then?" Eva asked, hoisting an eyebrow.

"Can we stop talking about this, and can you all just tell me where we're going?" I asked, raising my voice over them.

"We don't need to tell you," Nova said as she stomped on the brake a little too hard. "We're already here."

I turned to look out my window. It was so dark that I could see little outside of the harsh beam of Nova's headlights. I hurried to get out of the car with everyone else. We were parked off the side of the road where it ended near the cliffs above the beach. If I squinted, I could just make out the place where we had held the bonfire, a huge permanent heap of ash surrounded by logs worn smooth into benches by generations of witchy teenagers gathering there. It was the spot where Zale had introduced me to the origin story of Sedgwick Cove. But the benches were deserted now. No embers glowed among the ashes. And the others were walking away from it, in the direction of the woods.

"Where are we going?" I asked, jogging to catch up.

Eva's eyes, as she turned to answer me, were alight with excitement.

"We're going to the Shadow Tree."

8

I felt a frisson of fear skitter up my spine. "What's a Shadow Tree?" I asked.

It was Zale who answered, which shouldn't have surprised me. Zale loved to spin a good yarn.

"Witches all over the world have their traditions for celebrating Samhain, and Sedgwick Cove has its own special traditions that are unique to this place—kind of like the Litha Pageant."

"I'd rather not think about the Litha Pageant," I said.

"Right, yeah, sorry," Zale said, color flaming in his cheeks. "Not the best example to bring up, I guess." Zale himself had been the director of the pageant-gone-wrong and had been manipulated as thoroughly as I had been, so I imagined he'd like to forget about it, too.

"So what is the Shadow Tree, then?" I asked.

"As the new moon arrives—the same moon that will usher in Samhain, we gather at the Shadow Tree. A long time ago, the early witches to settle here discovered the tree in the woods. It is believed that Mary Vesper herself was the one to find it, and to declare that it was a special place."

"What's so special about it?"

"Mary Vesper was a spirit witch. She sensed a thinning of the veil there, and declared it an ideal place for communion with the dead, and consultation with spirit guides."

"Yeah, so don't feel bad if you don't notice anything special about it," Nova said over her shoulder with a wicked smirk. "What? Oh my goddess, I'm just kidding! Wren knows I'm just kidding, don't you, Wren?" she added, as Eva glared at her on my behalf.

"Sure," I said easily.

My relationship with Nova was... complicated. Our families had a long history of tension and competition, having been the first two covens to settle in Sedgwick Cove. In many ways, she resented me for being a Vesper and having the unstained legacy that came with the name. She resented her own family's blotted past, and so she found satisfaction in the fact that I was such an outsider to the culture, the traditions, even to my own powers. Behind the little barbed comments and jabs of humor at my expense, I knew there was a lot of insecurity and even jealousy, though what the hell she had to be jealous about, I still couldn't quite wrap my mind around. Nova was beautiful, rich, and a far more knowledgeable witch than I was. And yet, despite the resentment, we had come together to help each other. Nova had literally put her life on the line for me. Just a few months ago, we had faced down Veronica Meyers together, but she still acted like we were frenemies. As for me, I just tried to ignore the sarcasm and remember that, when it came down to it, Nova always seemed to have my back when it really counted.

"Anyway," Zale said loudly, pouting a little that his story had been hijacked, "over the years, we've developed a tradition of sending the youngest generation of the covens to visit the Shadow Tree as a sort of invitation to our ancestors to come home for Samhain."

My heart sped up a little. Why hadn't Xiomara told me about this place? If it was meant to be a good place for spirit communication, why hadn't we been there before? Would I be able to hear and see Asteria more clearly there? I sped up, falling into step right beside Zale.

"So it's like... what, a big group seance?" I asked.

He chuckled. "Not exactly. Come on, we'll show you."

I officially gave up on further questions as we trudged into the tree line and down a well-worn dirt path. The sound of the ocean became a muted rumble in the distance. The scant light from the sky was quenched by the canopy of leaves still clinging on, their fall colors muted in the dark. In another week, those leaves would blanket the ground instead, and the night sky would be able to peek into corners of the forest that had been hidden since the spring. Someone had set up lanterns along the path—they dangled from tree branches and blinked like fireflies from behind curtains of foliage. I could hear voices in the woods as well—laughing young voices full of excitement, and the excitement began to infect me, too. The path curved around several dense copses of fir trees and up an incline, where it emptied us out into a clearing, at the center of which stood a single, enormous tree.

The rest of the forest seemed to have pulled back in deference to the dominance of the Shadow Tree. It twisted up from the ground like the gnarled form of an old but powerful woman. The trunk was covered in misshapen knots and bulges, and the branches snaked around each other, bending improbably into the oddest shapes. It looked like something out of a fairytale, I thought, and then remembered my life had recently become stranger than fiction. The leaves on the tree were an otherworldly orange color that seemed impervious to the darkness around it, and not a single one had dropped to the ground.

"Some say it's the Crone, made manifest," Eva whispered to me, and for once, I didn't have to ask for further explanation. One of the very first lessons I'd had in the kitchen with Rhi, she had explained to me the symbolism of the Crone. She was one of three forms, the Maiden, the Mother, and the Crone, the three embodiments of the stages of a woman's life cycle, and the representations of the three stages of a witch's power. The Crone was the embodiment of the wise elder, a figure of deep knowledge and understanding that could only be attained by weathering the many storms of life, and embodying the lessons learned. She was a figure often overlooked or underestimated, when she ought to be listened to and revered. She was also the most deeply connected to ancestors who had gone before her.

On either side of me, Nova, Zale, and Eva had all stopped to stare in awe at the Shadow Tree, too. There was something more about it that drew the eye, apart from the shape of it. There was a magnetism there, a luring power, like it was whispering to us, calling us forward, and we were unable to ignore that call.

I was so entranced by the tree that I didn't immediately notice the other people who were appearing on all sides. Like moths to a flame, people were drifting out from the tree line in twos and threes toward the Shadow Tree. As I finally dragged my eyes from the tree and focused in on the other people in the clearing, I realized that all of these people were young like me. In fact, it seemed like every teenager in Sedgwick Cove was arriving en masse. They organically began to form a loose circle around the tree, and we walked forward to fill in one of the gaps.

Now that we were closer to the tree, I could see that there was a strange glinting light here and there among the branches. By squinting, I made out dozens of round objects hanging from the branches. For one confusing moment, I thought they were some kind of magic fruit I'd never seen before—they were curved and cast in shades of yellow and orange. Then I realized they were—

"Glass?" I muttered. "Are those made of glass?"

It was Nova who answered. "Lanterns."

"But... they're not lit," I pointed out.

"Not yet."

Slowly the circle filled in, until every gap disappeared naturally. It was like watching actors take their places for a play—everyone drifted perfectly into a pre-arranged spot, like they'd practiced it a hundred times before—which, I realized, everyone here had probably done, except for me. As the circle completed, an energy coursed through it like a current, making me shudder with a combination of anxiety and excitement. At the same time, the tree itself shuddered, waving its branches as though caught in a non-existent breeze. The lanterns made a gentle tinkling sound in the branches, like wind chimes. It was a warm, friendly sound, almost like an invitation.

The Shadow Tree was welcoming us.

"Now what happens?" I whispered, leaning into Eva. The clearing, already quiet, had now settled into a hushed silence.

"Just watch," she muttered back.

At first, I thought a breeze was whispering around us, but the air was still. No, it was voices, I realized—the faint muttering of every voice around the edges of the clearing, speaking in unison in a ghost of a chant, the words of which I couldn't understand at first. I turned my head to either side, to see that Nova, Zale, and Eva were all chanting along, lips barely moving, the words well-practiced and flowing like music. I watched and listened until, bit by bit, I was able to make sense of it. Before I knew what was happening, I had joined in, my voice disappearing into the shared susurration of the incantation.

"Crone, we call thy wisdom deep, shine your light to lead them home."

And then, as though watching a Christmas tree lighting in slow motion, the lanterns hanging in the Shadow Tree began to glow—just one or two, dimly at first, faint and flickering, elusive as fireflies, but growing brighter and multiplying as the incantation caught like sparks all over the great hunched figure. Within a few minutes, the entire tree was alight with blazing lanterns, a golden flame leaping in each glass belly. If I were the Wren I'd been upon first arriving in Sedgwick Cove, I might have been worried that the tree would catch fire, but the Wren I was today knew more of magic than that. Those flames were made as much of magic as they were of light and heat, and the Shadow Tree itself had clearly weathered the storms of ages huddled in her protective crouch. No, all I felt was overwhelming awe, and a deep sense of wonder.

The incantation died away as it splintered apart into "oohs" and "aahs" and applause, and there was something nice about the realization that I was not the only person who was impressed by the spectacle of the Shadow Tree—apparently, it was one of those things that just didn't get old, even if you'd seen it every year growing up. I suppressed a pang of jealousy. I'd missed this night many times that I should have been here. I was here now. I would never miss this again, if I could help it.

There was a sudden flurry of motion around the circle, and it took me a second to realize that people were going around handing something out to everyone. Beside me, Nova had a tall white candle thrust into her hand. A second later, I was holding one, too.

"What's this for?" I whispered, trying to keep the fear out of my voice. Chanting along to the incantation was one thing, but I really didn't like the idea of being thrust into participating in magic I didn't understand.

"Chill out, Vesper. All you have to do is light your candle from one of the lanterns. Then we're supposed to walk the flames to our own hearth," Nova muttered under her breath.

"Oh," I said, feeling myself relax. "Wait, do you mean we actually have to take the candle all the way home without letting it go out? On the shore road? That's impossible!"

"It won't just blow out, it's part of the spell," Nova said, a little snappishly. She obviously didn't enjoy having her participation in the tradition interrupted by my panicked stream of questioning.

I turned to Zale instead, just as he was handed a candle as well. His eyes were bright with excitement.

"Isn't this cool?" he asked, grinning broadly. "Now you know why we told you you'd just have to wait and see. No description does justice to the Shadow Tree."

Despite my confusion, I returned his smile. "No, you're right, it's incredible. But did I understand Nova? Are we all walking home from here to our own houses?"

"Yeah. You lucked out, you've got the shortest walk of almost anyone, with Lightkeep being so close to the North end of town."

"What about Nova's car?" I asked.

"She'll come get it tomorrow. Better to walk one way than both, because she's got the longest way to go," Zale said, raising his voice slightly so that Nova could hear him. She stuck her tongue out at him. As small as Sedgwick Cove was, the Claire family home, known by the locals as the Manor, was still quite a long walk. It was the southernmost building within the borders of Sedgwick Cove.

"Come on!" Eva prompted us, and we all moved forward as the circle in which we stood contracted.

Everyone was surging forward in their eagerness to light their candles. There was some playful elbowing and joking around as a few people tried to get their candle lit first, but most everyone took their time, greeting each other and laughing together.

"As you light your candle, you're supposed to reach out to your ancestors for guidance and connection during the time of Samhain," Eva said. Even as she said it, two boys stumbled past, laughing as one tried to light the other on fire with his candle. Eva rolled her eyes. "Obviously not everyone here takes that part of the ritual very seriously."

I laughed automatically, but as I turned back to the tree, I felt the weight of this moment crash down on me. Trying to connect with my ancestors—well, with one in particular—had been the sole focus of my energy over the last few days. Was it possible that this place, this ritual, might finally help me to get some of the answers I was looking for? Was this the moment Asteria and I could truly reach each other? I suddenly wished all these people were gone, and I could be here at the Shadow Tree alone.

I closed the last of the distance between myself and the tree in just a few steps. I reached out with a trembling hand and placed my palm on the rough, weathered bark of the tree's trunk, and closed my eyes. I tried to tune out everything around me. The tree felt more alive than it looked—something warm and pulsing coursed underneath my fingers, and though it was unexpected, I didn't pull away.

Asteria, if you can hear me, it's Wren. I need your guidance. I need it now more than ever. Please, if you can, try again. I still don't understand what it is you've been trying to tell me. Don't give up.

I thought about it for a moment, and decided that Asteria might not be my only Vesper spirit guide. There were generations of Vesper witches I'd never met, after all. I closed my eyes again and added, *Vesper witches, if any of you can hear me, I could really use your guidance now. If Asteria can't help me, maybe you can.* I felt myself wanting to apologize to them, though I couldn't seem to put my finger on what exactly I was apologizing for. For not knowing who I was for so long? For the fact I'd never reached out to them before? For my staggering lack of magical knowledge? I knew none of these things were my fault. But tonight was perhaps the first time in my life that I'd ever really thought about or felt close to them, and that, in and of itself, felt like some kind of offense. So instead, I simply thought, *I'll try to make you proud.*

I envisioned those words burrowing right into the tree, and then shooting up the trunk, out into the branches, and then into every leaf still clinging to the branches. I imagined them brightening every tiny flickering flame with their intention. Then I tipped my long white taper candle toward the nearest lantern, and watched as the tip of the wick blackened, curled, and then danced with flame. The sight of it nestled there in my hands was comforting, like getting to carry around my birthday wish after blowing out the candle.

Someone had placed their candle inside a larger lantern for safekeeping, and pulled out a fiddle. Music began to sing from the strings, slow and mournful at first, then rising into a kind of jig. People were clapping and singing along, laughing and dancing, swinging each other around. No one seemed at all worried that their candles would go out, as Nova had assured me, and I began to relax just a little. But though the antics of my fellow flame-bearers were entertaining, I longed to be left alone in the clearing. I wanted to know if there were other voices to be heard in the clearing, voices that could pass along the messages Asteria was apparently too confused to convey clearly. But no one seemed in any rush to leave or to quiet down, and so I had to accept that I would have to come to the Shadow Tree on my own another time. Maybe Xiomara and I could come together. We had connected with Asteria twice now by working together. Perhaps the third time would be the charm, and I'd finally be able to make sense of things.

Then, the fiddler, whoever it was, began to walk away from the clearing, and others began to follow. Candles were starting to drift off through the trees, like fireflies in twos and threes, as the kids who lived on the West side of town cut back through the woods, instead of taking the longer route by the shore road. A larger group was beginning a sort of procession back the way we had come, and I realized this might be my opportunity to be alone with the Shadow Tree.

"You ready?" Eva asked as she appeared beside me, candle in hand.

"Actually, not yet. I think I want to stay here for a little while," I confessed.

Eva's expression was a little confused, but she smiled. "That's cool. We can hang out for a while with you."

"Um, no we can't," Nova said bluntly, and then turned to me. "Look, I'm really not trying to be an asshole, but it's gonna take me over an hour to walk home from here."

Eva looked like she wanted to argue, which I appreciated, but I cut her off. "That's okay. Seriously, it's fine. I think I'd actually... I think I'd like to be alone here, if that makes sense."

Eva narrowed her eyes at me. "Are you okay?"

"Yes," I said, maybe a little too quickly. "Yes, I'm totally fine."

"Wren, the word 'fine' is like the biggest indicator that a person is not, in fact, fine," Eva said. "I suppose next you're going to tell me you were fine when you left my house last night?"

I felt the color flooding my cheeks as I stammered to reply.

"Look, Wren, you've been really supportive of me while I was working towards becoming a waterworker. You haven't been properly dry in months."

I smiled in spite of myself. "True. But you needed to practice."

"And so do you," Eva said gently. "For a lot longer than you think. I can see you getting discouraged, but you shouldn't be. You'll get there, just like the rest of us. And in the meantime, it's just... keeping your head down and doing the work. Now, the Shadow Tree is a powerful place for a spirit witch, so I'll leave you here by yourself on one condition."

I hesitated. "Okay..."

"Just be gentle with yourself. If things don't go the way you want, no moping. No beating yourself up. And don't sit here all night wearing yourself out. It's not worth it, and it won't help."

I suddenly found I was swallowing hard against something that felt dangerously close to tears. "Thanks, Eva," I managed to choke out. "I promise."

"Okay, then," Eva said, and then turned back. "I lied, there are two conditions. If I text you when I get home and you aren't safely back to Lightkeep, or at least on the way, I'm coming back here to drag your ass home."

I laughed, raising my hands in surrender. "Okay, okay!"

Eva narrowed her eyes at me again, making the universally recognized hand gesture for "I'm watching you" and then, with a wink, grabbed Nova's arm and started to follow the rest of the crowd back toward the path we'd come by.

I watched them all go one by one, the lights blinking out of sight as the forest swallowed them up. I didn't move. I just stood with my candle flickering in my hand, until at last I was alone with the Shadow Tree. I didn't feel nervous; instead, a sense of calm started to wash over me, the kind of calm you can find just by being in the presence of something warm and familiar. It was the same feeling, I realized, that I got when my mom and I would curl up on opposite ends of the same couch, or when Freya purred against me, or when I simply walked in the door of Lightkeep Cottage. I was connected to something in this clearing, and that connection was soothing. I allowed myself to enjoy the sensation for a few moments, just sort of basking in it, as the tree twinkled and winked in front of me.

I tried to focus my energy, like Xiomara had taught me. I cleared all the clutter out of my mental state, and tried to listen with more than my ears, to see with more than my eyes. The clearing was surprisingly warm and comforting, and yet, no spirit presence stepped into the foreground to speak to me, no new yet somehow familiar voice whispered to me. The longer I stood there alone, the sadder I felt. The magic of the place seemed to fade as the lanterns dimmed one by one, and went out. Had I been mistaken about the draw of this place? Maybe it wasn't the energy of ancestors at all—maybe it had been all the other excited witches surrounding me that had lent such an electricity to the atmosphere. Or— and this thought made my heart leap into my throat—maybe it was their connection to their ancestors I'd been feeling, because now that I was here alone, reaching out, no one was answering.

Tears sprang into my eyes as the last of the lanterns finally flickered and died. The Shadow Tree stood before me like a lifeless shell of a thing, no longer a source of wonder or awe, but just another reminder of my own disconnect from everything I was supposed to be. I was filled with a confusion and frustration that teetered on rage. How was it possible that I was in danger from dark and powerful forces for magic I could barely seem to find, let alone control? All the progress I'd been so proud of, the spells and charms I'd learned, the breakthroughs I'd had under my aunts' and mother's guidance, it all shriveled up into nothing in the emptiness of the clearing.

My phone buzzed suddenly in my pocket, making me jump. I pulled it out and found a message from Eva.

Are you heading back home yet, or do I have to come get you?

I checked the time on my phone screen, and saw that nearly an hour had passed since my friends had left. I blinked. Had it really been that long? My body seemed just as unaware of the passage of time as my mind —my legs didn't hurt from standing for so long, nor did my arm ache from holding the candle up. The message seemed to break the spell, though. I suddenly felt cold and tired. I was ready to go home. I should have just left with everyone else—what a waste of time. My mom would probably be wondering what happened to me, and I wasn't looking forward to the lecture I'd surely receive for staying in the woods alone.

I was just turning back to the path that would lead me back to Nova's car when, out of the corner of my eye, I saw my candle flame begin to sputter and dance violently. Instinctively I put a hand up to shield it, but there was hardly a breath of a breeze in the clearing, and anyway, Nova had told me the flame wouldn't blow out. And yet, as I continued to watch it, I felt that, at any moment...

The flame gave one last wiggle, and extinguished.

I stared at it, horrified. I didn't know what it meant when a magical flame went out, but I didn't think it could mean anything good. In desperation, I turned back to the tree, searching frantically for even a spark left behind where I could relight the candle, but I already knew the lanterns were out—I'd stood here and watched them die one by one.

Just as I thought my panic might choke me, a light appeared hovering at the edge of the woods. It was small and orange and leapt like fire—*was* fire, I realized. Just a tiny, disembodied flame, bobbing like a little head as though to say, *Come on.*

I looked down at my still-smoking candle, and then back at the flame hovering unsupported in the air, like an invisible person was holding an equally invisible candle. I felt a pull toward it, like it was silently calling my name. My fear vanished almost as quickly as it had come. Somehow, I knew that flame was mine—the same flame that had seemed to burn out moments ago atop my candle was now beckoning me forward. I didn't stop to think or doubt myself. I just stumbled forward toward the flame that, though it was silent, was calling my name.

As soon as I closed half the distance across the clearing, the flame blinked out of sight. I had about a second of heart-stopping fear, and then the flame reappeared, blinking back into existence maybe twenty feet into the tree line. I was so relieved to see it that I plunged recklessly forward to follow it, reaching the edge of the clearing and then leaving it behind all together.

It was like playing a game of hide and seek. Every time I got close to the light, it would disappear and then reappear further into the forest. If I'd been thinking even remotely clearly, I would probably have stayed right where I was, but rationality was not part of my process. I was acting purely on impulse, letting my emotions and gut and intuition guide me forward into the darkness. Something inside of me was so sure I was doing the right thing, that it didn't even occur to the rest of me—the rational, sensible side of me—to question it.

The little flame flickered and danced further into the trees, and I plunged after it. Having no feet of its own, the flame didn't seem to care about the fact that there was no path. Pulling out my phone and turning on my flashlight would surely have helped me, as I stumbled and tripped along through the underbrush, but I didn't even attempt it; I was afraid that if I took my eyes off the flame for even a second that it would vanish, and I would lose my chance to follow it and find out where it was going.

I knew I was going in the wrong direction to return to Lightkeep. I knew I didn't know the area well, and that if that little flame disappeared again, I would most definitely be completely lost in the woods. I knew, but I didn't care. I couldn't care. I was too busy making sure I didn't trip and kill myself on a tree root or get snagged in the brambles.

Once in a while, the flame would flicker and cast a shadow in such a way that made it seem like a figure was holding it. I felt no fear at this—something deep inside me was telling me that the flame was mine, and that whoever or whatever was carrying it was somehow mine, too. I felt no menace, no shiver tickling its way up my spine. Only a surety that, whatever I did tonight, I couldn't lose sight of that flame. It was the most important thing, to follow it wherever it led me.

After maybe half an hour of walking, the trees began to thin out, and the smell of the ocean got stronger. Even if I'd been blessed with a sense of direction, I don't think I could have anticipated where I'd come out after wandering the pitch-black forest for so long. At last I could see waving sea grass and open space out beyond the tree line, and then I noticed a shape looming up ahead, close to the cliffs. It took me a moment to recognize it, and when I did, I froze in my tracks, hesitating for the first time since setting off on this mad chase.

The flame was leading me right to the Sedgwick Cove Playhouse.

My mind began spinning. I knew I shouldn't be here. The Playhouse had been cordoned off since the summer, and I knew that the Conclave had set up security, now that we knew the Source was located beneath. If I kept going, I would be spotted, and then I'd be in trouble. But even as I hesitated, the flame itself came to a hovering stop. It drifted back and forth just inside the tree line, but it didn't continue toward the Playhouse. I took a few steps forward, and still, it remained where it was. My heart began to pound as I closed more and more of the distance between me and the flame. I was sure it would dart away as soon as I got too close, but it continued to let me approach. Finally, I was close enough that I could have reached out and touched the little flame. Then, with a sudden speed that made my breath catch in my throat, the flame shot toward me and rejoined the candle in a shower of sparks. The candle shook in my hand, but I managed not to drop it in my surprise. I stood for a moment, staring at it.

"What is it?" I whispered. "Why have you brought me here?"

The flame gave me no additional clue. It had to be the Playhouse, right? There was nothing else around here. I took a step forward, and then immediately tripped over something. Pure instinct made me protect the candle, and I held it aloft over me even as I sprawled face first into the earthy scent of moss and fallen leaves. The fall knocked the breath right out of me, and for a moment all I could do was lay there, gasping until my lungs started cooperating again. Still sucking in shallow breaths, I sat up gingerly and stared around for what I had tripped over. It was a boot. There was a black boot jutting out from under a nearby bush.

The boot was not empty.

I held my candle aloft, training the light lower to the ground so that I could get a better view. There was a pair of boots, heavy and black, laced high through shiny silver grommets, and from those boots stuck out a pair of long, slender legs encased in fishnet stockings under a pair of shredded jean shorts, and beside the shorts a slim hand, fingers outstretched.

Every cell in my body was telling me to run, but I stayed rooted to the spot, staring at the legs, at the hand, willing the owner to make some kind of movement; but all was terribly still. Even as I screamed inside my head that I didn't want to look, I held the candle out further, and bent down under the bush.

A tangle of dark hair half-hid the person's face, but I knew it the moment I saw it. With shaking fingers, I forced myself to reach out and feel for a pulse against the pale wrist, and felt nothing at all.

Jess Ballard lay underneath the bush, her eyes closed, her face peaceful. She was dead.

9

The world seemed to stop—the sound of the ocean, the flicker of the candle, all of it shifted into stasis as my mind struggled to wrap itself around what I was seeing. She was dead. The woman who had brought me the grimoire, who we were so sure would hold answers for the many questions we needed to unravel, was dead. I couldn't understand it. I couldn't make sense of it. She was alive two days ago. I'd sat with her—spoken to her. And now she was just... cold. Lifeless.

I had to get help. I pulled my hand back from her wrist, and saw something caught beneath it— an intricately knotted bracelet, rather like a friendship bracelet, lay among the leaves. I picked it up and stared at it. Something had sliced it clean through, and it didn't take me long to realize what it was; a small pocketknife lay open in the dirt, the blade still extended. I moved the candle closer to the knife, expecting to see blood, but the blade was clean. Scrambling back to my feet, I stumbled toward the edge of the woods and out into the far edge of the parking lot, to the theater. My legs barely held me as I ran, stumbling and sobbing, toward the theater itself.

There was no sign of anyone near the main entrance of the building, but I knew the security would be concentrating on the back side. I began to call for help as I jogged around the south side of the building. Within moments, a Sedgwick Cove police officer came running out from around the back, following the sound of my cracked and terrified voice. I recognized her as one of Zale's older cousins. I thought her name might be Maeve.

"What's wrong? Who are you, what—oh!" the young woman stopped at the sight of me, eyes wide. "It's Wren, right? Wren Vesper?"

"Yeah," I said, panting. "I... something's happened. There's a girl over in the... I think she's d-dead," I replied, the words barely forcing their way past my chattering teeth.

"Whoa, who, slow down," the woman said, reaching out as I swayed, and supporting me at the elbow. "What do you mean? Who's dead?"

"This... this girl. She... I recognize her. She's lying in the... the bushes over there, but—" I gasped against a sob, and more tears gushed down my cheeks.

"Okay, okay, calm down," she said soothingly, even as she pulled her walkie talkie off her belt. "This is MacFayden, requesting backup and an ambulance to Sedgwick Cove Playhouse." Then she returned the radio and said in a very calm voice, "Why don't you show me where you saw her, okay?"

Together we walked back toward the trees, she asking questions I couldn't answer, and me, too busy sobbing to say anything else coherent. My body went into fight or flight as we approached the tree line, and I froze where I stood, utterly incapable of getting any closer. I didn't want to see her again, the terrible stillness of her. Officer MacFayden turned back to me, her expression sympathetic, but also urgent.

"Can you show me where she is? You don't have to go in there, just... just point, okay?" she said soothingly.

I nodded, and then pointed a violently trembling finger to the clump of bushes right at the edge of the tree line. "She's right under there," I said, the words little more than a strangled whisper.

It was enough. Officer MacFayden nodded. "Did you see anyone else?"

I shook my head in reply.

"And you say you know her?"

"Y-yes. I only met her a couple of days ago. Her name is Jess Ballard."

Officer MacFayden crept forward, weapon drawn, crossing the last few feet of the grass and right up to the bushes. She disappeared behind them, and for a moment all I could do was hold my breath and wait. Maybe I was wrong. Maybe Officer MacFayden would reappear any second with Jess beside her, looking disheveled and disoriented, but otherwise unharmed. I found myself rolling the broken friendship bracelet between my fingers, like a talisman for good luck, hoping...

Officer MacFayden reappeared, and her grim expression shattered whatever fragile threads of hope I'd managed to spin in her absence. My knees gave way, and I sank into the grass. Everything felt dim and muffled, like I was watching it all from underwater. Officer MacFayden helped me to my feet and walked me over to her car, which was parked over in the corner of the theater parking lot. She sat me down in the back seat, and turned on the car so that the heater was blowing—I didn't realize until I tried to say thank you that my teeth were chattering like she'd just pulled me out of a frozen lake. Was I in shock? Probably. I'd never seen a dead body before outside of the very controlled atmosphere of a funeral home, and accidentally stumbling upon one, especially one I recognized, was not at all the same thing.

I watched through a kind of haze as more police lights blazed into the parking lot, followed by an ambulance. Then my mom's old Subaru swung into the lot as well.

Damn it. I should have realized they'd call my mom.

She jumped out of the car, leaving the door hanging open, and ran over to the small crowd of people gathered near the bushes, which someone was now cordoning off with yellow emergency tape. She spoke with one of the officers, who turned around and pointed right at the car where I was sitting. My mom came running over, her face starkly white, and opened the door.

"Oh, Wren, honey. Are you okay?"

I tried to nod. I wanted to be okay. But I wasn't. And so instead I burst into tears, and let my mother hold me like a child just woken up from a nightmare. She didn't ask any more questions at first, just shushing me and whispering soothing placations, until I had finally cried myself out and regained some control.

"We were just starting to get anxious that you hadn't come back from the Shadow Tree, but we figured you had probably done the full walk to the Manor," my mom said. "What happened, Wren? Can you tell me?"

I heaved a shuddering sigh. "I stayed behind," I admitted. "I know I shouldn't have stayed by myself, but I knew the way back and I felt really... comfortable there. I thought... my spirit powers... maybe it would be easier there. To connect, you know?"

"I certainly do. We've all felt it at the Shadow Tree," my mom assured me. "Go on."

"I... well, I didn't have any luck with a clear connection, so I was about to leave, and then my candle—oh, my candle!" I cried, suddenly realizing I wasn't holding it anymore. But then I spotted it in my mother's hand, the tiny flame still leaping about.

"I've got it, sweetheart. It's okay. Go on."

"The candle suddenly extinguished," I said, and then when I spotted the look of alarm on my mother's face, added "well, not really. I thought it had, but actually the flame just sort of... reappeared in the clearing. Somehow I knew it was the same flame, so I followed it, and it led me here."

"To the Playhouse?"

"Right to the edge of the woods there. When I reached that spot, the flame jumped back onto my candle. And then I tripped, and when I looked down to see what I tripped over—" The lump came back into my throat, and I choked on the rest of the sentence. Luckily my mom understood without my having to say it out loud.

"The flame led you right to her," she whispered, wonderingly.

I nodded.

"And she was already—?"

I nodded again, feeling another wave of sobs trying to shudder their way up.

"And you're sure it's Jess?"

"Y-yes."

"And you don't... you don't know how she—?"

"No," I said, my voice strangely high pitched. "I didn't see... there wasn't anything obvious. She looked like she... like she just laid down and went to... to sleep." At this point the sobs took control again, and I had no choice but to give myself over to them. I had no idea how long we sat there, until Officer MacFayden came back over and leaned into the car.

"Kerri, you can take Wren home. We can send someone over to ask questions tomorrow," she said.

"Thanks, Maeve," my mom replied, sounding relieved.

I shuffled out of the police cruiser and into my mom's waiting Subaru on numb feet. My mom put the candle wordlessly into my hand as she slid into the driver's seat. I no longer wondered at how it burned on without depleting the candle or dripping wax all over my fingers. I didn't wonder how it produced no smoke that discolored the upholstery on the interior of the roof. I kept my eyes fixed on the flame as a sort of anchor that kept me from spiraling back into the moment, and the place I'd just left behind. I watched it until we pulled into the driveway, and my mom opened my door and helped me out.

I felt like a ghost floating up the walkway and into the house. I moved toward the stairs, aching for the calm and peace of my bedroom, and the warm weight of my cat, but my mother applied just the slightest pressure to my elbow, steering me away from the staircase and through the living room to the kitchen, where Rhi and Persi were sitting at the table. When they saw us come around the corner, they jumped to their feet, their faces so white and drawn that I didn't need to wonder if they knew what had happened. My mom led me over to the big beehive oven in the corner of the kitchen. I'd only seen the fire lit there a handful of times during lessons, because the weather had not cooled enough for us to use the hearth. Now, a glass lantern hung in the arched beehive oven that nested above the fireplace. I understood without anyone explaining it—they had hung it there in anticipation of the flame still flickering in my hand. This lantern would be its home until Samhain came and went.

I stepped forward and tilted the flame to a waiting candlewick inside the lantern. It flared and sparked to life with a whooshing sound, the flame leaping through a rainbow of colors before settling into a steady golden glow. As I watched it, I could feel my mother's hand give my arm a gentle squeeze. A small, slightly dry hand slipped into mine—Rhi, standing beside me. Then I felt long fingers entwine with mine on the other side—Persi, letting me know she was there. We stood together in a knot of sisterhood, connected by hands, by blood, by hearts, all beating along to the same rhythm that led the steps, and minds, and hearts of all the witches who came before us. For the first time since seeing Jess' body laying there on the ground, I felt just a tiny portion of the horror melt away.

No matter what, we had this. We had each other. I could weather the rest.

* * *

WITHIN MINUTES of this quiet moment of connection, the dinosaur of a landline phone on the kitchen wall began ringing shrilly, shattering the kernel of peace we'd managed to find. As Rhi spoke in hushed tones to whoever had called, my mom's cell phone started buzzing. The inevitable chaos had finally descended.

When my mother hung up the phone, her expression was grave. She sat down with me at the table, and gestured for Rhi and Persi to join us.

"We need to decide what to do," my mom said.

"We already decided what to do," Persi said, her expression and posture truculent as she crossed her arms tightly over her chest. "We all agreed we wouldn't tell the Conclave about the grimoire."

"Yes, I realize that, Persi, but that was before the woman who delivered it to us turned up dead," my mom said, through clenched teeth. "Call me crazy, but I think that changes the situation just a tad, and requires a reassessment of our earlier decision."

"Okay," Persi said.

"Okay what?"

"Okay, you're crazy."

My mother clenched her fists, and exhaled sharply through her nose.

"Persi, that's not helpful," Rhi interjected.

"You know what's not helpful?" Persi asked, firing up. "Going back on our word to each other at the first inconvenience."

"Inconvenience?" my mother gasped, her voice rising an octave in her incredulity. "Persi, a woman is dead! That is a bit more than an inconvenience!"

"Okay, okay, bad choice of word, but you know what I mean," Persi snapped.

"No, I really don't, actually," my mom snapped back.

"Stop fighting, please, this isn't helping!" Rhi said, wringing her hands and looking back and forth between her two younger sisters.

"Nothing fundamental has changed," Persi said, holding up her hand to silence my mom, who was already opening her mouth to argue. "No, seriously. Think about it. The grimoire is still here. We still don't know who that woman is or how she found it. We need more information before we show our entire hand to the Conclave."

"Show our hand?" my mom ground out, rubbing her forehead. "Persi, this isn't poker. There's a damn sight more at risk than some chips on the table. That woman is dead. Someone killed her."

"We don't know that!" Persi said. "Maybe she died of natural causes!"

"Under a bush? Less than fifty yards from the Source?" my mom shot back.

"It's possible!"

"Yes, I'm sure that is the exact assumption the police will be operating under." My mom's voice was dripping with sarcasm at this point. Persi seemed to inflate, ready to begin shouting, but Rhi thrust out a hand toward her, her expression stern.

"Do not do it, Persephone Vesper. Do *not* start shouting. There's no time. The police and the Conclave will be here any minute."

Persi deflated with a sigh and a pout. "Fine."

Rhi chewed on her lip for a moment as her sisters looked on, waiting.

"We can tell them Wren met her. That she stopped by our house," Rhi said. "We have to, or they'll know we were lying. She asked for directions here, remember? If they ask around, they'll find out she was asking for Lightkeep Cottage."

"But she came to deliver the grimoire," Persi began, firing up. "How are we supposed to explain her visit if we don't mention the grimoire?"

Rhi opened her mouth, and promptly closed it again. "We can come up with some excuse, I'm sure."

"No."

All three heads turned to look at me, each face startled, like they'd been so busy arguing with each other that they'd forgotten I was there.

"No... what?" my mom asked.

"No. No more lying," I said, knowing the words were as much for myself as for them.

They all traded a look, and Rhi cleared her throat. "Wren, we can't just—"

"Yes. We can. We have to, starting with me. I knew about Jess. I knew she was coming before she ever showed up."

A stunned silence met my words, but now that I started, I couldn't stop. I had to keep going, letting the truth flow out, excising the wound that was poisoning me.

"Asteria warned me. She came to me in a vision when I was working with Xiomara, and she told me a girl would bring a book, and that I needed to trust her, and that she was connected to the Source."

"When did this happen?" my mom whispered.

"Right after the Litha Festival. I didn't know what it meant at the time, of course. It felt like gibberish, so I didn't say anything. And as the months went on and I couldn't connect with Asteria again, I sort of forgot about it. But then Jess showed up out of the blue, and I knew she was the girl Asteria had warned me about."

The staring felt like needles against my skin, but I plowed on, determined to say it all now that I'd started.

"I didn't know what book Asteria was talking about. No one ever told me about the missing grimoire, or I might have guessed," I said, trying to keep the accusation out of my voice. This wasn't the moment for pointing fingers. "But then Jess showed up, and because Asteria told me to trust her, I did. I sat down with her. I listened to her. I accepted her story as well as the book. Jess told me she was entrusted to deliver the book to me, specifically. I trusted that it was in my hands because it was supposed to be. And I don't believe for a second that the rest of you wouldn't have done the same."

I could tell that my mother wanted to argue, but she couldn't bring herself to do it. I watched as she swallowed all her objections, as hard as it was to worry them down.

"I'll admit that I didn't ask her enough questions. I was so shocked by her arrival, and by the lure of the grimoire, that I didn't remember what Asteria had said about the Source—not until Jess was long gone. I didn't say anything because... because I thought there might be a reason that Asteria came to me instead of to one of you. It felt like a confidence—one that I wasn't ready to break. I'm sorry if you don't agree with that, but I made the best decision I could with the information I had at the time."

Again, it seemed no one could argue with me, no matter how inclined she was to do so. Persi looked particularly ready to explode, but every time she made to open her mouth, the words seemed to get lodged in the back of her throat; and I knew it was because she was wrestling with the fact that she would have kept the same secrets I had.

"Once you all started panicking about the book, I realized I never should have let Jess leave, but by then it was too late. You all agreed that we should try to track Jess down, and since that's what I wanted too, I figured it was okay to keep my secret a little longer. After all, you wanted to keep the grimoire a secret from the Conclave, and that felt like a bigger deception than mine. I've been trying to communicate with Asteria since, and Xiomara's been trying to help, but... I can't get anything else out of her. She's... confused. I thought I'd have more time to figure it all out, but now..." My eyes filled with tears, and I had to swallow hard in order to keep talking. "But now Jess is dead. She's dead and I'm not sure if that's my fault or not, but in a way it feels like it is, so I'm not keeping any more secrets."

"Wren, you can't blame—"

"If the Conclave had known about Jess, maybe they could have helped to track her down before this happened. Maybe they could have helped us to prevent it. All I know is that I'm tired of lying. I can barely remember what version of the truth I've told to who, and I don't want to do it anymore. We need to tell the Conclave everything. We need to show them the grimoire, and everything that came with it. We need to tell them everything we've found out about Jess so they can track down her family. I'm sure they'd want to... to know..." I choked back another sob.

My mom, Rhi, and Persi all looked at each other, carrying on a silent conversation with their eyes.

"I don't think we have a choice," Rhi finally said. "I think Wren is right."

Persi chewed the inside of her cheek, arms still crossed over her chest. She didn't agree out loud, but she didn't argue either. My mom was still looking stricken.

"Wren, I'm sorry you felt like you needed to carry that secret all summer," she said, slinging an arm around my shoulders, and pulling me in closer for a hug. "You could have trusted me."

"I know," I said, and I meant it. "It wasn't about not trusting you. It was about feeling like the message was for me, and that I needed to be the one to figure out what it meant. It felt like a... I don't know, like a personal challenge or something. I wanted to prove to myself that I could master my spirit powers. But all I've done is make a mess of everything."

"Wren, this isn't your fault," my mom murmured, stroking my hair away from my face and untangling a tendril from my glasses, which were so badly streaked with dirt from my tumble in the woods that I could barely see.

I couldn't agree with that, and so instead I said, "It's been isolating, starting from scratch while everyone around me has grown up honing their craft. I'm not blaming you, Mom," I added quickly, because I could see my mother's face beginning to crumple. "I understand why you did what you did, and I'm not mad at you, not anymore. But I can't pretend that it hasn't had an impact, and that playing catch up isn't hard, because it is. But tonight at the Shadow Tree, I felt really and truly connected for the first time, not just to Sedgwick Cove, but to all the

Vespers who came before me. For the first time since I started my training, I felt like a link in a chain instead of just one person, groping around in the dark."

A sniff from beside me betrayed the fact that Persi, who generally seemed to be allergic to sentiment of any kind, was holding back tears. Rhi reached out and put a hand on Persi's shoulder, and Persi immediately slapped it away.

"I just need a tissue!" she hissed.

"Anyway," I said, "it's made me realize I don't have to do this myself—that I shouldn't do this myself. That grimoire, the Source, messages from Asteria, none of that belongs just to me; and even if they did, I need help. I need all the help I can get. That means you three, but it also means the Conclave, and anyone else we know we can trust. A woman is dead. We can't keep secrets anymore."

The three sisters didn't need to say anything aloud to realize they were all in agreement. They simply traded a knowing look around the circle, and Persi sealed it with a grumbling, "Fine." But then Rhi stood up suddenly, knocking her chair over and making us all jump.

"Okay, Wren is right. We can't keep the grimoire a secret. We should have known we couldn't. But that doesn't mean we can't protect it."

"What are you suggesting, Rhi?" my mom asked. "Whatever it is, we have to hurry." She had to yell the words at Rhi's retreating back, however, because Rhi had already turned and run out of the room. We listened in silent confusion while she rummaged around and cursed under her breath in the library. Then she appeared again, panting slightly, and with her hands full. I tried to make sense of the items I saw—a long curling strip of birch bark, a candle and box of matches, a raven's feather, and a length of green ribbon—but remained as confused as before. My mom, however, let out a soft "oh!" of comprehension, and Persi's face broke into a slow-blooming smile of understanding.

"A Binding. An excellent idea, Rhi," Persi said.

I wasn't completely clueless. I'd learned about the various types of Bindings used in witchcraft—whether it was to Bind two people together, or to Bind a person or an object from doing harm. But I was definitely still unclear on what exactly was happening as Rhi returned to the table. My mom spotted the look on my face, and took pity on me.

"Our biggest worry," she explained, "is that Ostara will convince the rest of the Conclave that the book isn't safe. They would never be allowed to destroy a coven's grimoire, but they could vote to lock it away or otherwise prevent us from using it, at least in the short term, while it's being examined."

"Would the Binding prevent them from using it?" I asked.

"No, it would Bind our coven to the book, so that we can't lose it again," she said.

"But... why didn't we just do that the first time? Then it never could have become lost," I asked.

"Ah, but you forget, our coven lost the book on purpose," my mom said. "They were trying to keep it concealed. Binding us all to it would have made it discoverable."

"You realize Ostara is going to expect this, right?" Persi said, her wicked smile fading. "It's going to be the first thing she checks for."

Rhi's smile only grew broader at these words. "Persi, sometimes the only conclusion I can draw is that you think your big sister is an imbecile."

Persi's mouth fell open. "I didn't say—"

"I've already thought of that," Rhi plowed on, laying the Binding implements out on the table. "That's why we're not Binding the book to us directly."

I frowned. "But you said we have to Bind it to our coven. Aren't... aren't we the coven? So how—?"

But as though in direct answer to my question, there was a sudden whirl of fur, and two shapes leapt up onto the kitchen table: Freya and Diana. Rhi grinned as she reached out and scratched Diana between her ears. Diana closed her one eye lazily, deigning to accept the show of affection.

"Oh!" I said, as the realization hit. "Will that... is that going to work?"

But Persi and my mom were also smiling broadly, and so I had my answer.

Together we sat around the table. Freya and Diana sat patiently as

Rhi plucked several long hairs—black for Freya and white for Diana—from their lustrously fluffy tails, to which indignity neither cat seemed to object. She placed the hairs inside the grimoire, right on top of the page with the Latin inscription, murmuring an incantation under her breath. As she did this, my mother lit the candle, and Persi began scratching a sigil onto the inner layer of the birch bark with the sharpened tip of the feather, her head bent low over her work, so that her curtain of dark hair hid her from view. After less than a minute's frantic scratching, she flung the feather aside with a triumphant, "Done!" And thrust the bark into Rhi's waiting hands. I caught barely a glance of the spiky, complicated sigil she created.

"What does it mean?" I asked, as it passed under my nose.

"It makes the grimoire discoverable. Wherever it is, the coven familiars will be able to see through any glamours or enchantments obscuring it with their inner eye," Persi explained.

Carefully, so that the bark didn't split, Rhi wrapped it carefully around the outside of the grimoire, and secured it with the green ribbon. She also secured several more black and white cat hairs into the knot as she pulled the bow tight. Then she hovered her hands over the grimoire for a few more seconds, her eyes closed in concentration. Finally, she opened her eyes with a satisfied sigh.

"It is done," she announced, dropping her hands to her sides.

Freya and Diana both sniffed at the book, as though inspecting her work. Then, as though declaring themselves satisfied, they leapt off the table and disappeared, tails whipping around the corner.

"Now what?" I asked.

"Now we remove all signs of the Binding, so the Conclave isn't clued in," my mom said. "And then, we wait."

We didn't have to wait long. Within a few minutes there was a sharp knock on the door.

"Here we go," Persi muttered, rising to answer it. "Once more unto the breach."

10

For the next hour, I sat on the couch with a cup of tea in my hands, answering question after question from Maeve and one of her fellow officers. Luckily, I didn't have to make up some kind of story about what I'd been doing in the woods, because like everyone else in Sedgwick Cove, Maeve was a member of a local coven, and therefore didn't even bat an eye as I described the ritual at the Shadow Tree, and the flame that led me to Jess' body. She simply nodded along calmly, and scribbled on her notepad.

While this questioning went on, the members of the Conclave arrived one by one. They never knocked or rang the doorbell, and yet my mother and aunts somehow knew when to rise wordlessly and open the door for them. I glanced at Xiomara as she walked through the living room, her eyes burning with a question she couldn't ask out loud. I excused myself from the officers with a mumbled, "Be right back," and went over to join her where she stood in the doorway. Xiomara gave Rhi a pointed look, and after a moment's hesitation, Rhi shrugged and returned to the kitchen.

"Are you all right, *mija?*" Xiomara asked.

"Yeah, I'm okay," I said, and watched her purse her lips at the lie.

"How much have you told them? About Asteria?"

"They know she contacted me in the spring. They know we've been trying to reach out since, but without success. I didn't get into the specifics of last night, only that Asteria is confused. But," I bit my lip, hesitating.

"*Escupelo*! Just come out with it, child!"

"I haven't told you everything."

Xiomara raised a single eyebrow, waiting.

"Just... don't be mad. It wasn't my decision. Well, it wasn't all my decision."

"What haven't you told me?"

"You'll see. The whole Conclave will know in a minute. Anyway, I'm sorry."

At that moment, Rhi brushed past us again and opened the door to Ostara, who swept in like a queen about to preside over her court. Despite the fact that it was nearly midnight, she was impeccably put together, makeup airbrushed and hair swept into an elegant chignon. In that moment, I realized that the reason she always ruffled everyone else was because she never looked ruffled at all, no matter how dire the circumstances. Then I wondered if it was a spell, which caused a hysterical bubble of laughter to force its way up my throat. I slapped my hand over my mouth to stifle it.

Ostara's arrival was like a silent command. Without her saying a word, we all stood up and followed her into the kitchen. I could feel the collective tension that bloomed at her appearance. The air was buzzing with it. Between that and the constant undercurrent of magic, I felt almost dizzy.

Ostara sat down at the table like a queen taking her throne and sighed, as though steeling herself. The rest of the Conclave sat as well, the witchy knights of the round table, except for Lydian, who shuffled up to it with the aid of her walker, and leaned heavily on it as she grunted and grumbled onto the little seat. Once she had settled, Ostara looked expectantly at Rhi who, as the oldest Vesper sister, was the matriarch of the coven by default.

"Let's start at the beginning," she said.

Rhi stepped forward. "Very well, Ostara, but I must warn you that the beginning is a lot farther back than you'd expect," she said, and placed the grimoire on the table.

The whole Conclave leaned forward to examine it. Xiomara realized what it was first, and began to mumble under her breath in rapid Spanish. Lydian chuckled incredulously, while Davina and Zadia both grew wide-eyed and still. Ostara stared at it uncomprehendingly at first. Then, we all watched as the realization swept over her, and the fear ignited in her eyes. She pushed back from the table, her chair squealing across the kitchen floorboards. Persi made a scoffing sound under her breath, indicating that Ostara was reacting exactly the way she expected.

"That... that can't possibly be... how... what is the meaning of this?" she gasped.

"That's what we're going to explain, if you can just get a grip on yourself," Persi said dryly. Lydian cackled wheezily in appreciation.

Ostara's features stiffened. "I'm listening," she said through pale, unmoving lips.

Rhi turned to me. "Wren? You're the only one who knows the whole story."

I swallowed hard, cleared my throat, and started to speak. I told them everything, everything I could think of, starting from my first warnings from Asteria that Jess Ballard was coming, to the moment I found her lying lifeless at the edge of the woods. I felt almost numb by the end, having gone through it with my family and then with the officers, and so it was easier now, just to let the details flow. When I had finished, my voice had grown hoarse and I felt a wave of exhaustion wash over me. My eyelids suddenly felt heavy, and I wanted to ask if I could go to bed, but no one was paying me the slightest attention now that I had stopped talking. Every pair of eyes was trained on the grimoire instead.

"I never thought... I thought it must have been destroyed long before now," Davina whispered.

"Not me," Lydian croaked in her ancient froglike voice. "I knew it was out there, bidin' its time, waiting for the right moment to reveal itself."

"It didn't reveal itself," Ostara snapped. "It was found."

"Says you," Lydian shot back. "I don't think there's a witch alive who could tame that book."

"And that is my fear exactly," Ostara said. "That grimoire almost ended Sedgwick Cove centuries ago."

"Be careful there, Ostara," Xiomara barked. "The book alone could do nothing. It took a witch to wield it."

"You think I don't know that better than anyone?" Ostara asked.

"And yet you do not speak of it. Your fear is not just of the book, but of the weakness that turned it into a weapon. Do not lose sight of that."

"I never lose sight of that. In fact, I rather think I am the only one who hasn't," Ostara said, each word forcing its way through her fiercely clenched teeth. "It works upon you all already, can't you see that? Drawing you in. Don't you feel it?"

All eyes fell on the book again, and several pairs were warier than before.

"What I cannot comprehend," Ostara went on, "is why we were not immediately summoned upon the arrival of the book. It is unfathomable that the three of you neglected to do so. Utterly unfathomable."

"Bullshit," Persi cried, rising from her seat, and glaring at Ostara with a look that surely would have cowed nearly any other witch in the Cove.

"Persi," Rhi said warningly, but Persi ignored her.

"We've asked for centuries—literal centuries—for the Conclave's help in tracking down this book," Persi went on. "Every matriarch in our family has begged and pleaded. And generation after generation the Conclave refuses, because in every generation there's a Claire standing in the way."

"Your mother never sought the Vesper grimoire," Ostara said.

"Asteria knew a lost cause when she saw one," Persi shot back. "She knew there was no point in arguing with you. This obsession with hiding the book has gone from caution to mania, Ostara. The power in that book is ours, and it's time for you to stop standing between us."

"So you admit you seek to expand your power!" Ostara cried, pointing a dramatic, perfectly polished finger at Persi, who snorted loudly.

"We seek only what is rightfully ours. Magic we have already honed, spells we have already perfected. We seek our history, our connection to our past. And you need to do some serious reflection on why you've always made it your business to stand in our way."

"I... that is not..." Ostara stammered, her normally porcelain cheeks flaming. I had never seen her so discomposed, and neither had most of the others, judging by the startled looks on their faces. Lydian, in contrast, was grinning broadly, as though she found the whole confrontation highly entertaining.

Persi leaned toward Ostara. "Is it really this book and our family you fear? Or is it rather your own weakness when faced with such a temptation?" she whispered.

Smack.

Ostara's slap resounded like a thunderclap against Persi's cheek, and Persi staggered. A collective gasp ran around the room, followed swiftly by Davina's bark of "Steady on, old girl!" and Xiomara's booming, "Ostara Claire, you forget yourself!"

All the angry color drained from Ostara's cheeks as she looked down in horror at her hand, as though it had betrayed her somehow, as though the blow hadn't been her at all.

Both my mom and Rhi had leapt to their feet, and my mom actually started toward Ostara, but to my surprise it was Persi who held her back.

"Don't give her the satisfaction, Kerridwen," she said, still looking at Ostara with a furious spark in her eye, and a smirk of satisfaction on her lips. "Well, well. I seem to have touched a nerve." She tossed her head, flinging her masses of black hair back from her face, to reveal an angry pink handprint blooming across her cheekbone. "Is this the leadership we can expect in Sedgwick Cove from this point on?"

"I didn't... I never meant to..." Ostara's words tumbled over each other as she struggled to distance herself from her own actions.

"Oh, I see. An accidental slap to the face, was it? Oopsie-daisy," Persi said scathingly. "And in front of two police officers, too. You're lucky I don't like paperwork, or I'd be pressing charges."

In the corner of the room, Maeve and her fellow officer shifted uncomfortably. It couldn't have been more obvious from their faces that there were several kinds of torture they'd cheerfully undergo, rather than have to arrest the head of the Conclave.

"You haven't had half the slaps you've earned, Persephone Vesper, and that's the truth," came Lydian's wheezy cackle. "Ostara, you should know better than to let her goad you like that, foolish girl. Too proud by half and not nearly as cool as you like to appear."

Ostara's nostrils flared, but she said nothing. Only a woman as old as Lydian could call Ostara Claire a "foolish girl" and make her feel like one.

"Let's move on. I propose the book be examined under the most carefully controlled of magical conditions," Xiomara said. "And I propose that the Vesper coven be a central part of that investigation. If we work together, we can ensure that everyone trusts the results."

"A fine idea," Davina said heartily, looking relieved that we'd finally arrived at a civilized discussion again.

"Ostara?" Xiomara asked, pointedly.

Ostara's face was twisted, her mouth pinched up as she choked down what I was sure must have been a very bitter pill. But choke it down she did, and when she spoke, her face relaxed again into her usual haughty indifference. "As you say," was all she would reply, but it was enough of a concession.

"In order for those conditions to be met, and to keep everyone safe in the process, we will need to remove the book from Lightkeep Cottage. I will not agree to this unless all the Vespers agree as well," Xiomara went on.

Ostara's posture stiffened again, but she didn't argue. Persi stared right at her, her eyes glittering with suppressed glee.

"I agree," Persi said, "as long as we are part of the investigation and, additionally, that we will be informed if the book is to be moved."

"I also agree," Rhi said quickly.

"And me," my mom said.

Xiomara turned to me. "And what about you, Wren? Do you agree?"

I looked around the room, at every pair of eyes now fixed on me. My initial thought was that I didn't understand why they were asking me. It wasn't as though they were going to make this decision based on what a kid thought. But Xiomara noticed my hesitation.

"I did say all the Vespers, Wren. I hope you realize that means you as well. This book was delivered into your hands, *mija*, and your grandmother helped to place it there. We do not yet know what that means, but I believe it is important. Asteria was my friend, and I will honor her wishes wherever possible. Therefore, we will not make this decision without you."

I looked around the Conclave—at Ostara's impassive mask, at Davina's encouraging nod, at Lydian's wrinkled toothless smile, and Zadia's stoic calm—and then back at Xiomara. Asteria trusted these women. She trusted Sedgwick Cove and the community she had always had here. If she needed help, these were the women she would have turned to. So, I would trust Asteria and turn to them as well. Because more than ever, I needed help.

"Okay. I agree," I said, "but I have a condition as well."

There was what might have been a skeptical snort from the direction of Ostara, but I ignored it. This was important.

"And that condition is?" Xiomara asked.

"That if I get another message from Asteria, and that message concerns the book, we will act in accordance with it, even if that means removing it from whatever this protective setting is, even if it means bringing it back to Lightkeep and even—" here, I paused, taking a breath— "even if it means using the magic inside it."

I could tell Ostara wanted to object. Every cell in her body seemed to have turned to stone, with the exception of her eyes, which were aglow with rapidly firing thoughts. I knew there was a battle raging there, a weighing and measuring and considering and, yes, even scheming. Finally, though, she made a movement that was part nod, part indifferent shrug.

"Very well," she said coldly, "but know that if any harm comes to Sedgwick Cove at the hands of that book, I will be holding you personally responsible, and the consequences will be your own to bear. I wash my hands of it."

Beside me, I felt my mother stiffen. Ostara was looking at me, not any of the other Vespers. I placed a hand lightly on top of my mom's to prevent her from jumping in, and replied. "I understand."

"Do you?"

"Oh, I think so, yes." I tried to keep my voice as calm and unconcerned as possible, trying to channel some of Persi's coolness even as my heart thundered in my own ears. And I wasn't lying. I felt recklessly right. Not for the first time, I wondered if Xiomara could hear my thoughts, because her mouth curved into the ghost of a smirk as she looked at me.

"Very well. So mote it be," Xiomara said. "We have much to discuss. Perhaps we can dismiss our officers here, unless..." she let the words trail off, demurring to the police. Maeve stepped forward.

"We'll check in with the team still over by the theater and update you with any relevant information. We'll be in touch tomorrow. We'll have to arrange further questioning, for Wren and perhaps for the rest of the Vespers."

I suddenly felt like I would pass out from exhaustion. I swayed a little in my seat.

"Wren, you need to go to bed," my mother said at once.

"I want to know what gets decided. About the book."

"We'll tell you in the morning, I promise," she said.

"You'll tell me everything? No secrets? No omissions to protect me, or whatever?" I demanded.

She solemnly held her pinkie out to me. I locked mine around it, smiling.

"If she doesn't, I will," Persi added, winking at me.

While the Conclave began to discuss the details, my mom and I rose to walk the officers out. Rhi and Persi followed.

"What will happen to Jess?" I asked Maeve as she stepped out onto the porch.

"We'll begin the process of finding her family so that we can notify them. And of course we'll be investigating how this happened, to make sure there was no foul play," she said, smiling sympathetically. Like all the women in Zale's family, she was very tall and broad, and there was something reassuring about her calm, solid presence. "In the meantime, we'll hold the body until such time as we can release it."

I shivered. I'd seen the body—touched it, even—but it still made my skin crawl to think of Jess that way. The door closed, and Rhi exhaled like she'd been holding her breath for hours. Then she immediately turned and smacked Persi on the arm.

"Goddess above, Persi! What happened to our plan?" she hissed.

Persi rubbed her arm, looking defiant. "Just because we have a plan doesn't mean the Conclave is going to agree to it! I had to hedge our bets!"

"By goading the head of the Conclave into an actual physical altercation?" my mom asked, though she looked more amused than anything. "You're going to bruise, by the way."

Persi tossed her hair in a careless shrug. "Nothing a bit of makeup and a light glamour won't conceal. Anyway, it was worth it to watch her lose that legendary control."

"And even more fun to threaten her with litigation," my mom added, grinning now. It was weird to see her and Persi on the same page, but they were certainly enjoying the Vesper coven victory at the moment.

"You think it will be okay?" I asked. "Letting them take the book?"

"Yes," Rhi said. "I trust Xiomara, at least, to arrange this as we discussed. And if Ostara decides to, well..." she paused here, searching for the right word.

"Go rogue?" my mom suggested.

"Yes, I suppose so. If Ostara... goes rogue, we've Bound the coven to the book. We won't lose it again, that's certain. We can be patient while the Conclave reassures itself."

"I was proud of you in there, Wren," my mom said, turning to me. "You really stood up for yourself."

I shrugged, unsure of what to do with the compliment, because it didn't feel true. I hadn't really meant to stand up for myself—I'd never been particularly great at that. But I did feel like I needed to stand up for the Vesper coven. For Asteria. I couldn't let her down, not now, not when I knew she was trying so hard to reach me.

Voices rose in the next room, reminding us all that there was a conversation going on that we didn't want to be left out of.

"Okay, off to bed," my mom said, planting a swift kiss on the top of my head.

"And you'll tell me everything tomorrow?" I reminded her. "Like... every single detail."

"Yes, I promise," she assured me.

I was still hesitating when Freya appeared beside me, winding herself around my legs once in a sinuous figure eight, before placing her front paws on the bottom step, and looking at me pointedly as though to say, "Coming?"

Her encouragement was the last little push I needed to give in. I bid my aunts a sleepy good night and trudged my way up the stairs, following Freya's twitching feather duster of a tail all the way to my room. As much as I wanted to fall face first into my bed fully dressed, I dragged on a pair of pajamas and brushed my teeth first. As I pulled my glasses off and my room swam out of focus, I felt a cold breeze brush over my arm, raising a row of goosebumps and making me shiver.

I looked over at my window, but it wasn't open.

"Huh."

I was too tired to investigate further. I curled up under my blankets, Freya tucked in the crook of my legs, and fell immediately, deeply asleep.

11

I woke to a sharp clinking sound.

I sat up in bed, rubbing at my sleep-crusted eyes. My first instinct was to look for Freya—she tended to be the culprit when it came to weird noises in my bedroom at night. But she was still curled up against the back of my legs, blinking up at me from heavily hooded eyes that told me she'd been just as soundly asleep as I had been, before that noise woke us up.

It came again, and this time I could tell it was coming from the direction of my bedroom window, the one right in front of my desk. I slid out of bed, my heart beginning to pound. My clock read 1:17 AM. I paused for a moment and listened for any other sounds from downstairs, but the cottage was quiet—the Conclave had departed while I slept so soundly, and from the muffled silence that lay over the house like a blanket, it seemed that my mom and my aunts had gone to bed at last. I approached the window, arms wrapped protectively around myself, listening again.

Clink.

This time I saw it as well as heard it—the noise was actually a small pebble ricocheting off one of the windowpanes. My pulse sped up. I didn't exactly have an abundance of adoring admirers—actually, I didn't even have one adoring admirer—so the thought that this was a moonlight tryst or some romantic gesture didn't even cross my mind. I did, however, have a surprising number of enemies, so it was with extreme caution that I leaned forward and risked a peek down into the garden below.

Bea stood in a flower bed, her anxious little face upturned. I swore under my breath at my window as I struggled to open it—the extreme humidity of the ocean air had swollen and warped the wood. Finally, I was able to shove it wide enough to stick my head out.

"Bea? What's going on? Is everything okay?" I called down in a whisper.

"I need to talk to you! Can you come down?" Bea hissed back.

"I'll be right there," I replied. I eased the window shut again and tiptoed out of my room, down the hall past my mom's room, down the stairs and out the front door onto Lightkeep Cottage's wide front porch. Bea was already coming around from the side of the house at a jog, and met me at the bottom of the porch steps.

"Bea, what's happening, you're freaking me out," I murmured. "Is someone in trouble? Is it Eva, or—"

"No, my family's fine, it's not that. But someone does need help," Bea said. She was wringing her little hands together, and biting at her bottom lip. "Do you remember when... when I showed you some of my sketches? Before Litha?"

"Of course."

"Well, lately it's been... hard. To draw, I mean," she said. "I used to see things so clearly inside my head. But now everything is... blurry."

"Blurry?"

"Yeah. Like, I can't... I can't see the way I used to."

I swallowed hard. I'd wondered if Bea might be having problems with her gift, too, since Xiomara and I were having so much trouble making progress, but Xiomara had been reluctant to ask her. Now, it seemed, I was getting the answer anyway.

"But then tonight," Bea went on, "for the first time in a long time, I could see! It was like I..." she pointed to my glasses, "...like I'd lost a pair of glasses, and then found them again. It came through so clearly, but it wasn't just an impression. It was a plea for help from someone."

"Who is it?" I asked.

"I'm not exactly sure," Bea admitted.

"Okay, well, where are they?" I tried again.

"I'm not really sure about that either."

"What do they need help with, can you tell me that?"

Bea shook her head.

I paused a moment to look at her, feeling lost. "Maybe I'd better just let you talk, then," I said. "I don't seem to be getting anywhere with these questions. What can you tell me?"

"Not much," Bea said. "But I can show you."

As I watched curiously, Bea tugged her backpack around to the front of her body, unzipped it, and pulled out one of her sketchbooks. She thumbed through the pages until she found what she was looking for.

A serious face with big dark eyes and masses of dark hair stared back at me. I recognized the mysterious half-smile at once.

"That's Jess Ballard!" I cried.

Bea looked relieved. "So you know her?"

"Yeah. Well, I mean, not really, but I know her name. She was the... she just died. Her body was down by the Playhouse," I said, shuddering. "Why are you drawing her?"

"She came to me. She said she needed help," Bea said. "Well, actually, she said she needed *your* help."

"My help?" I asked, frowning. "But she's... she's dead. How could I possibly be of any help to her now?"

Bea shrugged. "I'm not sure. But she's debating the whole dead thing."

"I... I mean, I get the denial, but I don't really think that's debatable. I mean, I saw her body. It was carried away in a body bag."

"I know, but this is what she keeps telling me," Bea said, and flipped to the next page in her sketchbook, which was filled with words and strange symbols instead of likenesses. I bent my head low over them, examining them. I saw the words, "back to my body" and "running out of time" and then a strange symbol over and over again, along with the words, "on her wrist," and then my own name: "Wren Vesper."

"I don't understand," I muttered to myself.

"I don't either, but she won't go away, Wren," Bea says. "It's like she's stalking me or something. I didn't know what else to do."

Bea's bottom lip began to tremble, the sight of which made my heart contract, like a giant fist was squeezing it. I hated to see Bea scared, and it was happening more and more now that she had confided her abilities to her grandmother.

"It's okay, Bea," I said, reaching out and patting her bony little shoulder. "You did the right thing. I just... I wish I understood this better." Even as I said the words, I felt an icy breeze on the back of my neck that raised violent goosebumps on my arms. "Is she... is she here right now?"

Bea nodded, gnawing at her bottom lip again. "She's following me around. She feels..."

Bea paused, searching for the right word, but the icy breath on my neck was causing more than just goosebumps. I could feel an alien feeling flooding through me, a feeling that I knew hadn't originated in me, and yet was coursing through me all the same, causing my heart to race, my muscles to tense.

"Afraid," I said, completing Bea's thought. "Afraid and... desperate."

Bea nodded, and her eyes shone with unspent tears.

"Did you tell Xiomara?" I asked.

"No."

"Why not?" I asked.

"She doesn't want Xiomara. She wants you," Bea said.

"It's okay," I told her. "We just need to... to find a better way to communicate. I'll be right back. Stay here, okay?"

I waited just long enough to see Bea nod before turning and running back into the house. I didn't go back upstairs, but instead darted through the living room to the library. Once there, I scanned the top rows of the shelves until I found what I was looking for.

"Bingo."

I grabbed the little stepstool and dragged it over to the shelves over the doorway. I stepped carefully up onto it, and retrieved a velvet bag tied closed with a length of gold cord that ended in tassels. It was the Vesper family spirit board. I clutched it to my chest, and ran back outside again.

I'd never used the spirit board before, but I'd seen my mother and her sisters use it. Asteria had left it with her friend Lydian, who had been responsible for discharging Asteria's will after she died. My mom and my aunts had used it to communicate with Asteria after she had passed away. She'd had a message for them, an important one, and the spirit board was the only way they had been able to communicate clearly enough to receive that message. I didn't know much about spirit boards, but after months of lessons with Xiomara to hone my spirit affinity, I knew the basics.

"Let's take this down to my mother's garden," I said to Bea when I had arrived, somewhat breathlessly, back outside. "I don't want to wake anyone up."

Bea agreed, and together we hurried through the garden gate, across the expanse of yard until we reached the door in the stone wall that led to my mother's garden. It had been locked up for years since we had fled, and so it had grown wild and feral in our absence. But in the months since we'd returned, my mother had been patiently and tenderly restoring it to its former glory, pruning and trimming and weeding and tending, by hand as well as by magic. Now, as we stepped through into the splendor beyond, it was hard to imagine that it had ever been neglected. Lush blooms glistened with dew all around us in the moonlight as we walked down the path to the little gazebo at the center, where I placed the spirit board on one of the stone benches.

"Have you ever used one of these before?" I asked Bea.

"Of course," Bea said, looking startled. "Haven't you?"

"No," I said a little bitterly. "I mean, not a real one. Your grandmother insists I have to practice without 'cheating,'" I said, rolling my eyes. Bea giggled as I unwrapped the spirit board and its planchette, and set them carefully on the bench. "But I've read about them. Should we do it together?" I asked her. "Two spirit witches are better than one, right?"

Bea smiled, and we took our places on the bench, sitting cross-legged on either side of it, and placing our fingertips lightly on the planchette. I had a vague memory of doing this once at a sleepover with Poe using a novelty Ouija board, but we'd giggled and cheated too much to even scare ourselves. Now I wondered, if we'd taken it seriously, would my latent magical abilities have turned an innocent sleepover into a terrifying paranormal experience?

For the second time, a frigid breeze sent shivers shooting down my spine. If Jess Ballard really was here, she was getting impatient.

"Okay, okay," I muttered. "Chill out."

Bea knelt on the opposite side of the bench, and together we placed the tips of our fingers on the planchette. Instantly, a hum of energy, almost like electricity, buzzed beneath the pads of my fingers.

"Whoa," I muttered. "Do you feel that?"

"Yeah," Bea said, her eyes widening. "I told you she really needed to talk to you."

Feeling jumpy now, I tried to channel my energy into concentration. I closed my eyes, and at once the planchette began to move. My eyes flew open. The planchette was whizzing around the board so quickly I couldn't register the letters.

"Hey!" I shouted. "You have to calm down! I can't help you if I can't understand what you're saying!"

At once the planchette squeaked to a stop. It was still vibrating with energy, but it didn't move again. I could have sworn I heard an exasperated sigh somewhere near my left ear.

"Thank you," I said. "Now, please tell me who you are."

Bea opened her mouth, but I shook my head at her. I might be relatively new to witchcraft in general, but I knew enough to know that establishing the identity of the spirit speaking to us was crucial. There were much darker entities with a vested interest in me, and I wasn't about to be tricked into trusting one.

The planchette moved slowly and deliberately across the board: J-E-S-S-B-A-L-L-A-R-D.

"Okay, Jess. I'm sorry, but I need to make sure. You came to Sedgwick Cove to pass something along to me. What was it?"

The planchette jerked to life again: G-R-I-M-O-I-R-E.

I sighed with relief. At least now I could be sure of who we were talking to.

"Thanks, Jess. Okay, now, what is it you need from me?"

M-Y-B-O-D-Y

I blinked down at the words. "I... I'm sorry, Jess, but I'm not sure your body will do you much good now. You're dead."

N-O-T-D-E-A-D

Bea and I looked at each other, her sad expression mirroring my own. Xiomara had warned me that spirits were often confused about where they were and what had happened to them. Apparently Jess didn't realize that she was dead, or at least she didn't want to accept it.

"Jess, I'm really sorry, I'm sure this is hard for you, but—

The planchette started whizzing over the board again, and this time I had to concentrate to catch all the letters.

N-O-T-D-E-A-D

N-E-E-D-T-O-R-E-J-O-I-N-M-Y-B-O-D-Y

I stared at the words, my heart speeding up.

R-U-N-N-I-N-G-O-U-T-O-F-T-I-M-E

"I... I still don't understand what you mean," I said. "Even if we brought you back to your body, what good would it do?"

L-E-T-M-E-E-X-P-L-A-I-N

Another icy gust blew through the garden, knocking Bea's sketchbook from the corner of the bench, and rifling the pages until it fell open to Bea's sketch of Jess and the other words she had written. I looked at it again. There was a symbol, drawn over and over again...

"What is this?" I asked, more to myself than to Jess, but Jess answered at once.

R-U-N-E

I looked again. I had been learning about runes in my spellwork, though this one was unfamiliar to me.

D-R-A-W-O-N-W-R-I-S-T

My stomach gave an uneasy squirm. If my mother and my aunts had taught me one thing, it was never to mess around with magic I didn't understand. "More damage comes from ignorance than from malevolence, remember that," Rhi had said sternly, and I had taken her at her word.

"Why?" I asked, playing for time. "What does it do?"

H-E-L-P-Y-O-U-S-E-E-M-E

I raised my eyes from the spirit board, expecting to trade an anxious glance with Bea, but to my surprise, Bea looked flushed and bright-eyed with excitement. She was already diving for her bag, and then she straightened up again, holding a black marker.

"Let's do as she says!" Bea whispered eagerly.

"Bea, this is... this could be really dangerous. I don't know this woman. I don't know what her intentions are. Aren't you worried this might be a trap or trick?"

"No, I'm not," Bea replied. "Don't you feel her energy?"

I hesitated. "I'm not sure what you—"

"Just concentrate on her," Bea said. "What do you feel?"

I closed my eyes and tried to relax my mind, like Xiomara had taught me. I imagined a web reaching out around me, seeking and tasting and feeling. It had never worked very well before—sporadically at best, and the impressions weak—but now, I had to brace myself against an onslaught of emotion that wasn't my own. It made me gasp, and I had to concentrate even harder not to be swept away with the tide of it. I identified the emotions as they shuddered through me: Fear. Desperation. Hope. But more important were the emotions I didn't sense: Greed. Hatred. Hunger.

My eyes flew open to find Bea looking calmly back at me, as though she knew everything I'd just felt, and what it all meant.

"You know it's pretty aggravating how much better you are at all of this," I said to her. "I'm supposed to be the powerful one here."

Bea's face split into an embarrassed smile. "You have five elements to learn. I only have one."

"Yeah, but still—"

Another frigid breeze bit at my face. It tasted like impatience. "Okay! Okay, I'll do it!"

Bea had already uncapped the marker and was reaching for my hand.

Reluctantly, I held it out to her and watched, holding my breath, while she carefully copied the symbol from her notebook onto the pale skin of the underside of my wrist.

The effect was almost instantaneous. Like a radio trying to tune to the right station, images and sounds started flickering in my head. At first, I heard only the scattered words of a language I didn't know, then the air around me grew heavy, like the air before a lightning strike. One moment I was staring at an empty garden, and then next, I blinked and there she was: Jess Ballard, sitting about six inches from my face. I gave a yelp and skittered back from her, whacking the back of my head on the gazebo pole. My eyes watered with the pain.

"Fucking finally!" Jess cried. Her voice, though clear, sounded like it was echoing up from the bottom of a deep well.

"It *is* you!" I gasped.

"What happened? Did it work? Can you see her?" Bea asked, face shining with excitement.

"Go on and draw that rune on her as well," Jess said. "And then she'll be able to see me, too."

Rubbing the back of my head, I moved back to the bench and replicated the rune on Bea's wrist. This time, I could hear that the unfamiliar language was coming from Jess—she was reciting some kind of incantation as I worked. A moment later, Bea lifted her gaze and spotted Jess.

"There you are!" Bea cried in delight. Despite her somewhat manic energy, Jess managed a grin.

"Nice to meet you, Bea," she said.

"This is wild—what was that, a spell? Are you a witch?" I asked.

"No, I'm not a witch. That was a kind of spell, though. It's called a Melding, and it helps the living connect with the dead," Jess explained.

"How can you be doing spells if you're not a—"

"Look, Wren, I promise I will explain all of this to you when I've got my body back," Jess said, a snap of impatience in her voice.

"Jess, I haven't been a practicing witch very long, but even I know there's no magic that can restore a spirit to a body once it's been severed by death," I told her, trying to keep my voice gentle, even as the rest of me practically vibrated with the excitement of actually seeing and talking to a ghost.

"I'm aware of that, Wren, but the thing is, I'm not dead. I'm Walking," Jess said.

"What's—"

"I used a Casting—that's what we call spells—to leave my body and take a spirit form. My body only *seems* to be dead. But I'm still tethered to it, and as soon as I return to it, I'll be walking and talking and breathing again."

"Are you serious?" I asked.

"I'll be happy to prove it to you," Jess said, and again, there was an undercurrent of impatience in her tone.

"You said, 'that's what we call spells.' Who's we?" I asked.

Jess let out a groan of frustration. "Wren, I appreciate you want answers, but I'm running out of time, here. I'll explain everything when I've got my body back."

"But if what you're saying is true, and you really can rejoin with your body, why do you need our help?" Bea asked in her bright, clear voice.

Jess's expression turned grim. "Because thanks to Wren and the Sedgwick Cove Police Department, my body isn't where I left it anymore."

I felt myself bristling. "Hey, how were we supposed to know you were doing some kind of weird zombie trick?" I snapped. "Your body was just lying there, no breathing, no pulse! Anyone would have thought you were dead!"

Jess rolled her eyes. "Yeah, okay, fair enough, but if we don't get moving, I will actually be dead. Are you going to help me or not?"

"If we do, do you promise you'll explain everything?" I countered.

Before Jess could reply, Bea piped up again. "Of course, we'll help you! What do we need to do?"

Jess's face split into a mischievous smile as she turned to look at Bea. "Ever broken into a morgue before?"

12

"I can't believe I let you talk me into this," Nova grumbled, as we piled into her car.

"I know. I'll make it up to you," I said, as I put on my seatbelt. "Bea, put yours on, too."

"I know how to drive a car, Wren," Nova snapped, as we jerked our way down the road toward town.

"If you say so," I muttered. The truth was, I had no other choice. Nova was the only friend I had with a license and her own car—and even that license was still only a few weeks old.

"Am I about to find out why my mother tore out of our house tonight?" she'd asked, by way of greeting. "Because she wouldn't tell me shit when she got back, but she looked pissed."

"Yes," I'd replied. "Yes, I'll tell you everything your mother wouldn't tell you, just get over here."

That had been enough. There was no stronger lure for Nova than somehow outmaneuvering her mother. Check and mate.

"I still don't really understand what we're doing," Nova said, as she barreled down the road. Lightkeep Cottage winked at us from the rearview mirror. I'd made Nova park a ways down the street so that no one would hear the car engine. Thank goddess she'd still been awake when I'd texted her.

"That makes two of us," I said with a glance into the back seat, where Jess was seated beside Bea, who looked wild with excitement.

"Look, unless you want me to slam on these brakes..." Nova threatened.

"Okay, okay," I said, and explained what happened after she, Eva, and Zale had left me alone at the Shadow Tree.

"Oh sure, the one time I insist on leaving an event early, and you find a body without me!" Nova grumbled.

"I didn't find a body on purpose, Nova," I cried. "And trust me, you're welcome to the trauma if you'd like it."

"Whatever," Nova said, tossing her hair. "So, then what happened?"

Wearily, I went through the rest of the night's events. My head was pounding.

"You have the Vesper grimoire? Like... *the* Vesper grimoire?!" Nova gasped, turning to gape at me.

"Road! Eyes on the road!" I shouted.

But Nova was pulling over to the shoulder and throwing the car into park.

"What is she doing?!" came Jess' echoing voice from the back of the car. "We don't have time for this shit!"

"Seriously!? No wonder my mother looked so frazzled when she got home. No wonder she wouldn't talk to me. Holy *shit*!"

I was surprised to see that Nova, who was almost pathologically unbothered by just about everything, was white as a sheet. Her hands, which were clutching the steering wheel, were shaking a little.

"Nova, can we like... deal with this later? We're kind of in a hurry here," I said.

"Why aren't you freaking out about it?" Nova asked, incredulous.

"Because I never heard of it until a woman handed it to me, and now that woman is literally haunting me from the back of this car! Nova, please!"

"Right. Yeah, we can..." Nova ran a hand through her hair and took a deep breath. "Wait, why doesn't she just wait until the morning? We can call over there and explain. I mean, it's not like people won't believe us. I'm sure this isn't even the weirdest thing they've dealt with, dealing with so many covens over the decades."

"I know, but Jess was adamant. She says she has some kind of... code of secrecy or something. She says people can't know what she is."

"And what exactly is she, did she say that? I mean, you're risking serious trouble to help her."

"She said she'd explain it all when she's in her body again."

"And you took her word for it?" Nova asked, her voice dripping with disbelief.

"Yeah, I guess I did."

"What's to stop her from going back on her word? I mean, seriously Wren, you barely know this woman. Why do you trust her?"

"Because Asteria told me to," I said quietly. "She came to me. She told me Jess was coming. And she told me to trust her."

Nova pressed her lips together, considering. Then she nodded once, grudgingly. "Okay, fine. And you say the ghost is in the car right now?" Nova's eyes darted from the road into the mirror, searching.

"Can you keep your eyes on the road please?" I asked, a little shrilly. "Yes, she's here, and actually she's not a ghost. At least, I don't think she is. Like I said, I still don't know exactly what's going on."

"I can't believe you're asking me to help commit felony breaking and entering, and you don't know exactly what's going on," Nova hissed through gritted teeth.

"Hey, you asked me to break into a prison a few months ago, and I agreed!" I shot back. "It's your turn."

Nova continued to grumble under her breath as we drove into the center of town toward Bea's house. Jess' nervous energy emanating from the back seat was so powerful, it made the air in the car heavy and cold.

"Can you try to calm down?" I muttered over my shoulder. "It's starting to feel like a walk-in freezer in here."

"Yeah, well, my body is currently in an *actual* walk-in freezer, so maybe cool it with the judgmental tone," Jess shot back.

I pressed my lips together and suppressed a shiver. Touché, not-ghost.

Nova rolled to a stop in front of Bea's house, and I saw the curtains twitch. A moment later, Eva and Zale came tiptoeing out the door and down the steps to the car.

"Okay, Bea, hop out," Eva said.

"What? No! I'm coming with you!" Bea cried.

Eva snorted a laugh. "*Cariña,* you have no business breaking into a building in the middle of the night."

"Oh, and you do?" Bea replied, crossing her arms over her chest. "If it weren't for me, none of you would even know that Jess needs help!" Bea scrunched her brows together in such a fierce scowl that Eva actually took a step back. I didn't blame her; it was like Bea was channeling Xiomara with that expression on her face.

Eva cleared her throat. "Yeah, but that doesn't mean you should get in trouble."

"It doesn't mean you should get in trouble either. Just get in, Eva, I'm coming whether you like it or not!"

Eva looked first at Zale, who shrugged, and then at me in a silent bid for help.

"We haven't got all night, here!" Jess shouted in that faraway voice.

"Okay, okay," I told her. Then I turned to Bea. "Bea, we'll take you with us, but only if you stay in the car as a lookout."

"Fine," Bea said, mollified. Eva and Zale slid into the backseat with her, and Jess vanished to make room for them.

Zale shuddered violently as he sat. "Holy shit, turn that AC down!" he exclaimed.

"It's not the AC, it's the spirit energy," I told him.

His expression lit up, and he looked eagerly around the inside of the car. "That's so sick. Is she seriously in here with us right now?"

"Let's get a move on!" Jess growled from somewhere near the trunk of the car. A moment later, Nova pulled away from the curb, and down the main drag.

There was only one morgue in Sedgwick Cove. The police station was too tiny to house one, and there was no real hospital within the borders. Instead, we had a single funeral home overlooking the sea, another of Sedgwick Cove's repurposed grand Victorian houses. There was a sign on the side of the building which read, "Blackleach and Graves Funeral Services." I actually giggled out loud when I saw it.

"What are you laughing at?" Nova snapped.

"Sorry, it's just... the name is a little on the nose, isn't it? I mean, Graves? For a funeral home? Come on, that's funny!" I explained.

No one else laughed, though I thought I heard Jess give a snort of appreciation.

"Okay, moving on," I mumbled.

Blackleach and Graves looked normal from the outside, but the services they offered were anything but. As Bea had explained it to me, because the various covens had their own unique funereal traditions, Blackleach and Graves served as a kind of staging area for rituals and spellwork. The rooms that typically held coffins and viewing areas were instead full of altars, candles, and all sorts of ceremonial items—from dried herbs and shrouds, to incense and pyre materials. And of course, in the basement, there was a morgue.

"Can someone explain to me why we have to break in?" Zale asked, sounding more hesitant now that they had actually arrived. "I mean, it's not like anyone around here is going to bat an eye at a spirit hanging around. I bet they'd just let us in."

"Jess says it's a secret, what she can do," Bea said, before anyone else could weigh in. "She can't risk the wrong people finding out."

"How does she know we're not the wrong people?" Eva asked.

Bea shrugged. "I don't know. But she's trusting us."

"Like I have a choice." I felt rather than heard Jess' sarcastic reply. "Desperate times, and all that."

We all got out of the car. This close to the water, the sound of the waves crashing against the rocks was a constant roar that masked the sounds of our approach.

"Are we sure there's no one here?" I whispered, as we mounted the steps into the wide front porch.

"Ms. Graves used to live on the top floor until a few years ago, but her arthritis got so bad, she couldn't manage the stairs anymore; so she took a ground floor apartment around the corner. It should be empty," Eva said, though she sounded like she was trying to convince herself as much as me.

Nova reached into her pocket and pulled out a tin.

"Since when do you know how to pick locks?" I asked her.

"Since about the age of seven, when my mother started locking the book cabinets," Nova said with a smirk. "Ironically, if she'd just left them unlocked, I wouldn't have had the slightest interest in them. Parents create so many of their own problems."

I was the only one who heard Jess snort with amusement at Nova's remarks. I stared around anxiously as we waited for Nova to fiddle around with the lock.

"Are you even sure your body is here?" I asked Jess. "It's not like you're a local. They probably had to get the state police involved, which means your body might be in some police morgue somewhere."

"I'm sure. I might be out of my body right now, but I'm still tied to it. I can feel exactly where it is, because it's constantly trying to pull me back," she said.

"So why don't you just let it? Pull you back, I mean?" I asked, genuinely confused.

"Because it's currently inside a zipped-up body bag stored in an airless freezer drawer," Jess replied dryly, "and if I let it suck me back in, I'll be trapped there, too. I might not be breathing right now, but on reentry I will start again, and I would very much like there to be oxygen available when that happens."

My stomach lurched at the thought. "Okay, good point."

"Got it!" Nova crowed, as the lock clicked and the door swung open.

We didn't have to worry about motion detectors or burglar alarms—no one in Sedgwick Cove went in for that sort of modern security, except for the occasional rich outsider who bought one of the waterfront estates. When I'd suggested we get one for Lightkeep Cottage, Persi had laughed in my face.

"Why deter a thief with loud noises when you could curse their bloodline instead?" she had asked. I had to admit she had a point. The

Vesper witches hadn't locked a door in centuries. Their magic had always been their protection, and most of the rest of Sedgwick Cove's population felt the same way.

There were a few seconds of confused fumbling as we all activated the flashlights on our phones, and the room was a terrifying confusion of looming shadows and swinging beams of light.

"How do we know where to—" Zale began, but Jess swooped past him, creating a chill breeze and eliciting a high-pitched scream. "She's near me! I think she touched me! Is she touching me?"

Even in the semi-darkness, I could see Jess's spirit roll its eyes. "Will someone please tell him I'm not the boogeyman? It's this way. I can feel the pull, come on."

"Jess says it's this way," I told everyone, and they all fell into line behind me. I didn't love being at the front of the group—cowering at the back was more my speed when it came to situations like this—but I had no choice, as we'd left the only other person who could see Jess out in the car.

We moved through three large, square, adjoining rooms by way of massive sliding pocket doors that squealed along their tracks as we shoved them open. Stacks of chairs were lined up against the walls, and empty plinths shaped like Roman columns stood around awaiting their crowns of funeral arrangements. Thick carpet muffled our steps as we followed Jess's slightly luminous form toward the back of the funeral home. Shelves on the walls held row after row of candles in every color imaginable, and the scents from all the jars of incense were enough to make my head spin. Eva let out a shriek as we turned a corner and found ourselves facing a row of figures blocking our way, but it was only a collection of statues depicting a multitude of goddesses, familiars, and other deities.

"If I die of a heart attack before we get out of here, do not let them put any of those creepy ass statues at my funeral, please and thank you," Zale babbled, trying to get his breathing under control.

"I'm starting to think we should have left *you* in the car," Nova hissed. "Seriously Zale, get a fucking grip."

We sped up so that I didn't lose sight of Jess, who was drifting along impatiently ahead of us, and watched her beckon us before disappearing through a solid door. I seized the handle, and was relieved to find that it turned easily under my fingers—no more time wasted picking locks.

We all agreed we could risk turning on the basement lights, since they couldn't be seen from the street outside, and everyone seemed to relax a little —we were still about to break into a room full of dead bodies, but at least we could see where we were going. Jess drifted through a room full of coffins and racks of shrouds and ceremonial robes to a second door, this one massive and made of metal. She drifted through it, and we pushed it open after her.

I had never in my life had the slightest interest in understanding what happened to people's bodies after they died—it was the kind of morbid mystery I was happy to leave unsolved. Now, as I gazed around at metal tables, rolling carts of sterile instruments, and a wall full of square silver refrigerator doors, I felt my stomach give a heave. Zale's face was pale and clammy looking. Eva looked like she couldn't decide between fascination and horror. Only Nova managed to cling to her general sense of ennui.

"Okay, now what?" she asked. "Do you think those freezer thingies are locked?"

"God, I hope so," Zale murmured. He was staring at the doors as though expecting them to pop open at any moment, like in a zombie movie.

I just wanted to get out of there as quickly as possible. "Jess, where are —" But as I asked the question, she appeared again, floating out from the wall of freezers looking relieved.

"I found it—I mean, me. My body. It's in this one," she said.

"You're sure?" I asked, my voice higher than usual as anxiety coursed through me. "Because I do not want to play musical corpses here. I only want to open one of those drawers."

"Yes, I'm sure! Do you seriously think I don't recognize my own body?" Jess snapped. "Now come on! I have no idea what the effect on my body will be from being stuck in there so long!"

"Does she know—?" Nova asked, and I cut her off by pointing to the correct door. Slowly, we all moved past the metal tables that dominated the middle of the room. Thank goodness they were empty. If there had been a human shape under a sheet or a toe sticking out with a tag tied to it, I might have lost all grip on my self-control, and run screaming from the room. We gathered around the door Jess had indicated, and I quickly realized they were all staring at me.

"What?" I asked.

"We agreed to help you, but this is your mission, Vesper," Nova said. "And that means you open the dead body fridge."

Realizing I had no argument to make, I sucked in a deep breath, held it, and yanked on the handle. The door opened with the slight hissing sound of broken seals. A gust of frigid air blew out in a fog, and we found ourselves staring into a narrow metal tube with a slab on a track, and an ominous black bag resting on top of it. I seized the handle on the metal slab and pulled hard. The slab slid out with a metallic screech, and the telltale shape of a body was revealed. Unable to stand the mounting tension, and afraid I would lose my nerve, I found the zipper with shaking fingers, and unzipped the body bag.

I had only a moment to process the Jess Ballard who lay in front of me —her skin so pale it was almost blue, her lips slightly parted, a peaceful look on her motionless features, before the spectral Jess Ballard at my side gave a sigh of relief and muttered, "Finally!"

A moment later, she was sucked back into her body like water down a drain, and what had been a corpse a moment before suddenly gasped to life again. Her back arched as the air flooded her stationary lungs, and then she sat up, a string of hoarse curse words streaming from her dry, cracked lips. With a gasp, she stared down at her body, and then sighed with relief.

"Thank God. I was worried they might have taken my clothes," she gasped through chattering teeth, as she looked down at herself. "Will someone help me out of this thing, please?"

Nova and Eva, their mouths hanging open, hurried forward with me to help Jess shimmy her legs out of the body bag. Zale had slid to the floor, and was sitting with his head down between his knees, taking great gulping breaths as he fought to stay conscious. We helped Jess as she slid down onto the floor, but her legs wouldn't support her, and we had to keep her upright.

"Sorry," she mumbled, looking a bit ill. "I... my muscles aren't quite... I need to warm up, I think."

"It'll be a miracle if you don't have hypothermia," Nova remarked, though her eyes were bright with excitement. Despite the creepiness of the situation, I could tell she was enjoying herself.

"Let's get her back up to the car. We can blast the heat," Eva suggested.

"And find Zale a barf bag," Nova added.

"I'll be okay, I just need a... a minute," Zale said in a feeble voice.

Nova and I stood on either side of Jess and put her arms over our shoulders so that we could take some of her weight. Eva yanked Zale to his feet, and let him lean into her as he tried to get his legs back under him. It was slow, noisy progress back up the stairs, and even slower through the completely dark upper level. At one point, my elbow nudged one of the statues, and I had to dive for it to stop it from falling and shattering all over the floor, which left Jess to collapse on top of Nova when she suddenly lost my support. Finally, though, we managed to get out to the car, where Bea's eager face was pressed up against the window.

"You did it! You found her! And she's... she's in there, right?" Bea asked, poking a little at Jess' arm as she slid into the back seat.

"Ow! Yes, I'm in here! How would I be moving if I was—wasn't—" But Jess' teeth were slamming together too hard for her to keep speaking.

Nova went around to the trunk and pulled out two sand-crusted beach towels, which we wrapped around Jess before cranking up the heat in the car. We all crammed in and drove up the street.

"Where are you staying?" I asked Jess. "You've been here for a few days, you must have been staying somewhere."

"The bed and breakfast around the corner from the town center, the one that overlooks the docks," Jess managed to eke out between her chattering teeth.

"That's Priscilla Baroni's place. Do you think we can take you back there?" Nova asked. "Or do you think they told Priscilla you were dead?"

"I doubt they told her anything in the middle of the night," Jess said. "I didn't have any identification on me when they found me, but I did have this." She reached into her jeans pocket, and pulled out a key on a brass keychain shaped like a cat.

"Let's get you back to your room, then, and we can decide what to do from there," Nova said, decisively.

We took a side street that cut us down closer to the docks, and pulled up in front of Baroni B&B. The porch light was on, but the lights inside were all dark.

"I don't think she can get up to her room by herself," I said to Nova. "I'm going to stay with her."

"Well, then I'm coming, too," Nova said. "What, like I'm going to leave you alone with this random woman who just Houdini-d herself into her own body? No way."

It was a show of solidarity and I was appreciative, but I didn't say thank you. Nova only rolled her eyes at anything approaching genuine emotion. So I nodded instead, which she ignored.

"I should get Bea home," Eva said. Bea had nodded off in the intense warmth of the car, her face pressed against the window, her mouth gaping. At the sound of her name, though, she jolted awake.

"I'm fine! I wasn't asleep!" she mumbled, rubbing her eyes.

"Yeah, okay," Eva snorted. "Whether you're tired or not, Xiomara will ground you for the rest of your life if she finds out what you did."

Bea looked mutinous. "But I want to know—"

"So do we," Eva cut her off. "We all want to know what the hell is going on. But that's going to have to wait for tomorrow."

"She came to me first!" Bea countered, crossing her arms over her chest.

"Bea."

Bea turned, startled to hear her name come out of Jess' mouth.

"Thanks for all your help," Jess ground out. "You saved my life, short stack."

Bea's cheeks flushed with pleasure. "You're welcome."

"I don't want you to get in trouble because of me," Jess said. "And it's safer if fewer people know what happened tonight. Can you help keep my secret? Wren can explain everything tomorrow, okay?"

Only a desire to keep being helpful could have talked Bea out of staying. She nodded solemnly and held out a pinkie.

"Aw, hell yeah, a pinkie promise," Jess replied, managing a smile. She hooked a shuddering finger with Bea's, and they shook on it. Then Bea rounded on me.

"Tomorrow?" she prompted, holding out her pinkie again.

"Absolutely. All the details. I promise, too." Taking that pinkie felt like swearing a blood oath, but I had no intention of breaking it. Bea had earned the right to know what was going on. I just had to figure it out for myself first.

"Zale, are you good to walk?" Nova asked, giving Zale a skeptical, sideways look as he pulled himself gingerly out of the car.

"Yeah, I'll be fine," he said, though it sounded more like a question than a statement. "I'm only a block from here. I think I just need the fresh air."

"I'll drop him first," Eva assured us, trying not to smirk. "I guess we can rule mortician out for your future career prospects, huh Zale?"

Zale flipped Eva a single, enthusiastic digit. Bea giggled, and the three set off down the sidewalk.

"Right," said Nova when the others had disappeared around the corner. "Let's get zombie woman inside, and then maybe she can tell us what the actual hell is going on."

13

Jess' fingers were still too stiff to manage the key, so I took it from her and let us in. We tiptoed through Priscilla's doily-covered sitting room and up to Jess' room on the second floor. I winced at every creak of the antique staircase, and almost cried when I saw there was a beaded curtain hung in the doorway at the top, but no one came out to investigate. With the massive influx of October tourists, Priscilla must be used to the sounds of constant coming and going, even late at night. The sign outside had announced there was no vacancy, as was usually the case all through the summer and fall, until after Halloween.

The longer she walked, the better control Jess seemed to get of her own limbs, but she was still shaking and shuddering like mad, and so I unlocked her room and let us all in. The place was a mess. The bed was rumpled and unmade. A pair of pajama pants hung over the back of a chair. At least six half-drunk iced coffees crowded the bedside table, along with an unopened bottle of water. She hadn't bothered to unpack her suitcase—it lay open on the window seat with a jumble of wrinkled clothes piled on top of it.

"Look, I know I owe you an explanation, but I'm still teetering on the verge of hypothermia here. I'm going to take a hot shower. Can you wait here for me?" Jess asked.

"We can wait," I told her. We watched her scuttle around, grab a bathrobe, the pajamas from the back of the chair, her cell phone, and a toothbrush. She shuffled out the door to the hallway bathroom she shared with the other guests on the second floor. When the door shut, Nova rounded on me.

"Wren, what the actual fuck is happening?" Nova hissed. "We've got her back in her body, so it's time for answers. Who is this woman?"

"I told you, I don't really know. She just showed up on our doorstep and handed me the lost Vesper family grimoire."

"But who *is* she? She's not a Vesper too, is she?"

"No. She says she's not a witch, but if that's true, I'd like to know exactly what she is."

"Oh, come on. She's got to be! How can she possibly explain tonight if there wasn't magic involved?"

"She didn't say there wasn't magic involved. In fact, she mentioned a "Casting", which sounds like spellwork to me. But if she's a witch, why wouldn't she just say that? I mean, she's in a town full of witches. Where better to tell the truth?"

"But that's just it, Wren," Nova said, and she dropped her voice even lower, so that I had to lean forward to hear her. "This could be the most dangerous place for her to tell the truth."

"You lost me," I said.

"Look, you already know about the Kildare Coven. They were banished forever from Sedgwick Cove because of the kind of magic they practiced. And as for my family, well..." Nova made a face. "We easily could have been booted as well, if they hadn't determined Sarah was the exception instead of the rule. But what we saw tonight?" Nova shook her head. "That kind of death magic is dark shit, Wren. Seriously dark shit."

I raised an eyebrow. "You didn't seem scared while you were watching it. If anything, you seemed... hyped."

Nova shrugged. "Well, yeah, it might be dark as fuck, but it was still awesome."

"Look, she said she was going to explain, so maybe we should just let her do that."

"Yeah, or maybe we should bounce before she unleashes some more unhinged death magic on us."

"Nova, I told you. Asteria told me I need to trust her."

Nova looked like she was battling with the impulse to argue with me, and I was pleasantly surprised when she swallowed her questions and shoved her curiosity down with an impressively unbothered shrug.

"Fine. But we still need to understand what the hell happened tonight."

"Agreed."

Nova looked around furtively. "Do you think we should try to search the room while she's gone?"

"And look for what?" I asked.

"I dunno," Nova shrugged. "Weapons? Additional dead bodies?"

I gazed around skeptically. "I don't know, Nova. It looks like it's mostly dirty clothes and leftover iced coffee in here."

Nova rolled her eyes. "We're not looking for the obvious, Wren. We're looking for what's hidden."

As much as I trusted Asteria, she was only human, living or dead, and therefore must be susceptible to the same weaknesses as the rest of us. So, I agreed that we should probably do just a bare minimum of snooping. Jess could still be hiding something—from Asteria and from us. Better to have as much information as possible when confronting her. `

Nova and I started on opposite sides of the room, opening drawers, feeling under the mattress and between the dresser and the wall. We moved as quickly as we could, knowing Jess could be back any second, and praying that she was taking her time defrosting her recently reacquired body so that we wouldn't be caught. I dug quickly through her suitcase while Nova stuck her hands into a pair of battered Doc Martins and the pockets of two oversized flannel shirts hanging on the back of the door.

"What's this?" Nova asked suddenly. She had opened a drawer in the bedside table, and pulled out a small leatherbound book.

"I don't know, a Bible? Isn't that what they usually put in hotel bedrooms?" I suggested.

Nova snorted. "Not in Sedgwick Cove. No, it's old, Wren. Like, *really* old."

I hurried over to join her. The book was made of battered, ancient leather, and the words inside were in a language I'd never seen before—neither of us could make sense of any of it.

"Any ideas?" Nova asked, after we'd closed it again.

"Not really," I said. "I know it's not French or Spanish."

"Or Italian," Nova added.

"It's... do you feel something strange when you touch it? A sort of... energy?" I whispered.

Nova nodded. "Yeah. This definitely isn't a normal book. It might be..."

"A grimoire?" I asked, the word falling easily from my lips, even as Nova seemed about to say it.

She nodded. "Witch or not, this is a spellbook of some kind, I'm sure of it."

We heard footsteps in the hallway, and Nova lunged for the bedside table, stashing the book back in the drawer, and sliding it carefully shut. But then the footsteps stopped, and we heard a muffled voice out in the hallway. Nova and I traded one silent look, and then both tiptoed over to the bedroom door and put our ears against it, listening.

I recognized Jess' voice right away, and the long pauses between her words meant that she was talking to someone we couldn't hear. Then I remembered she'd taken her cell phone along, and realized we were eavesdropping on her half of a phone conversation.

"I know. I guess this is going to be more complicated than I expected," she said with a sigh. "I know. I know. And you're sure it's not anywhere on our map? That's so weird. Yeah, I'm sure. Oh, come on, Cat, do you seriously think I can't tell?"

Nova and I looked at each other, but I could tell from the expression on her face that she was as mystified as I was. Without hearing the other side of the conversation, it was almost impossible to understand what Jess was talking about. Still, we kept listening.

"I don't know, I'll have to try again, but it will be tricky," Jess went on. "I may need to enlist the girl's help, and to do that I'm going to have to tell her at least part of the truth. Of course I won't. Fine. Will you please just let me handle it? I can slip under the radar much easier if it's just me. Yes, I'll keep you posted. Bye."

We heard Jess end the call and the footsteps started again. Nova and I scrambled as silently as we could back across the room, and just managed to resume our seats as the door opened and Jess appeared, clad in oversized pajamas, with her masses of dark hair damp and piled on top of her head in a messy bun that was still dripping onto her shoulders, leaving wet spots on her gray t-shirt.

"You two done tearing my room apart?" she asked, smirking. "Because I can go dry my hair, too, if you need more time."

I suddenly felt as though I had an obstruction in my throat. I threw a panicked look at Nova, whose usually bored expression harbored just an edge of anxiety.

"I... we didn't—" I began, but Jess cut me off with a casual flick of her hand.

"Please. I would have done the same thing. In fact, if you hadn't had a good snoop around, I would have written you both off as idiots," she said, throwing herself onto the bed and looking through her beverages for something she could still drink. "Find anything good?"

Again, Nova and I just looked at each other. Then Nova pointed to the drawer in the bedside table. "We found a book. A really old one."

Jess glanced at the drawer and nodded. "Thorough. I'm impressed."

She didn't seem angry, so I added, "We couldn't figure out what language it was in."

Jess laughed. "I've been studying it for years, and I still suck at it. It's Gaelic. Irish, mostly, though it's all antiquated, and so there's some Scottish Gaelic and old Britannic mixed in as well. I doubt anyone could read it who wasn't—" She cut herself off.

"Who wasn't what?" I asked eagerly.

Jess sighed, and took a long sip from the one iced coffee that still had any lingering fragments of ice in it. She seemed to be considering me, choosing her next words very carefully. Finally, she put the cup down with a sigh of resignation.

"What about her?" she asked, pointing at Nova.

"What about me?" Nova asked, bristling.

Jess ignored her, still staring intently right at me. "Do you trust her?"

I shot a glance at Nova, whose face was twisted with defiance and—more surprisingly—nerves. I realized that she wasn't sure of my answer. As for me, after everything Nova and I had been through together since I came to Sedgwick Cove, I was sure.

"Yeah, I do. She's literally put her life on the line to help me, and she came tonight to help you with no questions asked—or at least, with a lot of her questions left unanswered. I trust her completely."

Out of the corner of my eye, I could see Nova's cheeks were flushing. I didn't look at her, though, because among the many things I trusted about Nova was the fact that she would absolutely deck me if I caught her being even remotely vulnerable. Jess had no interest in how Nova was reacting. All she cared about, evidently, was what I had to say. And after I'd said it, she nodded once, decisively, and that seemed to be it. If I trusted Nova, apparently so did she.

"Okay, Vesper. Now that we've established you're both trustworthy, that means your word means something. So I need both of you to give me your word that you won't tell anyone anything I'm about to divulge to you, unless I tell you it's okay. It's for my protection, as well as the protection of the people I love. It will also keep you out of danger."

How could we not agree? We murmured the required promise.

Jess' shoulders relaxed, and her voice was a little less tense as she continued. "Good. Now, this conversation will probably be a little bit easier than it usually is, because you both already understand that the world is more complicated than most people believe," Jess said. "For instance, I don't have to convince either of you that ghosts are real. You already accept that as fact."

I nodded. Beside me, Nova did the same. It seemed like we were both holding our breath.

"I belong to a sort of... sisterhood. Our sisterhood has many families—we call them clans, and each clan is a separate bloodline that passes the same gift down through the generations. Correct me if I'm mistaken, but I think your covens work in a similar way?" she added, looking back and forth between us.

Nova and I locked eyes, each of us silently asking the other if we should answer. Here I'd been expecting answers from Jess, but I hadn't really been counting on giving any of my own. But she was giving us what seemed to be secret information, and so it didn't seem fair to refuse a trade in kind. A secret for a secret? Nova made a movement somewhere between a nod and a shrug, and that seemed to be enough discussion.

"Yeah, that's right," Nova said, as we both turned back to Jess. "And just like you, there might be some questions that we can't answer."

"Fair enough," Jess said. "Anyway, throughout history, members of our sisterhood have often been labeled as witches, and even burned at the stake or hanged for the mistaken association, so you'll have to pardon me if it seems like I'm trying to put distance between us. No disrespect meant. It's just that my only run-in with witchcraft prior to this was kind of disastrous. But we're not meant to wield your sort of magic, and I imagine the reverse is also true."

"Well, since our first run-in with your type of magic involved reanimating corpses, I think it's safe to say the feeling is mutual," Nova said dryly.

Jess snorted. "I like her. And technically, I wasn't a corpse. At least, not in the usual sense. Let me back this up, though, I'm getting ahead of myself. My sisterhood is called the Durupinen. We are the keepers of the gates between the worlds of the living and the dead."

A shiver, delicate and fluttering, shot up my spine like the fingers of a ghost.

"There are places in the world where the veil between the world of the living and the world of the dead are very thin—thin enough that trapped spirits can slip through with just a little help. As Durupinen, we help lead them to those places and provide that help, if they need it."

"So you're like... what, psychic mediums?" I asked.

Jess snorted. "Psychic mediums wish they were that cool. There are others out there who can sense spirits—we call them sensitives. But only the Durupinen have the control of the Gateways—we call them Geatgrimas, in our lore. But the point is, spirits who are lost find us—they seek us out, and we help them however we can, whether it's completing their unfinished business for them, or simply helping them find their way across to the spirit world."

"This is all super interesting," I said. "But I'm struggling to understand what it has to do with us and the grimoire."

"Well, I lied to you," Jess said. "About how I came across the book? I'm sorry about that. It's just that sometimes it's easier to interact with living people if I don't mention the ghost stuff. I thought you'd believe me more easily if I gave you a mundane story about how I found the book and tracked you down, instead of the real story."

"Which is?" I prompted impatiently.

Jess' expression softened. "Your grandmother. Asteria."

"But how—oh!" I gasped. Of course. *Of course.* "She came to you? As a ghost?"

"That's right," Jess said. "It took some time to understand exactly what she needed from me, but eventually I figured it out."

I frowned. "So I was her unfinished business?"

"Yes," Jess said. "She reached out to me several times because it was important to her that you have that book I delivered to you."

"And she didn't say why?"

"Unfortunately, no. Much as I'm careful with my secrets, it seems your grandmother is, too. She wouldn't tell me exactly why you needed the book, only that it was important to your family and to this town that you get it back."

Out of nowhere, I was swallowing against something in my throat, something that threatened to choke me with an onslaught of tears.

"Hey, are you good?" Jess asked, her eyebrows pulling together in concern.

"Yeah, I..." I tried to shrug nonchalantly, but only Nova could pull off shit like that. "I guess... I wonder why she didn't just come to me."

"Well, most people wouldn't be able to communicate with her in her current form," Jess said gently. "It's not that she didn't want to speak to you, I'm sure. She probably just didn't think she'd be able to make contact."

I knew she was trying to make me feel better, but her words just felt like a slap across the face. I tried to take the blow stoically, but I could feel the tears welling up in the corners of my eyes, like traitors. Here I was, working night and day to develop my powers, and Asteria had to find someone from halfway across the world to deliver a message to me.

"Wren?" Jess prompted, looking concerned now. "Have I upset you?"

"No, no, it's just... my gifts as a witch... well, connecting with spirits should be one of them. But I seem to have developed some kind of block. It's not progressing as well as my other skills."

"Wren, you've only been at it for a few months. You're doing fine," Nova snapped, sounding almost impatient.

"So you are a sensitive?" Jess asked. "And it's a new power?"

"I'm supposed to be," I replied. "And I'm not sure if it's new so much as... undeveloped. I've only known I was a witch since June."

Jess' eyebrows disappeared into the curling mess of her wet hair. "But isn't your whole family...?"

"Yeah. My mom sort of... ran away and hid it all from me. It was only when Asteria died that it all came out," I explained.

I watched with confusion as a smile broke slowly over Jess' face, followed by a chuckle that built into a gale of laughter. I stared, blinking at her as she seemed to come unglued.

"Jess? Are you... good?" I asked. Beside me, Nova looked as disturbed as I felt.

"I'm sorry," Jess choked out, trying to compose herself. "It's just... I'm starting to understand why your grandmother was drawn to me of all the Durupinen she could have connected with."

"What do you mean?" I asked.

"Well, obviously it was because of the book. I had handled it before, and knew where it was, but I wasn't the only one. No, I think it was because you and I have so much in common, Wren," Jess said.

"Why, do your spirit abilities suck too?" Nova asked. I whacked her on the arm and she grimaced. "What? It was only a joke."

"I think it's because Wren and I both came into our powers later than most," Jess said, focusing her gaze on me now, as the rest of her laughter died out. "My mom spent my whole childhood running from our legacy—literally. I moved more than twenty times before I graduated high school. She died when I was seventeen without ever telling me what we were. I had to figure it out the hard way."

For a moment, I felt like I couldn't breathe. I tried to imagine what it would be like, discovering I was a witch entirely on my own, and then trying to grapple with all the ramifications of that, without my mother and my aunts to guide me—without, in fact, an entire town full of people who could help me. I couldn't do it. I looked back at Jess to see that she was watching me carefully as I absorbed this information.

"I'm sorry, but I'm getting a bit off track here," Jess said, when I had sat in silence for nearly a full minute. "I was trying to explain what happened tonight, and I'm not doing a very good job. Can I continue?"

"Of course," I said, in need of a distraction from the complex feelings still roiling inside me, like a brew in Rhi's kitchen cauldron.

"I came here with only one purpose in mind, and that purpose was given to me by your grandmother," Jess said. "I needed to pass along that book. It took me a little while to find you—no one in this town is very forthcoming to outsiders, but I assume you already know that. Regardless, though, I found you and delivered your book. Mission accomplished."

"But that was two days ago," I said, momentarily distracted from my own insecurities. "So why are you still here? When you left my house, you made it sound like you were on the way out of town."

"Do you remember when I mentioned those places in the world where the veil between the worlds is thin?" Jess asked, waiting for both Nova and me to nod. "Well, Sedgwick Cove is one of those places. The

Durupinen keep track of those places—you can imagine why that would be important for us, seeing as we're supposed to be guarding them. But the thing is, we have no record of this place on our map. It's like it's been hidden or something."

"How do you know?" I asked. "That Sedgwick Cove is one of those places?"

"I can feel it," Jess said. "The same way I imagine you can feel traces of witchcraft. I realized I had to stay, to investigate and figure out what was going on. And so I have. I got a room here at this bed and breakfast, and then I started snooping around."

"And that led you to the Playhouse," I said, starting to feel at last that this story was starting to make some sense.

"That's right," Jess said. "But the Playhouse was heavily guarded, and so I knew I wouldn't be able to get near the place. Why is it being guarded, by the way? Do you know? It doesn't even look like it's open."

Nova and I traded a glance. We were getting into territory that meant a serious breach of secrecy. No one outside of Sedgwick Cove knew about the deep magic, and it was too dangerous to speak about it to an outsider, even I knew that. I cleared my throat.

"It isn't open. It's a summer theater. But there was an incident there a couple of months ago," I said, deciding on just a bit of the truth. "It was the site of some dark magic. The town has been... investigating it ever since."

Jess narrowed her eyes. She knew I wasn't telling her everything, but she seemed to decide that was okay, for the time being. She went on, "Well, like I said, I had to try to see why I was drawn to that Playhouse. So, I... well, I engaged in my own version of spellcasting so that I could perform my own investigation."

"And that meant killing yourself?" Nova asked, hoisting a single, skeptical eyebrow.

Jess smirked. "Not exactly. You see, the Durupinen have individual gifts—strengths that help them interact with the spirit world. For example, my sister is a Caller—she can actually summon spirits and exercise control over their actions."

I felt my eyes grow wide. "You mean she can... control spirits?" Even with my level of magical ignorance, that sounded malevolent. Perhaps my skepticism showed on my face, because Jess raised a cautionary hand.

"I know it sounds bad, but my sister Hannah is the gentlest soul you'll ever meet. Now that she fully understands her power, she only uses it in the most dire of circumstances, and then only for good. She's just one example. Some Durupinen are Empaths—they feel the emotions of spirits as though the emotions are their own."

"What about you?" I asked.

Jess gave a rueful laugh. "Me? Oh, I'm multi-talented. To begin with, I'm a Muse. That means that spirits use my artistic abilities to communicate. I drew your face several times, Wren Vesper, before I was able to fully connect with your grandmother."

The thought of my face in a stranger's sketchbook made me want to shudder, but it also triggered a thought. "Bea..." I began.

Jess was already nodding. "I know she's not a Durupinen, but our gifts are almost identical. I would be fascinated to find out more about how her abilities work, but of course there's been no time for that yet. I was in a bit of an emergency situation."

"So being a Muse wasn't the reason you wound up as a ghost?"

"Nope. That would be my other gift. Like I said, multi-talented," Jess said, flipping her hair sarcastically. "I'm also a Walker. That means I can use a Casting to leave my body and travel around in spirit form."

"How?" I asked, fascinated in spite of myself.

"With one of these," Jess answered, raising her left wrist to reveal several intricately knotted bracelets nested there.

"Oh!" I gasped, and reached into my pocket, pulling out the broken bracelet I'd found beside her body in the woods. "I found this sort of pinned under your arm when I found you in the woods."

Nova leaned over so that she could look more closely. I hadn't had much time to examine it before, but now as my eyes took in the complexities of the knotwork and the braiding, a creeping sensation began to wriggle its way over my skin. Different though our magic was, even I knew those bracelets were anything but ordinary.

After allowing us to gawk at her bracelets for another moment, Jess went on. "That one is cut through, because severing it is part of the Casting that allows me to leave my body. Once I escaped my body, I was able to roam freely without detection—or at least, without *complete* detection. There was definitely one woman down there at the Playhouse who sensed my presence."

"That would be Xiomara, Bea's grandmother," I explained. "She's the most powerful spirit witch in Sedgwick Cove. She's helping me to develop my own abilities." I fought the urge to add how badly that particular bit of training was going.

"I was lucky to evade her detection," Jess said. "Being a true Walker is a very rare ability. Other Durupinen who have attempted to cultivate it have typically descended into madness. It's a skill that can be much more curse than blessing, and I use it as infrequently as possible."

"But why?" Nova asked, her voice a bit breathless. "It sounds incredible, to be totally free of the confines of your body!"

Jess' smile was a little too knowing. "Yeah, that's the problem. Those who try it often lose their connection to their bodies, and desire instead to roam the world in their spirit form. That's when the madness sets in."

"And you don't? I mean, you haven't..." My voice trailed away as I struggled to find a polite way to ask my question. I mean, is there a polite way to ask someone if they're nuts?

Jess seemed to understand though, judging by the smile that played on her lips. "I've managed to avoid that particular pitfall so far. When I'm Walking, I'm still tied to my body. Though it appears lifeless, the body of a true Walker enters a state of stasis—like someone has hit a pause button. The body doesn't breathe or move, but neither does it begin to decay. It simply is, frozen in time, until the Walker returns."

"And so when Wren found your body—" Nova began.

"She understandably thought she had stumbled upon a corpse. Actually not the first time that's happened to me, believe it or not." For some reason she had to smother a grin, and her cheeks flushed slightly, like she was remembering something embarrassing, before clearing her throat and focusing on me again. "It was, however, the first time I was scooped up and thrown in a body bag."

It was my turn to flush a little now. "Yeah, I'm sorry about that. But how could I have known?"

"You couldn't," Jess said with a shrug. "And anyway, you rescued me. Let's call it square."

I smiled. "Fair enough."

"So what were you able to find out?" Nova urged. "I mean, about the uh... Playhouse?"

"Not much, actually," Jess said ruefully. "Besides the guards, there seemed to be some magical protections set up as well. There were invisible barriers I couldn't cross, and before I'd had much time to examine or test them, I heard the sirens. Then I had to abandon my investigation, and focus on getting my body back as priority number one."

I swallowed the urge to apologize again. She'd already agreed we were forgiven.

"So, I've already told you more than I should," Jess said with a sigh. "Now comes the point where I ask you for some honesty in return, and maybe a bit of help."

Nova and I looked at each other.

"Help with what?" I asked.

Jess crossed her arms. "I need to know what's under that Playhouse. And I need you to help me get in there."

14

"Did... did you hear what I said?" Jess asked.

It was a fair question, considering the fact that Nova and I were just staring at her as though both of our brains had stopped functioning simultaneously. I turned my gaze on Nova, and saw the same panic staring back out at me from her eyes that I could feel pumping through my veins.

"You... want us to take you under the Playhouse?" Nova repeated.

"Yeah," Jess said. "I can't very well know what we're dealing with if I can't even get in there to see it."

"I... don't really think that's going to be possible," I said.

"I'll do you one better. I know for a fact it's not going to be possible," Nova added.

Jess narrowed her eyes. "Why not?"

"It's... complicated," Nova hedged.

"I can keep up," Jess replied.

Nova looked at me again, silently asking me to jump in.

"See, the thing is, Jess... that place, under the Playhouse? It's sort of... off limits."

Jess rolled her eyes. "Yeah, I kind of sorted that out from all the security and the magical protections? Hence why I even tried something as extreme as Walking to get in there."

"Yeah, well that security is constant. We're talking twenty-four seven. And we're definitely not allowed in there," I said.

Jess raised one eyebrow. "I am speaking to the girls who just broke into a morgue and stole a body at the behest of a spirit, right? Or did those girls get impatient and fuck off while I was in the shower?"

"No, we're... it's not that we don't want to help you," I said quickly. "It's just, I don't think we can."

"We definitely can't," Nova added.

"Why?" Jess asked.

Nova and I traded anxious looks again.

"What happened there? What's with all the security? It doesn't seem like you knew anything about Gateways before I explained it, so what's with all the interest in that particular part of town?"

"Do you know how you said that there's like, a code of secrecy with your sisterhood, the Du—the Du-ruh... sorry, what was it?"

"The Durupinen," Jess repeated.

"Right. You have stuff you're not allowed to tell people because it protects you. We're in a similar situation here in Sedgwick Cove," I explained.

"It's been that way since the town was founded," Nova added. "I probably don't need to tell you that witches have been persecuted for centuries, because it sounds like some of you were even persecuted on our behalf. But when this town was founded, the covens that settled here agreed that the true nature of the town would stay a secret, for everyone's protection. And we take that seriously."

Jess was smirking, like she was expecting us to say that this was all a joke. "You do realize that your entire town is like... witch themed, right? I couldn't walk ten feet without tripping over a broomstick or a cauldron since I got here."

"Right, but that's why the protection is so clever. We project this image of fake, commercialized witchcraft to hide the real magic of the place. And it works. Visitors have no idea about the deep and abiding magical community that actually hides in plain sight here. They think it's all a show, like an amusement park."

Jess nodded. "Okay, yeah, I guess that makes sense. It's definitely clever. But then... you're saying that whatever is under the Playhouse is part of the secret?"

"It's not just part of the secret. It's the heart of it," Nova said. "You're asking us to show you the one thing we have to protect the most."

"Why? What is it?" Jess asked, and then caught herself. "Okay. Okay, right. You probably can't even say, can you?"

Nova shook her head. Jess closed her eyes for a second, clearly deep in thought.

"Okay," she said. "Okay. We can... we can figure this out."

Nova and I waited. I was pretty sure we weren't even breathing.

"Look, I'm not trying to get the two of you in trouble. You saved my life tonight, and that's not an exaggeration. But the fact remains that I need to get in to see what we're dealing with under that Playhouse; and, if the events of tonight have taught me anything, it's that I can't do it by myself. So, here's my proposal," Jess said, pressing her hands together, and choosing her words carefully. "I know what I'm looking for, and I'll be able to tell within moments if I've found it. If it's not a Geatgrima, I'll head out of town, no questions asked, and you'll never see me again. But if it is... well, I guess we'll have to have another conversation."

I looked at Nova, who was waggling her eyebrows and shaking her head in a way I absolutely could not interpret.

"Could we, uh... have a second to talk about this?" I asked.

Jess hesitated only a moment. "Of course," she said. "It's like three o'clock in the morning. I don't think we're going to solve this tonight, and I don't want either of you to get in trouble if you can avoid it. Why don't you go home, talk it over, and get in touch with me tomorrow. This is my cell phone, okay?" She dug around for a moment in the drawer of her bedside table, extracted a business card, and handed it to me.

I looked at Nova, but she was just staring blankly at Jess, so I pocketed the card and stood up, making the decision for the two of us. "Okay. But what about you? What are you going to do?"

Jess chuckled. "Well, given that multiple people in this town have only ever seen me as a corpse, I'm going to lay low and wait to hear from you."

"Don't you think they're going to come and search your room when they figure out where you've been staying? We might be a town full of witches, but our police officers can still do their jobs, and they're going to track you down."

"I won't be staying here," Jess assured me. "I'll find somewhere else to keep a low profile for the moment, but I won't be too far. Just let me know what you decide."

"What if we decide not to help you?" Nova asked, finding her voice at last. She was looking at Jess with a level, assessing sort of gaze.

"Then that's your choice, and I'll respect it," Jess said with an unconcerned shrug. "I respect that you need to protect your secrets, but I've got to protect mine too; and if I fail, the repercussions could be catastrophic. I respect you and your town, but that doesn't mean I'll just give up." Then she turned and looked directly at me. "I think your grandmother brought us together for a reason, Wren, and it's bigger than simply handing over a book. So think about it, and get home before the two of you get busted. I've got some packing to do."

Nodding, I grabbed Nova by the arm and pulled her out of the room. As the door swung closed behind us, I caught a last glimpse of Jess' face. She was gazing after us, a little wrinkle of worry creasing her otherwise smooth forehead.

* * *

"No."

"Nova, come on."

"No. No, Wren. Absolutely not. I can't even believe we're having this conversation. It's a non-starter!"

We were sitting in Nova's car, still parked outside the bed and breakfast. Well, I was sitting. Nova was, apparently, having a nervous breakdown.

"Nova can you just—"

"No! No, I cannot *just*," she replied, each word as sharp as a knife. "There is no *just* in this situation, Wren."

I sighed, which only seemed to infuriate her more. I turned to look out the window.

"I know what you're doing," Nova said, after a tense but silent minute. "You're waiting for me to calm down because you think I'm being hysterical, but the truth is that you should be hysterical, Wren! You should be freaking out right now!"

"Yes, because freaking out always solves things," I muttered.

"When it is a proportional response, it sure does!" Nova shouted, and then pressed her lips together, taking a sharp inhalation through her nose, and then blowing it out through her mouth. "First of all, I'm not sure if I believed a single word that came out of that woman's mouth. I mean, seriously? Gateways? Duru...whatever the hell she called them? It all sounds like bullshit."

I turned to look at her, amused despite my simmering aggravation. "Seriously, Nova? We live in a town populated by witches, and this is the hill you want to die on? That her magical community isn't believable?"

Nova rolled her eyes. "Whatever. It sounds fake."

"Well, so does our entire existence to anyone who doesn't live here, so maybe let's just assume that she's telling the truth."

"Why though? Why should we assume that?"

"Well, in the first place, we watched her re-enter her own purportedly dead body and come back to life, and somehow I think that's probably more than just some party trick or illusion. She's got magic of some kind, even if we don't fully understand it."

"Well—"

"And secondly, Asteria found her. She spoke to her, specifically. Everyone in this town has been drilling it into my head from day one that our covens are sacred, that our history is important, that our traditions are who we are. Hell, less than twelve hours ago, we were all standing around the Shadow Tree to honor exactly all of those things. And I'm sorry, but I don't believe that Asteria would just lead a fox into the henhouse and tell us to trust her. Do you?"

Nova chewed the inside of her cheek, but said nothing.

"No, of course you don't. In fact, I think you do believe what Jess told us. I think you believed every word that came out of her mouth, until the moment she started talking about the one thing that scares the shit out of you, and that's the Source."

"I'm not scared of the Source," Nova retorted.

"Yes, you are," I said. "We all are, aren't we? We don't understand it. We can't control it. And yet, somehow we have to protect it from the Darkness. It's okay to admit we're afraid of it. Of its power. Of what it can do. How it could tempt us."

"That's beside the—"

"And furthermore," I shouted right over her, so that she snapped her mouth shut again and glared at me. "It's okay to admit that that temptation has happened before. It's okay to admit that that makes us feel vulnerable, because it should."

"I don't do vulnerable," Nova muttered under her breath, as she stared icily out the window.

"Yes, you do. You just hide it better than most of us," I said. "Fear and vulnerability can be a good thing, you know. It keeps us alert and on our toes. It forces us to self-reflect and probe our own motivations."

"It's turned my mother into a monster," Nova said quietly.

"Not quite a monster," I said. "But yeah, there is such a thing as letting the fear spiral out of control. Your mom is probably guilty of that."

"My mom is *definitely* guilty of that."

"And she's not the only one. Look at my mom, fleeing this town and never looking back. The point is that the adults in Sedgwick Cove have let fear be in charge for a long time now. They let it take over. And I don't think this is any way to live, just holding our breath and being thankful for another day of not facing what we know is out there."

I sat in silence, and watched Nova's face as she processed everything we'd just said. She was less angry at least; the red was fading from her cheeks, and her jaw wasn't clenched. Finally, her whole body seemed to sag.

"Okay."

"Okay, what?"

"Okay, you're right. I'm scared about the Source. But that doesn't change anything. I don't think we should mess with it."

"Neither do I. No one is talking about messing with it, we're talking about identifying it. But if Jess is right and the Source is one of those... those Gate-whatevers... then we might actually understand the deep magic for the first time since the First and Second Daughters set foot in the Cove. Don't you think it's better to have more information than less? Don't you think we should arm ourselves with whatever knowledge we can find, even if it comes from an unexpected source? And Jess said that the Durupinen are protectors of the Gateways. She might actually be able to help us keep the Darkness from it!"

Nova let out a growl, making me jump.

"What?" I gasped.

"Why do you do that?"

"Do what?"

"Make it all sound so reasonable so that I can't argue with you!" she yelled, slamming her palm into the steering wheel.

I pressed my lips together as a barrier to the laugh that was threatening to burst out. If I pissed her off now, she'd turn on me again out of pure spite, and I knew it. I watched her nostrils flare for several seconds like the gills of a fish, counting her breaths. Finally...

"Fine."

"Fine... what?"

"Fine. I won't say anything. But I'm staying out of it, Wren. I'm not helping you. Whatever you're doing, I don't want to know, and if anyone asks, I am not taking any heat for you," Nova said, glaring at me. "And if this goes sideways and this Jess woman turns out to be a Kildare in disguise or some shit, that's all on you. Don't you dare ever say I helped bring her back to life or whatever the fuck happened tonight. Do you understand?"

"Yes." I would have preferred her help, but I wasn't going to push it. If the best I could get was her silence, I would take it.

"Damn it, Wren," she muttered under her breath as she started the car. We rode in silence all the way back to Lightkeep Cottage. She parked down the road from the house so no one would hear her engine. I took off my seatbelt and put my hand on the door handle.

"Do you want me to like... text you?" I asked.

"Not a word," she said.

"Isn't that gonna kill you, not knowing what's going on?"

She glared at me. "You're going to mess with the Source, and you think *I'm* the one who should be worried about dying?"

"Right. No text then," I said. I hopped out of the car and leaned down to the open window.

"Nova?"

"What?" she snapped.

"You're the only person I'd call to help me break into a morgue. Thanks."

"Whatever," she muttered, throwing the car into drive and speeding away—but not before I saw her lip twitch into the merest suggestion of a smile.

15

If anyone noticed the fact that I was zombie levels of tired at the kitchen table the next morning, they didn't mention it. Maybe they simply expected me to be practically comatose after discovering a dead body, and I probably would have been. The fact that I then went on an adventure to resurrect said dead body a few hours later was, apparently, an unnecessary piece of the puzzle.

"Would you like some tea, Wren?" Rhi asked me.

"Coffee. Turbo-charged," I muttered in reply.

Rhi bustled around the counter for a few minutes, and returned with a hot cup of coffee, which she set down in front of me.

"I'm surprised at you, Wren," my mom said from the chair beside me. I looked over at her, and saw that she was staring at me with narrowed eyes, like she was trying to read something printed on my face.

"Why?" I asked, my heart fluttering a little with anxiety.

"I thought you'd come storming down the stairs demanding to know what happened to the grimoire."

I couldn't believe it. In all the chaos of the previous night, I'd completely forgotten about the grimoire. I tried to keep my face impassive and my voice calm as I replied, "Give a girl a second, will you? I'm barely conscious yet." I took one scalding sip of coffee, and then looked pointedly at my mother. "So? What happened to the grimoire?"

"Well, the good news is that no one noticed the Binding," Rhi said, as she slid into the seat on the other side of me, with a slight creak in her knees. "Or if they did, they didn't mention it. Personally, I think most of the Conclave knows us well enough to know we wouldn't let that book out of our sight without tying ourselves to it somehow."

"Nothing they can do about it even if they did notice," my mom added, and there was definite satisfaction in her voice. "It can't be undone by anyone but a Vesper."

"Where is it now?" I asked.

"It's still here, in the library. But we agreed to move it to the lighthouse tonight," Rhi said.

My stomach dropped out of me. "What? Why?" I gasped.

I suppose it wasn't all that surprising that I'd have this reaction. The lighthouse had been the site of one of the most traumatic moments of my life, and that was the only association I had with it. My mom seemed to be expecting my panic, because her hand shot out and clasped mine, squeezing it tight.

"Wren, it's okay. The lighthouse has undergone a complete magical stripping down since Bernadette used it. It's probably the safest place on the Cove at the moment."

"Not to mention it's close to the Playhouse, which means the police details can keep an eye on both locations simultaneously," Rhi added. "Not that they'll be told what's inside, of course. No one outside the Vespers and the Conclave know about that."

I dropped my eyes to my mug and took another sip of coffee. No need for them to know that Nova was in on the secret, too.

"Today, the Conclave will be setting up the magical protections. When they are satisfied with the fortifications, they will let us know it's ready, and we will take the grimoire there," Rhi went on. "There we can examine it thoroughly, without fear of discovery or interruption."

I glanced around the kitchen. "And Persi?"

My mom smirked. "She's already over at the lighthouse. She says she'll be damned if she lets Ostara cast a single spell without watching her like a hawk."

I laughed. "Yeah, that sounds about right."

Suddenly, the phone on the wall—one of the many aspects of Lightkeep that made it feel like it was frozen in time—began to ring. My mom groaned, and dragged herself out of her chair to go get it. At the same time, my cell phone began to buzz against my thigh. I pulled it surreptitiously out of my pocket, and glanced at the notification.

It was a text from an unknown number. I pocketed the phone again quickly, just as my mother's voice rose.

"What do you mean, gone?" she was saying into the phone, her posture tense and still, like an animal caught in headlights. "How can it just be gone?"

Rhi turned, frowning, to watch my mother. Then she jumped up and ran into the library, returning a moment later with a relieved expression on her face. I knew she was checking on the grimoire which, based on her reaction, was still exactly where it was supposed to be.

But I already knew that whoever was on the other end of the line wasn't talking about a missing book. I braced myself, hitching what I hoped was an expression of mild curiosity onto my face. I saw my mom's eyes dart toward me several times as she listened. Then she hung the phone up and turned to face us, all color drained from her face.

"What is it, Kerridwen?" Rhi whispered. "What's happened?"

"There, um... there seems to be a..." she cleared her throat, "...a mix-up with Jess Ballard's body."

"What do you... you mean it isn't actually her?" Rhi asked, looking suddenly hopeful.

"No," my mom replied, running a hand over her face. "It's... it appears to be missing."

Rhi just stared at her, unblinking. "I don't... huh?"

"They took the body to Blackleach and Graves, to the morgue. But it's not there anymore."

Rhi was so pale, I thought she might faint. I reached out toward her, ready to brace her if she slumped over, but she managed to stay conscious.

"Someone snatched her body?" she whispered through white, unmoving lips.

"So it would appear," my mom said. "That was Maeve. There was no sign of forced entry. She—" The shrill ring of the phone cut her off again, and she groaned. "That'll be someone from the Conclave, goddess help us all." She answered it again with a wary, "Hello?" as Rhi hurried off to the library again, and returned this time with the grimoire clutched protectively to her chest. Instead of sitting back down at the table, she joined my mother over at the phone, and leaned in close to the receiver so that she could catch what the caller was saying.

My phone began to buzz again. No one was paying the slightest attention to me, so I slipped out of the kitchen, through the French doors, and out into the garden. My phone kept vibrating as notification after notification popped up. A quick glance showed me that Nova, Eva, and Zale were blowing up the group chat, but I didn't open it. Instead, I scrolled to the first text, the unknown number.

You make it back home okay?

It was Jess, that much was certain. I typed a hasty reply.

Yes, but they know you're gone. Did you make it out of town?

The reply came quickly. *I'm safe. Got out of the B&B without being spotted.*

A pause, and then... *Do they suspect you?*

No, I don't think so. Not yet anyway.

Did you talk to Nova? What's the verdict? Are you in, or am I on my own?

I hesitated. This was my chance to back out. I didn't have to help her. I didn't have to dig myself deeper into this mess. Then I looked down at Asteria's charm that I still wore around my neck, even though its spell was long since broken, and knew I'd already made my decision.

Nova's out, but don't worry, she'll keep her mouth shut. I'm in.

There was a longer pause, and then the reply appeared. *Thank you.*

Telling her she was welcome would be a lie, so instead I typed. *When?*

As soon as we can. I need to make some arrangements first. Monday night?

My heart throbbed like a wound in my chest. Monday was only three days away. I had no idea how we were going to pull this off with security crawling all over the Playhouse, security that was only going to get more intense now that Jess was missing. My fingers shook as I typed my reply.

Okay. I'll be in touch. Lay low.

"Wren?"

With a yelp of surprise, I dropped my phone on the flagstones. My mom was standing in the doorway.

"Honey, are you okay?"

"Yeah," I gasped, quickly snatching my phone back up, and making sure my texting app was closed. "Yeah, you just scared me."

"How much of our conversation did you hear?" she asked.

"Not much, but my friends are blowing up my phone," I said, holding it up. "They're saying the Conclave is flipping out because Jess' body disappeared from the morgue?"

My mom frowned. "How do they know about it?"

I attempted a roll of the eyes. "Come on, Mom, be serious. How often do you successfully hide stuff from me around here?"

She smiled sheepishly. "Touché." The smile faded at once. "This is a lot. Are you okay?"

I shrugged. "I think so."

"Because the Conclave will get to the bottom of this, sweetie. We'll have answers soon."

The words were meant to be soothing, of course, but all they did was make my heart start pounding like a bass drum.

"Yeah," I said with a forced smile. "Yeah, I'm sure we will. I'm uh... gonna go get dressed."

"Of course, honey. I'll let you know if I hear any news."

"Thanks," I said, and headed for the stairs. Once my bedroom door was shut behind me, I pulled my phone out again, opened the group chat, and scrolled the messages.

Z: *OMG THEY KNOW*

E: *they don't KNOW*

Z: *my grandmother keeps staring at meeeeeee*

E: *because you're probably acting weird just be normal.*
N: *imagine Zale being normal*
oh wait i literally can't

Cool, so everyone was melting down about as much as I was. This was going to devolve into chaos if someone didn't take control, and it looked like that person was going to have to be me.

We all need to talk. In person. Can you meet me at Shadowkeep at noon?

Zale and Eva replied at once. It was several minutes of being left on read before Nova finally agreed. I ran up to change out of my pajamas and threw my hair into a ponytail, and then stopped into the kitchen where Rhi and my mom were conversing in low voices.

"I'm headed out," I said.

"Where are you going?" my mom asked.

"I'm supposed to be opening this morning, remember? Busiest week of the year?"

My mother groaned. "Of course. Shadowkeep. I should have... do we really have to...?"

"Of course we do," I said. "Mom, we can't just close on a Saturday with all those tourists in town. Think of the complaints."

"She's right, Kerridwen. Not to mention it will look suspicious, and we don't want to give the rest of the town any reason to poke their noses into our business. Besides, what's the point of staying home? We're just going to pace around and drive each other nuts waiting for news. Might as well keep busy." She stood up and fetched a large basket of pre-wrapped scones and cookies off the counter. "Here, honey. Replenish the jars on the counter, and don't forget, we got the new branded wax paper bags in."

"Do you want me to come with you?" my mom asked.

I blinked. "Why? I know how to open. Besides, Persi should be there."

"Should" being the operative word. Between everything happening at the lighthouse and her frequent slipping away to visit Bernadette at all hours, I wasn't exactly counting on her.

My mom bit at her lip, and then sighed. "I know, I'm just... I'm just on edge with this whole..." She struggled for a few seconds as she tried to put it into words.

"The whole 'a-stranger-who-found-our-grimoire-turned-up-dead-and-then-the-body-vanished' thing?" I suggested.

She laughed humorlessly. "Yeah. That."

"Well, sitting at home won't change it," I pointed out.

"I suppose not," she said with a sigh, "but I'd feel better if this was all figured out."

"I know," I said. "But in the meantime, a crowded shop full of people is probably the safest place I could be."

Rhi was nodding and looking down at the grimoire, running her fingers over the cover gently. "I know we didn't want the Conclave to find out about the grimoire yet, but I must confess, I'm glad they know now. I don't feel safe keeping it in the house anymore."

"I agree," my mom said. She threw the book a baleful look, and then smiled up at me. "Go ahead, honey. I'll keep you posted about the lighthouse."

"And I'll be down to relieve you at lunch time," Rhi added. "Just have to jar and seal last night's charms. They're selling out like crazy."

I gave them both a quick hug and, after promising again that I would be careful, slipped out before they could think of another reason to keep me there. Guilt rippled through me, but I kept my lips pressed shut. It wasn't just that I thought I'd get in trouble for helping Jess get her body back. This might be my only chance to understand the Source, a chance not a single adult in Sedgwick Cove would allow me to take if they knew about it.

The truth was that none of the witches of Sedgwick Cove had ever fully comprehended the Source. It wasn't until just a few months ago that we even realized where exactly it was. Though we had drawn on its power for hundreds of years, we could neither understand it, nor claim it as our own. All we'd managed to do was stop the Darkness from taking control of it, and even that accomplishment was in danger of falling apart. But Jess wasn't a witch. She had information that we didn't, and it was possible she might finally help unravel a mystery that had underpinned this town and its residents for our entire history. As for me, I was the one the Darkness was after. I was the one it wanted to use to access the Source. Didn't that mean I should learn as much as I could about it? Wasn't I the one person who needed every bit of knowledge about the Source I could possibly find?

I knew the answer to that question.

I had to get off my bike and push it when I reached downtown—Main Street was too packed with people to maneuver through them safely while riding. It was barely nine o'clock in the morning, but people were already crowding the shops decked out in elaborate costumes, and lining up for the walking tours.

"—says they start at nine o'clock, but there's no tour guide here," a woman was saying loudly into her phone, while three middle schoolers dressed as the Sanderson sisters moped and grumbled beside her as the line behind them stretched down the street.

As I secured my bike inside the gate at Shadowkeep, movement caught my eye from where the glamour hid a secret staircase up to the second floor. I adjusted my gaze and watched as a young woman hurried down the steps toward me. It took me a moment as my eyes focused to see that it was Leila Nightjar. Her pretty face was twisted with worry as she hurried toward me, wringing her hands.

"Wren, hi! Is Persi around? I've been ringing the bell upstairs but no one's answering," she said, looking over my head toward the street, like she was worried she might be overheard.

I glanced at my watch. I was late, but only by a few minutes. "Yeah, I'm sorry about that, Leila," I said. "She's not here yet, but she should... well, actually, I'm not really sure when she'll be in," I hedged. With what was happening over at the lighthouse, I couldn't guarantee Persi would be at the shop any time soon.

"Oh." Leila's face drooped into such a pitiable expression, I wanted to hug her. She was carrying a bunch of flowers wrapped in brown paper tucked under her arm.

"Can I... is there something I can help you with?" I asked, a little nervously. I wasn't technically allowed to sell things out of the upper level of the shop yet, but if it was something simple...

"No, I... I just really needed to talk to her. That charm she sold me the other day, I...shit, I'm late," Leila said as she glanced at her watch. "Just... just have her call me?"

"Okay, sure thing," I called after her retreating back. "Um... I'll let her know!"

I watched Leila hurry away, and felt a pang of uneasiness. Persi was known all over Sedgwick Cove for her charms and spells she sold out of the top level of Shadowkeep. Had one of them gone wrong somehow? There was no time to worry about it. If Persi had customer issues, that was her problem to deal with—I had bigger issues at the moment.

I hurried to unlock the door, turn on the lights, and prep the store for opening. No matter how quickly I moved, it wasn't fast enough; as soon as people in the street saw that there were signs of life inside, they started lining up out on the porch, queueing all the way down through the gate and out onto the sidewalk. I was beginning to regret offering to open on my own, but at least it would keep me busy and distracted until my friends got there.

Finally, I unlocked the door and let in the excited horde, bracing myself behind the counter. Unlike the other days when dealing with the tourists, I found myself watching them closely, and wondering if any of them, like Jess, were not what they seemed. Did any of them know there was more to this place than met the eye? Did any of them have magic, or come from covens outside of the borders of Sedgwick Cove? Always, my eyes were peeled for Veronica Meyers, though I knew she would have to be out of her mind to show her face here again. Then again, she didn't have to show her face, did she? I understood enough about glamours to know that she could disguise herself against detection. But that would only work for a short time—all witches had the ability to see through a glamour if they thought someone might be using one, and I was nearly always on alert. I was so distracted examining the faces in the crowd and trying to sense glamours, that I didn't even notice when two very familiar faces appeared at the counter, right in front of me.

"Earth to Wren? Come in Wren!" Eva said, as she waved her hand frantically in front of my face.

"Huh? Oh, sorry. I'm kind of—"

"Freaking out? Losing your ever-loving shit?" Zale suggested.

"I was gonna say distracted, but sure," I said. I looked over their shoulders, and felt my heart sink a little. "No Nova?"

Eva's grin faded into a sad half-smile. "Yeah. She bailed."

"She told us to apologize for her, but she didn't actually sound sorry, so..." Zale looked over his shoulder. "Where do you want to talk? No offense, but this seems like the literal worst place to have a private conversation."

I rolled my eyes. "I realize that, but I'm stuck here for a while, and I didn't want to lose any time. You can wait for me upstairs. Come behind the counter," I said, dropping my voice. They ducked under the side of the counter, and popped up beside me. I went to the door and, making sure no one was paying too much attention, opened it for them to enter.

"I'll be up in a few minutes," I whispered after them, checking my watch. "Rhi should be here any minute, and I can take a break."

They nodded at me and ascended out of sight.

It felt like forever, but only about five more minutes passed before Rhi finally shoved her way through the door and across the crowded store to the register.

"Goddess above!" she gasped, raising her baskets above her head to maneuver her way through the throng of customers. "This is crazy, even for Samhain!"

"You're just in time," I told her, and pointed to the glass jars on the counter. There was now one lonely cookie left inside beside the pair of tongs.

"I'll get these refilled," she said with a sigh.

"And I'm taking my break," I said. "Just gonna pop upstairs." And I disappeared up the stairs before she could question me.

I found Eva and Zale wandering around and examining the shelves upstairs. They both dropped what they were holding, and joined me at once at the round table in the corner.

"We have to keep this quick," I told them in a low voice. "I don't want Rhi getting suspicious. You can both slip out down the outer staircase when we're done."

"Wren, seriously, what is going on?" Eva asked, and for once she looked anxious instead of intrigued. "That woman, Jess—"

"Is fine," I said. "She's safe outside of town and laying low for the moment. I'm going to tell you everything I can. I'm going to have to leave some stuff out, and it's gonna seem like important stuff, but it's not because I don't trust you. It's because I trust her and I gave her my word."

"You trust her?" Eva asked, narrowing her eyes at me. "A woman you just met?"

"Yes," I said. "I should probably start there."

As quickly as I could, I explained about Asteria's message, and about the grimoire. Their reaction to the reappearance of the grimoire was exactly the same as Nova's.

"Will you please keep it down?!" I hissed. "Do you want Rhi to come up here?"

Zale said something unintelligible, because his hand was now clamped over his mouth. I was looking at Eva, however.

"Nova doesn't want to get involved because... well, it's the Source. And the Claires—"

"Have a complicated history there," Eva said, nodding her head. "I get it."

"But do you get where I'm coming from?" I asked, not quite managing to mask the note of desperation in my voice. Luckily, Eva's expression was entirely clear as she nodded.

"Of course, I do," she said. "You can't grow up under Xiomara's roof without developing a healthy trust of the ancestors and their messages. If Asteria says we can trust her, then we can trust her. So what's next?"

I was so relieved that tears began to well up in my eyes, and I had to blink them impatiently away. "Thanks, Eva. I really... thanks."

Zale, meanwhile, finally seemed to have gotten a handle on himself. He pulled his hand away from his mouth, and asked in a strangled sort of whisper, "So is the Conclave flipping out over the grimoire? Because I assumed it was just over the whole missing body thing."

"Yes. And it sort of sucks that they were already on high alert, but now I think it might actually work to our advantage," I said.

"How?" Eva and Zale both asked together.

"Because, like I said, Jess needs to get under the Playhouse to examine the Source, and the grimoire has been moved to the lighthouse for safekeeping. And I think that might be exactly the distraction we need."

Eva frowned. "Meaning?"

"Meaning security has two locations to guard instead of just one. We have to draw them away from the Playhouse to the lighthouse, just long enough for Jess to get inside and get a look at the Source."

"And exactly how are we supposed to do that?" Eva asked.

"With a distraction."

Eva rolled her eyes. "Obviously, but what kind of distraction?"

I smiled. "The kind only a waterworker can provide."

16

The next two days were the absolute longest of my life.

Never had the hours dragged by so slowly. Never had I lived in such a constant state of torturous anticipation. Every time the phone rang, my heart leapt into my throat—I was sure we'd be busted, that somehow they'd figured out that we'd broken into the funeral home, or else they'd managed to track Jess down wherever it was she was hiding. Every time I heard my name, I jumped like someone had slammed a door. It was a damn good thing that everyone else at Lightkeep was as on edge as I was, or my mother surely would have noticed something was off. Instead, we were all walking on eggshells, waiting for news that never came, and then speculating endlessly on why it hadn't.

The difference, of course, was that I was the only one who was grateful it didn't come. No news was good news, as far as I was concerned.

For the first time since I'd begun studying with her, Xiomara canceled my spirit communication lesson with her. I answered a knock at the door on Sunday to find her standing there, her expression tight and grim.

"There is no point, *mija*," she said, her gravelly voice rougher and more hoarse than usual, like she hadn't slept. "Until I can get past my block and understand what is interfering with my spirit gifts, I see no reason to waste your time and mine."

"Is it really that bad?" I asked.

A spasm of emotion passed over Xiomara's face before she could suppress it. "My efforts since last we spoke have been met with nothing but silence from the spirit world."

I had no idea what to say. I was upset enough over my spirit gifts, but Xiomara had been practicing for decades. She had come to rely on her spirit gifts—to seek the regular counsel of the Marin witches long passed, and to draw on their magic to aid in her own. I couldn't imagine what it must be like, to feel like such an intimate part of yourself had been stripped away with no explanation.

"What about Bea?" I asked. I hadn't seen Bea since the night she arrived in the garden with Jess' message.

Xiomara shook her head looking, if possible, even more lost. "It is the same with her. No contact. And I've taken the additional step of going around Sedgwick Cove. I've spoken to every spirit witch in the Cove, as well as every witch I know who regularly uses spirit boards or other means of consulting with the dead. Everywhere it is the same. Silence."

I swallowed hard. Any lingering doubts I had about my decision to help Jess vanished on the spot. If everything she had told me was true—and I had no reason to doubt her—then she understood the spirit world better than anyone in Sedgwick Cove, and we needed her to help us understand just what the hell was happening.

"I'm... I'm sorry," was all I could think to say to Xiomara. The words felt useless, and sure enough she waved them away impatiently.

"I need to talk to Rhiannon. Is she here?" she asked.

"Yeah, she's in the kitchen, as usual," I told her. "Head on back."

Xiomara marched back toward the kitchen with all the familiarity her long friendship with Rhi had fostered. She pulled out a chair at the round table, and settled herself into it with a grunt by way of greeting. Rhi looked up from the three separate pots she had steaming on the stove and stepped away at once, lowering the heat.

"Xiomara! What is it? Did someone find... do we have anything new about—"

Again, Xiomara waved her hand like the questions were a fly that was annoying her. "No, no. I came to see you about Persi."

Rhi threw a look at me over Xiomara's head. We'd barely seen Persi since the night the grimoire was moved to the lighthouse. "Look, I know she's being a bit... protective of the grimoire, but you can't blame her Xiomara. We never thought we'd see it again, and—"

"It's not about the grimoire," Xiomara said. "Yes, she's being insufferable about it, but it's no more than we expected. No, this is about Persi and Bernadette."

Rhi froze where she stood. "What about them?" she asked, her voice utterly blank with bewilderment.

"You know that Persi's been visiting Bernadette?" Xiomara asked.

"Well, yes, of course," Rhi said, wiping her hands on her dish towel as she sank into a chair opposite Xiomara. "But surely no one is frowning on that? You know their history, Xiomara, they were..." Rhi stopped suddenly, glancing at me, before going on, "...they were so close. Surely you aren't going to begrudge her visitors?"

"No, it's not that," Xiomara said. "Goddess knows the poor girl's been through enough. It's only... well, you know Bernadette's gifts."

She said it in that loaded way that adults speak in front of younger people when they're trying to refer to things indirectly. I bit down on the inside of my cheek in annoyance, but otherwise kept my face impassive.

"Yes, I do," Rhi said, "and so does Wren, so please speak plainly, Xiomara."

I could have hugged Rhi, but I stayed where I was. I did know all about Bernadette's gifts. In fact, I'd found myself the subject of several of her prophetic paintings last spring when I first arrived in Sedgwick Cove.

Xiomara glanced at me, and then shrugged. "As you like. Bernadette has been very... prolific since she was removed from the Hold. I worry—or I should say, Ostara worries—that Persi's regular visits might be upsetting her."

Rhi tapped her fingers against the tabletop, looking pensive. "Is Ostara worried that Persi is upsetting Bernadette, or does she simply wish there were fewer witnesses to whatever it is Bernadette has been creating of late?"

It was hard to tell from where I was standing, but I thought that Xiomara might have betrayed a smile before she got her expression under control. My gaze darted to Rhi, whose quizzical expression relaxed into something resembling satisfaction.

So Rhi was right, I thought.

"If you could encourage Persi to... give some space, I think Ostara would appreciate it," Xiomara said, her tone the model of diplomacy.

"I would hardly expect you to come here and do Ostara's dirty work for her," Rhi said, and there was an edge in her voice that I rarely heard there.

"Consider it a personal favor," Xiomara shot back. "If Ostara had delivered the message herself, it would not have been nearly this friendly."

"Well then, why don't you deliver a message for me in return," Rhi said lightly.

Xiomara chewed her tongue. "I'm not a carrier pigeon, Rhiannon."

"Just this once," Rhi said, refusing to be deterred. "If Ostara spent less time trying to keep up appearances and more time focused on the actual needs of her coven—even the less publicly palatable ones—she'd have far fewer favors to ask of people, and a much more functional coven."

Xiomara snorted, but kept her face under control. I doubted Rhi had said a single word that Xiomara didn't agree with, but she could hardly say so out loud as a member of the Conclave. So instead, she stood up with a quiet groan and said, "I'll pass it along."

"And if you hear anything," Rhi added, as Xiomara turned to go, "about Jess Ballard or... or anything?"

"You'll be my first call," Xiomara assured her. Then she gave us both a tight smile and said, "I'll see myself out."

* * *

It took an impossibly long time, but at last, Monday came. Shadowkeep usually closed early on Mondays, and luckily, this Monday was no exception, despite the continued size of the crowds. I turned the closed sign over with a sigh of relief that felt like it came all the way from my toes. I'd barely turned around when Persi breezed past me to the back door.

"You can lock up, right?" she said, though it was more of a statement than a request.

"Yeah, but—"

"I've got to be somewhere," Persi said. "I don't want to be—"

A sharp rapping sounded behind me. As I spun to see where the sound was coming from, Persi gave a sigh and murmured, "Oh for goddess' sake, not again!"

Leila Nightjar was standing on the other side of the door I'd just locked, waving her hand frantically. I stepped forward to let her in when Persi cried, "No! Don't... I'll meet her around the back."

I watched, bewildered, as Persi motioned wordlessly to Leila, waving her hands toward the back door. Leila looked confused for a moment, then her face lit up with understanding, and she vanished across the porch in the direction of the back door. Persi, still muttering under her breath, followed, pausing only long enough to say to me, "Don't forget to set the alarm."

I stood for a moment, considering. Did I know better than to eavesdrop? Yes.

Did my curiosity coupled with my brimming anxiety get the better of my judgment? Also yes.

Navigating the old and therefore noisy floorboards, I crept my way toward the back door until I was close enough to put my ear against the crack. In a newer building, I might not have been able to make out the hushed voices on the other side, but Shadowkeep's warped and drafty old door provided the perfect place to listen.

"—told you that I can't do this right now," Persi was saying in a low voice.

"But why? I don't understand, I thought—"

"I was up front with you, Leila. I told you I was in a bad place. I told you I couldn't... that I wasn't ready for anything serious."

"I'm not talking about anything serious, Persi. I just want to make sure you're all right, but it's like you're ghosting me."

"I'm not ghosting you, all right? I just have... there's a lot going on."

"You've got time for Bernadette."

The pause that followed was so heavy with tension that I shivered on the other side of the door.

"Why do you know about that?" Persi finally asked, in an almost monotone voice.

Leila seemed to realize she made a mistake. "I... I didn't... I—"

"So you're, what? Stalking me now? Following me?"

"Of course not! But I... I've just been so worried about you."

"I can take care of myself."

"But you don't have to. Persi, I know you loved her, but you don't have to face this alone."

"Yes, I do." She spat the words out, like they were something foul and poisonous. "It's my fault, and I have to fix it."

"It's not your fault. Bernadette made her choices," Leila said, so softly it was almost a whisper.

"She made those choices because of me. I'm serious, Leila. Just... forget about me, okay? I'm not good for anyone right now, least of all myself. Go... find someone healthy for goddess' sake. Someone who isn't drowning in her own mistakes. All I'm capable of right now is dragging someone down."

I heard Persi's footsteps echoing across the porch. Leila called after her once, in a hopeless voice. Then there was maybe a minute of silence before Leila's footsteps followed Persi's away from Shadowkeep.

I felt weighted down as I moved away from the door—heavy with guilt that I'd spied on Persi, but also full of sadness. I was sad for Leila, who was obviously smitten with the chronically emotionally unavailable Persi, but more so for Persi herself. I knew that she was still visiting Bernadette. I knew she still had some lingering feelings for her. But I hadn't realized that those feelings were still so all-consuming. I couldn't say what

Bernadette was like before I came to Sedgwick Cove—by the time I'd met her, she was deep into her entanglement with Sarah Claire, and likely already losing her mind. But if Persi was still chasing that long-distant version of Bernadette, she was chasing a ghost. The thought made me sad, but also angry.

So much pain and sorrow, and for what? The Darkness left only misery in its wake, and this was just another example of the fallout.

I set out on my bike for home, preparing for an evening of make-believe. I pretended to have an appetite at the dinner table, forcing down bites of food, and moving the rest around my plate so that it looked like I'd eaten more than I really had. Then I pretended to read a book in the library until it was late enough that I could go up to bed without arousing suspicion. I feigned tiredness, even as my entire body was electrified with anxiety about the night ahead. I kissed my mom good night, went up to my room, closed the door, and waited.

17

Gradually, the cottage went to sleep around me. I listened for the footsteps, first Rhi's, then my mom's, as they made their way up to bed. The general sounds of life settled into the gentle rhythm of sleep, but still, I waited. I had to be sure.

At last, around one o'clock in the morning, I decided it was safe. I texted Eva and Zale to confirm our plan, and then texted Jess. I held my breath waiting for her response. Minutes ticked by. Had she been discovered? Finally, the reply came through, and I exhaled.

I'll meet you there. Thank you. Be careful.

I knew it was unlikely that I'd meet anyone on my way to the lighthouse—Lightkeep Cottage was the last house on the road to the cliffs—but that didn't stop me from looking over my shoulder every five seconds on my dark, solitary walk. I kept to the edge of the trees where I could, and kept my flashlight trained low and close to the ground.

I was the first to reach our chosen meeting spot behind a large, jagged rock. I could see the lights from the Playhouse parking lot through the misty haze that had settled over the cove like a blanket. I stood there, bouncing on the balls of my feet, until I heard footsteps and turned to see

Zale and Eva hurrying toward me, Zale looking almost painfully excited, and Eva looking anxious.

"No complications?" I whispered, as soon as they joined me behind the rock.

They both shook their heads. "I thought I was busted for sure when I realized *abuela* still hadn't come up to bed, but it turns out she dozed off in her seance room. I could hear her grunting and snoring from the top of the stairs," Eva said.

"Any sign of Jess yet?" Zale asked eagerly, looking around like she might pop out and yell "Surprise!"

"No, but she'll be here, I know it," I said, as much to reassure myself as to answer Zale.

"Is she gonna be in, like... ghost mode again?" he asked eagerly.

"You know, for someone who flipped out so badly at the sight of a body, you seem awfully eager to see another one," Eva said.

Even in the dark, I could tell that Zale was flushing with embarrassment. "I didn't flip out, I just... needed a moment. I'm prepared this time."

"Well, sorry to disappoint you, but as far as I know, she's staying inside the skin suit this time," I said, before turning back to Eva. "Did you bring everything?"

Eva turned partway around so that I could see the backpack slung over her shoulder.

"Thanks for agreeing to this," I told her earnestly. "I definitely couldn't do it without you."

"You might not be able to do it *with* me," Eva muttered.

"Hey!" Zale snapped. "Can it with the negative self-talk, queen. You've got this."

Eva gave him a tight smile that faded quickly.

"I'm sorry," I said to her. "It was shitty of me to put so much pressure on you right after you became a waterworker. Look, if you don't want to do it, I'm sure I can find another way to—"

"No," Eva said, and I was relieved to hear a hint of her usual determination in her voice. "I got this."

I grinned at her. "Yeah, you do."

The sound of a snapped twig, and then the shushing of footsteps broke into our conversation, and we all froze, listening. A moment later, Jess appeared from the edge of the woods with her hand raised in greeting.

"It's only me," she whisper-called to us.

I waved her over, and she joined us behind the rock. She was dressed all in black, though she had been every time I'd ever seen her, so that may have just been her wardrobe.

"Are we good?" she asked, looking at each of us in turn.

"Yeah, I think so," I said, and then turned to Zale. "What can you tell us?"

Zale grinned again, clearly happy that Eva wasn't the only one who could be useful in this operation. "I hung around in the kitchen while Maeve was over for dinner last night. My grandmother was talking to her about the security arrangements. Maeve confirmed that it's only two officers who patrol the area. They primarily stay in the parking lot of the theater, because that's where the only entrance to the cavern is; but every twenty minutes, they do a full walk-around of the building, which is when they get a visual on the lighthouse."

"What's in the lighthouse?" Jess asked.

"The grimoire you brought us," I told her, and then, when her face folded into a confused frown, I added, "It's a long story. I'll explain later."

"Right," Jess said, though it looked like she was swallowing back her questions with difficulty.

"So, we'll time our distraction for when they move around to the back of the Playhouse," I said, looking at Eva now. "And when they go to investigate, that's our chance to sneak into the cavern without being seen."

"What's this distraction?" Jess asked, "and are we sure it's going to work?"

"That's Eva's job. She's a water witch. And yes, it will work," I said confidently.

Eva nodded, her lips pressed closed. She looked like she might throw up.

"Now, once we're inside, how much time do you think you need?" I asked Jess.

"To confirm it's a Geatgrima? I only need to lay eyes on it," she said, "but to figure out what seems off about it? I'm not entirely sure. As much time as you can get me, I guess."

I looked at Eva, asking the silent question.

"I've been practicing," she said, "and I can keep it going for ten minutes. Beyond that... I'm not sure."

"That will be enough," I assured her, even as anxiety rubbed my already frayed nerves raw. I looked down at my watch, and felt my lungs freeze up. "We should split up now. It's ten minutes until the cops do their next set of rounds. You've got your phones, right?" I added, to Eva and Zale.

Zale nodded and held his up.

"I've got mine, but I won't be able to break my concentration to check it, so you'll have to use Zale as your point person for communication," Eva said.

"Ooooooh, yes, I am comms director!" Zale gasped excitedly.

Jess just looked at him like she was starting to regret every life choice that had led her to this moment. But then she turned to me, and with the air of someone steeling herself, she said, "Let's do it."

Zale kept staring at me, like he was waiting for us to initiate some kind of team handshake, but then Eva grabbed him by the collar and pulled him toward the beach. Jess gestured for me to lead the way, and I crept out from behind the rock, making for the edge of the woods. Once we were both obscured behind the tree line, we walked the perimeter of the parking lot, moving as quickly as we dared without flashlights, using the light that bled into the woods from the parking lot streetlamps to avoid tripping over tree roots. We passed right by the place where Jess had concealed her own body a few days previously, and kept going, until we were crouched in the bushes around that far north side of the theater's lot. I'd spent some time in this area—it housed the various outbuildings where they stored props, costumes, and set pieces. I remembered meeting Luca here, and had to swallow back a big pang of regret. However much I may have liked Luca, there was little chance I'd see him again; and besides, proximity to me would just put him into danger with his stepmother. She'd already used him as bait once, though in that instance it had just been a glamour of him. I couldn't bear the thought of endangering the real thing.

"Wren?" Jess's voice broke through my momentary distraction.

"Huh?"

"I said, how will we know when the distraction has started?"

"Zale will text us, but I think it should be pretty obvious. She's going to set it off over near the lighthouse, which we should be able to see from the other side of this building." I led her around the far side of the nondescript concrete box of a building, until we could just spot the lighthouse between two other outbuildings. I checked my watch again. Three minutes. Two...

Two things happened at once. My phone buzzed against my thigh, and we heard a voice over in the parking lot.

"Maeve? You take south, I'll go north," the voice said.

"You mean like every other time we've done it? Hecate's Wheel, Jacob, let's just get it over with, all right?" came Maeve's sarcastic reply.

Jess and I flattened ourselves against the wall as a beam of light rippled past toward the back of the theater. I pulled my phone from my pocket and checked the notification.

GO TIME!!! read the text from Zale.

"Zale says it's—" I began in a whisper, but Jess cut me off.

"Holy SHIT."

I followed her gaze to the lighthouse, and had to slap my hand over my mouth to stifle my own gasp. Three geyser-like jets of water were shooting into the air on either side of the lighthouse, forming a bubbling curtain of water around it, as though we were gazing on the world's largest decorative fountain. My mouth fell open just as a profanity-laden cry sounded from the other side of the theater, followed by sounds of running.

"Wow, Eva!" I whispered.

"When you said distraction, I thought... like setting off a firecracker on the beach or something," Jess breathed.

For a few more precious seconds, we stood transfixed at Eva's remarkable water magic. Then something in me snapped back to attention and I tugged on Jess' sleeve, pulling her toward the Playhouse.

"Let's not waste such a good distraction," I hissed, and together we ran for the building.

There were now two entrances into the cavern beneath the Playhouse. The first was through a secret door that the Kildare coven had ensured was built when the Playhouse was originally constructed. The second was through a gaping hole that my mother's own green witch magic had created when she took control of the surrounding foliage, and decimated the side of the Playhouse with a combination of violently expanding roots and vines that crushed the supporting wall to rubble. It was through this second, more easily accessible entrance that Jess and I now carefully climbed, picking our way through a minefield of rock and splintered wood, and a lush, almost jungle-like curtain of plant life that seemed in danger of swallowing the cavern completely. At last, we managed to fight our way into the chamber hidden within; and I looked around, feeling all the air go out of me like someone had just punched me in the gut.

I hadn't been down here since the night I followed the glamour-conceived doubles of the Gray Man and Bea, right into a trap. It looked exactly as it had after my mother and aunts had rescued us, and I found that my heart was beating so fast it felt like a flutter in my chest. I should have realized it would be difficult to be here again, to relive the trauma of that night; but in all my preparations and worries over this night's plan, I hadn't stopped to consider the effect it might have on me. My legs felt like water. A cold sweat broke out on my forehead, and my hands shook violently as I pressed them against the walls for support. But, even all of this was secondary to the sight of the Source itself, pulsating with palpable and visible energy.

As I was processing all of this, Jess was walking purposely across the chamber toward the Source. Her face, before it passed out of my line of sight, was alight with reverence, but without any of the hunger or malice that had lit up Veronica's face when she had looked at it. This realization alone restored just a little of my courage. It wasn't a mistake bringing her here.

The Source itself was little more than a pile of ancient rubble upon a battered stone plinth. Jess walked in a slow circle around its crumbled remains, which rose just enough on both sides to suggest that the rocks had once been built up into something more substantial—like an archway. I watched as Jess moved closer, and I felt an urge to warn her not to get any closer; but then I realized what was different now than the last time I'd been here—well, besides the fact that a madwoman wasn't pointing a gun at my friend.

The relentless pull of the Source was... muffled somehow. It no longer felt like an invisible magnetic force was pulling me toward it. I could still feel the attraction, and yet, it did not compel me, whisper to me, as it had when I'd first seen it all those months ago.

Jess dropped to her knees near the edge of the plinth, and seemed to be examining something. I started walking toward her, drawn not by that ineffable pull of the Source, but by my own burning curiosity.

"Is it... what you thought?" I asked, as I got closer. My mouth had gone dry, and I swallowed convulsively. "Is it a... a Gateway?"

Jess looked up at me, her expression very serious. "Oh yes. There's no doubt about it. A Geatgrima once stood here."

A great sense of relief washed through me. Answers at last. "How do you know?" I asked her.

"Well, let's look at the most concrete evidence first. The plinth is consistent with the design of other Geatgrimas I have encountered. You can see here, the runes that have been carved into the stones. These once ringed the entire platform, forming a Casting—what you might call an incantation, I suppose, or maybe a spell. Here, you can still see some of them, though time and damage have worn much of it away."

She gestured for me to join her on the ground, and after only a moment's hesitation, I dropped down onto my knees. She brushed some dust and sand away from the largest stone to reveal a shape almost like an arrow with a wavy shaft. Then she lifted two pieces of broken stone, and showed me how they fit together—revealing another symbol like half a sun with rays shooting out in spokes. The sight of them sent a shiver up my back and into my hair, though I had no idea what they meant.

"You can also see that the structure is still partially in place. These stones once stood in one large, solid archway. You can see this stone here used to rest right at the top," she pointed to another symbol which, to my surprise, I recognized.

"I've seen that before," I told her, tracing my finger through the air, mimicking the shape of the carving. It was like three spirals joined together at the center.

"It goes by many names," Jess said, nodding, "and has appeared in many forms and with many meanings. We call it a triskele, or a triskelion. What does it mean in your tradition?"

"I saw it in one of our family's books—a sort of textbook, I guess you could say, that I've been reading as part of my formal witch's training. It was used alongside a description of the witch's cycle—Maiden, Mother, and Crone," I said. "Each phase is different, but powerful, and they are all connected."

"In the Durupinen tradition, we think of this as three phases as well, but they refer to the phases of a spirit's journey: the phase within the living body, the phase in the Aether, when the spirit first leaves the body, and then the phase beyond the Aether, after the spirit has crossed fully over into the spirit realm. It is a central symbol to our sisterhood. Even if nothing else had still existed of the original structure of the archway, seeing this one stone would have been enough to tell me what we're dealing with here."

"How old is it?" I whispered.

"I won't pretend to be an expert on accurately aging a structure like this," Jess said slowly, "but I do know for sure that it was here for hundreds of years, before the witches settled Sedgwick Cove."

I couldn't wrap my mind around that sort of age, so I just nodded, and let the information roll off of me.

"Here's the thing, Wren. We have a problem here. A big, big problem."

I swallowed hard. "Just the one?" I asked, in a pathetic attempt at humor—an attempt that nonetheless elicited a slight smirk from Jess. "So... what is it?"

"Well, like I told you back at the bed and breakfast, I could sense a Gateway nearby, but I also knew that the energy, while still identifiable was... off. I would have wanted to see this place regardless, but the wrongness of that energy made me want to find it even more."

"Well, it's... it's all broken apart," I said, gesturing around to the rubble surrounding us. "I mean, that's what's wrong, isn't it? It needs to be... rebuilt or something?"

But Jess shook her head. "It's more than that." She leaned back until she was sitting on her haunches. She gazed around at the rubble as though it made her inexpressibly sad. "I've seen another Geatgrima in this kind of condition. It was also destroyed. Forgotten. But that wasn't what had broken it."

I found I was holding my breath, and forced myself to breathe as I listened to her.

"The truth is that, whether the archway stands to mark the place, the Gateway still exists. It should still be a location of safe passage for spirits to find their way through the veil to the spirit world. But this place— there's something wrong with it," Jess said, dropping her gaze again to the stones, and running a gentle finger over one of them. "Very, very wrong."

I thought about the Darkness. About the things I hadn't told her yet, because they felt at once too personal, and also not my secret to tell. I couldn't bring myself to say any of it. Not here, not when the clock was ticking, and any moment someone might come and discover us here. I swallowed hard, and still felt like I was choking on my own fear.

"Do you think you could explain this once we're out of here? We need to hurry," I said. "What else do we need to do to—"

"Wren?!"

I knew the voice that called my name. I leapt to my feet to find Persi standing inside the entrance to the cavern.

"Persi?" I gasped. "What are you doing here?"

"What am I doing here?" she cried. "What the hell are you doing here?!"

Her hair was wild, but not as wild as the expression on her face. She hitched her thumb back over her shoulder. "You know I don't trust them to keep a proper watch over the grimoire, so I've been checking in on it myself. Are you responsible for that aquatic spectacle out there?"

I smiled sheepishly. "Indirectly," I admitted.

"Well, I don't know what you think you're doing down here, but the Conclave will boil you in a cauldron if they find you here unaccompanied. Now, come on, before someone comes ba—" Her eyes darted from my face to the Source and then, inevitably, onto Jess.

Shit. *Shit.*

For what felt like an endless moment, I panicked, my thoughts racing, my heart thundering, trying to figure out just what I could say to explain away this impossible situation; but my mind was an absolute blank. And then...

"It's you!" Persi whispered.

My mind was racing to come up with an answer, but instead, a question exploded and derailed my attempts to explain. How did Persi recognize Jess? She had never seen her before—she hadn't been at home when Jess came to Lightkeep Cottage, and she'd never seen her body before I'd restored Jess' spirit to it.

"You know her," I said. It wasn't a question. Persi was looking at Jess as though she'd seen a ghost—ironic, given the circumstances, and yet it made no sense. How could she know this woman staring calmly back at her? "You know her," I repeated. "How?"

"I've... seen her before," Persi confirmed. "Who is she?"

"Wait, so you... you've seen her, but you don't know who she is?" I asked, feeling more confused by the minute.

"Who is she?" Persi repeated, as though she hadn't even registered my question.

"*She* can speak for herself," Jess said a little impatiently. "My name is Jess Ballard. And you are?"

Persi's face, already stricken with shock, now drained of all color. She swayed where she stood, and for a moment, I thought she was going to faint. Her arm shot out, and she pressed her hand against the wall of the cavern to steady herself. Unsure if she'd even heard Jess' question, I answered for her.

"Jess, this is my aunt. Persephone Vesper. Aunt Persi, this is Jess Ballard who, as it turns out, is not actually dead."

Persi was sputtering now, recovering both her voice and her penchant for ordering people around. "I don't understand. I can't... both of you need to come with me," she said sharply.

Jess and I exchanged glances.

"Please," Persi said, and there was sheer panic in her voice. "Now, before anyone sees us."

"Where are we going?" I asked.

Persi, who had already turned back toward the entrance to the cave, looked back over her shoulder at us as she answered. "You asked me how I know her," she said, pointing to Jess. "Come with me right now, and I'll show you."

18

We followed Persi out of the cavern in tense silence. When we reached the woods at the edge of the parking lot, I paused only long enough to extract my phone from my pocket, and sent a quick text to Eva and Zale. It took three attempts, because my hands were shaking so badly I could barely type.

We're out. Get out of there before they find you.

Then, I added, *Eva you were INCREDIBLE. most badass waterworker EVER.*

Zale replied with a thumbs up, and Eva with a string of heart emojis. I was dying to find out what was happening down on the beach, but there was no time for that. Persi had hijacked us, and we had no choice but to follow her. Jess seemed to realize we were at Persi's mercy as well, because she made no argument as she trudged along beside me, her expression grim and distracted. I had a feeling her thoughts were still back in the cavern with the Geatgrima. She'd said there was something wrong with it, and I still didn't know what that meant, but I had no doubt that's what she was focused on as we hurried along in the dark.

It took us fifteen minutes of tripping and cursing and catching our clothing on underbrush until we finally came out near the back garden of

Lightkeep. I hesitated, utterly unprepared to face my mom and Rhi, but Persi didn't head for the house. She continued instead to the gate, opened it, and then looked back at us, gesturing impatiently.

"Hurry! Before someone wakes up!" she hissed at us.

Jess gave me a wary look. I nodded in what I hoped was a reassuring way, and followed Persi's already retreating form. Only the moonlight glinting off her jewelry served to mark her path through the pitch-black garden beds. I heard Jess stumble and curse a few times behind me, but we hurried on, past the wall to my mother's garden, and along another path I rarely ventured down.

Because at the end of the path was Persi's workshop.

And nobody went in Persi's workshop but Persi herself.

I learned this lesson in one of the first weeks I was at Lightkeep Cottage. My mother was gone for the day, returned to Portland to deal with all the headaches of having to break our lease and move out of an apartment we'd lived in since I was three years old. I hadn't yet started my training in earnest, and so I was using my abundance of free time to explore the place that was now my home. I'd learned the ins and outs of the house, as well as the main garden areas. I decided I would go down and explore the parts of the grounds I hadn't yet spent any time in. Rhi had mentioned there were fruit trees, and I wondered what grew there, and if anything was ripe for picking.

I followed the path all the way out of the gardens, where it grew wilder and more untamed. Rabbits turned to statues at the sight of me, and birds sang their chirpy songs as they swooped from branch to branch, like they were warning each other about my invasion of their usually undisturbed haunts. I passed a greenhouse so overgrown and sagging that I knew it couldn't possibly still be in use, and followed the remnants of a tumbledown stone wall until I found myself facing a small, vine-covered building. It looked like a cross between a potting shed and a fairytale cottage—the kind of place I might have imagined a witch living in, before I relocated to a town full of them. There were riots of blossoms growing all over the roof and walls, and a tiny, crooked metal chimney puffed little purple smoke rings into the air. The walls were made of multicolored shingles cut to all different shapes and sizes, and there was a ring of perfectly smooth stones encircling the place, like a protective spell. I stood with my mouth hanging open, utterly enchanted, for at least a full minute before I rediscovered my will to move forward. Like Hansel and Gretel, I could not resist exploring this most unexpected and charming domicile, despite the decided lack of gingerbread and candy.

I hesitated on the doorstep—I knew I was still on Vesper property, because the boundaries of our land were marked with walls both physical and metaphysical. My mother had shown me the stone walls that looked like they were held together with sheer magic—and likely were—and warned me that the protections we had while at Lightkeep did not extend past those walls.

"Inside them, we are safe. Without them, we are vulnerable," she had said in a sing-song voice that told me she was merely repeating the words that had been drilled into her from her own wild, barefooted childhood wanderings.

I was inside our protections, and so this house belonged to our family, at least. Beyond that, I couldn't be sure. It was this connection that allowed my curiosity to get the better of me, and I turned the filigreed brass knob, and pushed the door inward.

I caught only a fleeting glance at the interior—the multi-colored flames leaping in the pot-bellied stove, the long work table, the shimmering fumes rising from a small cauldron, the sagging shelves full of jars and dried bunches of herbs and candles—before a whirlwind of dark hair and angry eyes flew into the gap, blocking my view.

"Let's get one thing perfectly clear," Persi had said. "You might own the cottage, but you are never ever to set foot in here. Ever."

The door had slammed in my face. And though I had glimpsed it again in my various explorations of the grounds, I never dared to so much as approach Persi's workshop after that.

And so, my heart pounded with anxiety as the little building came into sight, and when Persi opened the door and jerked her head impatiently for us to enter, I hesitated. It was only when Jess nudged me in the arm that I forced my feet to unstick themselves from the ground and shuffle forward, following Persi inside.

At first, I could see almost nothing, waiting in the darkness while Persi bustled around lighting candles and lanterns and, finally, the fire in the squat little stove. The firelight threw elongated shadows that stretched up the walls like long, creeping fingers.

"Sit," Persi said. It was more order than invitation, and Jess and I both obeyed, perching ourselves on two rickety wooden chairs that had been pushed up against the work table. Jess was looking all around her with a mixture of awe and curiosity. Persi flew forward and slammed a spellbook shut that was lying open on the table in front of us, and clasped it protectively to her chest before returning it to the shelf behind her. Then she looked between Jess and me, her gaze as sharp as knives.

"Explain," she said.

"Explain what?" Jess asked.

"Let's start with how you're alive when your body was sitting in the morgue a few days ago."

Jess and I locked eyes, silently asking each other who should begin and where. Persi, short-tempered at the best of times, gave a low growl of impatience.

Jess raised a hand in apology. "Very well. I'm the interloper here. I'll go first. But I must insist that we treat this conversation as confidential. You must give me your word that you will not repeat anything that I'm about to tell you. It is as much for your safety as it is for mine."

Persi's eyes darted fiercely from Jess' face to mine, and I nodded earnestly.

"Trust me," I mouthed.

Persi looked like she wanted to refuse just out of sheer spite, but she gave a sharp nod instead. Jess took this as the word she required and, with a calmness I envied, she began to talk. She explained about her own sisterhood, the Durupinen, and about how she came upon the grimoire. Then she went on to describe how she had sensed the Source and wanted to explore it, how I had mistaken her powers for her death, how I had helped her regain her body, and finally, how we had arrived in the cavern that night. Even Persi couldn't hide her increasing incredulousness, and by the time Jess had talked herself out, Persi's hands were pressed over her mouth, and her eyes were wide with shock.

"My... my mother...she spoke to you?" Persi whispered from behind her fingers.

"Yes. Many ghosts do. It's kind of... my thing," Jess said, though her tone was gentler now, like it had occurred to her in the moment that she was speaking to a daughter who was still grieving her mother. "She was adamant that the book be returned to Wren."

Persi's gaze, suddenly sharp, darted to me. "To Wren specifically?"

"Yes."

"And she came to me, too," I said, barely able to look at Persi. "The night of the Litha Pageant. She warned me that a girl was coming with a book, and that I should trust her."

"And you didn't think to tell any of us about that?" Persi asked.

I bristled a little. "I didn't know what it meant. And I'm not sure if anyone's ever told you this, but you don't exactly invite confidences."

Persi looked like she was biting back a retort, and then seemed to deflate. She ran her hands over her face and through her hair, taking a deep breath, before turning her attention back to Jess.

"So you mean to tell me that... that the Source is in fact one of these Gee—...geet—..."

"Geatgrimas," Jess said, enunciating clearly. "And yes, that's exactly what I'm saying."

It seemed we had finally reached the moment to ask questions, and I was not going to miss that opportunity. "Why would a Geatgrima give people access to magic?" I asked.

Jess furrowed her brow. "Look, I don't know much about how witchcraft works, so this is just a theory, but... am I correct in assuming that your powers are passed down through your bloodline?"

Persi and I both nodded.

"Well, as I said before, a Geatgrima marks the thinning of the veil between the world of the living and the spirit world. You could almost think of it as a tear in that veil. If your power comes from your ancestors, perhaps it is the proximity to those ancestors that amplifies your powers here. In other words, you are able to draw on your generational power because they are so close to you."

"So, then... do you suppose it's true of every Geatgrima? You said they're all over the world. Does that mean that witches are drawn to Geatgrimas wherever they are?" I asked.

Jess gnawed thoughtfully at an already well-bitten fingernail. "As to that, I can't say for sure. I feel as though the Durupinen would have records of something like that, if it was a historical pattern, and I've never heard of it. It's definitely worth investigating. But I think it's more likely that there is something unique about the Geatgrima here in Sedgwick Cove."

"Is that what you were talking about earlier?" I asked her. "When you said that there was something... something *wrong* with it?"

"Yes," Jess said. "This Geatgrima is... corrupted somehow. Twisted. I can't say for sure how or why it's happened, but that Geatgrima is not functioning the way it's supposed to."

I thought about Asteria and her confusion. I thought of Xiomara and Bea, and the fact that their connection to the spirit world seemed to be interrupted somehow. Could this Geatgrima be the reason why? Had something happened to it that was blocking their abilities—and my ability —to communicate with the spirits to whom they were usually so connected?

"What I don't understand," said Persi, "is how you wound up with our grimoire in the first place."

Jess shrugged. "As to that, I am as clueless as you are. I told Wren that I came by it in our library. That was only sort of a lie. It was found at Fairhaven, but a few rooms away from the library, in the bedroom of one of our apprentices. A small group of them were trying to use the spells in it for their own purposes. As you can imagine, that ended very badly for them, seeing as they were not witches and were meddling with power they didn't understand."

"But how did those apprentices get it?" Persi snapped. "Surely you looked into how such a dangerous book got into the hands of a bunch of students?"

"Of course we did," said Jess, in a slightly strained voice. "All of the clans involved were questioned, and the book had been discovered in one of their private libraries. They swore they had no idea where it had come from, only that it had always been a part of their family's collection, going back centuries."

"That still doesn't explain how they got it in the first place."

"You're right," Jess said. "It doesn't. But no one seems to know the answer to that question."

A silence stretched between us, Persi still reeling from the staggering revelations that had just been unloaded on her, and Jess and I waiting to see how she would respond to them.

It was a precarious situation we were in, and I think Jess could feel it, too. Of all the adults in the house, Persi would have been my last choice for who caught me sneaking around with a formerly dead woman in the very place we were all forbidden to be. Her tempestuous temper and general penchant for rash, emotional decisions meant that I could no better predict her response than Jess could, who had only known her for about twenty minutes. I held my breath, waiting. And then I remembered something.

"Persi, what did you mean when you said, 'it's you?'" I asked suddenly into the quiet.

Persi stared blankly at me. "What?"

"When you found us in the cavern and spotted Jess for the first time, you said, 'It's you.' How did you know who she was?"

Persi's face went even whiter than it had been a moment before. "I didn't know who she was," she hedged.

"But you recognized her somehow," I said stubbornly. "You said you were going to explain. Jess told you everything you wanted to know. It's your turn."

I could see her wheels turning behind the dark sparkle of her eyes. Finally, she sighed and stood up.

"I need to show you something," she said.

Jess and I watched in silent curiosity as she crossed to the far side of the shed, and opened a tall standing wardrobe in the corner. The top shelves inside were crammed with small bottles and jars and stubs of candles, but into the bottom were crammed several canvases, which she carefully extracted. She came over and laid them out, one by one, across the work table. Then she stepped back, her expression stricken, as Jess and I leaned forward to examine them. I heard Jess gasp beside me, but I couldn't tear my eyes from what was in front of me.

There were four paintings in all. One showed a woman standing on the cliffs with the Playhouse in the background. Another showed a woman's face painted like a sketch inside a book. The next showed the same woman standing inside a stone archway, her arms raised.

All of these women were the same woman. They were all Jess.

The fourth and final painting was the one that felt like it sucked my breath from my lungs. It was a single set of shoulders and a single neck upon which three heads sprouted. The first head was clearly Jess'. The second was mine.

The third was Sarah Claire's.

"What the actual fuck am I looking at right now?" Jess finally asked into the stunned silence. She looked sharply up at Persi. "Did you paint these?"

Persi shook her head, and so did I, because I already knew who had painted them. I recognized the style from the moment I laid eyes on them.

"It was Bernadette, wasn't it?" I asked. "Bernadette drew these."

Persi nodded. "Over the last couple of weeks. And these are just the ones she's finished. Her room is full of half-finished sketches and abandoned partial paintings. Wren, you're in a few. But Jess is in every single one of them."

"Who is Bernadette?" Jess asked. She pointed to the third face on the last painting, Sarah's face. "Is this her?"

I shot a look at Persi, but she gave no sign that she was going to answer. I realized that we had reached an impasse. To explain Bernadette and Sarah Claire, I would have to explain about the Darkness, something that I had successfully avoided up until this moment. Just as Jess had been careful about what she had shared about the Durupinen, I had tried to keep as many Sedgwick Cove secrets as I could. Talking about Sarah Claire would break open the entire history of our coven, but it seemed at this point that I had no choice. Jess was no longer an outsider in this story. She had been pulled right into the spotlight by Asteria, by me, and now, apparently, by Bernadette Claire. Knowing now how deeply Jess was tied to the Source, I felt like I had all the justification I needed to tell her everything. This was her story now, too.

And so I did. Starting with the same Sedgwick Cove origin story that Zale had told to me when I first came back home, I then took Jess through the whole story of my own encounters with the Gray Man—how I had thwarted first Bernadette and Sarah's attempts to help him access the Source, and then Veronica Meyer's plot to do the same. By the time I had finished, it was Jess' turn to pick her jaw up off the floor.

"I'm sorry," she said. "I'm... gonna need a minute."

"Take all the time you need," I said, "although I should probably tell you that it's my actual life, and I still don't think I've fully processed it."

Jess leaned forward in her chair, dropping her face into her hands, and taking several long, deep breaths. Then she sat up again, and said, "Okay. Sorry. I'm... I'm fine." Then she looked at me, alarmed.

"How are you fine?" she demanded.

A laugh burst out of me that I had to quickly stifle before it turned into a sob. "I'm... not really sure if I am, honestly."

"You poor kid," Jess muttered, shaking her head. "Man, we should really trade teenage trauma stories some time."

I smiled weakly, simultaneously wondering what Jess had been through as a Durupinen. I imagined there was probably a lot there to unpack.

"Okay," Jess said, shaking her head as though to clear it. "Okay, okay, okay. So we're not just dealing with a dysfunctional Geatgrima here. We're dealing with a Geatgrima that's been messed with by outside forces, some of them witches, and some of them...sorry, what is the Darkness exactly? Like, do we know, or...?" She was making a valiant attempt to keep her voice calm, but I could detect a faint tremor.

"We don't know," Persi admitted. "It certainly isn't human, and we don't think it ever has been. It could be demonic, but the only witch who has ever gotten close enough to learn its true nature was Sarah Claire, and she died before anyone could find out what she knew. What we do know is that it is powerful. Very, very powerful."

"Great. Cool. Fun times," Jess said, nodding her head over and over again. She took a moment to get herself under control again, and then said, "What about these paintings? This Bernadette, you say she was under Sarah's control. Possession like that can do real damage to the living host, trust me, I know. How is she now?"

Persi's face twitched as she struggled to keep her emotions under control. In all my explanation, I had never once mentioned that Persi and Bernadette had once been in a relationship—that was one secret that wasn't mine to tell.

"She is rarely lucid," Persi admitted. "She has long periods of catatonia. She doesn't speak or acknowledge anyone's presence. But then she has these brief periods of... mania, I guess you'd call it. That's when she produces these."

"Has she always been a psychic artist?" Jess asked.

Persi looked surprised. "Yes. How did—"

"I'm one myself," Jess explained. "We call them Muses in Durupinen culture. In fact, I drew your mother several times before she successfully managed to connect with me."

Persi looked stricken, and didn't seem able to reply. I, however, had more questions.

"You said she's not speaking," I said gently to Persi. "Does that mean that she hasn't explained any of these paintings?"

Persi blinked like she was trying to focus on me. "No. She mutters under her breath, but it sounds like nonsense. And once she finishes a painting, she's so exhausted that she sleeps for two days together."

I looked at Persi closely. There were shadows hidden underneath her makeup. She looked thinner, I realized, and fragile somehow, which was never a word I ever thought I would use to describe Persephone Vesper. This had been taking a toll on her for weeks, maybe even months, and she had suffered in silence, hiding it from everyone. I felt a pang of guilt—whether deserved or not—that I hadn't been paying close enough attention to notice. The conversation I'd overheard between her and Leila Nightjar suddenly made much more sense in the context of this realization.

Jess wasn't looking at Persi, though. She was staring, thoughtfully, at the last painting—the one that portrayed her, me, and Sarah Claire like a many-headed Greek monster. It made me almost queasy just looking at it, but Jess was deep in contemplation over it. Finally, she said, "This Sarah Claire. You say you exorcised her from Bernadette?"

"Yes," I answered. "Well, Persi did. I was just there to help."

"And what happened to her afterward?" Jess asked. "Sarah, I mean."

Persi looked confused. "She... she simply vanished. What could hold her here, if she had no host?"

Jess' expression was grim. "Nothing you've told me about how Sarah Claire reappeared seems to follow the norms of how spirits are supposed to behave," she said. "If she had truly crossed over when she died, Bernadette shouldn't have been able to bring her back. That's not how it works. Are you sure Sarah Claire had crossed over to begin with?"

"Are you asking if she's been haunting Sedgwick Cove for four hundred years?" Persi asked, sounding a little more like herself. "No, I don't think that's possible. Surely we would have seen a sign of her before now."

"Yes, probably," Jess said. "In that case, I think it might have to do with the state of that Geatgrima. As I said, it's not functioning properly. Once a spirit crosses through a functional Gateway, that's it. It's not a revolving door. But if the Gateway is damaged, maybe by whatever Sarah herself attempted to do to it on the night of her death—"

"Then maybe that was what made it possible for her to cross back through when Bernadette tried to communicate with her?" I finished.

Jess nodded. "Yeah. That's my working theory. And I'm guessing that unnatural crossing may have damaged it even further. Kind of like if you keep picking at a loose thread, and pretty soon you've unraveled half the garment."

"So what do we do now?" I asked. "How do we fix it? Because spirit witches are no longer able to communicate with their spirit guides. They've gone silent."

Persi sat up straighter at these words. "Xiomara?" was all she said, but I understood the question.

I shook my head. "Complete silence. And Bea, too. Xiomara told me it's been the same for every spirit witch in the Cove for weeks now."

"But why?" Persi asked, a note of desperation in her voice.

"I think Bernadette is telling us," Jess said, tapping her finger on the last portrait. "This has something to do with Sarah Claire. She's the key to this."

"But she's vanished," Persi said. "How do we find her?"

Rather than reflecting Persi's despairing expression back to her, Jess' face actually broke into a slow smile.

"Tracking down a rogue spirit?" she said, and her hand dropped to her hip, where a velvet pouch dangled from her belt. "Oh, that won't be a problem."

19

I would forever be impressed by my mother and Rhi for the way they handled the next hour. It was clear that Jess' existence could no longer be kept a secret, and that all we had learned about the Source was too important not to share. True, they both looked like they were going to pass out when Persi brought them downstairs and explained to them who the woman was standing next to me, but they recovered quickly. It was with a rapidly beating heart that I took my seat with them in the kitchen—the beating, magical heart of Lightkeep Cottage; and, by the still-flickering light of the candle from the Shadow Tree, Jess and I explained everything again.

It would have been enough shocking information to send anyone into a spiral, but my mother remained calm and focused, her eyes trained on the candle as she listened intently. Rhi was a bit less successful at hiding her shock, peppering our explanations with gasps and soft "Oh's!" of surprise, as she crumbled the cookie in her hands to a pile of cookie dust on her napkin with worried fingers. At last, my mother looked up at me and spoke.

"Well, I suppose it all makes sense, as wild as it is," she said, rubbing her hand over her face. "We've never understood the nature of the Source, but everything you say seems plausible."

"And Asteria knew," Rhi added, her voice no more than a whisper. "She knew we needed you here, Jess, so that you could explain all of this to us."

"I guess so," Jess said, squirming uncomfortably. "But as far as explanations, I don't feel like I'm doing a very good job. I mean, there's so much of it that I don't understand, so I'm doing a lot of guesswork here."

"Don't be absurd, this is all invaluable information. Here, have a cookie, dear, you look dead on your feet. I mean... well, you know what I mean," Rhi said, sliding the plate across the table. Jess took one with a nod of thanks, though she didn't seem to have any interest in eating it.

"Asteria also knew we needed the grimoire back," Persi said, "though how exactly it's going to help isn't exactly clear at this point."

"Well, Sarah Claire tried to use it all those years ago, the night she died," I said. "Maybe Asteria knew we'd have to use it now to fix... whatever it is that's wrong with the Source—I mean, the Geatgrima?"

Everyone started nodding along, as though what I had just said made sense. But just like me, no one seemed to have any idea what to do next.

"You said the grimoire is in the lighthouse now?" Jess asked, breaking the loaded silence.

"Yes. The lighthouse is actually Vesper property," Rhi said. "Oh, don't worry, it's incredibly well protected. When you were—or rather, when we *thought* you were dead—we didn't feel safe keeping it in the house. And since the Conclave was already so worried about it—"

"The Conclave is like, our local town council," I explained quickly. "It's made up of matriarchs from several covens, including the Claires."

"And you can imagine how the Claires feel about the reappearance of that grimoire, given what Sarah did all those years ago," my mother added.

"Ahh," Jess said, and then looked at me with dawning comprehension. "I'm guessing that's why Nova decided not to help us tonight?"

I nodded. "Her mother is the head of the Conclave. She doesn't agree with her mother on much, but there's not a Claire alive who wouldn't run screaming from that grimoire."

"The problem is," my mother said, "that we don't know what to do next, and without the grimoire we have little hope of figuring it out."

"Sarah Claire is still mixed up in this," said Persi, who had been unusually quiet during the whole explanation. "Bernadette may be... well, damaged by all of this, but this art is speaking for her; and as we all know, her art has always been accurate, even if we didn't realize it until it was no longer a prediction, but a reality."

"If Sarah Claire is still here earthside, she has been awfully quiet," Rhi said, sounding skeptical.

"Of course she has," I said, and felt four pairs of eyes turn onto me, making me blush. "I mean, why would she alert us to her presence? Why would she alert anyone who she couldn't manipulate or control? If Sarah was still here in Sedgwick Cove, we'd be the last ones to know."

"You mentioned that witches were having trouble connecting with their ancestors," Jess said. "Is that a fairly recent development?"

I nodded. "It's been a few months for me, but I'm not sure how much of that is because I'm just new at all of this. But even powerful, experienced spirit witches have been experiencing it for a few weeks."

"Then that leads me to believe that the damage to the Gateway—or at least, the majority of it—must be fairly recent," Jess said, more to herself than to anyone else. "Otherwise, why would there be such a sudden drop off in spirit communication?"

No one else could answer her question, and so we all just listened, waiting.

"I think—and I realize this idea might not be popular," Jess began, "but I think we should try to summon Sarah Claire."

"Summon her?" My mother's voice was sharp. "That sounds like an invitation for trouble."

Jess raised a hand. "I understand that. But we—the Durupinen, I mean—have very powerful spells to protect us from spirits, no matter how hostile they are. We could communicate with her without subjecting ourselves to any danger."

I could tell from the look that was passing between my mom and her sisters that they didn't buy that assessment for a second, but they didn't come right out and say it. Jess didn't miss the hint, however.

"Look, I know I'm a total outsider here," Jess said. "I don't know much about witchcraft, and from what I've experienced, I'm not particularly keen to learn more. But as ignorant as I am about your kind of magic, I can guarantee that you know even less about mine."

Jess let this declaration land, and though Rhi bristled ever so slightly, and Persi's face twisted like she'd been forced to swallow some unpleasant-tasting medicine, no one argued with her. She took heart from this lack of outward disagreement, and went on.

"Over the last eight years or so since I discovered I was a Durupinen, I have interacted with thousands of ghosts. Most were completely innocuous—just lost souls in search of help. Others were hellbent on destroying me and everyone I hold dear. I promise you, I know what I'm doing, as far as spirits go. What I don't have any experience with is this Darkness."

My mother and Rhi both looked startled to hear Jess speak of the Darkness. I felt guilt filling me up, and struggled to find the right words to explain, but it was Persi who stepped in and answered their unspoken question, before I was forced to.

"There was no choice," Persi said. "She's connected with the Source, just like Asteria told Wren. It made no sense not to tell her. If she's a... a Gatekeeper, like she says, and the Darkness is hellbent on acquiring a Gateway, then this is her business, too."

It seemed this made too much sense for either Rhi or my mother to argue about, and so they didn't try. Jess drew a bit of courage from their silence and, after giving them a chance to respond, pressed on.

"So here's what I'm proposing," she began. "You three get the grimoire back and try to find what magic Sarah Claire may have used on the night she stole it. Wren and I will attempt to summon Sarah Claire. If we can lure her out of hiding, we might be able to get enough answers to set this all to rights again."

"Absolutely not," my mom said at once. "I'm not letting Wren anywhere near Sarah Claire without me. My sisters can obtain the grimoire without my help."

Persi and Rhi looked at each other, and nodded in silent understanding. "We can do that," Rhi said.

Persi, with a sudden gleam in her eye, laughed. "Sorry," she said when we all stared at her. "It's just... going behind the Conclave's back— particularly Ostara's, always gives me joy."

Jess smirked. "Issues with authority, huh? Same, girl."

"How do we expect to lure Sarah Claire out of hiding when we're the very people she's hiding from?" I asked.

"We have to tempt her with something she can't resist," Jess said. "So we'll bring together all of the elements from the night of her death—the Geatgrima and the grimoire, together in one place. It will be easiest if we have something of hers, or at least, something that belongs to her bloodline. Does anything like that exist?"

My heart sank. "It used to, but it's gone now. Persi and I used it to exorcise Sarah from Bernadette. It was destroyed and thrown into the sea."

"Hmm," Jess said, looking crestfallen. "Yeah, that would have been ideal."

"The Claire coven has lots of heirlooms, surely," my mom said. "Is there really nothing else tied closely enough to Sarah Claire to be useful?"

"The grimoire," Persi whispered.

"Huh?" I asked.

She looked up and met my eye. "The Claire coven grimoire. Bernadette used it when she first brought Sarah back. She used it while Sarah was possessing her." She whipped her head around to look eagerly at Jess. "Would that work?"

"That would be perfect!" Jess said. "Where is it?"

"At the Manor under lock and key, no doubt," my mom said grimly. "Every coven jealously guards their magic, and the Claires are no exception."

"Do you think there's any way we could get our hands on it?" Jess asked.

"Ostara let us use that grimoire? Not a chance in hell," Persi said without hesitation.

"Actually..."

I hadn't meant to say the word out loud, but it had slipped out, and now everyone was staring at me. "Well... I just wonder if... if maybe Nova..."

Nova had already distanced herself from Jess and everything to do with the Vesper grimoire and the Source. I hadn't spoken to her since those texts the day after we broke Jess out of the morgue. She wasn't standing in our way, but she also wasn't helping. Could she possibly be persuaded now to do something to aid our cause?

"Do you think she could get her hands on it?" Jess asked eagerly.

"I don't like getting a child involved," Rhi said, wringing her hands on the table.

"Rhi, she's already involved. Every Claire is involved, at least indirectly," Persi said.

"And she's not a child, she's seventeen," I said. "The same age as me!"

Rhi's answering smile was sad. "You're both children to me, my love."

"It's not like we'd be asking her to be there when we summon Sarah," my mom said. "We don't want to put her in danger. We're just asking her to... borrow something for us."

"Do we absolutely need it?" I asked Jess.

"Not necessarily," Jess said slowly. "It is possible we could lure Sarah out without it. But the pull would be much harder to resist if we had something like the Claire coven grimoire in the circle."

"Then I'll try Nova," I said. "If there's anything we can do to hedge our bets, we should try it."

"Agreed," Persi said.

"Let's say we do successfully summon Sarah Claire. What then?"

"Then we find out what she's done to that Gateway so that I can try to repair it," Jess said. "If the Gateway can be restored to working order, then your spirit abilities should return, and your Source should be stable again."

"What are we waiting for, then?" Persi asked, half-rising from her seat, but Jess held out a hand to stay her.

"Hang on, now," Jess said. "There's another factor here, and that's the so-called Darkness. There's not much in the spirit world I haven't dealt with, but entities like the Darkness are above my pay grade. If we go through with this, what are the chances we summon more than just a ghost, and what the hell will we do about it?"

I watched my mom and her sisters look at each other in silent conference. Then my mom turned to Jess again. "The Darkness has been Bound from the Source since the last Covenant was signed. That said, if the Darkness ventures to rear its ugly head during your summoning, the Vesper Coven will be there to meet it head on."

I shivered, though whether from dread or excitement, I couldn't tell. Everything—every unanswered question, every fear, every half-understood warning and cryptic message—it all seemed to be coming together in this moment. And instead of running from it or waiting helplessly for it all to happen, we were walking right into it, battle ready.

I felt terrified. I felt elated. But as I looked at each of the four women sitting around me, there was one feeling that overwhelmed all the others.

I felt *ready*.

The phone on the wall rang shrilly, making us all jump. Everyone's expression immediately morphed into visible panic. Had someone spotted us? Had we left evidence behind? Had Eva and Zale been caught and forced to confess what we'd been doing? The bleak possibilities flashed through my mind, each more horrifying than the last. I watched with my heart in my throat as Rhi rose from the table and hurried to answer it.

"Hello?" she said, keeping her voice even. She listened for a moment, and then her eyebrows rose in surprise. "Oh! Sure, I can... hang on..." She placed her hand over the mouthpiece and called over to the table. "Persi, it's for you, honey. It's one of the nurses at the health center."

Persi's complexion went pale, and she rose to her feet. Nobody spoke as we watched her cross the room and take the phone from Rhi's hands, pressing it to her own ear.

"This is Persephone Vesper," she said, and then, "Oh hi, Jacinda, is everything—" She listened for a moment in silence. Then, so slowly that it felt like a dream, we watched as she sank right to the floor with a terrible moan.

"Persi!" Rhi cried, dropping to the floor beside her. "Honey, what is it? What's wrong?"

But my heart—or maybe something else entirely—was telling me. I didn't know how I knew, but I did. I knew it.

"Bernadette," I whispered.

My mother hurried over to her sister's side as Persi's voice rose in a keening wail, and then fragmented, like shattered glass, into heaving, broken sobs.

"No," she just kept saying over and over again. "No, no, no, no..."

Beside me, Jess was frozen with horror, waiting. It seemed to take forever for Rhi to prise the phone from Persi's hand, and place it to her ear again. She listened, stricken, as the nurse continued to speak. She closed her eyes and stroked Persi's hair, as Persi continued to sob inconsolably. Then she said, in a husk of a voice, "Thank you for letting us know." Then she rose slowly to replace the receiver.

We all stared at her.

"Bernadette Claire has... has passed on," she said quietly.

The words, spoken aloud, seemed to break Persi all over again. Her crying intensified, and both her sisters covered her shuddering body with their own, while Jess and I stood there helplessly. It seemed to go on forever, each second of grief stretched to a minute, each minute to an hour. Finally, though, Persi's sobs quieted enough that my mom and Rhi managed to get her onto her feet and, with one of them on either side supporting her, led her out of the kitchen and up the stairs to bed. Jess and I stood there for a few seconds in the echoing emptiness they left behind, and then Jess sank slowly down into her chair, looking shaken. I followed suit, my legs giving way completely so that I sort of fell into my own seat.

"They were in love," I said, my eyes focused on the phone on the wall. "Years ago. Even as Bernadette's powers started to pick away at her sanity, Persi stuck by her. I think she was the only person left who hadn't given up on Bernadette. She couldn't."

"That's awful," Jess said. "I'm... I'm so sorry."

I just nodded. I wasn't the one who needed to hear those words. I had never known the real Bernadette, and I could hardly be expected to mourn the twisted and dangerous woman she had become in recent years. But I could understand, even after all Bernadette had put me through, that this ending was not what she deserved.

My mother came into the room, looking bewildered and exhausted. She moved over to the stove and, perhaps just needing something to do with her hands, began brewing a pot of tea. Almost automatically, I used my nose to assess the ingredients: chamomile, lemon balm, lavender. She was brewing something to help Persi sleep. She came over and joined us at the table while the water heated, sinking heavily into her chair.

"How's Persi?" I asked.

She shrugged helplessly. "Heartbroken, though I think a part of her expected this. It's the guilt more than anything that's tormenting her. Guilt that she couldn't save her."

"It's not her fault," I said.

My mom smiled sadly. "Feelings like guilt and grief are rarely penetrated by anything so weak as objective reality."

"Did they say how she... how it happened?" I asked.

"By her own hand," my mom said. "I don't know any more than that."

The kettle behind her began to whistle, and she rose to take it off the burner. She pulled five cups down from the shelf, and lined them up on the counter, pouring tea into each one. Then she turned and placed two of those cups in front of Jess and me.

"Where is it you're staying, Jess?" my mother asked, as she set the cup and saucer in front of Jess with a gentle clink.

"Just one town over, in Camden," Jess said.

"I don't think it's a good idea for you to try to return there tonight. The police will be on high alert after what happened at the lighthouse tonight, and so too will the Conclave. We'd be happy to have you stay the night here. I... don't think we're going to be able to settle any more details tonight, not after... well..." She gestured to the phone.

"Of course," Jess said. "But I don't want to intrude on what is obviously a really heavy moment here."

But my mom was already shaking her head. "If you go, we'll only worry that you'll be caught. You'd be doing us a favor, not giving us another reason to worry."

Poor Jess. How was she supposed to argue with that? "Okay, sure, that would be great," Jess answered, "as long as you really don't mind."

"We don't mind at all," my mom said. "And that tea in front of you is something to help everyone sleep. It's up to you if you want to drink it, but it's an old Vesper family recipe, and it's very effective. At least eight hours of dreamless sleep, guaranteed, and a clear head when you wake."

"I never thought I'd voluntarily drink anything brewed by a witch, but that sounds amazing," Jess said.

My mom nodded. "We haven't got a spare bedroom, but I could—"

"Don't trouble yourself," Jess interrupted. "I can literally sleep anywhere. Just a couch will be perfect."

My mom nodded again, looking grateful. "There's a comfortable one in the library. Just let me take this tea to Persi, and I'll bring you down some linens and a pillow," she said.

We watched her load up a tray and carry it carefully out of the room. Jess looked at me, one corner of her mouth hoisted into a sad little smile.

"What a night," she said.

"Yeah."

"Do you think, with what's just happened... will they still want to...?"

"Bernadette's death is terrible," I said, "but it doesn't change anything. And I can't imagine Persi letting her final warnings go unheeded. It would be like letting her death be in vain, you know?"

Jess nodded, looking relieved. "Good. Because I'll have to proceed regardless, and I'll be grateful if we can do it together." She picked up her cup, took a long swig of tea, and immediately swayed in her seat. "Whoa."

"Oh yeah, sorry, that stuff works quick. You should probably go into the library before you drink any more. Here, I'll show you where it is."

I showed Jess where the library couch was and then, figuring my mom had enough to worry about upstairs, I ducked into the linen closet and grabbed two pillows, a sheet, and a patchwork quilt. By the time I delivered them to Jess, she was already curled up on the couch, struggling to keep her eyes open.

"This tea is... wow," she mumbled.

I laughed. "Yeah. It's good stuff."

"Hey, Wren."

I turned back to her. She was looking at me earnestly.

"It's going to be okay. We're going to figure this out."

I wanted to agree, to say "I know," and really mean it. But I didn't want to lie, so instead I said, "Good night, Jess."

20

The next morning felt like waking up in a world made of glass. Everyone moved quietly and slowly, afraid to shatter something... or someone. Rhi stood at the stove, the phone pressed to her ear, talking in hushed tones while she cooked feverishly. Jess excused herself out into the garden as soon as she woke, not wanting to bother anyone while she made phone calls of her own. My mother tried to take a tray up to Persi's room around nine o'clock, but returned with it still in her hands, along with Persi's undrunk cup of tea from the night before.

"She isn't in her room," she said, setting down the tray on the counter, and heading straight for the kitchen window. "But if I had to guess... yes, there's smoke coming from her workshop chimney." She turned to me and smiled sadly. "She's always been a solitary creature, pushing away anything that feels like help. She resents it. Always has, from the time she was a little girl."

Rhi turned and looked over her shoulder, the phone still jammed against her ear. "Do you think I should take the tray out to the workshop?" she asked, her tone skeptical.

"Not unless you want her to throw it at you," my mom replied. "Let's give her a bit of space, for now. Where's Jess? Has she eaten?"

I pointed toward the French doors, through which we could see Jess pacing the garden as she talked on her cell phone.

"She's been out there for a little while," I said.

"Well, I guess that makes sense," my mom said. "After all, this trip is obviously turning out to be more complicated than she expected." She took the plate off the tray and placed it in front of me instead. "Here, honey. Hungry or not, you've got to eat a little something. I'll make a plate for Jess, too."

At first, I put a bite of food in my mouth just to placate my mother, but the tastes that hit my tongue were so satisfying that, before I knew it, I'd cleared my plate. I looked over at Rhi, who winked. Either she'd bewitched my food, or she really was just that good. I decided I didn't care which one was the truth.

Jess came in then, pocketing her phone and smiling sheepishly. "Sorry about that," she said. "I had to make some arrangements. I thought I would be back home by now."

"I'm sorry you—" I started to say, but she waved me off.

"Don't apologize, Wren. None of this is your doing. I just have some very... overprotective people in my life who like to micromanage my risk exposure." Jess' lips curved into a smirk as she said it.

"Is it your sister? I remember you mentioned a sister," I said.

"Hannah? Yes, she wants me to stay safe, but she also usually trusts me enough to take care of myself. My partner, on the other hand, is another story entirely. If I successfully keep him from boarding a plane and storming the town of Sedgwick Cove, I will be lucky."

My face must have betrayed something, because Jess laughed. "It's not really his fault. His job is to protect Durupinen, and he was assigned as my guardian. You can see why, on several levels, he might be a bit concerned about the situation here."

I nodded. "I get it. My mom literally took me and fled."

"Exactly. I didn't exactly mention the whole 'Darkness' situation to him. That would have made his head explode."

"Won't he be mad that you didn't tell him?"

"Oh, definitely," Jess said unconcernedly, as my mom placed a plate of food in front of her. "But as long as I come home unscathed, he'll forgive me." She speared a bite of frittata and put it in her mouth. I watched as her expression shifted in real time from indifference to bliss.

"Oh my GOD," she mumbled, her mouth still full.

I grinned at her. "I know, right? Once a kitchen witch cooks for you, you'll never go back."

My mom sat down and slid a mug of coffee across to Jess, who took a sip and then moaned.

"Would you consider adopting me?" she asked weakly.

"I think if you help us figure out the problem with the Source, you'll have your pick of any coven to adopt you," my mom said, smiling.

"So, um… about that… the Source, I mean, not the adoption thing," Jess said, cradling her coffee mug. "Where do you think we're at with that? I don't want to be insensitive, with everything that happened last night, but…"

"No, I understand," my mom said. "We'll still help you, but… yes, we need to regroup and figure everything out. You don't know Persi very well, but I do. I don't want to underestimate what we've undertaken to do, but at this point, I fear our biggest challenge will be to keep her from storming off in the equivalent of an emotional tornado, and trying to set it all right herself."

Jess nodded. "Honestly, I relate. I'm the chaotic sister in my family as well."

Rhi hung up the phone with a sigh, and joined us at the table with two more plates, setting one down for herself and one for my mom, before sinking into her chair. "What a sad situation," she said with a sigh.

"It's been sad for a long time, Rhi," my mom said pointedly.

"Oh yes, of course," Rhi agreed. "I suppose I meant… what a sad ending."

"I think we have to consider the possibility that we might have to do this without Persi," I said. I looked up from my plate to see both my mom and Rhi staring at me. "I'm not trying to be insensitive. In fact, it's the opposite. Persi needs time to process this. She needs time to grieve. If we throw her into a dangerous situation, don't you worry she might... I don't know, do something reckless or dangerous?"

Rhi and my mom traded a look that told me all I needed to know. This was exactly what they worried about.

I felt something brush against my ankle, and looked down to see that Diana and Freya had both entered the kitchen, probably lured in by the smell of food. Rhi crumbled some bacon up, and dropped it onto the floor for them.

"Look, let's just talk things through a bit," I suggested. "What needs to happen first? What did we decide before everything fell apart last night?"

"In order to move forward we need the grimoire back, which will be a feat in itself, because I don't think we'll be able to remove it by ourselves. I think at least one Conclave member will need to help us undo the enchantments, and I'm just not sure who would be willing to do that. Xiomara maybe, but we'd have to explain a whole hell of a lot," Rhi said.

"And we need to get our hands on the Claire coven grimoire, if at all possible," Jess reminded her.

"And that's a big 'if,' especially now with... well, things just got very complicated for the Claires," Rhi said.

"I think it became impossible, actually," my mom said and, when Rhi began to argue, she cut her off. "Oh come on, Rhi, be serious. How are we supposed to just turn up on their doorstep and demand a priceless family artifact with no explanation? 'Oh, sorry for your loss, but can you please hand over the symbol of your family's deepest power while navigating a terrible loss?' It's ludicrous. We can't possibly."

"I could talk to Nova," I suggested again. "She might help us."

My mom was shaking her head. "I don't want to get Nova in trouble."

"Mom, aren't we past worrying about things like getting in trouble?" I asked incredulously. "Besides, she's already involved! She helped me get Jess' body back. She was basically the getaway driver."

"I don't know, Wren..." my mom hedged, but I could hear her weakening.

"Look, just let me try, okay? I think it might be the only chance we've got," I said.

My mom raised her hands in surrender. "Fine. I don't like it, but then, I don't like any of this."

"Can I help at all?" Jess asked. "Do you want me to come with you, and help explain, or...?"

"No!" I said quickly. "Sorry, no offense, but I don't think you'd help our case. She's already trying to distance herself from you, and I don't think seeing you standing there will make her feel any better about helping us."

Jess nodded good-naturedly. "Good point. I'll stay here."

Figuring I'd better not waste any more time, I excused myself from the table, and ran upstairs to shower and dress as quickly as I could. By the time I trotted back down the stairs, my wet hair scraped hastily into a bun, my mother had gone out to the garden and pulled together a stunning assortment of flowers, which she arranged into a white ceramic pitcher and tied with a wide sage green ribbon.

"Take these with you," she said, thrusting them at me. "I'll feel better if you take something to acknowledge Bernadette."

"Great idea," I said, taking the pitcher into my arms and breathing in the heady aroma of my mother's blooms. "They're beautiful, Mom."

"Good luck," Jess said to me, smiling tightly.

"Thanks," I said, returning the smile with a grimace of my own. "I think I'm going to need it."

* * *

It took several minutes to figure out how to safely secure the flowers into the basket on my bike, but I managed it. Downtown was as busy as ever, but I barely paid any attention to the crowds, except to make sure I didn't ride right into someone—my mind was too busy trying to decide what the hell I was going to say. I was suddenly struck with the awful notion that I might be confronted with the entire Claire coven when I arrived at the Manor—after all, that's what families did in the wake of a tragedy. They gathered together. The thought was enough to make me want to turn around, but I kept pedaling determinedly forward. There were more important things at stake than weathering a bit of embarrassment.

Luckily, when I pulled down the slope to the Manor's long drive, there was only one car in the driveway, and that was Nova's. I leaned my bike against the fence, and made my way to the front door with the pitcher of flowers, balancing it awkwardly in one arm so that I could knock on the door. A minute or so later, Nova answered it. My heart sank when I saw her red-rimmed eyes and pink nose above her pajamas.

"Hey," I said.

"Hey."

"I, um... I'm so sorry about Bernadette," I said, feeling my own throat get tight. "My family wanted me to bring these over."

"Thanks," Nova said tonelessly. "Come on in and we can put it with the others."

She turned and walked down the hallway, and I hurried to close the door behind me and follow her. She led me into the family's sitting room, where a half dozen other floral arrangements were already adorning the surfaces. I placed ours carefully on a small end table by the window, and turned to join Nova on the sofa.

"Where is everyone?" I asked. "I thought the house might be full of people."

"It will be by tonight," Nova said, picking at a crumpled tissue she had balled up in her hand. "All the Claires will be here for a vigil. But for right now, my mom and everyone are down at Blackleach and Graves making arrangements."

"How... how are you?" I asked. It felt like pulling the pin from a grenade, asking that question to Nova Claire, but she surprised me. Rather than blowing me off or snapping at me, she just stared out the window.

"I don't know. I feel kind of numb," she said. "Which is weird, because Bernadette really has been gone a while now, but... I guess maybe a part of me was still hoping we'd figure out how to fix her. Which is obviously stupid, but..." She shrugged.

"It's not stupid," I said. "I think that's a natural part of mourning someone who's technically still here." I thought about my friend Poe and her *lola*, who was starting to slip away from dementia. She was still there, living in Poe's house, and yet she was already gone.

"Yeah, well. At least we can move on now," Nova said, still not looking at me. "Put all of that shit with Sarah's ghost behind us."

The mention of Sarah was like an invitation for me to pivot the conversation, and I took it, my heart knocking against my ribs like a fist against a door. "That's actually, uh... one of the reasons I stopped by."

Nova turned to look at me, frowning her confusion. "What is?"

"Sarah Claire."

Nova's whole face tightened like a mask. "What about her?" she asked through unmoving lips.

I could tell I was close to losing my nerve, but I plunged forward anyway. "I, um... I went last night. To the Source. With Jess."

Nova closed her eyes. "I'm pretty sure I told you I don't want anything to do with this. Like seriously, Wren, I don't even want to know what—"

"She was right. Jess, I mean. The Source is one of those Gateways she was talking about."

Nova's eyes flew open, and she stared at me. "Be fucking serious."

"I am. I promise. But there's something wrong with it, Nova. It's not working the way it's supposed to, and it's cut all the spirit witches off from their spirit guides."

"Wren, just because you still suck at your spirit abilities doesn't mean the Source is messed up. You can't expect—"

"It's not just me. It's every spirit witch in Sedgwick Cove. Xiomara has spoken to all of them. All their spirit guides have gone silent. Even Bea can't draw them anymore."

I watched the cracks form in Nova's determination not to believe me. She bit at her lip, clearly trying to find a way to explain away what I was telling her.

"Persi caught us," I continued, "and she already recognized Jess because of Bernadette."

Nova stood up suddenly, dropping her tissue to the floor. "What the hell do you mean, because of Bernadette? What does Bernadette have to do with it?"

"She's been... has anyone told you that she's been drawing and painting in the hospital?" I asked.

A spasm of emotion crossed Nova's face, and I knew her answer before she spoke it. "No. They told me she... that she wasn't communicating, and that visitors were too upsetting."

"Well, that was kind of true," I said. "She hasn't spoken at all or written anything down. But she has been communicating in her own way, with her art."

"Nobody told me," Nova murmured. "No one... they said I shouldn't go, that she was too unstable."

"That might have been true. Persi said she went back and forth from manic to catatonic. But she showed us the paintings Bernadette's been making. She had taken several of them, and... and every one of them showed Jess' face."

"She was still getting visions," Nova whispered.

"Yeah. And there was another painting, a sort of woman with three faces. One face was Jess' and the second was mine. But the third... well, the third was Sarah Claire."

"Why?" Nova asked in a strangled voice. "Why, what does that even mean?"

"We're not totally sure. But Jess thinks we should contact Sarah Claire. She thinks she might still be here, even after Persi exorcised her."

Nova was already shaking her head. "No, that's not possible. Sarah's gone. She has to be gone."

"Bernadette didn't seem to think so," I said.

"How do you know what Bernadette thought? How did anyone know? She was... she was crazy. Broken. That painting was probably just... just *nonsense*."

"Do you really think that?" I asked gently. "Or do you just want it to be true?"

"Go home, Wren," Nova said, turning her back on me and looking out the window again. "I don't need this today."

I jumped to my feet. "Nova, I know this is the worst timing ever, and I'm sorry I have to bring up painful stuff."

"Do you?"

"Do I what?"

"Do you have to bring up painful stuff? Because you could just... not."

"Nova, if this was only about sparing your feelings, I'd never talk about Sarah Claire again. But this is bigger than us. We think Sarah might still be here, and that might be why the Source is all messed up. We need to talk to her, and it would be a lot easier if we had something of your family's to lure her in—"

Nova spun around, her expression so vicious that I took a step back in alarm.

"What of my family's? What are you talking about?"

"Well, the mirror is gone, of course, but..." I swallowed hard, steeling myself. "Well, Jess thought that your coven's grimoire might work just as—"

"You have got to be fucking kidding me. You came here to ask me to steal something from my own family? And our *grimoire* of all things?!"

"No!" I cried. "No, of course not! I just thought maybe we could... could borrow it. It's important, Nova. If we're ever going to free this town from Sarah's actions, we need to understand—"

"Get out!" Nova shouted. She picked up a bud vase off the nearest table, and flung it at me. I ducked out of the way just in time, and it shattered against the wall.

"Nova, please—"

"GET OUT!"

She reached for a much larger vase as I turned and fled for the front door. I didn't stop until I was on my bike and had pedaled far enough away that I couldn't see the Manor anymore. Well, actually, I couldn't see anything anymore due to the tears that had welled up into my eyes. I blinked them away and wiped them on my sleeve, furious with myself. I shouldn't have come. Nova would probably never speak to me again, and I didn't blame her.

Back at Lightkeep Cottage, my mother spotted me from the garden, and hurried over to the fence.

"Well?" she asked.

I just shook my head. My expression must have been bleak, because she opened the gate and hurried over to put an arm around my shoulder.

"It's okay, honey. We'll figure something else out."

"I shouldn't have gone."

"You had to try."

"No, I didn't."

I shrugged her arm off my shoulders and walked back into the house, feeling miserable. My mom took the hint and didn't follow me. I needed some time to myself. I looked around for Freya, hoping to curl up with her, but she remained elusive, and I convinced myself that I probably didn't deserve cat snuggles. I laid down in my room and stewed in my own misery until the sun started to dip behind the tree line, and Rhi called everyone down for dinner.

Jess didn't ask about Nova as I sat down, so I assumed my mother had told her about my disastrous attempt to get the grimoire. Rhi hovered over near the window, biting at her lip.

"Do you think we should check on her?" Rhi asked. "She hasn't come out of the workshop all day."

"She really should eat something," my mom said, nodding. "Maybe we can just take her a plate, so she can still be alone, if she prefers?"

"Yes. Yes, that's a better idea than dragging her to the table," Rhi said, her expression clearing up. She began to pile food onto the table. I watched Jess' eyes go wide as Rhi handed her a heaping plate of roast chicken, potatoes, gravy, asparagus wrapped in bacon, and a steaming, buttered popover.

"This woman should open a restaurant," she murmured to me. "I've never eaten so well in my life."

We all ate in silence for a few minutes before my mom finally said, "We should try to decide what to do next. Jess, can we still summon Sarah without the Claire grimoire?"

"I've got other methods we can try," Jess said, nodding. "They're more complicated and less reliable, but they can definitely work."

"Well then, I guess the next question is when?" Rhi said. "How long do you need to prepare?"

Jess considered, chewing thoughtfully. "It will depend on how hard it is to get my hands on a few items," she said. "There are some specialty herbs and gemstones and stuff that—"

"I don't think that will be a problem," my mom said, trading a smile with Rhi. "We'll take you over to Shadowkeep after dinner."

Jess looked dubious. "Really? Because when I peeked in the window the other day, it looked pretty... well..."

"Yes, that's the tourist level," my mom explained. "We keep the good stuff upstairs. I think we'll have everything you're looking for, and if not, we'll know where we can get our hands on it."

Jess grinned. "Excellent."

We finished eating, and Jess and I helped to clear the table while my mom went to change out of her dirt-smudged overalls, and Rhi put together a plate of food to take out to Persi. She carried it out to the front door, and then called to me.

"Wren? There's something on the porch here for you!"

Puzzled, I put down the plate I was washing, turned off the water, and walked out to join her at the front door, wiping my hands dry on a dishtowel. "What is it?"

"I don't know, honey, it's just got your name on it," Rhi said, pointing to one of the rocking chairs. Then she continued down the steps and out through the garden to take Persi her food.

I looked down at the seat of the chair. There was a square package wrapped in brown paper, with a note tucked into the string. I picked up the note, which had my name scrawled on the front, and opened it.

I don't want Bernadette's last message to go unanswered.

Sorry I threw that vase at you, even though you kind of deserved it.

Also if anything happens to this grimoire I will kill you myself.

Nova

Heart thrumming, I tore open the paper. The grimoire lay inside.

I turned to run into the house to tell my mom, when Rhi's voice suddenly rang out from behind me, and I swung around again to see her running from the direction of the garden, the plate of food still clutched in her hand.

"She's not there! Persi's gone!" she called out.

I opened my mouth to reply, but my mother appeared in the doorway behind me at that moment, making me yelp instead.

"Are you sure? Maybe she's just refusing to answer," my mom said.

But Rhi was shaking her head. "I opened the door. It was unlocked. She's gone."

All the color drained from my mom's face. "We've got to find her."

Rhi made an exasperated sound. "I know we do, that's why I—"

Jess appeared in the doorway, too, having heard everything. "I'll help you. We can split up. Where might she have gone?"

"Jess, that's a lovely offer, but you can't help us, honey, the whole police force is looking for you," my mom said. "But you and Wren can stay here in case she comes back."

"I don't want to stay here!" I said. "I want to help look!"

My mom rounded on me. "Wren, can you please just cooperate? I'll feel much better if at least one member of our family is home and safe."

"I'm not a child, Mom, you don't have to—"

"Look, not to interrupt the teenage rebellion, but... isn't that Persi coming down the road?" Jess asked.

We all turned to look in the direction she was pointing in time to see a figure walking slowly down the shore road from the north. It was undoubtedly Persi. Her long tresses of black hair whipped around her face in the wind, just as the long skirts of her black dress whipped around her ankles. Her feet were bare, her arms crossed tightly over her chest, and her makeup ran in smokey tear tracks down her face.

Rhi dropped the plate she was carrying, and started jogging toward the end of the driveway. We all followed her as she began to call Persi's name.

"Persi? Persephone! Are you all right? What's happened honey, where were you?"

Persi didn't answer. She just continued walking toward us, her face oddly blank.

We spilled out from the end of the gravel drive into the road, my mom wringing her hands, Rhi still shouting Persi's name. Jess bobbed anxiously from foot to foot.

"Do you think she's okay?" Jess asked. "Where do you think she went?"

"I don't know," my mom replied, her voice thready with anxiety. "The only things up that way are the Shadow Tree, the Playhouse and—"

"The lighthouse," I interrupted. "Look."

At that moment, appearing over the little hill in the road came Diana and Freya, flanking Persi on either side. A chilly mist was blowing in off the ocean, wrapping the three of them in a swirling haze. No one moved. We just stood there, transfixed, watching the three of them get closer. At last Persi stopped walking, still a few yards away from us, and the mist parted enough so that we could see her more clearly. Her arms weren't just crossed over her chest. They were clutching something against her body. She grasped the something with both hands, and held it out so that we could see it.

"It's the Vesper grimoire," Rhi murmured, stunned.

"It can't be," my mother gasped. "She couldn't have removed it."

Persi was walking toward us again, and now she was close enough to answer.

"I couldn't remove it, no," she said, "but they could." And she looked down with a nod of acknowledgment, first to Freya and then to Diana.

Of course. The grimoire had been bound to the cats. I stared in disbelief at Freya, who sat back on her haunches and began to groom herself unconcernedly. I barely managed to clap my hand over my mouth before an incredulous laugh burst from my lips.

Persi walked right up to Rhi, and held out the grimoire to her. Rhi hesitated only a moment before taking it reverently into her own hands.

"We have the Claire grimoire, too," I said, holding up the package. "Nova came through after all."

Persi grimly nodded her satisfaction. "Then it's tonight. We end this tonight."

21

Persi disappeared upstairs, and emerged half an hour later having washed her face and changed her clothes. No one asked for details about what had happened in the lighthouse. There would be time for that later. For now, we were focused on the night ahead, and what we were planning to do.

We waited for all the shops to close downtown, and then my mom took Jess to Shadowkeep to restock her supplies. Jess returned gushing about how the Shadowkeep inventory could rival the one the Durupinen used at Fairhaven.

"Fairhaven sounds amazing," I said to her. "I hope I can see it one day."

"Oh, we'll definitely have to get you over there for a visit," Jess said, grinning. "You know most of our secrets now. And there's no better place for a spirit witch to practice her craft."

Rhi called us all together at that point for a planning meeting around the kitchen table. The two grimoires lay in the middle of the table, ancient and exuding their own unique airs of magical power.

"I've been wondering about the Vesper grimoire," Jess said. "You mentioned that Sarah used it to try to help the Darkness gain control of the Geatgrima—sorry, the Source. But you don't know what spell she used?"

"Nobody does," Rhi said. "Well, I suppose Mary Vesper might have, but she took that secret to the grave, and I don't think she'd tell us even if we tried to contact her with the spirit board."

"We couldn't try even if we wanted to," I reminded her. "Spirit contact is cut off. That's what we're trying to fix."

"Oh, yes, of course," Rhi said.

"Well, that will be one of the things we try to get out of her once we have her where we want her. If Sarah really is still around and she answers our summons, she'll be drawn into the circle, and she'll be trapped there," Jess said. "Then we can question her and figure out what she's done to the Gateway, and therefore how we might be able to reverse it."

We began to formulate our plan. Of course, my mother wasn't happy until we'd worked out every single logistical possibility. She came up with scenario after scenario—"Well, what will we do IF"—over and over again, until they became so far-fetched that I had to put my foot down.

"Mom, next you're going to ask what we do if aliens descend in a spaceship and abduct us," I cried. "We are as prepared as we can be! At some point you will have to accept that we can't plan for every single variable! It is literally not possible!"

My mom flushed, and raised her chin defiantly. "Well, excuse me for wanting to be prepared."

"You're very thorough," Jess said, smiling kindly at her. "But I promise you, I have a lot of experience with ghosts. Yes, even ghosts as dangerous as Sarah Claire," she added, as my mom made every indication of interrupting. "In fact, I just finished dealing with one in Scotland that makes Sarah Claire sound like a fluffy little bunny rabbit. You've taken a huge leap, trusting me as far as you have. I'm just asking you to trust me far enough to solve this, okay?"

My mom hesitated only a moment, and then nodded.

"Sorry about that," I said to Jess as we all got up from the table. "She's like… crazy overprotective. It's the whole reason we left Sedgwick Cove in the first place."

"Don't apologize," Jess said. "I think it's sweet. Besides, it's probably good for me, having someone like your mom around to ask those kinds of questions. I'm more of a charge-ahead-and-make-it-up-as-I-go kinda gal. Drives my sister crazy. This is better. Well, maybe not as fun, but definitely safer."

She grinned, and despite my nerves, I grinned back.

It was agonizing, waiting until midnight, but finally it came. We set out up the shore road, Rhi driving my mom's car, and the rest of us cutting as quietly as we could through the woods up to the Playhouse. Rhi had a basket of baked goods and a thermos of hot chocolate on the front seat beside her. The plan was for her to tempt the police on duty to have a snack and then, when they'd passed out from the sleeping potion she'd laced the food and drink with, we'd be able to enter the cavern unnoticed.

Jess, Persi, my mom, and I waited in the trees, shivering with the cold, until finally we saw Rhi flagging us down from the parking lot. We hurried out to meet her where she stood beside the car. Sure enough, Maeve and her fellow officer were slumped on the ground snoring, their expressions peaceful, half-eaten cookies on the pavement beside them.

"I don't like this at all," Rhi said, bouncing anxiously on the balls of her feet. "There's going to be hell to pay when the Conclave find out what we've done."

"And they'll forgive us as soon as they realize Xiomara and the rest of the spirit witches have their powers back," Persi snapped. "Come on, Rhi, pull yourself together. There are things worth getting in trouble for."

Rhi nodded, though she still looked like she wanted to cry with guilt as we all worked together to pick up the two officers and move them into their cruiser. Once we had shut the doors on them both, we moved swiftly for the Playhouse. Rhi took her lookout position by the front door so that she could keep an eye on the parking lot, in case anyone arrived or the officers started stirring. My mom stayed with us as far as the hole in the side of the building, and then stayed posted beside it, in case anyone tried to enter that way.

"You shout for me if you need me in there," she said, her tone sharp with anxiety.

"Of course, Mom," I said.

"I'll be right next to her," Jess assured her.

"And I'll be there, too," Persi said.

There had been no arguing with Persi. She demanded to be inside, where Sarah was going to be; and no one dared say no to her, not with the state she was in. Still, Jess was eyeing her warily as we made our way into the cavern.

The cavern should have been dark, but there was a strange glow from the Geatgrima that bathed the whole space in an eerie, bluish light. Persi had been here before, but now that she understood what the Source was, she didn't seem able to take her eyes off it. She walked in a wide circle, taking it in from every angle, with an expression of awe on her face. Then, that expression twitched with a spasm of emotion.

"Is this where... did Bernadette..." she choked out.

"It is the place her soul would be naturally drawn to, if it were working properly," Jess said gently. "But as it is damaged right now, I don't know if she would have been able to Cross here."

Persi nodded, struggling to keep her face under control. Jess threw me a look, and I went over to Persi.

"Is this going to be too difficult for you?" I asked her.

She whipped her head around to glare at me. "Of course not."

I waited for her to meet my eye, as defiant as her gaze was. "This is important," I said quietly. "We're only going to get one shot at this. You need to be focused. For Bernadette."

Something sharp in Persi's eyes melted. The defiance drained away, and only quiet determination remained.

"I know. I promise," she said huskily.

I turned back to Jess. "We're ready. What do I need to do?"

Jess waved me over to her. "You can help me set the circle. Come on over here."

I joined Jess about ten feet away from the Geatgrima. We set to work —or rather, she set to work, and I handed her the things she needed to do that work: chalk, candles, gemstones. It was remarkable how much our magic had in common, even though the incantations and rituals surrounding it were very different. I tried to commit as much of it as I could to memory, but she worked swiftly and quietly, and in the end, I gave up and concentrated instead on making sure I had whatever she needed ready in my hand. At last, she stood up and inspected her work, looking satisfied.

"Okay, the circle's ready, but we still need the bait to set the trap. Wren?"

I handed her Casting bag back to her, and pulled my own backpack from my shoulder and onto the ground. I extracted the grimoires and held them out to her.

"And we're sure the protective spell on the grimoires will hold?" Jess asked, looking down at them with wary eyes.

"Yes," Persi said, because she was the one who had cast it. "She'll be able to see them, but she won't be able to touch them."

"Good, good," Jess said. "Okay, set them in the circle, Wren, and let's get this show on the road."

"Like this?" I asked, setting them down and adjusting them arbitrarily.

"Perfect," Jess said, and then stilled my hands by placing her own on top. "Seriously, Wren. You can't screw this part up. If it's inside the boundary of the circle, you did it right."

"Right, sorry," I said, backing away and rubbing my sweaty palms on my jeans. "Now what?"

"Now, I summon her, and we see if she answers. There's definitely some lingering spirit energy here, and it's not coming from the Geatgrima. If I'm not mistaken, she's been here very recently. Once she's trapped in the circle, we can question her. Go take your spot and wait. You too, Persi."

Persi jerked out of a kind of trance, tearing her eyes from the Geatgrima and hurrying to join me behind a wall of jungle-like vines that still hung like a curtain from the ceiling of the cavern. By parting them slightly, we had a clear view of Jess, the circle, and the Geatgrima itself.

My pulse boomed in my ears as I watched Jess settle herself out of sight beyond the boundary of the circle. She knelt down, closed her eyes, and began to concentrate. As she did so, I felt a ripple of energy expand outward through the cavern. Beside me, I felt Persi shudder and knew that she felt it, too. I had to remind myself to breathe as we waited.

We didn't have to wait long.

The temperature in the cavern, already chilly, began to drop. Beside me, Persi's breath was coming out in sharp little puffs, like a steam engine. But it was more than cold that permeated—it was also a tidal wave of intense emotion—fear and hope and curiosity and anger, all twisted together. It hit me like a fist, and I reeled back from it, trying instinctively to stop it from tangling itself into my own feelings, confusing me. I glanced at Persi. She had noticed the change in temperature, but that seemed to be all. I turned back to the circle just in time to see a figure shiver into existence within it.

"She's here," Jess murmured from beyond the circle. "She's been here all along."

I would have known her anywhere. Sarah Claire's spirit. Persi stiffened beside me, and I laid a steadying hand on her arm, as much a gesture of warning as it was of support. I could see from her expression that she would have liked nothing better than to leap across the room and tear Sarah to spectral shreds. Persi did not look at me but she did nod once, sharply, a gesture which seemed to say, "Yes, I know. I'll behave myself."

Sarah seemed to be all thin limbs and wild hair and huge, dark eyes that were focused entirely on the Claire grimoire. Jess was right—her connection to it had drawn her right in. She drifted toward it with an expression of bemusement, like she recognized it, but couldn't place it in her memory. She sank into a crouch to examine it, and that was when she saw the Vesper grimoire as well. The change that came over her face was terrifying. An absolutely feral hunger swept over her features, and a keening moan of longing burst from her lips. She dove toward the book, and then gasped in alarm when she found she could not touch it. Her fingers clawed desperately at thin air, never able to come within an inch of its battered leather cover. She unleashed a scream of rage and then turned, eyes combing the ground, and settling on a nearby piece of rubble. She reached for it but, because it was outside of the boundary of the circle, she could not pick it up. Her eyes went wide with rage as she realized what had happened: she was trapped.

Persi made an incredulous noise beside me. "It worked," she muttered. "I can't believe it actually worked."

I could. I'd seen the extent of Jess' magic before.

Sarah began to scream with frustration, throwing herself against the barrier of the circle in all directions, noticing the chalk upon the ground, and shrieking even louder. After all, witches used circles too. Her voice rose to a crescendo, the ferocity of her energy making the very air vibrate.

"Stop."

It was Jess' voice. She spoke quietly, and yet it cut through Sarah's cries completely, and silenced her at once. She stepped out from her hiding place, her gaze trained on Sarah with a mixture of anger and pity. Sarah glared at her, but seemed too wary to speak at first.

"I said stop. Stop now. It's over," Jess said.

Sarah cocked her head to one side, and looked Jess over from top to bottom in a swift assessment. Then she curled her lip in disdain.

"You are no witch," she spat, but even in her condemnation there was something like doubt. The statement almost became a question.

"You're right. I'm not," Jess said, "and every moment I spend in this town makes me more grateful for that."

Sarah didn't seem to register anything but the first few words. She peered at Jess more intently now, as though trying to read her, like a book in a strange language, or tea leaves in the bottom of a cup.

"No, not a witch, and yet... and yet there is something about you."

"I get that a lot," Jess said with a smirk.

"What are you?" Sarah hissed.

"I'm the one who's here to crash your party and ruin your fun," Jess said, rising from her circle and tucking her chalk back in the velvet pouch at her waist. "Now tell me what you've been doing to this Geatgrima."

Sarah's eyes widen. "What is this word you use? I do not know it."

"Yeah, and that's only the first in a long list of things you don't know, which is why you shouldn't be messing with it."

"You... you speak its name. You..." She drifted up against the edge of the circle, coming as close to Jess as she could. "You are... connected, somehow. I feel it. The essence of the Source—there are traces of it in you." She pointed an accusatory finger at Jess' face. "Explain yourself!"

"You first. I asked you what you're trying to do to the Geatgrima."

But Sarah wasn't listening. She was looking at the Vesper grimoire again.

"How did you come by this book? You are no Vesper. No witch," she hissed. "You have no idea of the forces you are meddling with, mortal. Undo this magic. Give it to me."

"No, Sarah. You will never use that book again," Jess said firmly. "It was never yours to begin with, and you have done more than enough damage with it."

Sarah's face spasmed with emotion. "You cannot stop me. This is my destiny."

"There's no such thing as destiny," Jess declared. "There are only the choices we make and the natural consequences of those choices. Now, you still haven't answered my question, and I'm running out of patience with you. This Geatgrima is damaged—unstable. The damage is recent, and I know that you caused it. What have you done to it?"

Sarah's face twisted with anger. "I do not seek to damage it. But it resists me."

"Of course it does," Jess replied. "Would you let someone tear you to shreds without fighting back? If you're not trying to destroy it, then what are you trying to do?"

"It is none of your concern."

"Oh, I think you'll find it is," Jess said, dropping the light conversational tone. "You said it yourself. There's something that connects me to this place, and I am sworn to protect it."

"It does not belong to you," Sarah hissed. "It belongs to him, and I am the key. I am the only one who can unlock its power for him."

"Him?" Jess asked, and for the first time, her calmly confident tone faltered. I saw her eyes dart over to the corner where we were hiding.

I nodded my head. "The Darkness," I mouthed to her, and watched her go pale.

Sarah continued to rave, oblivious to our aside. "It calls to me. Me and me alone. I am the pentamaleficus. I am the only one who—"

Jess shakes her head. "Again, you misunderstand. It calls to you because it calls to every spirit. Even before your spirit leaves your body, it can feel that pull. It's not because you're special. It's not because you alone can master its power. It is universal and unmasterable. I say again, you do not understand what you are messing with."

"Do not presume to understand the Source!" Sarah shrieked, her face twisted with a mad rage. "Only he... only I can..."

"Sarah."

I didn't remember making a conscious decision, but suddenly I had spoken aloud. Not only that, but I stepped out from the hiding place we'd been concealed in. I felt Persi's fingers claw at the back of my shirt to pull me back, but I was already out of her reach. Suddenly, I was there, fully visible, and Sarah's eyes nearly bugged out of her head. She went as still as a statue, looking, for a moment, like a flickering hologram in a film.

"You."

The one word sent a shiver of sheer terror up my spine. Never had I heard a single syllable infused with so much pure hatred.

"Yes, it's me."

She shifted as I stepped forward, and I realized she was trying to put herself between me and the Geatgrima.

"It's over, Sarah. You have to give this up."

Sarah threw her head back and laughed, a dangerous sound devoid of humor and brimming with lunacy. "You expect me to stand aside for you? To give up the greatest triumph of my life and my afterlife? What a pathetic little mouse he has tried to replace me with. How could he have ever thought you worthy?"

"I don't know," I said, suppressing the stinging truth of those words. "But I don't want to be chosen, Sarah. I don't want to replace you."

"Then you are a fool, and just as unworthy as I knew you to be. But he doesn't need you," she said, and turned to gaze at the Geatgrima again. "I will penetrate the secrets of this place, and he will welcome me back to him."

"Sarah, this is delusion," I said. "You are no longer a pentamaleficus. He cannot use you anymore."

She spun around, her face rendered inhuman with rage. "I CAN FIX IT."

"Your powers are tied to your bloodline, and you no longer have a body. No blood, no body, no powers. I know it's hard to accept, but you must accept it."

"I cannot," she replied in a strangled whisper.

"Why? I don't understand."

"You haven't seen what I have seen. What could be. What *will* be. If you only knew—"

"Then show me."

Sarah's eyes went wide. "What?"

"Show me. You say I would understand if only I could see. So, show me."

Sarah's face split into a smile of bleak amusement. "You would fall so fast, pentamaleficus. You would turn in the moment and flee this place, straight into his embrace."

"Prove it."

I didn't know where this recklessness was coming from, but it seemed, at least partly, to be a desperation to understand. This girl had stood in the very same position that I was in now. The Darkness had wanted her— tempted her. But where I had resisted, she had given in. And I wanted to know—I *needed* to know why.

"Show me!" I shouted again.

Sarah held out her hand. I stepped toward her.

"Wren, no!" Jess cried out. From the corner of my eye, I saw her start toward the circle, reaching for me.

But I had already made my choice. Without stopping to think, without considering the consequences, I stepped over the boundary of the

circle, right out of my own reality.
    And into Sarah Claire's.

Back to the Beginning

I'm standing alone in the forest.

It is dark and warm, the kind of summer night that lies upon you like a heavy blanket. The air moves sluggishly in my lungs as I trudge through the underbrush, and my hair sticks to my face and neck like clinging cobwebs.

I am not afraid. The forest is familiar to me.

Despite the deepness of the dark, I know my way. My feet, bare and filthy, pick easily between the tree roots and stones that litter my path. I am seeking something specific, and I pay not the slightest attention to anything else around me in my search for it.

Not the silence.

Not the mist unfurling in tendrils between the trees.

Not the feeling of eyes on the back of my neck.

I have only one aim in mind, and that is to find yarrow as swiftly as I can. The fevers in the village have outpaced our stores, and it is imperative that I find more so that we can make more of the salve that has been easing symptoms. My mind's eye is full of labored breath and red flushes on cheeks, and sparkling, distant gazes. We could lose some of our community tonight, if I do not hurry.

At last, the close set trees give way to a clearing, and I see it: an abundance of yarrow, like lace dotting the high grasses. I drop to my knees, weak with relief, and begin to harvest with swift and grateful fingers.

I reach for a stalk. Then another. Then another.

I stop.

I turn.

It has penetrated my notice at last, that feeling of being watched. I do not *think* I will find someone standing at the edge of the clearing behind me, I *know* it. I know it as surely and effortlessly as I know my own name. The knowledge doesn't frighten me. I have never met anyone or anything in these woods that I need fear, and so it is only with curiosity that I turn and gaze upon him for the first time.

He is a stranger, in every sense.

His shape is that of a man—a young, broad shouldered man with dark, wide-set eyes and a square jaw. He wears a loose white shirt, open at the collar, and a pair of worn, brown woolen breeches. His feet are bare, and oddly long. Even in stillness, he is graceful.

It is in this grace, in my awareness of it, that the strangeness unfurls itself. I know before he moves what his stride will be like—loping, easy, silent—and this knowledge helps me to know that I am not looking at a human man. Not a true one. Whoever this stranger is who looks so calmly at me, he is not a man as I have known men.

And I have known men. Known them and found myself quickly bored of them.

I rise slowly to my feet. Still, I am not frightened. As I survey the figure, I twirl the stalk in my hand thoughtfully. The stalk... the yarrow...

The fever.

Fear rips through me then, and I chastise myself for being so easily distracted from my purpose. It does not matter who this figure is. I have no time to spare for him.

"You do not ask who I am." His voice is melodic, a song at once familiar and strange.

"I care not who you are."

"How can that be so? I am a stranger on your land. Surely you wish to know who I am?"

"Whether I do or do not wish to know does not matter now, sir," I say, keeping my head bent. "I must hurry."

"In what must you hurry?"

"I am gathering yarrow. I must gather as much as I can find."

"To what end?"

"To create a salve that can put an end to the fever." Even as I say it, I feel a bead of sweat trickle the length of my neck, and down into my blouse. A frisson of fear skitters through me. It cannot be sickness, surely, only the heat of the summer, the weariness of the long hours.

"I can help you."

The words catch on the night, hanging over me, and I still my busy hands. "Why would you help me?"

There is a pause. "You ask why?"

"Yes." And because I wish to accuse him, I raise my eyes to him. "You do not know me, and you do not know the fever of which I speak, for if you did you would turn tail and flee. You have no reason to care, or to help me. And so, yes. I ask why."

The man has closed half the distance between us, and yet there was no rustle of grass beneath his feet. He is just as still as before, but now I can see into his eyes, down, down...

I pull my face away and will my gaze to the frothy white bloom of yarrow still clutched in my hand, waiting for the answer I have compelled from him. And after a moment, he gives it to me.

"I can feel your distress. It has overrun this place, tangling with the air and clinging to the moisture from the sea. It drags and claws at me. I wish to alleviate it. Will you deny me this wish? For it will ease your suffering as well as mine."

All my life, I have known if someone is lying to me. Even as a child, I could hear it at once, the sharp sour note of it on the tongue, or else see the shadow of it crouching in the pupil of the eye. It is part of my spirit gift, for the essence to reveal itself even when the mortal form tries to hide it. Now, though I know it a risk, I look the man in the eye again. This time, bracing for it, I do not fall. Instead, I stare, as though into a mirror, at a reflection of my own pain. It throbs in my head and in his eyes with the same, aching rhythm, like our pain shares a single heartbeat.

"Is this true? I ask in a whisper that skitters across the silence. "Do you really feel my pain so acutely?"

He does not answer out loud. Instead, I feel an invitation—no... a dare?—drop into my head like a coin into a well. He dares me to find the lie I suspect him of. But though I probe and search, I can find no trace of it. He does not lie to me. He seeks to help—for his own benefit, perhaps, and yet the result will ease both his pain and my own.

Too many graves. We have already had to dig too many graves.

"Very well," I say. "What is the price?"

I know this is no man, and therefore I know his magic is not human. I am bargaining with something I don't fully understand. This is dangerous, but the fever is also dangerous. I choose the danger which stands before me, because at least its consequences will fall to me alone. The fever takes indiscriminately.

"I do not ask a price," the man says.

"There is always a price."

"Not today."

I search again in his eyes, in his voice, for the lie. I cannot find it. More sweat trickles down my back. The yarrow wilts in my hand. Precious time slithers past us as I wrestle with my indecision.

"Yes. If you truly ask no price, I accept your help," I say at last.

The man says nothing. He only nods, one corner of his mouth curving into the ghost of a smile that I can pretend I have not seen. Then he sinks to his knees in the clearing, rolls up his sleeves, and presses his long-fingered hands to the earth.

He bends his head and closes his fathomless eyes. His mouth moves over words I cannot hear, but I know instinctively that I would not understand them even if I could hear them. He sinks his fingers into the earth, the fingertips disappearing as the deep brown soil envelops them. All at once, I can feel a humming in the earth beneath me, a current of power that courses through the ground and buzzes like a hive of bees against the bare soles of my feet. I can feel it is magic even as I recognize that it is no magic I have ever encountered before. Like the figure kneeling before me, it is *other*.

What begins as a thrill of dread becomes a thrill of excitement. It surprises me, but I cannot suppress it. I can feel it tingling in the roots of my hair.

His hands close on two great fistfuls of earth and he stands, the soil trickling in tiny eddies from between his fingers. He does not approach any closer—perhaps he can feel my skittishness—and instead extends his hands out toward me.

"You must take it," he says. "Take it and sprinkle it on the doorstep of every dwelling in your village. The fever will be gone with the dawn."

I hesitate. Even for magic, it seems too good to possibly be true.

"And the fever will spare them?" I ask. "All of them?"

"All of them."

All at once the soil slipping between his fingers seems too precious to waste, a priceless treasure about to be borne away on the breeze. I hurry forward and extend my basket out so that it waits beneath his outstretched hands. He opens his fists and releases the soil into two heaps on the waiting bed of cheesecloth.

"Do not waste time," he tells me in his melting voice. I raise my eyes from the soil in the basket, and find his face again. I mean to thank him, but I cannot. I am lost in the black wells of his eyes.

A crow caws loudly in the air above us. It startles me, and I blink.

The man who is not a man is gone.

For the next hour, I creep from cottage to cottage, from makeshift shelter to tent, sprinkling the enchanted soil on each threshold from the spoils of my basket, but not before returning an armload of fresh yarrow to the waiting belly of our cauldron. I hope the soil will work, but I am not ready to gamble the survival of our covens upon its efficacy.

But the man who was not a man told the truth. As the sun rises, the fog of confusion and fear of hovering death clear, like the mist; and by midday, we have made our last weary rounds, and can confirm that every fever has broken, every frail being has been released from its grasp. I tell no one of the soil, nor of the thing that had given it to me.

But that very night, and every night after, I dream of him.

* * *

The dreams deepen over time, like love. Or hatred.

At first, I dream as I have always done—my dreams peopled with those I know, and also those who have gone before me. Sometimes they speak to me. Sometimes they merely watch over me, guiding my actions by the gentle weight of their presence. But in the background of these dreams, there he is—a hovering figure in the distance, easy to ignore, if I choose.

But I never choose.

As the weeks go by, he grows nearer. I can make out more of him—the unshaven plane of his cheek, the dirt beneath his fingernails, his slightly parted lips, like he is always just on the cusp of saying something out loud. Still, I do not approach or speak to him. I am waiting, but he is waiting, too.

We are learning about each other.

I wonder if this is the hidden price I must pay for the magic that cured my village—that I have carved out a place in my brain for him, and he has taken up residence there. And yet, he does not feel like an intrusion. Can one really be an intruder when someone has opened the door and allowed you inside, if only on the threshold?

Yes, that is exactly it. He stands upon my threshold, neither asking for nor taking the liberty of further admittance. He simply... is.

He is patient. I am not.

When I can glean no more of him from watching him in the distance, it is I, not he, who approaches closer. It is my choice—at least, I see it as my choice. Perhaps I never had a choice.

Now I chase him through my dreams. I turn to look at him, and he fades away. I call out to him, but I have no power there, for I do not know his name. I find myself looking for him, searching for him. I try to get closer, but he never lets me get close enough to answer the questions that poke at me like needles.

Then, one night, as soon as my eyes close, I see him.

Just him. No one else. The guides, the familiar faces, they've all fled to further reaches of my mind. Here, it is only him and me, alone for the first time since that night in the clearing. In fact, as the setting resolves around me, I realize we are in that very clearing, standing at opposite ends, looking at each other. I raise a hand, if not in greeting, at least in acknowledgment. He raises one as well. Then his knees buckle and he falls to the ground.

I forget how to breathe. My heart turns to a lump of ice in my chest as I lurch forward without thinking, stumbling across the clearing to get to him. Is he injured? In pain? What could have taken him to the ground like that? The tall grasses around me pull at my skirts and wrap around my limbs, preventing me from reaching him, like warnings I am determined to ignore.

I am halfway across the clearing when he raises his head, eyes dark and sparkling with agony. Still hunched upon the ground, arm wrapped around himself protectively, he whispers to me from cracked lips; and though he is still so far away, I can hear the words as though spoken into my ear.

"Help me."

My eyes fly open. I am no longer in my bed, but in the middle of the bedroom floor. The candle beside the bed has long since gone out, and the room is wrapped deeply in shadow. I peer over at my sister, but she is still soundly asleep, mouth open, snoring softly. I tiptoe over to her, and place my hand over her head. I close my eyes, and a gentle flickering series of images plays foggily in my mind—baking bread, drying herbs, watching butterflies unfurl from their cocoons in the milkweed—she is in the tight grasp of her dreams. She will not hear me go.

I slip down the stairs, and out into the moonlit garden. My feet carry me forward without conscious thought. I am not even sure my eyes are open. I am reaching out into the air for him, trying to find his energy, like a beacon I can follow. My heart is pounding hard and high, and I feel like I can't breathe. A vague fear is gripping me tightly.

It is not fear of him. It is fear *for* him. I must find him. I must help him if I can.

My mother has said that I could navigate the Sedgwick Woods in my sleep, and that's how I feel—like a sleepwalker in a terrible dream that I can't wake up from. Why do I feel such emotion for this being I have no real knowledge of? Why does it feel like it is my responsibility—mine and mine alone—to make sure he is safe? I cannot fathom it; it frightens me, but the fear I feel over the depth of this strange connection pales in comparison to the feeling I fear at the thought of his demise.

The forest yields to me. No brambles snag at my clothes, no roots pull at my feet. I arrive at the edge of the clearing once again, and stare around wildly. At first, I see nothing. The silence is absolute, other than the sounds of my own ragged breathing. Had I misunderstood? Had the dream been something else—a premonition perhaps, or a trick? It hadn't felt that way. My grasp of the dream state has always been strong, my interpretations accurate.

Then there is a feeble flicker of movement close to the ground, so small, I nearly miss it. A hand rises above the gently waving grass.

I hear him at last. His voice, again, at once distant and so close: *Help me.*

I am across the clearing in a heartbeat, and then freeze like a deer scenting a hunter at the sight of him.

He smiles up at me—a smile that is also a grimace of pain. "Do I look that terrible, then? I suspected as much."

I want to turn away, but I don't. I take in every horrible detail. His deathly pale complexion, mottled with gray; the beads of sweat glistening over his face and chest; his labored breathing that contorts the muscles of his neck from the effort. And worst of all, standing out all over his body, is a deeply contrasted web of black veins, pulsing sluggishly.

"What... what has happened to you?" I manage to whisper.

"If I knew, I imagine I could deal with it myself," he replies, in a hoarse ghost of a voice.

I drop to my knees beside him, my hands hovering uselessly over his wracked and pulsating body. I feel helpless, lost, and yet desperate to try something.

"I must understand the nature of this illness. I must perform a revelation," I whisper, somehow sure he will know exactly what that means. Unsurprisingly, he nods, like this is what he both expected and dreaded by calling out to me.

"It will hurt," I say unnecessarily.

He nods again, grimly. "Do it. Please."

It is a spell I have performed countless times as a healer, but I know at once this will be no ordinary revelation. The man on the ground in front of me is not an ordinary mortal man, and whatever I reveal is unlikely to be a mortal man's ailment. Still, I must try.

I pull at the buttons of his damp and filthy shirt, but my fingers are shaking too badly, and so I simply tear, so that his heaving chest is exposed. The veins are bulging against his skin, like they are struggling to break right through. Bracing myself, I place my hands against his chest, startled at the bitter cold of his skin, and close my eyes.

Seek it out. Draw out the poison. Reveal the bane.

A barrage of images hits me with the force of a fist, but I do not remove my hands from his skin. Instead of giving in to the impulse to push the images away, I lean into them even as they repel me, and I try to make sense of what I see and feel.

Grasping specters of clawed hands...

A cave, the scent of the ocean...

A stone archway...

The man in front of me, his hands pressed to the stones, his bare foot crossing the threshold...

Agony. Cold. Ripping. Tearing.

I pull my hands away, the flesh on my palms and fingers aching and burning with cold. I look down at them. They are covered in frost that begins to melt in the warm gasps of my startled breaths. I look down into the man's agonized eyes.

"You saw it?" he asks.

"Yes."

"I sought only to understand, but..."

I feel a tiny prickle on the back of my neck. A lie? I brush the feeling aside. He's fading before my eyes.

"I do not know this magic," I tell him. "But it is of the spirit. You've been... invaded. Possessed. There are natures here that are not your own."

"Can you help me?"

I bite at my lip. He needs help. He will not survive whatever this is. And yet I do not know.

"This may be beyond my skill. I can promise nothing."

"Can you promise to try?"

The plea in his voice almost breaks me. I think of the soil. Of the fever that vanished like a nightmare with the dawn.

"Yes. I promise to try."

He presses his lips together in a thin, colorless line as he nods and closes his eyes. Waiting.

Waiting for me. I can barely breathe with the weight of the fear pressing down on me, suffocating me. I do not fear to try. I fear to fail. To fail *him*.

I have nothing, no tools to aid me, and somehow I know there is no time to retrieve them. I ball my hands into fists, stretch them wide again, and place them back against his skin that burns with cold. I can see it now, in every vein, this cold energy. It is what is killing him. It must be exorcised, like poison from the bloodstream. I raise one hand to my throat, my fingers already numb, and fumble for the chain that hangs there, tugging it free from the collar of my night dress. I stare at the object that dangles from it: a tiny glass vial which contains a protective charm.

Whispering an apology to the goddess, I bring the tiny vial down hard on a rock, and it splinters apart into a dozen diamond-bright shards. I take the largest of these into my right hand and, before I can talk myself out of it, I bring it down against the man's skin and press down ruthlessly.

His back arches as the pain hits him, but he makes no sound. I watch in fascination as blood that is not blood beads up around the cut I've made above his chest. It is dark and thick and bubbles like something rotten. It should repel me. Instead, I place my hands on either side of the wound and begin to chant. The words fall off my tongue easily in a long, unbroken chain, words I have used a thousand times before, over a thousand ailing bodies, but not like this. Never like this.

Still, beneath my fear and uncertainty, I can feel them beginning to work. The flesh beneath my fingers is warming as the icy cold energy pours out of him. At first, it rises in a thick fog only from the cut I made in his skin, but as I chant it begins to pour from his nostrils and his eyes. Then he opens his mouth in a silent scream, and it billows up from his throat. It surrounds us, draping the entire clearing in a deathly cold fog. Then the fog begins to swirl and divide and coalesce all around the clearing. I watch, wide-eyed with shock, as the fog forms... figures. Like humans, but composed of bitterly cold smoke.

If I am to lose control of my magic, it is at this moment. My shock is almost enough to shake me from my concentration, but my training—or perhaps sheer instinct—allows me to cling to my resolve, allows my lips to keep moving, and for the words to continue to tumble out without my conscious effort. I cannot fathom what I have drawn from the shaking body beneath my fingers, but I know this is like no healing magic I have ever performed, or will ever perform again.

At last, my spell has run its course. No more mysterious fog pours from the shuddering figure beneath my fingertips. His muscles release, his spine sinks back to the earth, his desperate gasps settle into the deep, even breathing of one in deep sleep. I do not remove my hands—I seem unable to do so—but I do tear my eyes from him to stare around at what has manifested in answer to my call.

They are ghosts. Spirits, severed from their earthly bodies. They surround us, agitated, pacing like animals facing down a threat. I have seen the same postures, felt the same defensive energy, from animals who are hurt and cornered—ready to fight for their lives even as they realize their chances of survival are slim. Waves of deep animosity roll off them as they circle us. I can feel it washing over me, dizzying in its strength. They begin to close in on us, and I begin to panic. I do not understand what these things are. How can I protect him from them? I raise my hand in malediction.

The figures stop, and I realize they understand me. I open my mouth to ask the obvious question, but a tingling realization now coursing through my body answers. These are spirits—or something akin to spirits. I can barely hear their distant voices, their whispers borne away on the night air, before they can reach me. And yet, I understand they are calling out to me.

It is a warning. It burrows into my bones and nestles there, like a frightened animal.

As I stare at them, trying to understand, they shiver, and fade. The cold vanishes with them. We are alone.

The sound of his groan startles me, and I turn back to the figure lying limp in the grass. His breathing, once shallow, is now steady. The deep black of the veins beneath his skin has vanished. His eyes flutter open, and his dark eyes find mine.

"I cannot feel them anymore," he whispers through cracked lips. "They're gone."

"They are," I reply, as I press the back of my hand to his forehead. It is no longer icy against my skin. "But how did they come to be there in the first place?"

At first, I do not think he can answer. He is weak, his eyes rolling in his head as he struggles to keep them open. Just as I feel sure he has fallen into unconsciousness, his hand reaches up and snatches at my fingers. He squeezes them with a strength that startles me.

"I knew I saved you for a reason," he whispers. "Oh what power we shall gather, my little one."

* * *

We are bound together now. I can feel it.

He has saved my life. I have saved his. It is a deep magic that cannot be undone.

As the days go by, he waits for me. I see him in the trees. On the cliffs.

In my dreams. He is closer now than he was. I can no longer ignore him, but I do not go to him. Not yet.

I am afraid. Not of him. Of myself.

The truth is that I know he is dangerous, and this knowledge only makes him more fascinating to me. I want to understand him. I want to be closer to him. This is why I am afraid. Because despite knowing better, despite all I have learned and all I have done, I do not run from him. I seek him. What does this say about who I am, and who I have grown to be despite all I have been taught?

There have always been kinds of magic that are off limits. From my earliest years, I endured scoldings about the things we must never wish for, the power we must never crave. We are instructed to humble ourselves, to respect the magic we have, and to be grateful for it.

And I am grateful. I am also hungry.

Hungry to hurt those who hurt me. Hungry to savor control when I am told to let go. He has never denied himself in this way. He is the hunger personified.

This is what he whispers to me in my dreams. These are the words carried to me in the wind by the cliffs, and in the rustle of the leaves in the forest, and I finally begin to understand. He is the presence we have always known to lurk here, the abomination that fed on the magic and twisted it to its own vile will. We have protected against him. We have shunned his energy and his influence. And yet, he has managed now to creep under my skin, to beguile me with promises and visions that live as deeply hidden in my own heart as they do bare and exposed in his outstretched hands.

You do not need to dream in shame of this power, he whispers to me. *You can reach out. You can take it. We can take it together.*

At first, I try to reason with myself. I do not want this power for myself alone. I want it for all of us, all the witches of the Cove. I wish to protect us, to enrich and empower us. Who should wield this power, if not us? Have we not proven ourselves worthy, the proper stewards of this place, and all its secrets?

But I am the one person I cannot lie to. I know the truth, and soon I accept it. I do not want this power for myself. I want it for us. For him. To witness what we could do with it together. He has promised to show me, and I am dangerously close to accepting that invitation.

At last, one night, my reserves of will power run dry. I wake from a dream, sticky with sweat, and gasping for something more than air. I do not stop to think. Just like the night I saved him, I simply open the door and run. My feet—and my heart—know where to find him.

The cave is tucked into the cliffs, a treacherous climb that leaves me bleeding, and drenched to the skin. The sea nearly plucks me from my path, the wind tears at me, but I tame them. By the time I stagger into the cave to face him, I have proven a power that even he must respect.

"You have come to me at last."

"I have."

He smiles, and I am undone.

"Why do you call me here?" I ask.

"You already know."

I swallow hard. I do know, but my fear twists my knowledge into questions. I shake it away, and find my resolve again. "Show it to me."

He reaches out his hand, and I take it. The connection that radiates through us is both terrifying and elating. He turns and leads me deeper into the cave, squeezing through the fissures in the rock, until it opens into a wide cavern. It ought to be pitch black inside the cavern, but it is not. The whole space is lit with an eerie glow, bleached like moonlight, and this glow emanates from a tall stone archway in the center of the cave.

I am not sure whether I pull away, or if he lets go of my hand, but suddenly I am moving forward on bare and bleeding feet, drawn by the inexorable pull of this archway. I walk in a slow, deliberate circle all the way around it, taking it in from every angle, trying to understand the storm of emotions coursing through me as I stare at it.

The archway stands on two circular stone platforms stacked one on top of the other, made from the same pale, weathered stone. There are symbols and words carved into the face of the platforms all the way around, but I can make sense of none of it. It is a language I do not know, and the symbols, like runes only unfamiliar, are still more strange. But most unnerving of all is the feeling that pulsates through my body, like blood in my veins—an almost dizzying draw, like a thousand strings have been tied to every true part of me, and are all pulling me forward.

"What is it?" I whisper.

"I don't know. But it contains the secret of the Source. The deep and abiding magic that draws all here, like moths to the candle flame. I have found it at last, but it is like a door without a key."

"I have seen your power. Surely you do not need me."

"Oh, but I do. I lack the one thing I need to understand this place."

"And what is that?"

"A soul."

These words should send me running. Instead, I draw closer to him, as though I could fill that emptiness.

"I have watched and I have waited," he says, and raises one hand to stroke my cheek. "I have tasted your power, and it is greater than any witch who has ever walked these shores. You have command of the five, and yet you do not use it. Your gifts are deep, yet you do not chase them to their depths. Why?"

"Fear."

"Why do you fear it?"

"No." I shake my head. "Not my fear. Their fear."

I do not need to explain further. He knows the coven from which I come, the community that I have called my home. We have always trafficked in caution and concealment. Only my own coven knows the extent of my magic, and they demand I keep it hidden.

He can hear my thoughts. "Is that not the reason the witches have come here? So that they do not need to hide anymore? And yet, here you are, hidden away like something shameful among the very people who should celebrate you."

My cheeks flush with a flood of emotion I do not expect, and am powerless to conceal. Tears swell unbidden in my eyes, and I blink them away, angry with myself. I do not want him to see my pain—only my strength. But—

"Pain is strength," he whispers. "Use it. Claim it. Do not let them deny you. I have seen what you can be—what you will be. Do you wish to see it, too?"

A frisson of fear shudders through me, but I do not bow to it. I steel myself, and look up into his eyes instead; and it is like falling into two deep pools, falling... falling...

The vision hits me like a bolt of lightning. Raw magic coursing through me, as I rise from flame and crashing wave and swirling winds, the earth cracking beneath me, the collected intention of a thousand ancestors gathering in my fingertips. My eyes are stars glittering in an endless sky, my hair a billowing cascade twisting like vines, ensnaring all within my reach, pulling it within my control, as a gown of seafoam and blossoms and fire rises to envelop me, as every living thing in the Cove and beyond kneels at my feet, like to a queen. Their fear sustains me. Like air, it fills my lungs and my heart and my spirit, and I feel infinite. I am infinite.

I blink, and find myself breathless and panting, staring into his unreadable face once more.

"Do you see now? Do you see what you can be? What we will be, together?"

"Yes."

"The key to that power is here." He nods his head at the archway behind him. "Together we can unlock it, and all you have just seen will come to pass. All you need to do is take my hand."

I look down at his outstretched hand, like a promise. I take it.

He is the Darkness. He is terrible. He is beautiful.

And I serve him.

* * *

Torn from my host, I am lost.

I had known it could only be temporary. Even our shared bloodline could only protect her for so long. As the days passed within the walls of the prison, I had felt her mind deteriorating, driven mad by the unnatural joining of two souls within a single body. Soon she would be useless to me, and I would have to abandon her to find another.

But then the Vespers come. They destroy my best-laid plans. Again.

I can feel it again—the inexorable pull of the Source. I fight against it, as I did all those years ago, but I am weak and tired from the effort of clinging to Bernadette's mortal form. I do not know how long I can resist it. This is the moment I almost give up.

Like the tide dragging at the grains of sand on the beach, the Source pulls me closer. I plead with the Darkness to find me, to save me, but I am met only with silence. With no body, and no magic, I am nothing to him anymore. I am no longer pentamaleficus. I am only shade and shadow. I am an echo of dust.

At last my will crumbles, and I find myself wandering the beach, drawn to the entrance of the cave. It is over. I have nothing left to fight for, no shred of hope that I can rejoin him. I prepare to give myself up to the Source, to let it swallow me. I do not know or care what awaits me on the other side. If it is not him, it may as well be nothing at all.

But I am not alone. A woman stands between me and the entrance to the cave.

She sees me, of that I am certain, and yet my sudden presence does not surprise her. She stands with hands calmly folded in front of her, her expression impassive. She is waiting for me.

"Hello, Sarah."

"You know who I am."

"I do."

"Who are you?"

"I am the woman who can give you everything you've ever wanted."

I laugh, because this is absurdity. She smiles.

"You don't believe me," she says.

"I do not."

"You ought to. The Darkness awaits your return, and he is not patient."

My laughter dies. My mind goes still.

"Who are you?" I repeat.

"My name is Veronica Meyers. I am a member of the Kildare Coven."

"That name means nothing to me. You are nothing to me."

"Not yet. But hear me out. The Kildares came to Sedgwick Cove after your time, but it is your legacy that we have striven to come into."

"My legacy." The words sound so strange, spoken from living lips. I was a pariah in life, and in death perhaps even more so. It is inconceivable that this woman speaks the truth. "What do you know of my legacy?"

"I know you were the first pentamaleficus to walk this stretch of shore," the woman says. "I know that, together with the Darkness, you sought to harness the great and terrible power of this place." She looks behind her, at the cave's entrance.

She knows, I realize. She knows what this place is. How can she know?

"And now I know he seeks another in your place. Another, more powerful witch to help him fulfill his destiny."

"She is not more powerful!" The words explode from me. "It is only because... because I cannot... I no longer—"

"You no longer have a body through which to channel your power," the woman replies. "But what if you did?"

All I can do is stare. She looks calmly back at me.

"I do not understand," I finally say.

"You need a body. We need to unlock the mystery of the Source. Let us do so together."

She appears so calm, so assured. All I can do is laugh.

"I fail to see the humor," the woman says.

"There is much you fail to see," I reply. "I cannot possess you indefinitely, and I am not interested in a temporary body that will deteriorate with every moment I spend inside it. You will lose your mind before you can grasp even a fraction of what the Source can do, and then your body will be useless to me. What foolish bargain is this you seek to make?"

But the woman still smiles. "I am not proposing you use my body. Another will be provided."

"Foolish woman. It must be a witch, or I cannot inhabit it. The body will rot."

"And a witch it shall be. Our coven is willing to sacrifice one of our own for this cause."

"You lie."

"I promise you, I do not. If you can prove to us that you can unlock the mystery of the Source, we will give you the body you require to rejoin your master fully. And to prove it, I will Bind the promise in blood to seal it." She lowers a hand, and brushes it against her jacket, revealing the glint of a knife holstered at her hip.

If I still had a heart, it would surely be pounding now. "What do you gain?"

"You promise to share the knowledge with the rest of our coven. You teach us how to access the magic."

"You claim to know my legacy, and yet you seem ignorant of the nature of who I serve. If you wish to access the deep magic, then you will have the Darkness to contend with."

The woman's smile grows. "Then we shall contend with him. Do we have a bargain?"

I hesitate. My last attempt to crack open the Source went terribly wrong. There is no guarantee that it will go right this time. And even if it does, the Darkness surely will not be pleased that I shared the secret with another coven. I study the witch before me. She is confident—ludicrously so. She does not understand the Darkness the way I do. She does not comprehend the full extent of his power, or she would not be so foolish as to propose such a plan. What does it matter if I share the secret with her? The Darkness and I, together in our power, will crush her and her coven to dust.

We stand there, two witches in the dark under the blood moon, each sure she will get what she desires.

Only one of us is right.

"A bargain," I whisper.

22

I was flying through the air as I entered my own thoughts again, just in time to land on my back with a merciless thump. I lay gasping, all the air gone from my lungs, head spinning, teeth chattering with cold.

"Wren! Talk to me, kid, are you okay?"

It was Jess' voice. I felt her hands pressed to my forehead, slapping gently at my cheek, shaking my shoulder. I wrenched my eyes open, and saw her terrified face swim into focus, only to be shoved roughly aside as my mother and Persi took her place.

"I'm... I'm okay..." I managed to force out. "I... she showed me... I understand."

"I know," Jess said. "I saw it, too. I was in the circle." She sounded as badly shaken as I felt.

The three of us: Jess, Sarah, and me, all joined together through the same memories. Bernadette's painting made sense at last; she'd foreseen that journey, and now I had lived it.

I felt three pairs of hands help me up into a sitting position, but all I wanted to do was bat them away. I didn't have time for this. I didn't want to be coddled. I finally understood. My blurry vision began to resolve, and I focused it right back onto Sarah Claire.

She still hovered within the boundaries of the circle. Our strange connection through her memories had not managed to free her from the trap Jess had laid.

"What happened, Wren?" my mother asked. "Are you all right? What did she show you?"

"Everything," I said, and I could hear the wonder in my own voice. "I know how she first encountered the Darkness. He saved her life—the whole village—and then she saved his. And then he promised her power... so much power..."

I met Sarah's gaze. She looked triumphant, like she had just proved an unprovable point beyond a shadow of a doubt.

"And so now you see," she said in a voice vibrating with emotion, "why I cannot simply let go. I have seen it, what will be mine."

"Oh, Sarah," I whispered. "I'm so sorry, but that's just not true."

Her mouth twitched like she was swallowing a curse she longed to hurl at me. "Of course, it's true."

"He showed you your desire. He showed you what he wanted you to see, because he needed you. He tried to steal the power of the Gateway, and he nearly died. He knew that whoever tried next would likely be a sacrifice. He used you."

Sarah was shaking her head violently. "You know nothing, child. Nothing of which you speak."

"You think he didn't try to show me those very same things?" I asked. "That night at the lighthouse, do you really believe he didn't try to convince me the way he convinced you?"

She wanted to shout, I knew, but the words wouldn't come. Her body convulsed with the words she wasn't speaking.

"When I walked into the ocean, I saw it—the same vision he showed to you, or a version of it, anyway. The Darkness and a witch, as one, a new and terrifying being with dizzying power. He showed me what he thought I would want—what he thought every witch must want, because it is the only thing a monster like him thinks about. But he was wrong. I didn't want it, and it's the only reason I was able to break his grip on me."

"All your words have proven," Sarah hissed, "is that you are weak. That is why I am still here."

"No, Sarah," I said, and there was sadness in my voice. "The weakness is your own."

Sarah lunged at the barrier of the circle again, making all of us jump.

"You're still here because you let someone else manipulate you," I said.

"Someone else? Who?" Persi asked.

"Veronica Meyers," I said. "She found Sarah after the Litha Pageant. She bargained with her. If Sarah could unlock the mystery of the Source, they would sacrifice a member of their coven to restore her to a body. She could live again, and fulfill what she calls her destiny—to be the pentamaleficus joined to the Darkness in unbridled power."

Sarah raised her chin defiantly. "As I shall be."

"No, you won't. Veronica exploited you the same way the Darkness did. She understood you, because she is just like you—she wants what you want. Do you really believe she would share that power with you if you laid it at her feet? She counted on you to be too desperate to pass up her offer, and so you were. And so you've been here ever since, toiling away for another master who will cast you off at the first opportunity."

"The Kildare witch is not my master! She is a means to an end!" Sarah shrieked.

"No, you are the means, Sarah. You've been here ever since, making desperate attempts to strip power from this place. And now you've all but destroyed it."

For the first time, I saw real fear cross Sarah's face. "It is not destroyed," she said.

"Not yet, but it is damn close," Jess chimed in. "Because of this." And she held up the Vesper grimoire. She must have grabbed it when we were released from Sarah's memories. It now lay in her hands, its pages open. "Seeing your memories has filled in the gaps. I understand now what's happened."

Sarah hardly seemed to hear her. She was staring with ravenous greed at the grimoire, like a predator tracking prey.

"The spell you used that night all those centuries ago was a risk. You did not understand the nature of the Source any better than the Darkness did; and despite all your years of experience as a witch, you made the same mistake that a group of foolish young Durupinen would make centuries later, when they tried to strip the power of a Gateway for their own. They survived because I intervened before it was too late. But you were not so lucky, Sarah. No one arrived in time to save you, only to clean up your mess as best they could. But damage was done that night that couldn't be undone. The Source itself was weakened—not irreparably, but enough that, years later, when another misguided witch of your bloodline tried to call you back, it began to crumble."

Everyone in the room was listening to Jess now, mesmerized at these revelations.

"I suspected it was your return that destabilized the Gateway further, and now it's clear that I was right," Jess went on. "No spirit should be able to return to the world of the living once she has Crossed. It should be impossible, but here you are. It was a destructive act, your return. It goes against the natural order of things. You took a small hole and forced it wider. You were unknowingly destroying the very thing you claim to revere."

Sarah's expression was shifting now from anger to disbelief. Fear was skittering across her features, as each word Jess spoke fell terribly into place. I picked up the thread.

"And then, when all your efforts had failed, and your last desperate attempt to hijack Bernadette's body had been thwarted, Veronica convinced you to help her. But in your determination to deliver on your promise to her, you've done more damage still. This Gateway is crumbling. Any further attempt you make to access its power could be the attempt that destroys it forever. And just imagine how much that would anger your master. Cut off from the possibility of such limitless power... because of you."

At last, it seemed, we had found the words that could pierce through Sarah's delusion. It was like watching a house of cards collapse behind her eyes, to be replaced with a spark of utter terror.

"It's not true," she whispered. "It's not true. I can still fix it. I can still—"

"Sarah. Enough."

The voice was soft, and at first I did not recognize it. All I knew was that it hadn't come from any of the women grouped around me. Only by following Sarah's startled stare did we realize who spoke.

Bernadette stood in the entrance to the cavern, her form slightly shimmering, a dull glow lighting her up from within, so that she shone without casting any light around her. She looked like a dream made real in her simple white nightgown, her hair billowing around her, caught in a breeze no living person could feel. Her face, for the first time since I met her, looked serene and untroubled. The visions and doubts that had tortured her in life had fallen away in death. She was free.

Free, but not free. She was still here. Trapped, as long as the Gateway was compromised.

I could hear a dry sobbing sound, and I knew it was Persi. I tore my eyes from Bernadette long enough to see that my mother had moved in close to Persi, supporting her, yes, but also preventing her from running forward. Bernadette was not here for Persi. She had eyes only for Sarah, and her gaze, as it locked on its target, was full of understanding and sorrow.

Sarah's face spasmed with shock at the sight of Bernadette's ghost, and she had to fight to get it under control. Even when she resumed her disdainful manner, though, her voice betrayed her, trembling with suppressed emotions.

"Bernadette. I wondered if you would survive our time together. I see you succumbed to weakness in the end."

"Only a witch as power-hungry as you would consider death a weakness, Sarah. I suppose that's why you've fought so hard against it since I brought you back. That should have been my first warning when I made contact with you. But I was too sure of my own motives to question yours, not when we connected so well. I understand that connection is not what I thought it was. It was only your manipulation."

"You are a fool, Bernadette Claire. We could have had power beyond comprehension—power beyond reckoning."

"No. You knew from the moment you took over my body that I would only be a temporary vessel. Your promises to me were as empty as the Darkness' promises to you."

Sarah had gone so still that she seemed, for a moment, like one of Bernadette's own renderings—a painting made manifest. She and Bernadette were locked into each other with such intensity that they felt like the only real things in the room, the rest of us faded to the insubstantial equivalent of ghosts.

Bernadette broke the silence. She took one deliberate step forward. "I have seen into your heart, Sarah Claire, because you let me in. I know you better than you know yourself. I see into it now." She held out a hand. "Free yourself, my blood sister. Break his hold on you. Show the courage you could not show in life. Choose to begin healing the damage you've wrought."

Sarah wavered. "How?" she asked.

"Step through with me," Bernadette said, gesturing to the remains of the Geatgrima. "You are the missing piece that is out of place. If you Cross back now, the Source can begin to heal itself. All of it lies with you."

Sarah's eyes began to gleam with the ghosts of tears. My goddess, was it working? I felt like I could see her resistance crumbling away in real time.

Bernadette was still speaking in the same, soothing tone. "Imagine that, Sarah: the chance to undo all the wrongs. No one gets such a chance. Do not squander it."

"I... I can't," Sarah whispered, but it sounded like a plea rather than a declaration. Jess' hand tightened on my arm. She sensed it too, the weakening.

Bernadette walked slowly forward until she reached the outer edge of the circle. She extended her hand. "Come with me. We will Cross together. All will be healed. Two Second Daughters, rewriting our legacy."

Sarah drifted to the very edge of her magical cage. She looked down at Bernadette's hand, and then nodded. Beside me, I heard Jess murmur under her breath, and felt the invisible barrier between the two spirits vanish. When Sarah reached for Bernadette's hand, she was free to take it, to step outside of the circle. Bernadette smiled, and led Sarah toward the plinth upon which the remains of the Geatgrima stood.

We all held perfectly still. Any moment now...

It happened in the space of a breath. Sarah turned her head, and her eyes fell on me. Something twisted in her expression—a feral, animal something, and though she spoke no words, I could hear the thought echoing in my own head.

If the Darkness wants her, he will have to take us both.

She launched herself at me, face wild, hands outstretched, malice and covetousness burning in her eyes. There was no way to stop her. All I could do was close my eyes, and brace for her invasion.

A burst of cold air...

A blood-curdling scream...

My eyes flew open just in time to see Bernadette and Sarah collide in midair, to watch as Bernadette, expression grim with determination, her arms wrapped in an embrace around the very woman who had torn apart her life. And in that embrace, Sarah Claire was carried straight through the Geatgrima. Their entwined figures shivered in the air above the plinth for a fraction of a heartbeat, and then vanished.

No one moved. No one spoke. Everyone was afraid to trust what they had seen, to believe it could really, truly be over.

But the moments ticked by. Persi gave a dry sob, and the stillness shattered like spun glass. My mother loosened her grip on my arm, and I felt the blood rush down to my numb fingertips. On my other side, Jess scrambled to her feet and moved cautiously forward, until she stood with one foot upon the plinth, still and expectant. At last she turned, and the hope in my chest bloomed in perfect synchronicity with the smile on her face.

"It worked," she said, her face eloquent with relief. "The Geatgrima is restored. Can you feel it?"

And before I could even answer, a whisper brushed past me, gentle as a butterfly wing.

Well done, my little bird.

I laughed, even as the tears came into my eyes. "Thanks, Asteria."

Epilogue

Asteria came to me that night. I heard her voice, not from without, but within, calling to me from the inside of my own—head? Heart, perhaps? Regardless of exactly where it came from, I woke at once full of the knowledge of exactly where I would find her.

I hurried down the stairs and out the door into the garden, in nothing but a t-shirt and flannel pants. I should have been shivering with cold, but it couldn't seem to touch me. My grandmother felt like a flame inside me, protecting me and keeping me warm.

My bare feet padded purposely through the frosty grass, following a path my heart had already chosen. I reached my mother's walled garden, which was never locked anymore, and pushed the creaking old door inward.

Frost and cold could not touch this place. The trees were rich with foliage, and the flowers bloomed lush and colorful, like hothouse plants. Asteria sat at the center of the garden on a bench, waiting patiently for me. I felt the smile bloom on my face, like one of the flowers nodding in the gentle nighttime breeze.

"Asteria."

"Hello, my brave girl. Come sit beside me."

I sat. She was real, and yet she was not. I could see her, but only if I didn't look too hard. I could feel her, but only in the way one might feel the wind or the brush of a butterfly wing. She was a suggestion of herself.

"You look better," I told her. "And you sound better, too. Like yourself."

"Sarah's desperate magic twisted our means of communication. We were all lost and confused—separated from ourselves and our living coven members. I could not reach you, and when I tried, I could not make sense of what was happening."

"But it's better now?"

"All is as it should be. You have done so well," she said to me. "The Source is safe and stable again, and the spirits beyond it are connected with their loved ones again."

I wanted to smile. I could feel it trembling at the corners of my lips. But then I felt my face crumple, along with my happiness.

"Why do you despair, my love?"

"Because it won't last, will it?" I asked. "It can't. The Darkness won't stop its pursuit. It will never rest."

"That is true," she said. "I wish it were not so. But like the Vesper witches that came before you, you will stay the watch."

I felt a lump in my throat. I didn't want to stay the watch. I didn't want to always be waiting for the next attack. I felt trapped, my momentary relief curdling into despair.

"Couldn't we... couldn't we just leave this place?" I asked, a note of desperation coloring my words. "We can still be a coven somewhere else, can't we? Why do we have to stay? Why is this our fight?"

Her smile was slow and sad. "Do you not feel this is your home?"

"Of course, I do, but..." I shrugged. "I've known other homes. We could begin again somewhere new, couldn't we?"

"Oh yes, I suppose we could," she said. "But let me ask you this: could you really turn your back on this place, knowing that the Darkness might find a way to consume it? Could you find contentment, always looking over your shoulder, waiting for him to reappear?"

I wanted to say yes. The word was right there, stuck in my throat, threatening to choke me. But my lips wouldn't give up the lie, because that's what it was. I hated it, but it was true.

Asteria understood my silence. I could sense every one of my bitter, hurt, and angry feelings passing through the space between us.

"There's one thing I still don't understand," I said.

"Just one?" Asteria asked with a hoarse chuckle.

"Well, one that's pressing on me," I clarified. "How did you know about the grimoire? It's been lost for such a long time. Generations of our coven have sought it to the ends of the earth, and never tracked it down."

"Ah," Asteria said. "In life, I could never have unraveled such a secret. But in death, we share in the collective knowledge of our coven. The moment I passed into the spirit realm, I knew all that had been kept from us, for our own protection. And when Sarah Claire began her attack on the Source, I knew from whence help must come, and I sought it at once."

"You contacted Jess."

"That's right."

"But how did the Durupinen come to possess the grimoire in the first place?" I asked.

"Would you like me to show you?" Asteria asked.

"Can you?" I asked.

"Oh, yes." Asteria said. "With your spirit gifts, I can share the memories with you. You already know how it works—Sarah showed you many of her own memories, I believe."

I shuddered. I wished I could unsee those memories. They felt like intrusions inside my brain. But somehow, I didn't think that anything Asteria showed me would feel the same way.

"It will be rather… disorienting at first. But you have earned these answers, my little bird, if you want them."

I hesitated only a moment.

"I want them," I whispered. "I want to understand."

"Close your eyes," Asteria said. "And brace your mind."

I dutifully scrunched my eyes closed, but before I could figure out how to follow her second instruction, an icy blast of memory hit me like a violent ocean wave, dragging me under, tossing me through my own mind like a ragdoll. For several long moments, it was nothing but a howl of sound and flashing images and deep, biting cold. But then I managed to steady myself and the images slowed, the sounds resolved, and I found myself once again dropped right into a memory that was not my own. There was no pain this time—though whether that was because I had chosen to experience the memory, or because the memory came from my own bloodline, I couldn't say. Also, this time, I seemed to be an observer, rather than reliving someone else's experience from their point of view. This realization calmed me, and I began to take in the details around me without the haze of fear or confusion.

I found myself sitting in Lightkeep Cottage as it had been when the very first Vespers lived there—I recognized it from Sarah's memories, though the scene was much crisper and clearer than when I had seen it through the lens of her memories. Beside me was Mary Vesper. She knelt on the braided rug in front of the hearth, her hair a tangled mass around her chalk white face. She had smudges of dirt and blood on her cheeks, and her eyes were dark and wild with fear.

She was staring down at the grimoire, which sat in her shaking hands.

I understood. It was the night of Sarah Claire's betrayal—the night of the Covenant. The Darkness had been thwarted and cast out, and yet the terror remained, sharp as a knife. In Mary's hands, she held the grimoire. She looked at it like it was a beloved pet that had attacked her. Then she looked behind her and saw her two sisters asleep on a bed in the corner. They were curled up together like cats, their curls tangled like their fingers as they held hands in their slumber. Both looked the worse for wear from the night's events—scratched and bruised and dirty, their skirts torn and their hands streaked with blood.

I watched a decision crystallize in Mary's mind—she would protect them. She would protect all of them, every witch that called Sedgwick Cove her home now, and for generations to come. Dear as it was, she could not justify the grimoire's continued presence under their roof. It was too dangerous—too tempting. It had yielded the magic that had almost destroyed everything. It could not stay, and she could not destroy it. It was too closely tied to her coven, imbued with their very essence. To destroy it would be to destroy their own gifts, and she could not do that. She did not speak aloud, but I could understand her thoughts, nonetheless.

She must hide the book. But where?

There had been markings on the Source—she had seen them. She closed her eyes, and began to draw in the ashes of the hearth the symbols she could still conjure in her mind's eye. When she finished, she looked down at what she had created, and shuddered. She knew at once they were correct. The sight of them sent strange energy skittering through her veins, just as they had done when she laid eyes on them in the cave. She placed her hand over the symbols, her palm facing down, and focused her inner eye.

Show me the place, she begged the goddess. *Show me the place that holds the answers I seek.*

And bursting clearly into my mind, just as it burst clearly into Mary's, was the sight of a castle set in the countryside, a mighty yet beautiful fortress of stone, crowned with four towers. And carved over the great arched doors to the castle was the triskelion, a symbol Mary knew well, and which she had seen carved atop the archway in the cavern. Mary hurried to her feet. She must tell no one, not even her own sisters. She would hide the book, and she would take the secret to her grave.

Then I had to brace myself against a violent barrage of images, each bursting on my mind like a wave, and dragging me under to the next: using a love potion and a glamour to secure her passage aboard a ship; standing, drenched upon the deck of that same ship, arms raised to the sky, casting powerful magic to see them safely through a storm; riding upon horseback, sleeping in barns, gathering herbs and plants to dress a wound on her leg; and at last, standing upon the threshold of the castle itself, weak with exhaustion, and gratitude that the mercy and wisdom of the goddess had carried her so far.

Next, I saw Mary standing across from a woman with red hair that cascaded down her back almost to the ground. This woman wore a richly embroidered purple gown and, at her throat hung a silver pendant with the very same triskelion symbol, winking with gemstones in the firelight. She was looking down at Mary with an expression of deep consideration.

"Come with me," the woman said, and led Mary through hallways hung with tapestries and torches, through a great hall and then out into a courtyard, at the center of which stood a very familiar-looking archway.

"I can't believe it," Mary whispered. "It's the same. It's exactly the same."

"They stand all over the world, and it is our job to protect them," the woman said. "But I admit, the threat you speak of is... disturbing. This Darkness... what is its origin? Its nature?"

"As to that, I cannot truly say. It is not human, nor do I think it ever has been. It is powerful. And it feeds on the power of the Cove, and the power, it seems, has its source in the archway. I do not think the Darkness will ever rest until it can consume it completely."

"We have no magic to combat such a being. It is unknown to our lore and our Castings," the woman said, frowning. "And you are sure your magic can fend it off?"

"It has been Bound from the deep magic. It is powerful blood magic. I believe the Source will be safe," Mary said. "Safe from the Darkness, that is. I fear what human greed can do."

The woman smiled, a wise and knowing smile. "Yes, we must always protect against our own worst natures, mustn't we? So it is not the Darkness you fear?"

"Certainly I fear it," Mary said. "But it seems the Darkness needs a human servant to carry out his machinations. I do not want to hand that servant to him. Therefore, I ask that you take this book, hide it, and protect it. It contains the magic that any servant of the Darkness would require to assist him."

"Does this magic not exist in the spellbooks of others of your kind?"

"No. This grimoire is... it is unique in its power and in the way the magic comes to its pages. I risk my own coven by speaking more plainly. But I beg that you take me at my word. We both want to protect the same thing, do we not, even though it be for different reasons?"

The woman's expression softened. In that moment, I knew that she trusted what Mary had told her.

"You hand me the key to immense power in surrendering this book," the woman said. "That speaks of great humbleness. Even I, unschooled in your ways, can sense the magic you possess. Why do you not seek this power for yourself?"

"The Vespers do not abuse our power," Mary said sharply. "But I can no longer trust the other covens in our village. I wish to remove the temptation, for all our safety, and for the preservation of the deep magic. Please. I think it will only be safe with those who understand the nature of the Source, and who are already sworn to protect it."

She held the book out to the woman, and the woman took it into her hands.

"We will guard it carefully," the woman promised, "and return it only to a Vesper."

"No living Vesper will seek it," Mary said, "for I shall take this secret to my grave. Only a Vesper from beyond the grave will ever seek to retrieve it, and if that is the case, you can be sure she has been sent by me, and that the book is needed to protect the Source."

"An alliance between witches and Durupinen," the woman said, shaking her head incredulously. "I never would have believed it. But then again, what are we all, but women persecuted for our power? Perhaps an alliance was long overdue."

"Perhaps," Mary agreed.

I emerged from the memories as from deep water, gasping for air and shivering with bone-deep cold. Asteria still sat beside me, smiling gently.

"Mary was the one who hid the book," I said. "She... she gave it to the Durupinen. But why didn't they protect it, like they said?"

"They did try," Asteria said. "But they encountered their own enemies and shifts of power through the centuries. The book was never lost completely, but its significance and origin was lost to time."

"But it still came to our aid when we needed it," I said in wonder. "Somehow it found its way back."

"It certainly did," she agreed. "Perhaps that, too, is part of its magic."

We sat for a few moments in the quiet of the garden.

"Will I still be able to talk to you?" I asked her.

"Not quite like this," Asteria said. "But once I Cross, I will become one of your spirit guides, my little bird. You can always reach out to me, and I will always be listening. Just like the flame that guided you to Jess that night at the Shadow Tree, all the Vespers will be here to light your path."

"I wondered if that was you."

"It will always be me, little bird."

I had to blink tears from my eyes so that I could see her clearly. "I'm obviously not happy any of this happened—Bernadette, and Sarah and everything the spirits went through, especially you—but I am glad I got to sit and talk with you one last time. Like this."

Her smirk of a smile broadened. "A silver lining, indeed."

THE NEXT DAY when I came downstairs, it was to find Jess waiting on the couch for me, her things all packed up on the floor beside her.

"Hey. I wanted to make sure I said goodbye, but I didn't want to wake you."

"You're leaving already?" I asked, with a sinking feeling.

"Yeah. I've got some serious paperwork waiting for me back at Fairhaven. This whole adventure was... not exactly as advertised," she said, smirking.

I smiled sheepishly. "Yeah. I guess we did kind of turn a simple delivery job into a struggle over immortal souls."

Jess shrugged. "It happens more often than you'd think. To me, anyway."

"Do you really think the Source—I mean, the Geatgrima, is healed?" I asked.

"I am definitely going to send some people around to double check my assessment, but from everything I can observe, yes. That Geatgrima is now in perfect working order."

"You mean other Durupinen will be coming here?" I asked, perking up.

"Yes, I expect so. But this time we're going to have my people call your people, so to speak, and go through the official channels. That means my Council and your Conclave will have to butt heads and figure it out."

"Does that mean your Council will explain how you seemingly came back to life? Because I don't think I would do a very good job."

Jess laughed. "Don't worry, they'll take care of it. The Council has gotten very adept at cleaning up my messes. And this way, with everything out in the open, we can work together without all the subterfuge. I don't think either of our orbits would be happy if we went rogue again, do you?" she asked.

"Probably not. But speaking of witches and Durupinen butting heads, Asteria showed me something last night that answers a lot of questions."

And without further ado, I explained the vision Asteria had brought to me, and watched as Jess' expression grew more and more astonished.

"You mean to say the witches of Sedgwick Cove and the Durupinen of Fairhaven have been working together for centuries and we just... forgot?!" she gasped.

I shrugged. "A lot can happen in four hundred years, I guess. The connection got broken somehow. Anyway, it explains why the grimoire took so long to resurface."

"Well, I never thought I'd be grateful those apprentices messed with witchcraft, but now I guess I am. I'm not sure I would have been able to help Asteria otherwise," Jess said with a bewildered shrug.

"About that," I said. "I've been wondering. You said the apprentices were trying to take a Geatgrima's power for their own. But aren't you already connected to the Gateways? What more power could they have been looking for?"

Jess opened her mouth, and then closed it again. "That's going to have to be a story for another day, Vesper. I could stay here another month and still not have the time to explain that whole situation."

She stood up, and slung her bag over her shoulder.

"I'm not a big one for mushy goodbyes," she said. "And besides, I'll see you again soon. You owe me a trip to Fairhaven, remember?"

"I've never been out of the country before," I said. "I'll have to get a passport!"

"And brush up on those spirit witch skills," Jess said with mock sternness. "There'll be a test on all the castle ghosts before you leave."

I felt my smile slip off my face. "Thanks, Jess. Seriously. I couldn't have done this without you."

Jess gave me a brusque one-armed hug. "I know you've still got this whole Darkness thing hanging over your head. I know a little something about being born into a role you want no part of. But I've seen you in action, kid. That Darkness doesn't stand a chance."

I couldn't be so confident, but I still felt a little of the weight lift from my heart at Jess' words.

A knock sounded on the door, and I got up to answer it. Bea was standing on the porch, her expression eager.

"Is she still here?" she asked, peeking around the doorframe.

I laughed. "You just caught her. Come on in, Bea."

I noticed as Bea passed, she had her sketchbook in her hand. "Hey, I wanted to ask you. Since we fixed things last night, have you noticed anything at all with your—"

Bea cut me off by holding up her sketchbook so I could see her latest. There knelt Xiomara at her boveda, head bent, a candle burning by her elbow. The space around her was crowded with figures, fainter and less defined, but still very much present, one of them with a hand placed lovingly on Xiomara's shoulder.

I looked up from the sketch and felt the smile break over my face. "Well, I guess that answers that!"

Bea nodded, and then plopped down on the sofa beside Jess, who put an arm around her shoulders and smiled.

"I'm glad you stopped by," Jess said. "I couldn't have left Sedgwick Cove without thanking you."

Bea looked slightly startled. "Me? Why would you need to thank me?"

"Are you kidding?" Jess asked. "You answered my call for help. You ensured I got my body back. I owe you my life, Beatriz Marin. That means I'm in your debt. So if this spirit gift of yours ever gives you any trouble, you know who to call, okay?"

Bea flushed, grinning broadly. "Okay."

Jess sighed and rose to her feet. "Well, I'd better get going. Your mom recommended I escape before the Conclave descends, and I'm gonna take her advice."

"Wait!" Bea said. "I'm not just here to say goodbye. I have a message for you!"

Jess frowned. "For me?"

But Bea was already flipping through her sketchbook to another page, which she then turned and displayed to Jess, whose mouth fell open.

On the page was a sketch of a young Asian man with high cheekbones and a sarcastic smirk. His hair swept dramatically over his forehead, and his eyes sparkled with an untold joke.

"He told me to tell you that he knows he can reach you himself, but he's not going to because the two of you are in a fight."

Jess blinked. "We are?"

"Yes, because you didn't let him pack your fall looks for foliage season in New England, and he says you probably looked like a hibernating goth the whole trip, which offends him," Bea announced.

Jess shook her head in exasperation. "That tracks. Thanks, Bea."

Bea shrugged. "You're welcome. And if it makes you feel any better, I think your clothes are cool."

"It does, kinda, yeah," Jess laughed.

And with that, Bea skipped off to the kitchen, following the smell of the cake Rhi had just taken out of the oven.

* * *

THAT EVENING, feeling restless, I went out onto the porch to look at the stars. There had been a solar flare, and people were saying we might be able to see the aurora borealis in New England. But instead of a light show, I found Persi sitting out on the steps.

"Oh, sorry," I mumbled, turning to head back inside.

"No, it's okay, Wren. I think for the first time today, I could do with some company."

Being alone with Persi instantly made me anxious, but I sat down beside her. She was looking up at the sky, and there was an unwrapped parcel in her lap. Among the pile of brown paper and string was a beautifully carved driftwood bird, its wings stretched wide in flight.

"That's pretty," I said, pointing to it.

She looked down at it as though she'd forgotten it was there. "Yeah, it is," she sighed. "Leila Nightjar made it for me."

"She seems... nice," I ventured.

Persi managed a small smile. "Yes, I'm sure she is. Persistent, too, which I admire, even if it is driving me mad at the moment."

I had vague ideas of something encouraging to say about new beginnings and giving people a chance, but I didn't have the courage to speak them out loud, so I swallowed them instead.

"I'll be fine, you know," Persi said, wrapping her arms tightly around herself. "Everyone's treating me like I'm made of glass right now, but it's not necessary."

"Sure," I said.

"It's not like we were still... I mean, it had been a long time since... anyway, I'll be fine."

She had brought Bernadette up. It felt like the only chance I might get to say what I wanted to say, so I took it.

"Bernadette could have slipped away quietly, but she didn't," I said, and paused, so that Persi could tell me to shut up, if she wanted to. When she didn't, I went on, "She hung on. She fought. And when her body gave out, she still stayed, just so she could fix not only what she'd broken, but what Sarah had broken as well," I said. "That's quite a legacy, in the end. I'm sure Ostara must be proud."

"I don't care what Ostara thinks," Persi said fiercely.

"You must be proud, too," I said quietly.

Persi pierced me with an arrested look. Then she sighed.

"I am proud. But then, I was always proud of her. I hope she knew that."

We sat together in silence then, gazing out over the stars as they winked into view one by one, until the sky was peppered with them, and the water sparkled with their reflected light. Sedgwick Cove lay under those stars as it had for hundreds of years, as it would for generations to come, a haven for families like mine to live without fear.

And I would do all I could to make sure of that, whatever may come.

About the Author

E.E. Holmes is a writer, teacher, and actor living in central Massachusetts with her husband and two children. When not writing, she enjoys performing, watching unhealthy amounts of British television, and reading with her children.

To learn more about E.E. Holmes and *The World of the Gateway*, please visit eeholmes.com

Printed in Dunstable, United Kingdom

74809942R10170